As the Fallen Rise

Sadie Hewitt

Developmental Editing by Jamie Johns
Copy Edit and Proofreading by Mozelle Jordan
Cover art by Rebecca Frank

Paperback ISBN: 979-8-9876432-0-4
E-book ISBN: 979-8-9876432-1-1

To my husband,
who spent countless hours watching me write and
supplied me with love and coffee.
My sisters,
who ripped this book up one side and down the other.

As the Fallen Rise is a paranormal/urban fantasy where all things wicked, dark, and dangerous collide.

This story includes elements of battle, hand-to-hand combat, anxiety-inducing situations, blood, kidnapping, graphic violence, death, graphic language, on-page consensual sex, and blackmail.

Readers who may be sensitive to these, please continue with caution.

PROLOGUE

AGNES

Year 1635

To any passerby, the cottage in the middle of the clearing was just another ordinary home. The timber exterior was patched together with heaps of mud and the thatched, matted roof was threatening to disintegrate under the constant drizzle of April rain. The pathway leading up to the cottage was merely trodden, dead grass and the gardening boxes overflowing with weeds. Even the local peasants had snubbed their noses at the hovel and turned away, not bothering to give a second look. As unassuming and demure as the outside was, however, the interior was the exact opposite.

The glow from the hearth was warm and inviting against the fogged, glass windows. A cauldron simmered over the open flame, the smoke swirling lazily around the dried herbs tethered to the thick beams that made up the ceiling. And despite the appearance of the crumbling roof, there was not a single drop of water leaking onto the dirt floor. A small bed was pushed into the far corner of the cottage, heavy quilts draped over the hay-stuffed mattress. Books lined the shelves, only a few of them older than the woman who was perched on the edge of a chair, her arms folded tightly over her chest.

Agnes was young even when compared to the others seated in her cottage. But, at the very least, she was still too old to be seated at the crest of the semi-circle of six males and one female, each representing a faction of daemons created by the Princes of Samsara, listening to the beings argue with each other like schoolchildren. She unraveled her arms, rubbing her eyes with the palms of her hands.

"Allow us access to your lands," a silver-haired male growled to another, his fangs threatening to strike as he bared his teeth. He leaned forward to rest his forearms on his knees, his wool tunic shifting with the movement. "We're being slaughtered. These humans have been emboldened by the Paladin Society. We need a safe-haven."

The counterpart, a lithe, auburn-haired Fae with dark, leathered wings, simply rolled his brown eyes. Fingers steepled in his lap, his back had stiffened with the vampyre's sudden shift. "Even if you could make it to any Fae gateway by the next equinox, I struggle to see how this is a problem that needs to land on the shoulders of my people," he replied, his voice undertoned with a calm chill. His hands parted, one reflexively inching toward his left hip, where a short sword was typically sheathed in a leather casing. That is, if Agnes had not demanded its removal. "If the vampyres were better at disguising themselves, maybe they wouldn't be getting slaughtered. You need to teach your kind to not be so...obvious in their hunting patterns."

The vampyre male flared his nostrils, rage broiling within his blue eyes. He leaned back, his arms crossing over his chest, as he took in a long, frustrated breath. "The problem, *Adair*," he spat the name as if it were acid burning his tongue, "is that if the humans are coming after us, they will soon be after you as well. We should consider banding together. There is only so long before the Paladin Society comes knocking on the Fae gateways."

Phorcys, the sea-dwelling triton with fins of midnight jutting from each forearm, was slowly nodding his head. He leaned over to mutter something into the ear of the dragon shifter, Fuzanglong. The dragon shifter chuckled under his breath, the deep rumbling stirring the large pearl embedded in the center of his chest, which glistened under the firelight. The ghoul, Urzuc, seated to the far right of Phorcys, made an attempt to join the conversation, but Phorcys shoved him away with a quick flick of his wrist, while covering his nose in a failed attempt to rid himself of the rancid stench of decay emitting from Urzuc.

The ghoul sat back, glowering at the two through cloudy eyes. The Fae male, Adair, snapped his gaze over to Agnes. "And what does *he* have to say about all this?" Adair asked sharply, the tips of his leathery wings twitching with irritation. "Surely, *he* can come up with some way to keep these vampyres happy."

Agnes sighed through her nose, surveying the company gathered in her home before she answered. "You've known for the entirety of my four hundred and eighty-six years, Adair, that my equal in Samsara is Eligos. I've never had contact with *him*. It would be suicide."

Adair bristled from her response, shifting uncomfortably in his seat. "Then surely, Eligos— "

"Surely, Eligos has enough on his plate dealing with Samsara rather than weighing in on council affairs," Agnes interjected, running a hand over her dark, braided hair. She leaned forward in her seat, placing an elbow on her knee and her chin on her fist. "And, surely, we have no interest in getting the princes involved."

The daemons sat in silence, weighing her words care- fully. They knew what it would mean to summon a prince without permission— instant death for them and everyone they loved.

A spark of satisfaction shot through Agnes' body. As council emissary to Samsara, it was her duty to relay in- formation back and forth between each faction and act as a moderator or protector when the time called for it. The Princes of Samsara had not been to Earth for thousands of years due to the work of the Mage. Agnes intended to keep it that way.

Agnes rose from her seat and wove her way toward the cauldron that threatened to bubble onto the open fire. She reached into the hearth, stirring the cauldron three times with an iron spoon, whispering an incantation over the liquid within. The daemons watched her apprehensively, and she appreciated the power she held over them. It was rare for a woman in 1635 to have that sense of control. She cleared her throat.

"Adair, if you won't open your lands to the vampyres, I cannot force you," she started. Adair sat up a fraction taller. "But, you can use your influence over the humans to incline behaviors in a different direction while you're outside of the Court of Wind and Storm."

Adair narrowed his eyes. "What would you have me do?"

Agnes reached above her, snapping a piece of dried garlic from the bushel. Her nimble fingers peeled the outer skin before tossing it into the cauldron. The potion hissed in response, a billow of steam unfurling into the cottage. "Tell them..." she paused momentarily to stir the potion once more. "Tell them vampyres cannot stand garlic."

Ryrreia, a succubus and the second female in the cottage, let out a throaty cackle of a laugh. Her black hair slid across her shoulder as she arched her back, thrusting her breasts out to rub along the vampyre's upper arm. "Do you hear that, Darragh? Garlic." The words came out like a feline purr, her full lips pouting as she surveyed him through hooded eyes.

Darragh, ignoring Ryrreia completely, despite her hand running up his inner thigh, gaped at Agnes in disbelief. "You'll bet the future of vampyres on *summer asthma?*"

It was Agnes's turn to bristle. "Don't be foolish, Darragh." She reached into the hearth to stir the potion for a third time. "I'm seasoning them for you." She looked over her shoulder to wink at the vampyre male who drew back a small smirk in return. "Besides, sophistry works wonders in protection against humans. Not everything requires a violent response." She turned back to the cauldron, grabbed a glass bottle off the mantle, and pulled the cork from the rim. Slowly, she lifted the iron ladle and poured a portion of the contents into the bottle. The liquid was viscous, similar to honey, and smelled like a pot of beef stew that had cooked for too long.

"Here," Agnes stated, shooing Ryrreia away from the vampyre and straightening her arm to hand the bottle to Darragh. He took it hesitantly, wrinkling his nose at the look of it before tilting his head back and downing the contents as if it were a pint of ale, shuddering softly.

"And that was?"

Agnes picked up another bottle, emptying a full ladle of potion into it before pushing the cork back in. "So you won't burn during the daytime. I'll bottle up as many as I can. Distribute them to vampyres you meet along the way. So long as my magic endures, whoever takes the potion will be safe from the sun. That should dissuade Paladin from hunting the ones immune, at the very least."

Darragh looked at her in wonder." How—how did you?"

She brushed him off. While most locals referred to her as a witch, she preferred the term, Mage. A Mage with magical abilities passed down from mother to daughter through her bloodline, thanks to the King of Samsara himself. Abilities to tap into the energy of the earth and use it to protect the daemons: devils and djinn, vampyres and shtriga, the fae, wolf shifters, sirens, dragons, ghouls, and succubi. There was only one Mage at a time—could only be one Mage at a time. Nature determined the rising after the previous one passed on. There had been a short twenty years between herself and her predecessor, though there was nearly two hundred years before that.

"His kind can go in the sun," the wolf-shifter male, Gawin, growled with a thick finger pointed accusingly at Darragh, "but still nothing for the wolves? We want the ability to shift at any time, not just the full moon. You've known this for centuries now, Agnes."

Agnes stilled. These creatures lived on the precipice of war at all times, mandating a balancing act that she learned to walk over the centuries. She had momentarily forgotten Gawin was in the room and would have never flaunted her ability in front of him had she remembered.

"*Your* kind," Darragh shot back, swatting the man's hand away, "isn't being hunted to extinction. *Your kind—*" he paused for dramatic effect, "just needs to stop *breeding like the rabid dogs you are.*"

The shouting between the daemons started again, the cycle only broken for short bouts of time. Agnes let out an audible sigh, dropping the ladle into the cauldron with a clank and pocketing a glass bottle of potion. She had been hoping this cycle would last more than thirty minutes.

Agnes lifted her fingers to her mouth and let out a sharp whistle, one that she knew would be painful against the sensitive ears of the daemons. The room quieted instantly; all sets of eyes turning to look at her. "I think we all need to take a breath," she announced, reaching for the door behind her and yanking it open with authority. "Each of you need to exit my cottage and keep fifty paces away from anyone else.

Count to three hundred, then come back inside." Her tone was sweet, yet firm. Children, indeed.

There was a pregnant pause before the daemons began to stand, one at a time, grumbling under their breath as they passed Agnes on their way over the threshold. Darragh and Adair exchanged shoves as they attempted to cross through the doorway at the same time.

Agnes managed to suppress her eye roll before she closed the wooden door with a snap behind them.

She could still hear the muffled arguing outside of the cottage, and she felt her teeth clench with impatience. She needed to open a window. She needed to take a breath of fresh air. She needed to remove the stench of Urzuc, the ghoul, from her cottage.

She wound her way through the empty chairs to the back door, that faced the forest. Her fingers clasped around the wooden handle as she pulled it open, feeling a rush of relief as the chilled air hit the exposed skin of her face and forearms. The sheen of sweat that had collected in a thin layer dried almost instantly, and her skin pebbled under the abrupt shift in temperature.

"I know you're there," she called into the darkness, her breath swirling in the cool mist in front of her, "May as well come out now."

A moment passed by before she heard the crackle of dead leaves under feet and the rustle of branches being parted by hands. A tall, muscular man emerged from the thicket nearest the door. Agnes smiled at him as she leaned against the door frame; a smile that she knew he could still see even with the clouds covering the moonlight.

He walked toward her, a swagger in his step that she had become accustomed to over the past seventy-five years. He cocked his head at her as he approached, his hands stuffed into the pockets of his waistcoat.

"How did you know it was me?" He asked in his Irish brogue, with a grin that lit up his handsome features.

Agnes surveyed him, her gaze raking over his green eyes, his dark hair that was pulled into a short ponytail at the base of his neck.

She let out a snort of derision that any noble, human or otherwise, would have considered unladylike. "The first council meeting in thirty years? I knew you would be eavesdropping the moment it was announced."

He feigned astonishment, placing a large hand on his chest. "How was I supposed to know there was a council meeting tonight? I haven't been near another vampyre in three years." He paused to look up at the sky, a few stars managing to peek between the break in the clouds. "What did our fearless leaders have to say for themselves this time?" Agnes ignored him, fishing into the folds of her apron.

She snapped her fingers to get his attention before pressing the glass bottle into his hand.

He pinched the bottle between his forefinger and thumb, bringing it up to eye level. He stared at it warily for a moment.

"Is this that sun potion you've been working on for the last few months?" he asked, his eyes narrowing as he continued his stare-down of the vial. "Because I've had about enough of your experiments. After that last one you gave me, I had blisters for weeks on my—"

"Yes, Cian," Agnes interrupted, her arms crossed over her chest. "This is the sun potion I've been working on. And it *will* work, I promise." Or she hoped it would work. She was sure she would hear from Darragh if it didn't.

He tilted it toward her as a toast. "To your good health, then." He tipped the glass back and Agnes watched as the thick liquid slid into his mouth. He gagged, his hand darting upward to cover his nose. "God, that taste is otherworldly." He shuddered as he recovered, and pointed a finger toward Agnes. "If I get any more blisters, I'm coming after you."

She sent him a sly smile, pushing herself off the door frame with a shrug of her shoulders. The raised voices around the corner of the cottage were only getting louder. It was time to intervene once again. "I look forward to seeing if you have those blisters or not, then." She reached into the folds of her apron for a final time, pulling out a handful of vials she had prepared for this moment. She knew Cian would turn up. He was too nosy not to. "Hand these out to others you may come across. It should protect you from Paladin for the time being." She looked toward the forest, the depths concealed between the thick tree line and the night sky. She had heard they were in the area, more than likely looking for her.

Cian raised his hand to his brow in a mock salute that made Agnes truly roll her eyes. "Until next time then, Mage." He returned her expression with a darkened smirk of his own before slipping back into the thicket, disappearing into the black.

ONE

GREER

Present Day

Greer Myers stepped from her Jeep Wrangler, the gravel driveway crackling beneath the sandals on her feet. The humid, summer heat was brutal under the mid-afternoon sun. It was only made bearable during her two-hour drive by the wind howling through the open windows. She desperately needed to repair the air conditioning in her vehicle, but was lacking the financial means to do it.

She would rather suffer the mid-summer consequences than admit to her mother that she needed the help.

Greer let the door snap shut behind her, adjusting the canvas bag she had pulled onto her shoulder before exiting the car. Perspiration trickled between her shoulders, soaking into the back of her tank top. She felt the sweat everywhere—the bridge of her nose where her sunglasses sat, the fringes of her hair that were plastered to her brow, the backs of her thighs beneath the knee-length, flowy skirt that was patterned with flowers and greenery.

She pulled a claw clip from her bag and twisted her hair around her finger, securing it with the clip at the back of her head. Her neck felt immediately cooler with the removal of her wavy, brown locks.

The drive, though uncomfortably hot, was necessary and one that she had been tapped to do by the head researcher in the anthropology department at the state university. Greer had been hired in as a newly minted graduate, working under Henry Hahn as he studied the local Native American tribes within the Pacific Northwest region. It was her first solo interview, and she was determined to prove her capability of exceptional work.

This interview was crucial. Greer had discovered the artist through a local museum exhibit, one where the woman had donated her story-telling paintings to the museum for a six-week period of time. The painting that had caught Greer's eye In particular was of one depicting two creatures circling one another in a clearing. Henry was interested in the details of the painting; Greer was interested in the details of the artist.

The dwelling at the end of the driveway was a simple log cabin. Each log puzzle-pieced on top of the other, culminating at the ends with a gooey, black chinking that sealed the seams of the wood together. Some of the chinking, either from the heat of the sun or from age, had begun to drip down the sides of the cabin.

To Greer, the house looked like it was bleeding.

Greer's gaze flicked up as the door to the cabin creaked open and a woman stepped onto the wooden porch. She was older than her voice sounded over the phone with wrinkles and laugh lines etched into the bronzed skin of her face. Her long, black hair was braided into two plaits that ran down each side of her chest. From a distance, Greer could tell the woman's dark eyes were kind in nature, though somewhat wary of a newcomer on her property.

"Hi!" Greer called out, waving to the woman with a trembling hand. "My name is Greer Myers. We talked on the phone yesterday?"

The woman's wary gaze melted away as she stepped off the wooden porch and onto the packed, dirt pathway that spliced through the herb gardens planted in the clearing. "I had a feeling that was you," she replied as she reached Greer, holding out her hand to shake, "I'm Deborah. Thank you for making the journey out to see me." She gestured toward the house, the front door still ajar at the top of the porch. "Thank you for having me," Greer responded with a smile, as the woman led her through the garden. Greer watched as the tips of Deborah's fingers brushed along the leaves of the plants as she walked by, and a small smile crept onto Greer's lips.

They climbed up the porch stairs and entered the house, the air only a few degrees cooler in the shade. The windows were thrown open, letting the gentle breeze waft through the small, yet open floor plan. Paintings and woven baskets hung from the walls while brightly colored, patterned rugs lay haphazardly on the wooden floors. Dried herbs hung in the kitchen, giving off a sweetly spiced scent when the breeze curled through them.

"Can I get you anything to drink besides water?" Deborah asked, heading into the kitchen and pulling a cabinet door open. She reached in, taking out two tall glasses.

Greer slowly followed behind her, stopping in front of a clay pot seated on the coffee table. It was decorated with variously colored beads, faded from the sun's rays streaming into the room day after day. She bent down to study the pot and the intricate details of the beading that she knew told a story.

"That was made by my grandmother," Deborah explained, handing the glass of ice water to Greer. "She was an artist as well."

Greer straightened with a jolt, turning to look at Deborah and taking the glass from her outstretched hand. She took a deep gulp, enjoying the rush of cool liquid on her dry throat. "This is perfect, thank you."

"What is it that I can help you with?" Deborah went on, gesturing for her to take a seat on the opposite side of the coffee table.

Greer set her canvas bag on the floor, leaning it against the accent chair. She reached into the bag to pull out a recorder from the inside pocket, holding it in the air between them. "Do you mind if I record you?" she asked nervously, a fluttery feeling flipping in her stomach. "It would just help me take better notes later."

"Of course," Deborah said, taking a sip of her own water. She relaxed against the back cushion of the couch as Greer set the recorder between them. Her hands shook as she pressed the play button in the middle of the device and a red light flickered on.

"This is Greer Myers in Washington State on June the twenty-first. Oh, it's the summer equinox." She smiled to herself before continuing on. "Interviewing Deborah Hodgins." Greer slid her foot from her sandal and tucked it under her backside as she shifted in the seat. "I am part of a team at the state university in Oregon, researching how different societies culture's shape their beliefs, whether it be religion, folklore, creatures." She paused to reach down and remove a photograph of Deborah's painting from the front of her notebook, placing it on the table next to the recorder. "I came across your painting in the Klamath exhibit not too far from here. Would you be able to tell us more about it?"

Deborah picked up the photograph, studying it for a moment. Blurry trees in the background gave way to a humanoid predator in the foreground. Fang-like teeth protruded from his gumline, his mid-length hair pulled into a ponytail at the base of his neck. His clothing was old; late 1700s if Greer had to guess. His hand was wrapped around the base of a tree, hugging it tightly to his chest as he stalked the tree line close to the village where the tribe resided.

"This was my favorite to paint," Deborah said with a sigh, lightly running her fingers along brush strokes that created the chained necklace hanging around the man's neck. A jagged and green gemstone dangled from the chain. She placed the photograph back on the coffee table and slid it to Greer. "My grandmother used to tell me stories, passed down from her grandmother and hers before that. A monster who lurked in the trees after dark. He would whisper your name in the wind, beckoning you into the forest before dragging you into the night."

A shudder went up Greer's spine as she leaned in, placing her chin in the palm of her hand. "Did you ever hear what that creature was?"

The woman's head danced back and forth for a moment. "Yes and no." She took another sip of water from her glass. "My grandmother said it was a demon; her grandmother called it a trickster. What they did say was that there were many creatures in the forest, but this one craved the taste of humans. If you heard your name called from the trees, you were never seen again."

Greer was scribbling frantically in her notebook. She looked up to Deborah, her lips turned downward. "You said other creatures. You don't believe it was just the one?"

Deborah shook her head, her smallest finger playing in the condensation that built up on the side of the glass. "That creature wasn't indigenous to our lore," she said quietly, looking up toward Greer. She sucked in a breath. "The stories of this creature came with the arrival of the white man from the east. I was raised in southern Oregon, where my ancestral home is. We had myths surrounding coyotes and water monsters. Dog-like creatures that acted like tricksters." She tented her fingers on the photograph and twisted it back toward her, picking it up once again. "I think that's why I'm drawn to him. Brown hair, a beautiful face. He was strong, powerful, fast. He didn't actually appear in my family's stories until my great-great-great grandmother met him."

Greer's face turned from intrigued to stunned. "Your family saw him?"

"Oh yes," Deborah answered gravely, nodding her head. "My great-great-great grandmother was playing in the water as a child, close to dark. She was swept away from the river after a downpour of rain during the dry season. This man jumped in to save her, pushing her back onto the shore. Later that night, when she was tucked into bed, she heard a whisper come from the forest. She snuck out of her home, following the voice. It didn't call to *her*, it called to a man in her village, but she followed it just the same. She found herself in a clearing, squeezed between a couple of large bushes, when two coyotes appeared. They took after the voice, chasing it deeper into the forest. She could hear unearthly snarls and growls; a fight had broken out. The creatures circled back to the clearing, running at speeds hard to see. The man who had saved her, his arm shredded from the claws of the coyotes, was battling them. The way they moved...it was other-worldly."

Greer tapped her pen on the notebook, her brow furrowed in concentration, enthralled by the story. "So, what happened next?"

Deborah shrugged a shoulder, slumping back into her chair. She turned to gaze through the closest window, her mind wandering to a place far away. "I'm not sure," she finally said, her voice cutting through the silence. "My grandmother said they were all scared away by a branch breaking in the bush when she changed her position. Others in my family have said the creatures just moved on after their fight. What I do know is this," she paused to lean forward again. "That man came back thirty years later when my great-great-great grandmother was a mother herself. She saw him lurking in the woods at night, whispering into the wind like he had all those years before."

Greer went quiet as Deborah finished her story. She shifted forward to pull the photograph toward her. She lifted it off the table, studying it.

"How would you feel about dinner? You've come all this way." Deborah stood from her chair, shuffling into the kitchen. "I picked fresh vegetables and herbs from my garden this morning."

Greer was in the process of opening her mouth to decline when her stomach grumbled. The thought of dinner made the back of her throat thicken with hunger. "I could probably stick around for some food," she said, as she pressed the power button on the recorder, effectively ending the interview.

As Deborah pulled the fresh vegetables from the refrigerator and began chopping them, Greer stood at the stove to sauté the onions thrown into the pan.

"If you were born in Oregon, how did you end up here?" Greer asked, stirring the pan of onions and olive oil. Deborah smiled, tapping the golden ring on her finger with the tip of her knife. "I met my husband in college; he was from Washington. We moved up here shortly after we got married." She gestured at a shelf opposite the small dining table, nestled into the corner of the kitchen, where a wedding photo was perched. "We built this house nearly fifty years ago. He passed away from a stroke just after our forty-eighth wedding anniversary."

Something inside Greer's chest cracked open as she stirred in the green peppers Deborah had tossed in with the onions.

"I started painting when I was young," Deborah went on, now cutting a chicken breast, "but began painting the stories passed down from my family back in the eighties. I wanted to preserve the stories important to my tribe."

"They are beautiful," Greer said. She took the cutting board of chicken from Deborah's hands, pouring the cubed meat into a separate pan on the stove. Deborah leaned over to coat it in olive oil before giving the pan a good shake. The smell of cooking meat paired with oregano and salt only made Greer grow hungrier. "I'm going to see your exhibit again this weekend."

Deborah beamed. "I hope you enjoy it. Those paintings are my pride and joy."

The sun peaked and then set by the time dinner was finished. The cooled breeze ruffled the fringe on the rugs and blew away any remaining humidity from the afternoon. Greer had spent the evening asking Deborah about her childhood, her marriage, and her artwork. She hadn't meant to spend as much time there as she did, but something about the woman made her feel warm and safe.

Once her notebook and recorder were packed away and the dishes were washed from dinner, Deborah had laden her with homemade pastries for the drive back home.

Greer turned to face Deborah, pulling a small wooden box from her canvas bag. "For you," she said with a small smile, "as a thank you for meeting with me."

Deborah grasped the box and slid the lid open, revealing the tobacco leaves piled inside. Her face broke into a wide grin, and she reached over to pull Greer into a tight embrace. Her spiced cedar scent wafted up Greer's nose as they drew each other closer, just as the last of the sun's rays set over the tops of the trees, casting them into shades of darkness only broken by the candles Deborah had lit after their meal.

"Do me a favor, young one," Deborah said, as she pulled away. She reached up to cup her hand on Greer's cheeks. "Never stop in the woods after dark. You get in your car and you drive straight home."

Perhaps it was the warning coupled with the seriousness in her tone, but Greer felt her hair stand on the back of her neck. She nodded stiffly as her mouth grew dry, and her eyes widened apprehensively. "Yes, yes, of course," she replied in a strained voice, biting the inside of her cheek. Greer clambered into the front seat of her Jeep Wrangler a few minutes later, placing the paper plate of pastries on the seat next to her. She sat in the silence for a moment, watching Deborah blow out each individual candle in the windows of the living room. Then, she drew the curtains tightly shut, encasing the log cabin in darkness.

What Greer expected to be sounds of the forest around her, she heard nothing except the wind rustling the leaves on the trees. No crickets, no chirping of birds, no buzz of mosquitoes. She turned over the engine of the vehicle, rolling down the windows to air out the stuffy, humid cabin.

"Greer."

A whisper was carried on the breeze, an unearthly call that made her stomach clench painfully. Greer's head whipped to the window as her hand rose to grip her throat. She sucked in a slow, uneven breath, as her fingers trembled against her neck. Her eyes felt frozen, unable to close as her heart thudded against her chest.

"Greer."

She watched the tree line, horrified to hear the crack of branches, as if a large animal were moving just on the other side of the brush. A wild scent came next on the wind, a metallic tangy scent that reminded her of blood and wet undergrowth. It was unnatural, one that was foreign to her.

Slowly, she reached into her canvas bag and removed her cell phone. She clicked on the flashlight, and the resulting light flooded the driveway, sweeping across the forest. It was when the light landed on a pair of reflective, bulbous eyes that she blinked, her mind curling toward a startling blank. The eyes disappeared from view, but the humanoid shadow that darted toward the clearing made her head recoil from the window, her own gaze wide and staring.

Shocked out of her frozen state, she threw the Jeep into reverse and gunned it out of the driveway, not looking back to see the creature withdraw into the trees and disappear into the darkness.

TWO

"Yes, I got home safe," Greer said into the phone the next morning, jogging down the carpeted stairs of her apartment building. "I didn't call you, because there was nothing to talk about." She pressed her hip into the metal crash bar of the door, pushing it open with a quick shove. The fresh, misty air flooded her cheeks as she began to cross the parking lot toward her Jeep.

"No, mom. My trip to Morocco is in six months, not six weeks." She paused again as her mother continued her interrogation on the other end of the line. "Yes, I am still going alone. No, I am not booking a tour for it. No, I am not canceling it to pay for the air conditioning in my car. I've been saving for months now. I will be fine."

Greer pinched her cell phone between her ear and her shoulder as she dug into her canvas bag to find her car keys. "Mom— mom, I have to go." Another pause. "Because I have to drive. Yes, I'll call you later. Love you too."

She flicked her phone into her bag and let out a sharp sigh of frustration. Her mother, Celeste, was the polar opposite of her. Where

Greer had wavy, brown hair and bright, gray eyes, her mother had straight, blonde hair and brown ones. Where Greer was carefree and loose, her mother was rigid and tense. Where Greer was friendly and outgoing, her mother was paranoid and unpleasant. Opposites in almost every way that mattered.

Because of this, Greer and her mother had butted heads her whole life, finally forcing Greer to choose a college ten hours north of her hometown in northern California. She enjoyed the hiking scenery, the salty air, and the rocky terrain that Oregon had to offer. More importantly, she liked that it kept her mother at arm's length. That was one of the main reasons she decided to take the job at the university rather than going back to her hometown.

Unlocking her car door, she glanced toward the direction of the forest. It was still dark beneath the cloudy sky and rising sun. Droplets of rain had begun to roll off the greenery that hung on the trees, pooling into the cracks in the pavement. She took a deep breath in, savoring the early morning smell of fresh, wet earth.

What she didn't expect to see was the silhouette of a man standing just inside the shadows of the tree line, staring at her.

Greer looked away for a moment as she went to open the car door before her heart started, an uncomfortable heat creeping into her cheeks. She snapped her gaze back toward the forest, to the same spot where she knew the man had been standing less than a second before.

No one stood there now.

There was no rustle of trees or falling of leaves to indicate someone had been there at all. She glanced around the parking lot, taking in the joggers on the trail and people headed into their respective offices for the day. Not one of them seemed spooked over a person in the woods.

She shook her head, taking a sip of the coffee she held in her hand. Her mind had to still be overactive from meeting Deborah the day before.

She opened her car door, tossed her work bag onto her passenger seat, and drove toward the university.

It was barely a fifteen-minute ride before she pulled her car into the staff-allocated parking lot. Reaching into the glove compartment, she removed her badge and slung its lanyard around her neck. The rain was now coming down in droves as she jogged up to the building, her bag settled firmly over head to protect her hair.

She swept off the water from her canvas bag as she hit the front door, her heels clicking against the marble tile of the lobby.

"Hey there, Greer!" the security officer, Roger, called out to her. He waved a casual hand as he buzzed her into the building. She waved back, a grin spreading across her lips. "Working on anything good this week?"

She shrugged as she pulled open the door, holding it from closing with the toe of her black pumps. "Spent the last few days at the museum up the coast cataloging recent discoveries from the Klamath tribes. Henry asked for my assistance in collaborating on an academic paper about socio-cultural ties and how they may have contributed toward the oral accounts of different creatures in the forests around here."

The older man took a sip of coffee from the mug gripped between his fingers, an expression of interest flashing on his face. If there was anyone in the library more knowledgeable than Roger, Greer would have been shocked. Working there longer than she had been alive, Roger spent most of his days picking the brains of the university's sharpest minds. "You should look in section ten on the second floor.

I heard from one of the librarians that there was a shipment of new Klamath and Modoc texts delivered over the weekend."

She tipped her own to-go mug in his direction as she slipped her toe from the doorway. "Thanks, Roger! You always know how to give a hand." He waved again as she clicked down the narrow hallway toward the elevator.

Tucking her coffee into the crook of her elbow, she punched the button to take her down to the basement level. A quick trip to the small office she shared with two other post-graduate hires to unload her bag, then she would dive headfirst into the tenth section of the second floor. Upon arriving, the elevator opened with a ding and she readjusted her coffee into her hand before she walked inside, taking a sip of the hot liquid in her mug. The elevator shuddered with a jolt, descending slowly into the depths of the library.

The light to her office was already on, the glow like a halo on the threshold against the darkened hallway of the basement. Greer bent down, opening the door with her elbow.

"Oh, gosh, you're here early!" There was a flurry of activity behind the tall pile of books stacked on Erin's desk. She popped her head over the mountain of documents, blonde hair bound in a tight bun nearing the top of her head. Her freckled cheeks were flushed against the otherwise pale skin of her face.

Greer laughed as she set down her bag on the chair opposite Erin. "I'm actually here on time for once." The coffee cup slid out of her hand, landing with a thud on the wooden desk. "It is you, my dear, who is early."

They worked closely together, having been hired by Henry in the same month, and were learning how to link the knowledge they had into a career. Currently, their time was being filled with academic research into social and cultural norms of societies around the world.

These days, Greer spent most of her work week at museums around the state helping to register new archaeological finds, while Erin stayed locked in their office, reading texts to support claims and beliefs held by whatever society they were researching at the time. It was a bit broader than Greer would like, but it was an entry-level position into the field. Erin stepped out from behind the desk, stooping to scoop up a pile of papers that had fallen onto the ground. "I wasn't expecting you or Daniel until closer to nine this morning."

Greer peered at her phone, zipping the black stone of her necklace back and forth along the silver chain. "Erin, *it is* nine in the morning. I can't believe I beat Daniel here." She glanced back up toward her friend, who was inspecting her own cell phone.

"Damn, time has just flown by this morning." Erin paused to look up at Greer, her green eyes bright in the fluorescent lighting of the small space. "I found some interesting oral accounts that had been recorded and shipped to the library in the past couple of days."

Greer grinned, moving her bag to settle into the chair behind the wooden desk. "Something that Roger put into your ear, perhaps?" She picked up the coffee mug and took another sip.

Erin returned the smile. "He does know when all the good stuff comes in." She shuffled some of the papers around, giving Greer time to look at her.

Erin was, by most people's definition, stunning. Aside from her blonde hair and freckles, her green eyes reflected sunlight on even the cloudiest of days, and her body was tall and curvy, normally clad in some sort of romper or jumper. Today, it was a blue, floral jumper. Her feet were clipped into a pair of brown, closed toe flats.

A slap of papers pulled Greer from her thoughts and her gaze shifted over to the stack Daniel had placed onto her desk as he entered their office. "Look at the detail woven into this basket; it's absolutely exquisite," he started, as Greer flicked through the photographs of beaded necklaces and basketry.

Greer made a noise of agreement at the back of her throat. "Is this from an exhibit?" she asked, pointing toward the painting of Kemukemps, a trickster within Modoc storytelling, that had been completed by a local member of the tribe. "The styling looks similar to the artist I interviewed yesterday."

Daniel adjusted his thick-rimmed glasses, peering down at her through brown eyes. "It was gifted to a museum a couple hours north of here for the summer exhibit. Are you thinking of making a road trip?" He took a sip of his tea and honey, steam still rising from the top of the mug. Greer took a deep inhale, smelling the light citrus notes from his beverage. "I think it would be worth wandering up there to see what else they have," she answered, thumbing back through the photographs and setting a few of them aside. "Especially if the artist isn't Deborah. These local artists know more about passed-down traditions than any academic researcher. It might put us on the track Henry is looking for."

Daniel dropped into his own office chair a few feet away from Greer. The office space, small enough that the three of them could touch each other if their arms were spread wide, was cozy despite the fluorescent lighting. Glass jewelry and small, clay pots bedecked the shelves Greer had hung over the past year, while books lined the gaps between the area not yet taken up by art. Colorful paintings Daniel had collected over his years of travel hung from the walls, taking up nearly every inch of white space given to them. The office smelled like the inside of a brand-new book, combined with bold coffee and the floral scents of tea. Erin usually had some sort of soft, acoustic music playing from her laptop while they worked.

The office was one of Greer's favorite places to be. "What's on the docket for today then?" Daniel asked, switching his computer monitor on with a click of his finger. "You'll have to tell us all about the trip to Washington."

"Deborah was great. She gave me a ton of wonderful information for me to go through today." Greer paused to reach into her bag to retrieve the recorder from the inside pocket. "Since Erin took my only job of browsing the new collection that came in— " Erin's lips curled into a smirk. "— I'll get to work creating a manuscript of the interview for Henry to read over." She kicked off her heels and crossed one ankle over the next as she pulled her laptop in front of her and got started.

The sun set was quickly setting over the top of the buildings by the time Greer had packed up her laptop and left the library. She found a street spot to park her car only two blocks from the restaurant, a miraculous feat considering how busy the area closest to the university was.

"Greer! GG! Over here!"

Greer stood on the tips of her toes to see over the throng of people who had gathered at the hostess stand near the front of the restaurant, Crossroad Brewing Company. She managed to spot her best friend, Delia, waving frantically from her perch at the booth. Greer maneuvered through the crowd, nearly slipping on the wet, wooden floor when she cleared the last group engrossed in their conversation about the recent win by the university's football team.

"Delia, Paige! Hi!" Greer said with a laugh when she reached the table, stripping off her sodden coat and hanging it on a hook between the two booths. "How early did you have to get here to find a table? It looks crowded."

Delia stood from her side of the booth and wrapped Greer in a tight embrace. "We got lucky. Paige's new contract is supplying the brewery with large stock items, so the owner had the hostess sit us right away." She paused to hand Greer the beer list. "Which also means the first flight of drinks is on us."

Greer leaned forward to reach beyond Delia and squeeze Paige's hand. "You deserve it, you've been working so hard lately."

Greer took a seat in the booth opposite Delia and Paige, her eyes flicking between her two closest friends. Delia had been her roommate since their undergraduate years, having taken the chance to move away from her hometown in southern Texas. Paige, on the other hand, Delia had met at a sorority party during their junior year. Paige was a local, born and raised, and had decided to forgo college to get into the family business of restaurant wholesale and distribution.

Paige had come with one girl and left with Delia. They were still inseparable nearly six years later.

Delia tucked her curly, brown hair behind her ear. "Tell us all about your first solo interview. It had to be a success."

Paige interlocked her fingers with Delia's, placing a kiss on the temple of Delia's bronze skin. The three chatted for some time before placing drink orders- one Barrel Aged Stout for Delia, a flight of IPA-Style beers for Paige, and a flight of Pilsner and Blonde Style beers for Greer.

Greer sat back in the booth, taking in the clinking of glasses and soft conversations from the tables around them. She glanced at the exposed metal beams; the brew tanks seen through a window cut out behind the bar. A waiter waltzed by, an aromatic heap of nachos steaming on the plate in his hand. Her stomach growled. The last thing she had eaten was take-out sandwiches from the deli down the street from the library.

"Dels, what's the status of your brothers?" Greer asked, pulling herself from her thoughts as she took the last sip of beer from her small glass. "Have you heard anything?" Delia's lips downturned as her shoulders slumped. "No, nothing. I've been filing motions for the last few months.

The latest one is in the federal circuit. There's been no word on when, or if, they'll take up the case."

Delia was raised with her two brothers until her mother died of cancer just after her twelfth birthday. She flipped through foster home after foster home until she found a group home for queer youth in one of the major cities.

Shortly after her graduation from high school, she learned her brothers had been adopted into a family through a closed system. She had not been able to find them since. That had fueled Delia's desire to become a lawyer.

She had recently accepted a position as a junior associate in one of the larger firms in the area. She was enjoying her corner cubicle just as much as Greer was enjoying her shared basement office.

"We're going to find them," Paige said soothingly, placing a gentle hand on Delia's thigh. "We're going to get you back in touch with them if it's the last thing I do."

Greer believed it.

The three shared an appetizer and a second round of drinks, spent a few minutes laughing at the band of men near the bar, who were lauding over the Washington Commander's missed field goal attempt, and then paid the bill with the waiter.

Greer donned her coat, still damp from the summer rain, and exchanged hugs with both Delia and Paige.

The air was cool when she exited the restaurant, but at least the rain had stopped. She tucked her hands into her pockets as she stepped over a puddle in the alleyway that led to the parking spot of her Jeep. The weather was unseasonably cold, despite the temperatures of the day before.

Greer's heels tapped against the cracked pavement of the alley as she walked in and out of the shadows between the two brick buildings. The wafting smell of old frying oil was in the misty air. She swallowed thickly as she picked up the pace of her steps, choosing to ignore the roiling build-up of panic that had set into her stomach. She shook her head to rid the thought, silently attempting to convince herself that her mind was being overactive yet again.

"Hello, darling," a voice drawled from behind her. The hair on the back of her neck prickled at the sound.

She spun on the tips of her toes, spotting the man half-hid- den in the shadows beyond the dimly lit street lamp. She turned her back on the man and continued her walk down the alley. She had her fair share of run-ins with drunken bar-goers, particularly in college, and knew it was best to just ignore the threat while keeping your wits about you. Being alone with him in the alley, though, was making her increasingly nervous.

"Aw, where are you going, sweetheart?" he crooned. Greer heard his footsteps splash through the rain-soaked

cracks in the pavement. "Don't you want to have a bit of fun?"

She reached into her bag to pull her keys from the inside pocket, placing one in between her pointer and middle fingers in case she needed a weapon. Her Jeep was in sight, just on the other side of where the alleyway spilled into the main road. Her heart pounded in her chest as she power-walked toward the busy street.

"I don't like it when I'm ignored," the man growled, much closer than he had been moments previously. She felt her stomach flip as his hand wrapped around her upper arm, spinning her to face him.

His breath was rancid, a mixture of liquor and stale beer, and she cringed as the smell broke through her senses. She could just hear the rumblings of conversations as people passed by on the main strip.

"Let me go!" she cried out in a trembling voice, hoping the noise would attract sober patrons into the alley.

She yanked her arm against his grasp, but he held steady against the motion. His other hand jerked upward, his fingers gripping at her throat. They slid along her skin, his nails tearing painfully at her flesh, eventually catching on her necklace. The chain broke away, the gemstone clattering to the ground. She fought to break his grip, but the hand wrapped around her neck only tightened. His eyes, glossy and rimmed with red, were unable to focus. At that moment, Greer knew he would not remember attacking her the next morning.

Her hand was wrapped around his forearm, struggling to pull his hand away from her. She let out a strangled yell, putting every ounce of strength into breaking his grip. It was then she felt it.

A sudden pulse of energy from deep within her soul vibrated, rattling her bones. That pulse shot from her fingertips, entering the man's forearm. He let out a terrible, earth-shaking scream as he cradled his arm to his chest, collapsing to the pavement. Black spider-webbed etchings coursed through his veins like a poison, cracking and burning him from the inside.

Having heard the commotion, the alley flooded with people. A woman approached Greer, placing her hands on Greer's shoulders. "Hey! Hey, are you alright?" the woman asked, shaking Greer gently.

"What the fuck— "

"Look at his arm— "

"What did that— "

Greer didn't answer, her vision blackening in the periphery. It darkened entirely, and she didn't feel herself collapse to the pavement.

THREE

The rays of the sun, bright and cheerful, poured in through the slit between the curtains. It was too sterile, the vine- gary scent of cleaning supplies and overly bleached towels sweeping over her senses.

Greer groaned, her eyes opening to reveal a whiteboard with the date and *Nurse: Odette* written in neat, curling letters. She turned her head, taking in the half-empty saline bag hanging from the metal IV pole and the plastic side table clad with an opened box of tissues.

"Greer? Oh, my baby!"

Blonde hair covered her vision as her mother leaned over the edge of the bed to plant a kiss near a laceration on Greer's forehead.

Her brow furrowed as she glanced up toward Celeste. "What—where am I?"

Celeste pushed Greer's hair from her temples with cold fingers, tucking the locks behind her ears. "You were attacked last night. I got a call from the police. I drove here as quickly as I could."

Greer lifted her hand, her fingertips gently touching the bandages loosely taped to her neck. Her eyes widened, remembering what had happened the previous night.

"The man— there was— "

"I think that's what we would all like to know." Greer's head whirled toward the open doorway, the inside of her skull pounding against the too quick movement. A police officer stood in the doorway, his blue uniform stiff and pressed. The golden badge on his chest gleamed under the bright lights, and his hand rested on the gun tethered to his belt. His eyes were kind as they studied her, his gaze pained, and his brow wrinkled.

"May I?" he asked, gesturing toward the empty seat opposite her mother. His black shoes squeaked against the smooth tile with every step.

Greer nodded, though she had the distinct feeling that the question was rhetorical.

"Is this something we can do later?" Celeste asked, her fingers curling in the white sheets near the edge of the bed. "She just woke up. It's been a long night."

"It's best to get these details while they're still fresh," he responded firmly, but not unkindly. He shifted his belt as he sat, the wooden chair groaning under his weight. "We saw the video tape from the alleyway, but can you tell me what happened last night? In your own words?"

Greer squinted her eyes, focusing on the patterned, white blanket covering her legs. Everything was too white here; It reminded her of her mother's house. "I was at Crossroad Brewery Company with some friends," she began slowly, her voice hoarse. She licked her chapped lips, making the cracked flesh burned. "I— I was headed back to my car when a man grabbed me."

The police officer leaned forward to place his forearms on his thighs. "Did you get a good look at him?"

Greer shook her head, swallowing thickly. "No, no. It happened so fast. One minute, he was on me and the next..." She trailed off, the vision of the man's blackening flesh at the forefront of her mind. She cleared her throat before continuing on. "What happened to him?"

The police officer shifted, the wooden seat groaning once again. "He was brought to the hospital with severe burns. He succumbed to his injuries late last night." He watched Greer with a sharp stare. "Is there anything else you can remember?"

Greer felt her heart stutter at the news. Dead. He was dead. She thought back to his sour breath, his hands on her neck, the pulsing power that thrummed from her fingertips. She lifted her gaze, her eyes connecting with the officer's. "No, nothing. I tried to fight him off, but he just..."

The officer sucked in a breath. "There was a second body discovered, a young woman. She wasn't much younger than you. She was tucked behind one of the garbage bins in the alleyway. Do you have any information regarding her identity?"

Greer blanched. "Wh—what? A body? No. No, I don't.

How did she— was it the same man?"

The officer watched Greer closely, assessing her for a moment before responding. "We don't believe so. It seems to be some kind of animal attack. She was covered in bites." This time, Celeste was the one to reply. "Animal bites?" she asked sharply. "What kind of animal does *that* in a city?" "We're trying to locate more video footage to see if it was a stray mountain lion. As of right now, that is all I can say."

"Was she drained of blood? Her neck broken?" Celeste pressed, a pink flush creeping up her neck. "What did you do with the body?"

Greer groaned at the questions, her head falling back against the flat pillow behind her. The interrogation was typical of Celeste; it had been for Greer's entire life.

"Like I said," the officer interjected, his tone indicating the end of the conversation, "that is all I can say about an active investigation." He stood from his seat, adjusting his belt back to center. "I'll leave my card on the table here, just in case you can think of anything else." His thick knuckle tapped the table where he had set the card.

"Thanks for stopping by," Greer said quietly, earning a clucked tongue and an eye roll from her mother.

The officer tipped his head at her before crossing the threshold, his sneakers squeaking all the way to the elevator at the end of the hall.

Celeste opened her mouth to reprimand Greer, no matter that all of this was out of Greer's control, when a second person flit into the room.

The woman was tall and athletic, her pronounced muscles evident through the tight, purple set of scrubs she bore, and her red hair was braided, swinging with every step she took. She seemed to glide over the floor, so light that her weight never shifted from one foot to the next.

It wasn't any one of those things that caught Greer's eye, though.

It was her massive, iridescent wings that protruded from her back. They seemed to shimmer under the bright lights, held together by thick bands of tissue. Greer glanced over to her mother, who was busy scrolling through the home screen on her phone.

Greer said nothing, but kept her lips parted as the woman introduced herself as Odette, the nurse on duty. Even the doctor who entered the room after her didn't seemed to notice, though Greer considered that perhaps, he was used to them.

"How is your pain?" Odette asked, logging into the computer with quick taps of her fingers. "I brought some more Tylenol around, but I can certainly get something stronger if you need."

"Erm, Tylenol is fine," Greer hesitantly responded, watching the doctor lift the bandages from her neck. "These are looking great," the doctor started, replacing the bandage. "No evidence of infection. Of course, we administered a tetanus shot when you arrived and ran antibiotics through your IV. We can get you home by this afternoon." He turned to the nurse. "Odette, would you start getting the paperwork ready?"

"Of course!" she exclaimed after scanning the hospital band around Greer's wrist. She handed Greer a small cup with two pills inside, along with a cup of cold water. "I'll get it going right away."

"Great," the doctor replied, pumping a pea-sized amount of hand sanitizer onto his palms and rubbing them together before turning back to face Greer, "Glad to see you're awake and doing well."

Odette took Greer's blood pressure and listened to her lungs, leaving the room soon after she entered the vital signs into Greer's chart on the computer. She navigated her wings through the opening of the doorway as she went. Greer glanced over to her mother, who had placed her reading glasses on the bridge of her nose. "Did you not see her huge wings?" Greer asked, tossing her thumb in a gesture over her shoulder.

Celeste cocked a brow. "Wings?" She reached up to feel Greer's forehead. "Are you feeling alright?"

Greer looked back at the empty doorway, listening to the beep of a heart monitor as a patient's slippered feet whispered over the linoleum floors. "Yeah, of course," she finally said, as she settled back into the bed. "Everything is completely fine."

Greer returned to work a couple of days later. She was desperate to put some space between herself and Celeste, who had booked a hotel room near her apartment building for the unforeseeable future. Delia and Paige had stopped by for brief respites of time when Celeste had gone to the grocery store, but she never strayed far.

"Are you already back in the office?" Henry asked that morning, his dark brows high on his forehead. His fingers tapped against the side of the doorframe. "I had human resources send an email approving additional time off."

Greer tossed him a tight smile. "My mother has decided to stick around for a little while longer."

Erin snorted with laughter as she tucked her nose deeper into the crevice of her book.

Henry's lips upturned in amusement. "Ah, I understand." He entered the office, adjusting the top button on his gray, wool sweater. "I read over the transcript of your interview with the artist. Excellent work. I've submitted it, along with the grant paperwork to continue our research. Pending approval, we can afford for you to attend a few conferences in Arizona during the next academic year. In the meantime—" he paused to drop a trifold brochure onto her desk. "The artist is in town for the unveiling of her paintings at an art exhibit. Want to see if you can connect anything else?"

Greer picked up the brochure and turned it over in her hand. "I can head over there today if you want me to." She lifted her gaze to catch Henry's. "This museum isn't too far from here."

"Head out now," he said with a nod. "Grab some lunch for us on your way back, if you would. I can only eat so many deli sandwiches at Daniel's behest."

Daniel's head snapped up as he removed the wireless headphone from his ear. "If you three would make up your minds," he said in a playful tone through gritted teeth, "I wouldn't have to make the decision every day."

"Dealers choice then," Henry responded with a low chuckle. He exited their office with a quick wave. The soles of his old, brown loafers squawked with every step.

The sound made Greer wince as flashbacks from earlier of the police officer in her hospital room came to mind. She folded the brochure in half before stuffing it into a pocket of her bag and placed her laptop into standby with a quick press of the power button.

Greer pulled into the parking lot of the art gallery nearly twenty minutes later. She approached the black front doors, the pair bracketed by iron sconces with piped-in flame, and saw small gatherings of people through the windows. She reached forward to pull open the right door and immediately heard the low murmurings echoing through the gallery. Her heels clicked against the smooth concrete flooring, passing each painting hung on the brightly lit, white walls.

"Champagne, miss?"

Greer glanced over to see a nicely dressed man carrying a tray of six champagne flutes, each lined with links of bursting bubbles floating toward the surface of the glass. She politely declined and moved deeper into the gallery. The paintings done by Deborah were raw with thick brush strokes coating the canvases. Each told various stories of the legend of creation, snowstorm spirits, and how old age came into our world. She was following a series of paintings telling the story of the last, when she felt an arm brush against her. "Fascinating, isn't it?"

Greer turned her head to see Deborah. Her salt-and-pepper hair was still braided into two plaits, but beaded earrings now dangled from her earlobes. Her brown dress was embroidered with the same beads and leather sandals on her tanned feet.

"I heard about what happened," Deborah went on, glancing toward the gouging cuts at the base of Greer's throat. Greer reached up to fix the collar of her turtleneck, but Deborah placed a gentle hand on her forearm. "There are all kinds of creatures in this world that want to cause pain. Not all of them are human."

Greer felt her body stiffen and still. She shuffled on her feet as a ringing in her ears grew louder with each passing second. "I'm not sure what you mean," she managed to say. Deborah continued her act of studying her own painting, but drew in a deep breath to say, "We all felt the pulse of power you created. It opened a window for us, a surge of light in our darkened world."

Greer began to pick at the cuticles of her fingers as she bit her lip with unease. "What is happening to me?" she asked in a hushed whisper. She felt Deborah's fingers enclose around her wrist once again.

"Others will come for you now. You need to ready yourself."

"What does that—" Greer began to say, turning to look down at Deborah.

The woman was gone, pulled away by a patron inquiring on the price of an art piece displayed under a spotlight. It left Greer with a roiling stomach and a weight in her chest. She hesitated for a moment before fleeing the gallery.

FOUR

G reer was dreaming again. It was the dream that had been recurring in the week following the attack in the alleyway. It always started the same.

She woke on a dry river bed, the cracked clay bifurcated only by sandy trails where the water once flowed. She pushed herself to a standing position and allowed a quick sweep of the landscape. The limestone rock walls were deeply fissured from the erosion of the wind that whistled through the canyons. In the distance, she spotted the rock spires that rose from the ground and arched into unsteady formations. The blue sky was open and endless against the horizon, and the air should have been warm with the glow of the sun baking the clay beds into thin layers of shale.

But it wasn't warm. Not for any living thing that resided here.

The frigid wind sliced at her exposed skin, chapping her lips and numbing her fingers. She wrapped her arms around her chest and tried to ignore each breath that sawed her throat. A crack sounded in the canyon where the rock wall gave way. The rocks shifted and tumbled into the canyon near where she stood.

Instinctively, she knew she had to move. She had to run. She was being hunted.

The tang of limestone dust was thick on the wind that twisted through the dry ravine, and it took a shockingly small amount of time for her tongue to be coated in it. She kept running despite her throbbing feet. She didn't know how long she ran, but the spires in the distance never seemed to grow closer.

An unnaturally large shadow passed over her, the wing-span of the creature covering the width of the riverbed. She glanced upward, but saw nothing save for the streaks of white clouds that moved across the sky. Every animal seemed to be hiding from the creature, as the skittering of mice and lizards through the dried grass went silent with every pass of the shadow.

There was nowhere to hide. No fissure large enough to tuck into, no clear path to ascend the canyon wall.

A surge of power crackled through the air and her skin prickled under the energy shift. Two leather boots landed on the thin shale with an ear-splitting snap. The force of the boots sent shock waves through the earth beneath her, and the silhouette of the stranger encapsulated her body in shadow.

Her eyes would rake over the man in front of her. She would take in the brown leather armor held into place by brass buckles at the shoulders and waist. The gray, feathered wings that spanned many arm lengths and connected through the thick muscle at his back. The dark hair swept into a bun near the back of his head, loose locks shifting near his tightened jaw with every gust of wind. Finally, she would connect her stormy gray eyes with his cerulean blue ones.

This is where the dream would fork—becoming what Greer differentiated as the good dream or the bad dream. In the good dream, they would watch each other warily until his hand lifted to rest on her shoulder. In a flash, he would unsheathe a dagger from his hip and thrust it into her gut. She would let out a whoosh of air as her muscles clenched around the blade. She would have enough time to look down to study the leather-wrapped hilt and the three emerald gemstones embedded in a horizontal line. She would look into his eyes once more as the blood crawled up her throat, leaking from the corners of her mouth. She would choke on the thick, red, blood spraying onto the cracked clay when she coughed. She would fall onto her knees and crumple to the rock beneath her. It would be over. and she would be dead.

In the bad dream, his hand would lift to cup her cheek. They would say nothing to one another, but she would know that her soul recognized him as a part of her. He would bend down to pull her into his arms and his wings would open with a powerful *thwap*. They would rocket into the air as he carried her away from the desolate canyon. She would nuzzle her nose into the crook of his neck and breathe deeply. A musky sandalwood would fill her nostrils, and a heat would pool in her core. He would sense it too, tightening his grip around the backs of her knees and her waist.

They would land on the butte that overlooked the canyon, and he would kiss her deeply. His full lips would smile against hers and, in that moment, Greer knew that she would never fit so perfectly into anyone else's arms.

His kiss would land on her once more. Then he would slip his knife into the spaces between her ribs. He would pull back from her, and his eyes would glisten with tears unsaid. Her fingers would wrap around the straps of his leather armor in a struggle to hold herself upright. He would walk her backwards until her heels hung over the precipice, and she could feel the loose rock sliding beneath her feet.

He would kiss her one final time and then he would let her go. She would fall, her arms reaching out toward him as she barreled down to the canyon floor. Each breath agonizing, each second sending him deeper into the ether of the sky. Her body would crash against the rock, and she would feel her bones shatter on the impact. The last thing she would see would be him watching her over the edge of the cliff face.

Greer awoke with a sharp intake of breath and her hand grasping at her chest. That night, it was a bad dream. A very bad dream.

Her bedroom was still dark. The dim street light from the parking lot was barely discernible against her pulled curtains. She could hear Delia's soft snoring through the wall they shared. She was tangled in the floral sheets gracing her mattress, surrounded by the pile of throw pillows she used as decoration.

She was home. She was safe.

Despite using those words as a mantra, she couldn't shake the intense feeling of unease that settled into the pit of her stomach.

Greer swung her legs over the edge of the mattress and leaned to grab her cell phone from the side table. She clicked on the home screen, wincing against the deluge of bright light.

Six in the morning.

She sighed and scraped her hand down her face, moving it to rub the back of her neck. She slumped her shoulders and let her hands fall into her lap. There was no point in attempting to go back to sleep—it was going to evade her anyways.

It took her only a few minutes to dress into a pair of joggers and a long-sleeved shirt. The café down the street opened in the last thirty minutes, and she figured getting a coffee was a better use of her time.

By the time Greer slipped away from the apartment building, the city had begun to wake up. The morning hustle and bustle of commuters whizzed past her, splashing puddles of water from the overnight rain onto the sidewalk, and the diner nearest her home was wafting the scent of frying bacon from its vents. She passed by the windows and spotted the older regulars sitting at the countertop. They sipped their coffee from faded mugs and one waitress was already pouring a refill from the steaming pot she held in her hand.

It wasn't quite dawn yet, the dark sky was just beginning to shift into the bluish-orange hue that preceded the sun, but the streetlamps lining the sidewalk had already begun to flicker. She took in a deep breath to calm her nerves, but to no avail.

Greer tugged on the door to the café, the familiar ding of the bell sounding above her. The earthy, early morning scent shifted into the spicy fragrance of coffee grounds as she stepped inside.

The long ordering counter was stacked with espresso machines, bean grinders, and pre-filled coffee carafes. Bottles of various flavorings topped with white hand pumps lined the glass separating customer from employee. The chalkboard bolted to the wall above the counter had *summer coffee special: iced pistachio rose latte* and *try our salted caramel affogato today!* hand-written in a neat font. The line was already three deep with patrons waiting near the cash register, the two employees behind the counter busy frothing milk and pouring drinks into cardboard to-go cups. Greer made it to the front of the line. She ordered a lavender honey latte for herself and a coconut mint iced mocha for Delia, both from the recommendations printed on the laminated menu near the cash register. With one final sweep around the café, coffees now in each hand, she spotted a familiar sight tucked into the far corner.

"Hey. Odette, is it?" Greer said, approaching the nurse hovering over her open book. "I think you took care of me when I was in the hospital earlier this week." She tried to keep her eyes averted from the wings that hung from her back, the tips scraping the tiled floor.

The woman lifted her head, a small smile tugging at the corners of her lips. Her red hair was pulled into a fashionable bun at the base of her head, any fly-aways slicked back. "Yes, I did. It's so good to see that you're doing better." She returned her attention to the book, wings fluttering at the motion, but Greer sat in the seat opposite her.

"I just—" Greer paused, biting the inside of her cheek. "I can't help,...but wonder. I'm sorry if this is a bit forward, but I study cultures for a living and—" She sucked in a deep breath, hoping the question wouldn't come across as offensive. "Why are you wearing wings? I noticed them in the hospital and—"

Odette went preternaturally still, her gaze still fixed on the page in front of her.

She slowly lifted her head, and Greer noticed that she had gone starkly white. Odette's hand wrapped around the to-go mug, denting the sides with her fingertips. "I—I don't," she started in a hushed whisper, as she glanced at Greer. Her eyes were wide with fright. "You can't possibly see them."

Greer furrowed her brow in confusion. The reaction was unexpected. "Of course, I can see them," she replied, gesturing toward the wings, "Can't everyone—" She trailed off to look over her shoulder. She realized for the first time that not a single person was giving a thought to the woman with wings in the corner of the café. Her breath turned shallow.

Oh God. Not again.

Odette slammed her book shut and shoved it into the bag dangling from the back of her chair.

"Wait, wait—" Greer started. The legs of her chair screeched against the tile floor as she stood. "Don't leave, please." She reached out to grab Odette's arm, but managed to graze the wings instead.

Greer watched as Odette's back stiffened. Odette whirled, her own hand encircling Greer's wrist. "Never, ever touch a faerie's wings," she said in a deadly calm, her eyes narrowing onto Greer's slackened and stunned face. The patrons of the café had begun to notice the stand-off, their shoulders squared to the altercation between Odette and Greer. It had gone quiet, the only noise being the steady drizzle of new coffee being brewed into a carafe behind the counter.

Odette seemed to realize they had attracted attention. She withdrew her hand with a sharp jerk and began to maneuver around the baffled early-morning crowd. Her wings were tucked in tightly to her back, lifted so as to not drag on the floor.

"Odette, wait. *Wait*," Greer said, as she attempted to follow Odette's trail through the busy coffeehouse. "Please, I need help. *Please*."

Odette spun one last time as Greer hit the sidewalk. The sky was beginning to lighten, streaks of orange painted against the dark canvas. "I am not going to be dragged back into this," she hissed, shoving a pointed finger into Greer's chest, "You will stay away from me." With that, she stormed off and turned the corner at the end of the block, disappearing from view.

Overwhelming panic began to boil in Greer's stomach, her breath turning into quick and shallow pants. She squeezed her eyes shut and hoped against all odds that she could wake herself from the dream she must still be having. She felt her hands tremor, the hot coffee sloshing through the opening in the lid and onto her fingers.

"You must know why you could see them," a voice called from behind her.

Greer's shoulders grew rigid as color rose back into her cheeks. The voice wasn't that of the man who had attacked her, that man was dead, but the physical response to the unknown man behind her was the same nonetheless. She whipped around to find herself staring at the man a few feet from her.

He held an aura of power about him. It was an old and arrogant power, one in direct contrast with the leather jacket and black jeans he wore. Silver rings banded his fingers and he played with them as he spoke, spinning them around. Whether it was a calming technique or out of pure habit, Greer wasn't sure.

He ran a hand through his short, dark hair and his green eyes bore sharply into hers. "The power you sparked has alerted all of us to your presence," he went on, jaw tightening as he crossed his arms over his chest. "And has alerted you to our presence. Her glamour no longer holds under your gaze."

The words, so similar to Deborah's, hit Greer like an arrow to the heart. "We don't know each other," Greer responded defiantly. She went to turn away, to walk back toward the direction of her apartment building, when the man was suddenly in front of her.

His scent washed over her, one of old leather and bold aftershave, as he looked down at her. "I know more than you think," he bent down to retort in her ear. His breath grazed her bare neck, and she felt a shudder claw up her back.

She lifted an elbow and shoved him away. The green, jagged gemstone that hung from the black cord around his neck bounced on his chest. "Stay away from me or I'm going to scream," she warned. She gave him a wide berth as she continued to walk away from the café.

"No, you won't." His tone, flecked with an Irish accent, was sure and condescending. It caused a flutter of annoyance to flare within Greer.

Greer picked up her walking speed, but he adjusted with ease. "Yes, I will."

"If you were going to, you would have done it already." She inhaled deeply, nostrils flaring.

His lip curled in a smirk. "That's what I thought. You know, I've been studying your ancestral line for centuries now. Been guarding it since the last one was killed. I back-tracked through history until I found every daughter born. And do you know what I discovered?"

Greer continued her march down the sidewalk, not bothering to acknowledge him. He went on regardless.

"I found that you aren't where you're supposed to be."

She snorted with derision. "And where am I supposed to be?"

"Six feet under, I presume."

Greer's steps faltered and she tripped over a raised crack in the sidewalk. She assumed he meant from the attack days ago. Her skin prickled, her body awash in fear. "I got away from him, didn't I?" she said, her voice calmer than she felt internally.

He shook his head. "I meant you should have died with your mother twenty-six years ago."

She jerked her head upwards, fastening her gaze onto him. "My mother is still alive. You have the wrong person." She continued her pace into the parking lot of her apartment building, the sun now beginning its ascent over the tops of the trees.

The man dipped into the long shadows of the forest. He lifted his hand to run a finger over his lower lip, studying her. "I quite think I have the right person," he called after her, as she thrusted the door of the building open. "And I quite think we're not done having this conversation."

The last of his words cut off as the thick, metal door swung shut behind her. Greer flew up the first flight of stairs before stalling at the window that faced the parking lot. She peered down, her stare passing over the emptying lot.

The man had disappeared.

She craned her neck, leaning over the windowsill to see where he would have walked off to, but she didn't see him at all. Only the cars zooming down the street and the pedestrians headed to early morning classes remained. She did spot her mother's car idling under the carport, though, and she let an aggravated sigh slip through her nose.

She took a sip of the coffee, the light taste of lavender brushing over her tongue. She pushed the conversation with Odette from her mind and wanted to forget the interaction with the strange man who accompanied her home entirely.

She stomped up the last flight of stairs, awaiting the arrival of her overbearing mother.

FIVE

CELESTE

Celeste Myers saw red.

Her ears pounded as her vision tunneled on the man who was walking with her daughter. The man she suspected wasn't entirely human. She recognized the subtle signs. The unnatural stare of predator versus prey, the shift into the shadow as the sun tipped over the tops of the trees. And, of course, there was the speed in which he moved as soon as Greer entered the apartment building.

Her throat dried, and she bit back a yell of anger that threatened to escape from between her lips. Her knuckles whitened as she fisted the steering wheel instead.

She was lucky she had decided to stop by Greer's apartment. She was lucky she had the foresight to check on her daughter, to make sure that she was caring for herself following the attack from that animal.

Greer had begged her to go home, had pleaded with Celeste to allow things to return to normal. But Celeste knew that nothing would be the same now. Things had changed. Greer had changed.

Celeste had prayed to the universe and to any God from any religion that her daughter wasn't it. Wasn't one of *them*. She always knew the possibility was there. She had known the moment she watched her father slice through the neck of the woman they had tracked down. Had known from the moment she decided killing an infant wasn't worth what she had trained her entire life to do.

She tried to play it off in the hospital when Greer's eyes grew wide and she mentioned the nurse having wings, but she knew then. She knew her daughter had been tapped as the next Mage.

Celeste put her car into drive and pulled out from under the carport, entering the morning traffic on the main road. There were only a few places in town that man would have gone. She had scoped out the possibilities on her way into town. In fact, she had even begun an internet search on her phone the moment she heard her daughter's attacker had been mysteriously killed in the assault. Celeste knew that others would be coming for her.

The first house was abandoned. Most of the windows on the first floor were broken, glass still sprinkled on the sodden and warped, wooden porch. Thin sheets of plywood covered the openings from the inside, but cracks between the sheet and the windowsill showed an empty living room with peeling wallpaper.

Celeste knew it wasn't the luxury most men of his caliber tended towards, but the house was close to the university campus, and the roof seemed to be in decent shape. The students that walked by the house didn't give it a second look. It was a decent hiding spot.

Celeste sped by it anyways.

The man would have needed to cross the street to reach it- the street that was already bathed in sunlight. No, the house he was residing in was going to be on the right side of the road so he could use the forest for shelter during the sunrise and sunset.

She approached the second house, located on a secondary street that broke the forest into two. The house was set back from the road, built in a time when people favored front yards to back ones. The chain link fence surrounding the house was barely held upright by the metal posts in the ground.

She pulled her car off to the side and put it into park. This house was even more derelict than the first. The roof had caved at some point, mossy mold growing on the shingles still intact. The owner hadn't bothered to cover the broken windows with plywood, leaving the interior of the house to be subjected to whatever weather blew on that day instead.

In Oregon, it was rain. Celeste hated the rain.

She watched the house for a time and waited to see if any movement came from the other side of the stripped frame. When the house still appeared empty after a thirty-minute block, she started up the car and pulled back into the street once more.

The third house still backed the forest, but it was a twenty-minute drive from the first two and located closer to the outskirts of town. Celeste figured there was a way to cut through the forest if one chose to. Even though this house was further from the university, she also knew that creatures like him preferred solitary houses if given the opportunity. They were better to keep victims in.

She rolled to the foot of the gravel driveway and put the car into park. The air was mistier out here and smelled like what she thought others would describe as fresh. She thought it smelled like pig shit, hay, and a third unknown scent. Wrinkling her nose, she stepped from the car.

The house was an old farmhouse style with white siding, two stories, and a wrap-around porch. A wooden swing was set into the corner of the porch, facing a pole barn with two large hydraulic doors, perhaps for the wife to watch her husband tinker on equipment during the summer evenings. The porch itself needed to be resealed, but the dark, red stain soaked into the wood near the front door told Celeste that the couple wasn't going to be fixing it anytime soon. Then, she realized what that third scent was. The sickly, pungent mustiness of a decaying body. It had been quite a long time since Celeste had smelled it for herself, but it was one that she would never forget. She figured it was the previous owner, caught unawares when the man moved into town.

If the owner's body was decomposing somewhere close to the house, that certainly meant the man now inside of the house had removed his head as soon as they were done feeding.

Celeste crossed the grassy yard, passing by a small garden gnome and a copper wind spinner in the shape of oak leaves, before ascending the steps of the porch. The wood was sturdy and strong under foot, another sign that the death of the owners was recent. She tip-toed to a window, peeking through the crack in the curtains. There was movement on the other side. She was right.

The breeze brushed her blonde hair over her shoulder as she backtracked to the front door, rapping her knuckles on the glass insert. She stepped back, her hand wrapped tightly around the hilt of the silver stake she had pulled from the car before exiting.

The door was yanked open to reveal the same man from earlier. His leather jacket had been removed and hung on a hook near the door, leaving him in only a black T-shirt. He smiled down at her, a feral and unkind one that would have made a lesser person's skin crawl. Celeste only held her head higher.

"Hello, I'm looking for the owner's of the house. I'm from the gas company."

The man looked down the front of her white blouse and blue jeans and back up again. He leaned a forearm against the door frame above his head, sliding around the toothpick he had between his lips.

"You didn't think that would work, did you?" he said mockingly. "I smell her on you. You must be mommy."

Celeste jerked the silver stake upward, aiming for the man's heart. He took a step backward, chuckling under his breath.

"Easy, easy." He paused to snap his fingers, and two more men appeared behind him, baring their sharp fangs. "What was your plan here? You're outnumbered."

Celeste glanced briefly over his shoulder. She eyed the dark-skinned male with coiled hair, his arms crossed over his chest. Her gaze flicked back to the first.

"Leave town," Celeste said in a low growl, "or I will kill you."

The man took another step back, splaying his hands out to his sides. "I actually don't think you will. I think you're a bit out of practice." His grin pulled into an all-knowing smirk as he tucked his hands into his pockets. "An active member of the Paladin Society would never walk into a vampyre den alone." He clicked his tongue at her parted lips and raised brows. "Of course, I know. I recognize the markings on your blade."

The two men still in the hallway chuckled under their breath.

"Now, I could just kill you," the man continued, shrugging a shoulder. His head danced back and forth as if he were seriously considering it. "That just seems like an awful headache. We can't have bodies piling up here." He stopped to pull the toothpick from his mouth. "Well, more bodies than there already are. Mister and Missus Camper have been so accommodating. You should see the bathtub in the master bathroom."

"It has jets," the third vampyre, a pale fellow with bright, red hair and a long nose, interjected with a grin of his own. "I think I'll just send you on your way though," the first man went on, sliding his fangs out from under his gumline. "I'm sure you and I will become fast friends." Celeste let out a low hiss from between gritted teeth.

"You will leave Greer alone." She pointed the tip of the blade at him.

"Greer? Is that her name?"

Celeste knew her mistake immediately. There was power in a name. There was a reason none of these men had given her their own. She drew her face into a blank expression, and the man's lips split into an ear-to-ear grin. "Oh. We are out of practice, aren't we? How long has it been? Twenty-six years?" He sucked a tooth. "As far as leaving her alone, that is far less likely."

"You don't know if she is— *her*," Celeste said. She could feel the shakiness in her voice. It signified weakness. Weakness was something her father would not have tolerated, but as a mother, Celeste wasn't sure how to rid herself of it. "She awoke the magic," the first man pressed on. The dark-skinned man shifted from side to side on his feet in the background. "The book has awoken. We can sense her presence now—" He leaned forward, dropping his voice into a dramatic, hushed whisper. "— So, we came like a moth to a flame."

Celeste sneered. Jerking her hand up once again, she caught the unsuspecting man on the underside of his chin with the blade. He grunted in pain as his hand flew to the mark. The two vampyres behind him made to take steps forward, but he shooed them back with a flick of his wrist. "She needs to know who she is," the man started, his chest heaving with restrained control, "She needs to know *what* she is before it's too late—"

"She needs to know *nothing*," Celeste retorted, her teeth clenched tightly together. "I'm her mother. I get to decide—"

The man took a threatening step forward. Celeste held her ground despite her rapidly beating heart. "You are not her mother. You are her kidnapper. Holly Hawkins was her mother, and Greer should know what you have done."

The name *Holly Hawkins* was one Celeste hadn't heard in decades. She jolted backward as if she had been shot in the gut. The wooden planks of the porch creaked as she took a step from the threshold of the door. "You don't know if Greer is— "

"Your reaction said everything I needed to know about your *daughter*." The last word was spat out in a condescending drawl. The man placed the toothpick back in his mouth, a gleam of triumph shining in his eyes. "I wonder what sweet, sweet Greer will say when she learns you butchered her real mother like a steer."

Celeste's eyes flashed in rage. "I am her mother, and I will protect her. From all of this."

The man rested his hand on the knob of the front door. "Her mother might have been able to, but you killed her. Now, I guess we'll never know."

With that, he shut the door in Celeste's face and bolted the lock behind it.

SIX

"You can't hide the password to the copy machine," Erin said, her elbows set firmly on her desk as she looked over at Daniel. "We all need to use it!"

"Henry trusted me with it, knowing I wouldn't copy or print anything frivolous," Daniel retorted. "If you need something copied, give it to me, and I'll take care of it for you."

Erin groaned in frustration. "Daniel, this is ridiculous. I'll just ask Henry for the passcode myself— "

"That's fine," he responded airily, waving the post-it note toward her. "Just remember that he's going to bring up last year's Christmas party."

Erin balked. "They were serving maple bourbon espresso martinis! It was hardly my fault what happened— "

A sharp knock on the open door silenced the two and drew Greer away from the documents she had been pretending to catalog. In truth, her mind was flicking between Odette, the strange man, and the disappearance of her mother's car first thing that morning.

"You can have the passcode, Erin, but under strict scrutiny," Henry said from the doorway.

Tea spilled over the side of Erin's mug as she jumped in surprise. Daniel let out a bark of a laugh that he quickly covered with a series of forced coughs.

Henry turned to look at Greer. She noticed the buttons on his green knit sweater vest were done incorrectly. "I came to check in with you. I wanted to see how you were feeling." Greer nodded in response. "Everything is fine. I'm just going over these last documents Daniel found in the archives." She paused to hold up the stack of photographs. The top half flopped over onto the side of her hand and Greer caught something from the corner of her eye. Turning her head, she studied the painting she had interviewed Deborah over. The man in the foreground, his fangs ever-present, with his hand wrapped around the tree. And the thick, jagged stone that hung around his neck.

Greer stilled as her eyes narrowed in on the necklace. She felt her breathing hitch in her throat as she laid the stack down on her desk and flipped back to the photograph. "I have to go," Greer said in a hushed voice and immediately stood from her office chair. "I— I have a lead on something. I have to go." She closed the lid of her laptop and hurriedly stuffed it into her canvas bag, followed by her notebook, a pen, and the photograph.

"Enthusiasm," Henry was saying as Greer sped past him, canvas bag banging against her back as she jogged down the hallway, "That's what I like to see out of my researchers. Now the passcode— "

Greer didn't bother yelling down the hallway that she had placed a post-it note of the passcode in the top drawer of Erin's desk just last week. Instead, she pressed the button to summon the elevator. She swayed back and forth on her feet as she waited.

The elevator finally clanged to a stop on the basement floor and Greer entered the car, pushing past the group of interns making their way off. They tossed dirty looks her way and she mumbled an apology as the doors shut behind her.

Her speed quickened as the elevator released her on the ground floor, giving her barely enough time to wave goodbye to Roger, whose brow was furrowed. She slowed to a power walk long enough to fish her car keys from the inside pocket of the canvas bag and unlocked the driver's side door.

The door opened with a quick tug, and Greer dumped her work bag, as well as the lanyard around her neck, onto the passenger seat. She shoved the key into the ignition and the engine roared to life a moment later.

She paused. She didn't know the name of the stranger, let alone where he lived, where he worked, or what he did during the day. She slumped back against her seat, taking a shaky breath. The city wasn't egregiously large by any stretch of the imagination, but it would certainly take most of the day to search. She glanced at the clock on the dashboard— three in the afternoon.

Perhaps she would get lucky and stumble across him on campus.

Greer did not, in fact, get lucky. She spent most of the afternoon and evening driving her car through the university campus, into student housing, crossing the busy downtown financial district, and slicing through the suburb neighborhoods of the locals. She had even mustered up the courage to do one pass along the same strip where the brewery was located, though her chest had tightened at the sight of the alleyway.

The car rolled to a stop in the lot of her apartment building a few hours later and she defeatedly shoved the gear selector back into park. Greer let her head fall against the headrest as the palms of her hands rubbed at her eye sockets. It was ridiculous of her to think she could easily track this man down. It was even more ridiculous of her to think that he might have anything to do with the painting. It was made in the image of a story from two hundred years ago; it was impossible that he had anything to do with it.

Grasping the handles of her canvas bag, she stepped out of her Jeep and shut the door behind her. There was one more place to look and it was within walking distance. Greer smoothed out the white shirt she had tucked into the band of her patterned maxi skirt and began her walk toward the coffee shop. Her strappy sandals slapped against the pavement as she went and she was thankful the rain had stopped for the day, as the cars driving home for the night could no longer splash puddles of water onto the sidewalk.

She entered the café just as the sun fell behind the tops of the trees and took a quick sweep of the interior. The coffeehouse was slower than it was this morning, and Greer felt her stomach drop at the empty leather seats surrounding the lit fireplace.

One employee, her curly hair tied back with a blue bandana, was wiping down the empty tables with a wet rag. She glanced up toward Greer and sent her a small smile. "Closing in fifteen," she said, before pocketing the rag into the front pocket of her apron. She bent down to flip the chairs onto the table, readying to mop the floor.

Greer sucked in a breath of disappointment. Sighing through her nose, she figured she may as well purchase something while she was there.

She headed to the left of the cash register where a wall of pre-bagged coffee beans, mugs made from local artists, and glass pour-over coffee makers were settled onto the shelves built into the wall. She grabbed a bag of coffee beans, labeled Snickerdoodle, and tucked it into the crook of her arm. She fumbled with her wallet as she slowly walked toward the cash register, where a second employee had stopped cleaning the espresso machine to ring up her order.

"This it?" the woman asked, her youthful face looking up at Greer with wide eyes.

"I just needed a restock, I guess," Greer responded with a tight smile, handing the bag and her debit card over to the employee.

"Do you always find yourself at coffee shops or is this just a happy coincidence?"

Greer's head jerked upward as she whipped around, a few thick locks of brown hair loosening from the knot on top of her head. Her heart soared as she locked eyes with the dark-haired stranger, his ring-clad fingers wrapped around a leather-bound book.

"You," Greer took a small step toward him. "I've been trying to find you." A tap on her upper arm had Greer looking over her shoulder. The employee held out the bag of coffee and the debit card. "Oh, so sorry," Greer said, as she unceremoniously stuffed both into her canvas bag and shifted it back up onto her shoulder.

The man looked pleased at her statement, biting his lip to hide the smile that was threatening to pull at the corners of his lips. "Were you now? It hasn't been so long since we've seen one another."

Greer's cell phone vibrated against her hip. She dug into her bag and pulled it out, rolling her eyes when she caught the caller ID *mother* on the top of the screen. She clicked the phone off and dropped it back into her bag, but didn't quite miss the flash of anger behind the man's eyes when he, too, saw the name on the screen. She felt the phone vibrate one more time, signaling a voicemail. She ignored it.

"I have questions for you," she started, leading him from the coffeehouse.

He pulled the door open with one hand, keeping the book tucked tightly against his waist. "I would think you do considering I told you about your mother— "

"Not that," Greer cut him off as she crossed the threshold and onto the sidewalk. The summer air was thick with grilling hamburgers from a house across the main road, the smoke rising above the garage roof. Her stomach rumbled at the scent. "I still think you have the wrong person for that." She paused to pull out the folded photograph from her bag. "I'm an anthropologist at the university. Part of my research is with native tribes in the Pacific Northwest." She unfolded the paper and held it out to him. Their fingers lightly brushed and she quickly withdrew her hand back to her side. "I recognized your necklace in the painting, and I was curious. Is it an heirloom or some sort of relic? It's unusual in its shape— " She trailed off, watching the man with an inquisitive gaze.

He studied the photograph for a beat, his head tilting to the side as he looked at it. Greer had the sudden urge to tuck the stray hair that had fallen onto his forehead back with the others, but held against the thought.

He cleared his throat and looked up at her with a smirk. "She did get my likeness, didn't she?"

Greer's brows flew to her hairline. "You can't be suggesting that—"

He held out the leather-bound book, and she took it into her hands. She felt the book begin to hum beneath her touch, but ignored it to watch the man. He reached behind his neck and unclasped the black cord. He placed the gemstone into his palm, holding it against the photograph of the painting. The resemblance was certainly uncanny, Greer couldn't deny that.

"That doesn't answer my question—" she began, but the man interrupted her.

"It was given to me by a good friend some years ago," he said, wrapping the gemstone in his fist. "She thought it would give me good luck on my endeavors. I've worn it ever since." He stopped to clasp the necklace back into place and glanced back down at the photograph. "The artist who painted it did a good job. Even got the edges right." His eyes narrowed as they darted back up to meet Greer's. "Who did you say the artist was?"

"I didn't."

"Hmmm." He returned his attention to the book in Greer's hands. The humming had transitioned to a heavy vibrate in the meantime. "I think the grimoire wants something from you."

"The grimoire?" Greer looked down at the book. She had assumed he placed some sort of device on the inside cover to create the humming sensation.

"A witch's manual," he pressed on. The sleeves of his leather jacket creaked as he folded his arms over his chest. "It must recognize you. I haven't seen it do that in many, many years." Greer tried to hand the book back to the man, but he held his hands up in surrender. "That's not mine. It's yours."

She scoffed as she shook her head, looking off toward the tree-covered mountains in the distance. She turned back to him after a moment. "This isn't mine. You just gave it to me to hold onto." She held it out to him once more. He ran a thumb over his lower lip as he rocked from heel to toe and back again. "Open it. If it's yours, you'll be able to read it. If not, I'll take it back and apologize for wasting your time."

She let a frustrated sigh escape her lips as her gaze dropped to the book.

The brown leather encasing the pages was old and worn. She didn't know why she was nervous as she unwrapped the single strip of leather that held the covers together, letting it dangle toward the ground. It opened with little difficulty, despite the apparent age of the leather, and she found herself skimming the page she had flipped to.

At first inspection, Greer noticed the paper wasn't paper at all, but thick parchment. It was yellowed and torn, the edges not matching up with the others, creating a haggard look about the grimoire. The black ink, curled against the parchment in thin strokes, sat on the surface of the parchment rather than absorbing like modern day paper would allow. The words on the parchment bore little resemblance to anything she had read before and they seemed to be a list of ingredients for a kind of spell work.

This book was old. It was very, very old.

She shut it quickly to protect the pages from the water dripping from the awning above them.

"And?" the man said, impatience tipping into his voice. "And what?" Greer responded in the same tone. "It's a book. A very old book. You should take better care of it, otherwise the ink will fade."

The man went preternaturally still. "The ink?"

"Yes, the ink." Against her better judgment, she opened the book once more. She didn't allow her finger to touch the page as she pointed out the swirls and dips of the handwriting on the parchment. "You should take this to be treated by a person who can do restoration work. I have a contact in my phone; I can give you the number— "

"I didn't know it had ink," the man said, with a shake of his head. "I assumed it did, of course, but I've never been able to read it."

Greer stared at him as she reached up to rub her brow. "You've never read it? Why is it in your possession?"

The streetlamps flickered on as the sky crossed over into true night, bathing them in an yellow glow.

"I can't read it," he reiterated, his green eyes boring into hers. "Just like you could see through that faerie's glamour, just like you killed that man with a single touch. The grimoire hides itself from those who do not possess the capability to perform its magic."

"I didn't kill— "

"You may not have meant to, but your magic certainly did. It awoke when you were endangered and protected you from harm. You have been tapped as the next Mage, like it or not."

Greer felt the book bounce against her thigh as she dropped her hand to her side. She didn't even flinch as the old, leather cord scraped the pavement. "This isn't funny," she managed to croak out, her throat tight and thick against the panic building in her body. She had tried her best to forget about the attack. She felt her skin crawling, his hands around her throat, his fingernails scratching against her neck.

"It's not a joke," he responded firmly. He dropped his voice to a whisper as he stepped toward her, an attempt to keep the passersby from overhearing, and placed a hand on her upper arm. She felt the calluses on his palm tickle her bare skin. "Take it home with you. Try a few of the spells I assume are in there. When you can show me what you can do, I'll answer more of your questions."

Her lips parted as she looked down at the grimoire once again. She bit back the overwhelming desire to throw it into the street, where an oncoming truck had whizzed by. She swallowed and sent a fleeting look back toward the man.

"I don't even know your name."

His lips pulled into a slight frown as he squinted down at her. He seemed to be trapped in uncertainty. He scrubbed a hand down the shadow of a beard that pricked his jawline. "Cian," he finally said, after much hesitation. "The name is Cian."

"Greer," she replied almost at once, sticking out her hand.

He took it in his own, his fingers devouring hers, and shook it.

Her attention turned toward the mountains in the distance and she took in a breath to ask a final question. When she swept her eyes back to where Cian had been standing, she was taken aback when she realized he had gone. She looked around to see if she could spot the back of the man's head in the oncoming crowd of college students headed toward the bars for the night, but he was gone.

Had it not been for the grimoire still firmly clutched in her fist, she would have wondered if he had been there at all.

SEVEN

The grimoire was set in the middle of the wooden coffee table, directly in between a bowl of decorative wicker balls and a single candle shaped like a green succulent. Greer sat with her clenched fists tucked under her chin staring at it. Her heel bounced against the beige, carpeted floor of her living room. She half expected the book to do something fantastical and found herself disappointed when it didn't.

"This is ridiculous," she muttered under her breath, standing from her perch on the gray, microfiber couch. "Absolutely ridiculous." She didn't know why she was even entertaining the idea of her being the only one who can read the damn thing.

She padded into the kitchen and tossed a frozen meal into the microwave, leaning against the counter as she waited. The scent of chicken alfredo filled the room, the plastic container popping under the accumulated steam.

She glanced back over her shoulder at the leather grimoire as she bit the inside of her cheek. If there was any time to explore the book alone, it would be now. Delia was working late at the law firm and was expected to meet Paige for their date night afterwards.

The microwave dinged, pulling Greer from her thoughts. She opened the door and took the plastic tray out by her fingertips, dropping it quickly onto the counter. She hissed under her breath as she sucked on the end of her burnt finger. It was already reddening, with the skin swelling under a newly forming blister.

A vibrating noise sounded behind her. She watched with renewed interest as the book danced across the glass of the table. Wiping her finger on the leg of her pants, she slowly walked over to the grimoire. It stopped moving when she approached it, halting in place as if it had been stationary the entire time.

She sank to her knees at the long-edge of the table and reached forward to slide the book toward her. It hummed playfully at her touch. Curiosity getting the best of her, she opened the book to the first page, the spine so threadbare that the book lay flat against the surface.

She pinched the first piece of parchment between two fingers and studied the quality. It was not as worn or torn as she expected, leading her to believe magic may have something to do with how well preserved it was. No, that couldn't be. Cian certainly had some sort of preservation work done to it. That had to be it.

With the lightest touch, she ran her fingertips down the parchment. The black writing was smeared in some places, as if someone had slid their hand across the ink before it had the time to dry.

She tilted her head to read the first page: *Grimoire VII, 1556.* Her eyebrows rose in response. Over four hundred and sixty years old. She turned the page once again and noticed the same looped handwriting scrawled across the parchment.

Page after page contained spells for protection, healing, and sleep, potions for walking in the sun, shifting outside of the equinox, and fire resistance. Drawings of various creatures and crystals were scratched into the margins.

One section of the book was devoted entirely to plants. Alongside a drawing of each organism were lists of how long each plant needed to be in the sun, how much water it required for survival, and what each part of the plant could be used for.

Chamomile for relaxation. Echinacea for healing wounds. Valerian for sleeplessness. Ginger for nausea.

It was clear to Greer that whoever had owned the book dedicated quite a long time compiling different ways to treat illnesses and diseases. She found it fascinating how much was known all those centuries ago.

She carefully turned back to the first page of the book and read over the first spell once more. It was written in a language that she didn't recognize. Somehow, someway, she knew exactly what it said. She stretched out her arm, holding her palm open in front of her. Closing her eyes, she repeated the first word that appeared in the grimoire. "*Suundias.*" She cracked open her eyes. Nothing happened. She dropped her hand into her lap. "This is stupid," she said under her breath. She couldn't do magic, couldn't be a witch. She let another sharp sigh exit her nose and adjusted on her knees. One more time. She would try one more time.

Greer narrowed her eyes as she considered what she knew about witches and magic, beyond the green skin and the hairy mole just on the upper lip. Every movie, every book, every character required emotion to conjure their power. They dug deeply into themselves to pull out that shred of magic they needed.

Her thoughts returned to when she had been attacked, to when everything had changed. She pushed past the churn in her stomach and her mouth began to dry as she took a hard look at what she had been feeling when it happened. The overwhelming sense that she had to flee. The terror when she realized she couldn't. The panic when his fingers wrapped around her throat.

She held these feelings in place as she whispered *"Suundias."*

A jet of flame burst from the candle on the coffee table. The wax melted instantly, creating a green puddle where the succulent once was. The fire spread across the wax and easily overtook the clay bowl. It cracked under the heat, splitting it in half just as the blaze caught the decorative wicker balls.

A cry of panic leapt from Greer's chest. She instinctively threw her hands toward the flame as if she could put the fire out herself.

Suddenly, a deluge of water dumped from above and extinguished the blaze. The fire hissed in protest as the flames turned to steam, rising up to the ceiling in billowing rolls of vapor. She sputtered, wiping the water from her eyes.

The coffee table, the glass warped and scorched under the heat, was soaked with water and newly hardened green wax. The mixture dripped onto the carpet, where puddles of water and wax were forming within the fibers. The couch, the acrid scent of singed cloth joining the smells of over-cooked clay and burnt wicker, was just as wet.

Greer was frozen in shock. Her sodden clothes clung uncomfortably to her body and her hair had curled into lanky, slick knots and tangles.

Her ears were ringing and she knew the fire alarm in the kitchen was noisily trilling, but the sound was muffled to her. It was only when pounding on the door, shaking the wood in the frame, that she came to, leaping from her knelt position at the end of the table.

She stumbled to the door and yanked it open, revealing her neighbor from across the hall. The gentleman was older and recently widowed, wisps of white hair stuck to the sides of his head. His eyes were etched with worry as he surveyed her.

"I heard your yell— " he started to say, but Greer had already turned from the door.

She grabbed a wet pillow from the corner of the couch and waved it in the air underneath the fire alarm. Droplets of water flecked the cabinets and countertop with each swipe Greer made. The trilling halted after a long moment, and she shakily turned back to the doorway.

"I— I'm really sorry, Mister Kulikowski," she stammered, gesturing over her shoulder toward the ruined coffee table. "A candle tipped over and set everything on fire."

Astonishment painted her neighbor's wrinkled face. "A candle did that?" His tone was filled with disbelief as he glanced past her and took in the scorched table.

"It was a big candle."

He returned his gaze to her. "And you're okay?"

Greer nodded, a tight smile pulling at her lips. "I threw a bucket of water on it. I just need to clean up."

"Do you want a hand? I have a free night— "

"No!" The word came out abrupt and harsh. Her heart tugged as he flinched, taken aback. "I'm so sorry, I just mean I don't want to bother you with it. Delia will be home soon; it shouldn't take me very long."

He studied her for a beat before inhaling sharply. "Okay, then. As long as you aren't hurt."

"Not hurt at all, but thank you for checking on me."

He sent her a final curt nod before shuffling back to his own apartment, the door clicking into place behind him. She shut her own door, sighing deeply before assessing the damage in front of her.

Interestingly enough, the grimoire situated in the middle of the warped table was perfectly content. A ring of water and wax surrounded the otherwise dry surface under the book, the leather left untouched by the heat or flame that had overtaken the table.

"Don't be silly, I'm just glad you're okay!" Delia laughed as Greer palmed the bill and slid it toward her.

Four margaritas, two mango and two passion fruit, a basket of chips with salsa, one chicken enchilada plate, and one chorizo burrito.

The clean-up from the night before had taken Greer longer than she anticipated, and Delia had come home to find her best friend picking dried wax from the fibers of the carpet. She had locked eyes with Greer, took in the wrecked living room, and immediately got to work helping Greer clean the damage.

Greer owed her. Big time.

"Do you remember when we could down a pitcher of these, *each*?" Delia lamented over the mariachi music playing through the restaurant speakers.

Greer looked up from her wallet to see Delia peering into her glass, swirling the ice around with her cocktail straw. "I remember hugging the toilet like I was requesting sanctuary."

Delia snorted. She reached up to readjust the claw clip that held her tightly wound curls into place. "Well, I remember those tattoos we got after our graduation night out." She paused to hold up her arm where a thin, dainty arrow had been inked near her wrist.

Greer lifted her arm to touch Delia's wrist with her own, where a matching tattoo was placed in the same space. "You mean you barely remember. You had to take Tylenol for a week afterwards though."

Delia glanced down, her lips puckering in thought. "Luckily, the tattoo artist deterred us away from the original idea, otherwise I would have your misspelled name on my ribcage."

It was Greer's turn to laugh. "Grere? Yeah, we were lucky that the tattoo artist recognized our lack of sobriety, but not lucky enough that he decided to tattoo us anyways."

"It was a dingy loft above a hole-in-the-wall bar close to campus. What did we expect? Both have since closed, by the way."

"I guess we'll always have something to remember him by."

"Are you headed straight home?" Delia asked as she gathered her purse into her arms. "I'm hoping the musty smell of the carpet is gone. I left every fan I could find running."

"You go ahead. I'm going to head to the indie bookstore down the street. Erin gave me a recommendation I wanted to check out."

Greer stood from her side of the booth and tossed her purse over her shoulder. She followed Delia through the heart of the restaurant, winding through the tables filled with the clinking of glass against wood, murmuring conversations pebbled with sharp laughter, and waitresses delivering steaming hot plates of Mexican food.

The smells of sautéed peppers and frying meats wafted after her. It streamed into the sidewalk as Greer pushed the door open with her hip.

The restaurant, located a handful of blocks past the coffeeshop, was one of the more popular places on their side of town. Decently priced, good food, and top shelf margaritas made it a staple for students at the university. It also helped that it was within walking distance of the apartment Greer shared with Delia.

The humidity of the summer evening hit Greer like a brick when she stepped onto the sidewalk. Stars speckled the dark canvas, covering the clear sky above the mountain pass. Wayward crickets chirped as a gaggle of college students waltzed by, arms hooked into one another, as they headed toward the row of fraternity houses just off campus.

Greer waved to Delia and peeled off toward the bookstore. It was set in a brick building between a record store and an antique shop. The sign above the large display window blinked. The fluorescent light was well on its way to needing replaced. A blue open sign hung from a silver chain in the glass insert of the front door, swinging idly under the breeze from the air conditioner vent.

The bell chimed as she entered the shop. The Friday night street noise silenced as the door shut behind her. She waved a greeting to the owner, a plump, middle-aged man with thick glasses and a curly mop for hair. He looked over the edge of his book with a smile before returning to it.

Greer headed toward the back bookshelves where she knew she could find the romance novels, her footsteps muted against the worn carpet. Her fingers grazed the spines at eye level, the books vertically lined in alphabetical order based on author name. She plucked one off the shelf and tucked it under her arm.

The bell chimed once more as she knelt down to inspect the bottom shelf, her leggings pulling at the knees.

"You're looking at the wrong book."

Greer groaned as she stood and looked over her shoulder. Cian, leaning against a standalone bookcase with his arms crossed over his chest, was looking down at her. He had ditched the leather jacket, instead wearing a slim fit, black shirt that hugged his shoulders and biceps. She noticed, for the first time, a Celtic knot tattooed on the inside of his upper arm.

"Are you following me?"

He clicked his tongue. "Rich question, considering last night you were looking for me."

She turned back to the bookshelf.

"Have you tried anything from the grimoire yet?"

She heard him let out a sharp sigh from the back of his throat. "No," she lied smoothly in response, plucking a second book from the shelf. She stood, tucking the book under her arm with the first.

There must have been something in her expression, because Cian's lip curled into a smug smirk. "Liar. What happened?"

It was Greer's turn to sigh. "I...I almost burnt down my apartment building. No big deal."

"So, you believe me then? About your ancestry?"

Greer rolled her eyes, keeping her back to him. She pulled a third book from a shelf and flipped it over to read the summary before replacing it. "I believe you think it to be a conspiracy of sorts. I'm not sure what to think." It was the truth. She had stored the grimoire in the back of her closet underneath a pile of weekend bags. It hurt the anthropologist in her, but she figured if the book couldn't get burnt or wet, then a little dust would be fine.

Cian was quiet for a long minute before he clucked his tongue impatiently. "You almost burned down your apartment with magic and you still don't believe in it?"

She turned toward the small section containing true crime thrillers, sweeping her eyes along the spines. "I could have just as easily knocked over a candle."

"Do you truly believe that?" She didn't.

He had pushed himself off the bookcase to follow her. Reaching out, he placed a firm hand on top of the book she had attempted to remove from the shelf, holding it in place.

She inhaled deeply, the scent of his aftershave overtaking the aura of the gently used books. "What do you want from me?" she asked, a bite entering her tone. She turned her gaze up to meet his, realizing how close he stood. She took a step back.

"I want you to try with the grimoire again." He took a step forward, closing the gap once again.

Her jaw clenched as she returned her attention to the books. She stayed silent.

His lips pinched together as he tapped his fingers against the book he still held into place. "Holly Hawkins," he finally said, his posture stiffening with frustration.

"What?" she asked, brows knitting.

"There was a murder of a woman named Holly Hawkins twenty-six years ago in Polson, Montana. If you want to know why you should care, start there."

"Or you could just tell me," she retorted through gritted teeth, throwing her hands up into the air. The books she had clenched under her arm tumbled to the ground.

"I want to keep my leverage, thank you. If you want your questions answered," he said, leaning forward to whisper in her ear, "then take another look at the grimoire."

A shiver went up her spine at his breath on her neck as he turned away.

"I'll check in with you later, yes?" He wriggled his fingers over his shoulder, not bothering to say more of a good-bye.

The bell chimed as he exited the shop, leaving Greer alone between the shelves.

EIGHT

The weekend came and went.

Greer had been manipulated into spending Saturday with her mother, who was still holding her ground and refusing to return home. They tooled around the city, had brunch at a ritzy restaurant near downtown, and took a hike on a popular trail in the mountains. Delia, knowing how tenuous Greer's relationship was with Celeste, made sure to stay busy with Paige.

Greer was exhausted, mentally and physically, by the time Sunday night rolled around, and she found herself looking forward to the work week. If only to get away from Celeste.

She grabbed the ceramic mug from under the Keurig, filled to the brim with newly brewed coffee, and set it on her desk. While the report she needed to write was open on her computer screen, her attention was pulled elsewhere. Holly Hawkins. That's the name Cian had given her.

Holly Hawkins.

Greer mindlessly tapped her fingernails against the side of the mug, staring at a crack in the laminate surface of her desk.

"Stop that."

Greer's gaze lifted, and she was surprised to see Erin staring pointedly at the mug in her hand.

"Stop what?" Greer asked, her head tilting. Her brown waves slipped over her shoulder, spilling down her chest.

"The tapping. You've been doing it all morning."

Greer let go of the mug and dropped her hands into her lap. "I'm sorry, my mind is elsewhere— "

"Your mother is in town," Daniel finished for her, as his fingers clacked away on the keyboard, not bothering to look up from his own computer screen.

Greer grimaced as she slumped back into her office chair. "That obvious?"

Neither of her office mates replied, only solidifying their answer.

Greer let out a soft sigh. "I'm going to go for a walk," she announced after a moment, sliding her chair back. She smoothed out her floral-patterned dress as she stood and adjusted her sleeves. "I'll be back in a few minutes." Her sandals clicked against the floor as she exited the office and turned toward the elevator.

She pressed the button to call the car, waiting in the hallway with her arms crossed over her chest. Her mind flashed to Cian, to his insistence on her using the grimoire again. The elevator dinged as it arrived and the doors split open, revealing the wooden panels on the walls and the bright lights set into the ceiling.

Her finger hovered on the button to the third floor as she entered. The third floor was a silent floor, reserved for students and staff who required removal from the hustle and bustle of the main two floors in order to work. It was mostly made up of private rooms clad from floor to ceiling with glass walls so security could make sure no one was doing drugs or hooking up on the tables.

Greer went up there when she was frustrated with her research. The windows overlooked the forest-covered mountains that stood erect over the city, and the scenery could break her through even the densest mental block.

Instead, she scanned her employee badge on the reader and pressed the button to the second level of the basement. Her heart thundered in her chest as the elevator jolted and then descended. The doors separated when it halted into place and she stepped into the archives of the library. Spanning the length and width of the floors above, the basement subfloor was filled with floor to ceiling metal shelving units. Each shelf was stuffed with books, boxes, folders, and additional organization methods overflowing with loose papers. It smelled dusty and old— the number of people who came down here was minimal in comparison to the upper floors. This was especially true considering one needed an employee badge to enter.

The archives were kept cold to preserve the older documents, and Greer tightened her gray sweater around her shoulders as she exited the elevator. A fluorescent light near the back of the archives beamed brightly, casting long shadows from the shelving units. Metal carts lined the far wall and each was stacked with documents that needed to be restocked by the library graduate interns who worked the evening shift.

She walked toward the middle of the floor, where a circle of computers sat on antique wooden desks. Each computer was ancient in their own right and took a few moments to turn on. They only had the capability of pulling up the location of archived documents and were typically used by said library graduate interns.

Greer sank into a seat opposite a computer, the screen thick and curved. She powered up the unit and waited the few minutes it took for the machine to boot on.

She had done a quick internet search of Polson, Montana over the weekend, but abandoned it just as fast when her mother tried to peek over her shoulder to see the screen. Greer had gotten far enough to know that Polson was a small town in the northwest corner of the state with a population of just under four thousand. It was nearly an eleven-hour drive if she started in the parking lot of her apartment building and sat on the shore of a decently-sized lake.

The screen fluttered to life, landing on the form that linked archive locations to the search engine. Greer rhythmically tapped her fingers on the keyboard as she thought, anxiously biting her lip.

She chewed on the inside of her cheek before typing in *Hawkins, Holly, Polson, Montana* into the search bar and clicked enter. A small hourglass popped up on the screen, turning over and over again to signify the computer was working. Her heart leapt into her throat when the search came up with a single location.

Aisle four, shelf sixteen, bin twenty-three.

Greer grabbed a post-it note and a pencil from the corner of the desk, scribbling the location down onto the bright pink paper. She stood from her seat, the metal legs scraping against the linoleum tile, and headed deeper into the archives.

She found the aisle in record time and was unsurprised to learn it was located in the criminology segment. She repeated the shelf and bin numbers like a mantra as she slowly made her way down the aisle, stopping when she reached the correct vicinity. Hands trembling, Greer reached up to pull the single, thin folder from a shelf labeled Pacific Northwest Cold Cases. She grasped it for a moment, tracing the opening of the folder with her pointer finger. She had the distinct feeling that, if she decided to look in the folder, her life would shift forever.

And she wouldn't be able to shift it back.

She sucked in a breath and opened it anyways.

The folder contained a handful of documents that had been released by the detectives in the last twenty-six years. The stack mostly contained crime scene photographs, but a yellowed cut-out from a newspaper called The Lake County Leader rested in there as well as two additional written documents. She thumbed through the photographs, each more gruesome than the next.

The first was the body of a woman in a chair, her hands tied behind her back with a white, fraying rope. Her brown hair bracketed her face as her chin dropped down to her chest. Blood had dried to her shirt in a large stain, dripping onto the fronts of her jeans. Her arms were covered in bruises and stab wounds. The attack was seemingly brutal, as streaks of blood painted the ceiling above her.

The second picture revealed her autopsy photos and a copy of the report. Greer tilted her head as she looked at the woman on the metal slab and the up-close photograph of her face. Her brown hair was matted with blood and a thick, jagged cut opened her neck from one ear to the next. Her lips were full, but pale, and her nose was straight and long. She was a beautiful woman. Her date of birth in the corner put her at age twenty-eight at the time of her death. Just two years older than Greer.

Greer turned to the copy of the autopsy report. The woman's name was scrawled on the top of the page in hurried, block writing, and underneath was an address for a house located on Seventh Street. A series of boxes sat atop the printed diagram of the human body, splayed out with the hands positioned palms up near the hips. Two boxes were checked in the same hurried marks, one for violent and one for homicide. Various measurements, including body temperature and liver color, followed.

The next document contained a series of information concerning every wound and mark on her body. Some were obvious, such as the bruises to her face and arms, as well as the slit to her throat. Others, such as the stab wound to the gut that nicked the woman's liver and the fractured left wrist, were only found when Greer skimmed the report. Various arrows pointed to each wound on the diagram, each corresponding with a wound detailed in the handwritten note.

Greer dropped her gaze further down the document to see *Manner of death: blunt force trauma to the head and cut-throat injury resulting in exsanguination.*

Holly's death was slow, torturous, and brutal.

Greer grimaced as she took a second look at the autopsy photos before tucking them at the back of the pile. The third photograph made Greer's stomach clench with unease. It was a picture of a baby's nursery. The walls were painted a light pink and an old crib was tucked in the corner of the room. A white changing table, the paint chipped, stood directly to the right of the crib. The closet doors were thrown open, the infant clothes missing from the empty hangers hung on the rod. White, plastic letters hung above the crib spelling the infant's name: Greer.

Greer felt her throat constrict as she paced the aisle. Her swallowing turned thick as the backs of her eyes burned with tears. She flipped to the last photocopied document: a missing child report.

The form was completed to the best of the police officer's ability. The age of the infant was estimated to be female, five weeks old at time of abduction, the address the same as the autopsy report from its mother. Vague details were given in the report, but the child was Caucasian with brown hair and gray eyes.

Greer froze.

A missing infant named Greer with gray eyes? And the mother—her locks of brown hair and the long, straight nose that looked so similar to her own.

She barely made it back to the trash can near the computers, emptying her stomach into the bin.

Greer had made copies of the photographs and documents when she recovered enough to work the copier. She folded the papers, tucking them into her work bag when she reached her office twenty minutes later.

Erin looked alarmed at Greer's pale, sheen appearance, and Henry sent her home early, chalking it up to side effects from the assault she was still recovering from.

Greer sat in the front seat of her Jeep Wrangler, staring at the steering wheel. Students swept past the car on their way to the library, using the employee parking lot as a short-cut. The summer breeze smelled sweet and fresh through the cracked windows, ruffling Greer's hair as it blew.

But Greer felt none of it. She was numb. Empty. Dulled.

She made an attempt to clear the lump from her throat as she turned the key in the ignition, pulling away from the lot and entering into the mid-day traffic. The sun was out, the rays heating the black pavement under her tires and glaring through the windshield. She threw on a pair of sunglasses as she drove.

The drive was instinctive, and she barely thought about where she was going as she wove through the city streets. There was only one person she wanted to talk to.

She pulled into the parking lot of *Quincy and Astor Law Firm*. It was located in an office building, the front door opening to a hallway containing a handful of businesses. She held the door as a man exited, talking excitedly into his phone with a leather briefcase held in the other hand. She walked down the hallway and entered the law firm through a gray door. Glass windows, metal caging criss-crossed through the panes, allowed a peek into the office. The carpet from the hallway extended into the lobby, which was painted a calming, deep blue. Four white, cushioned seats, finished with cherry wood armrests, were positioned around a matching coffee table clad with women's and men's health magazines.

A saltwater fish tank bubbled behind a set of the chairs, and it coated the lobby in a light algae scent. An older woman sat behind a glass window, her tortoiseshell reading glasses perched on the end of her nose.

Greer trembled as she approached the receptionist, who recognized her from the number of times she visited Delia for lunch. The receptionist waved cheerfully and buzzed Greer through the locked door leading to the lawyer's offices in the back.

There was a quiet murmuring of paralegals on the phones and the shuffling of papers from one place to the next. She followed the hallway past the paralegal's cubicles and a conference room with a large wooden table, the scent of copier toner on the air-conditioned draft, and stood at the threshold of Delia's cubicle.

"I'm looking at it now," Delia was saying into the receiver, the phone pinched against her shoulder as she toggled the mouse, "It looks fairly ironclad, but I'll have John Quincy take a second look before the trial." She paused to listen to the other end. "I don't think that's necessary." She glanced up, seeing Greer in the doorway. "Let me call you back, Mike." She hung up the receiver and immediately shot up from her office chair. "Greer, what—?"

Greer entered the cubicle, her chest heaving with the effort to choke back tears. Trembling, she reached into her work bag and pulled out the bundle of papers. She handed them over to Delia, collapsing into the chair used by clients.

Delia unfolded the papers and leaned against the edge of the desk, crossing one ankle over the other. She rubbed her chest as she viewed each copy with a furrowed brow before reaching the final photograph. Her eyes widened with surprise, and she straightened to standing as she took in the nursery and the missing infant report.

Delia's gaze darted up to meet Greer's. "And you think...?" She trailed off. "Where did you find this?"

Greer opened and closed her mouth, wracking her brain to think of an explanation. "A man tracked me down and gave me Holly's name. He thinks I'm this lost infant."

Delia's lips parted as she read over the autopsy report once more. "Have you—your mom is still in town."

Greer knew what her best friend was hinting toward. She shook her head. "I didn't— I just thought of you." She shifted in her seat. "I don't know what to do."

Delia smiled softly at her, love shining brightly from her eyes, as she sunk into the seat to Greer's left. She leaned over and grasped Greer's arm, squeezing gently. "This sounds like a hard conversation you need to have with Celeste."

Greer groaned, placing her forehead in her hand.

Greer did nothing about the documents for the rest of the week. She put it to the back of her mind during the day, focusing entirely on the new batch of research Henry had assigned her to sort through. At night, she sat cross-legged in the middle of her bed and studied every detail of the photographs, memorized every word of the documents.

She hadn't mentioned anything to Celeste yet, but she knew it was only a matter of time. The longer she waited, the heavier she felt the tug in her gut.

By the end of the week, Greer was seated alone at the bar of the Mexican restaurant. She was in the process of finishing her third margarita, biting at the black cocktail straw stuck between a clump of ice cubes.

"Drinking alone usually indicates someone is at an all-time low."

"Jesus Christ," Greer mumbled, rubbing her forehead as Cian dropped onto the barstool next to her.

"It's been a week," he pressed, flagging down the bar- tender with a twitch of his wrist.

"And?" she scowled as she took a sip of her drink. "And did you look into Holly Hawkins?"

Her name was a shock to Greer's system.

Greer reached into the pocket of her jacket and pulled out a folded copy of the news article. She had taken to carrying it with her, tucked away where no one else could find it. She tossed it onto the wooden surface of the bar and slid it toward him with two fingers.

Cian picked it up and folded the paper. His eyes moved back and forth as he skimmed it. Greer already knew what it said.

October 17th, 1996

A shocking scene has rocked the community of Polson this week when resident Holly Hawkins, 28, was found dead in her two-bedroom home on Seventh Street at 7:15pm.

The Polson Police Department announced October 17th, 1996 a joint investigation between local law enforcement and the Montana Department of Justice. At this time, there are no suspects and no persons of interest in the case.

Holly Hawkins was discovered during a wellness check when neighbors called the police for suspicious noises. It was discovered that her five-week old daughter, Greer Hawkins, had been taken from the home.

The community has come together to purchase a gravestone for Holly Hawkins, and she will be buried at Polson City Cemetery pending investigation.

A sizable award is being offered for any information that leads to the arrest of the person who killed Holly.

Cian finished reading the article and looked over to her. His studying gaze watched her for a long minute before the bartender returned with his drink; a whiskey sour. He reached forward to grasp the glass before taking a sip.

"The woman posing as your mother cannot be your mother. If she was, you would have control of your magic." Greer turned her head, her eyes connecting with his.

"Why are you doing this?"

He sat back in his seat, swirling the glass in his hand. "You're the Mage—"

"I don't know what that means."

"Your ancestral line is one of witches that were created to protect us."

Greer took a large swig of her margarita, finishing it off. "Who is us?"

Cian bared his teeth at her. A pair of sharp fangs descended from his gum line.

Greer stilled, staring dumbfoundedly at the newly protruding teeth. She slowly lifted her gaze to look him in the eye. "You're—you're a...?" she trailed off, the margaritas roiling as her stomach clenched. She was going to be sick.

"I was born in Macroom, Ireland in 1532," he said quietly, leaning forward to rest his forearms on the edge of the bar. "I was turned into a vampyre in 1562 just after my thirtieth birthday."

Her stare shifted to the condensation dripping down her glass. She did the math. That made him forty hundred and ninety-one years old. She took in a slow, deep breath. "Do you kill people?"

"Yes."

"And feed on them?"

"Yes."

"Why haven't you killed me?"

"Can't. Your magic protects you."

She narrowed her eyes. "How do I play into all of this? What did Holly Hawkins have to do with all of this?"

Cian's rings clinked against the side of the glass as a waitress brushed past him holding a tray of drinks. She sent him a flirty look over her shoulder and his lip curled into a smirk. He winked at the waitress before turning to look at Greer, whose cheeks heated as she scowled.

"We've talked about this. You make progress with your magic and then I will answer any questions that you have."

"Why do you even care?" she shot back in frustration, garnering the attention of the bartender.

"When your ancestor was the last Mage, she made a potion for me that allowed me to walk in the sun. When she died at the hands of the

Paladin Society, the magic of the potion died with her. I need you to remake it."

Greer massaged her temples with two fingers. "I can't do that," she said with a bitter, humorless laugh. She paused again, biting a lip. "What is the Paladin Society?"

Cian took another sip of his drink. "You get me that potion, I'll get you answers."

"Don't expect that to happen," she retorted, handing her debit card over to the bartender.

"Then don't expect anything from me," Cian said, a bite of irritation in his voice. "Don't forget, I can wait you out. I've got the time."

Greer couldn't help the second scowl that tugged on her features.

NINE

CELESTE

There was a pounding on the door.

Celeste groaned, turning over amidst the pillows and tangled sheets of the hotel bed. She glanced at the clock through locks of blonde hair.

Eight in the morning. Who in their right mind would pound on the door at eight in the morning?

"Mom?" The door shook in the frame. "Mom, are you awake?"

Celeste's eyes flew open at the sound of her daughter's voice. She tore the sheets from her legs and leapt from bed, adjusting the hem of her silk pajama bottoms as she went. She unlatched the chain lock and unbolted the door before cracking it open to reveal Greer on the other side.

"What are you doing here?" Celeste asked groggily, wiping the sleep crust from the corners of her eyes. She opened the door further and stepped aside.

Greer crossed the threshold. She held a cardboard drink carrier containing two to-go cups in one hand and a paper bag in the other. She held them up. "I bought cinnamon rolls from the diner by my apartment."

Celeste let the door swing shut. "You know I don't eat that."

Greer rolled her eyes. "Since when? Cinnamon rolls used to be your favorite."

Celeste bristled. She had never liked when people knew personal information about her and she certainly wasn't used to it now. "It's been a long time." She crossed her arms over her chest. "You would know if you made an effort to visit once in a while," she added for good measure.

Greer set the paper bag on the wooden dresser that held the flat screen television. "Suit yourself then."

Celeste took the silent minute to drag her stare up and down her daughter's body. Hair drawn into a loose braid. The too-short jean shorts with the frayed hem, her tight, white tank top that showed off toned shoulders, the brown Birkenstock sandals with golden buckles. She hadn't even bothered to paint her toenails.

Greer noticed Celeste looking and rubbed the back of her neck. "Mom, can we not do this today?"

"Do what?" Celeste asked innocently enough, but the tone was implied.

"This," Greer said, pointing to the space in-between them, "I didn't come to fight over my clothing choices. If I wanted to do that, I would have moved back to San Francisco five years ago."

"You won't move back to San Francisco, because I am still in San Francisco."

Irritation flashed over Greer's face. She scoffed. "Okay, I'll get right to it then." She paused to reach into her canvas bag and pulled out a folded piece of paper. "I found this in the archives while doing research for a project. I wanted to know what you thought of it."

Celeste took the paper from her hands and unfolded it. *Polson, Montana*. She felt her stomach jolt in response, her facial features opening a fraction in surprise. Those stupid, reckless, fucking vampyres...

Celeste recovered just as quickly, returning to the calculated expression she typically used. "I'm not sure what you want me to think of this," she responded coolly as she lifted her gaze. She noticed Greer had been watching her closely, eyes narrowed. "What is it?"

"A cold case," Greer said, "involving a woman and a missing infant."

"That much I got from the article, honey."

Greer took in a slow, deep breath. "I was curious what you thought about the missing infant named Greer with gray eyes."

Celeste let out a forced laugh as she crumpled the paper in a ball with both hands. "Do you think the infant is you?" Her brows rose when Greer said nothing, but rubbed her upper arm in discomfort. "Do you hate me so much that you think I'm not your real mother? Or is it that you just wish I wasn't?"

Greer's mouth slackened as she sputtered, "Are you serious, mom? You have to admit, this is fishy. When Cian came up and-" Her lips clamped shut.

Celeste jumped on the mistake. "Cian?" The vampyre told Greer his name. Not a good sign. "Who is Cian?"

"Look, it— it doesn't matter," Greer started again, playing with the end of her braid. "You and I, we've never seen eye to eye. And this woman, Holly, has similar features to me. It's just—"

Celeste cocked her head. "Similar features? What, she has brown hair like half the population in the United States?"

Greer's lips pinched into a tight, white line as her expression soured. "Forget it, mom. Just forget it. If you aren't going to take me seriously—"

"You're accusing me of murdering a woman in cold blood and stealing her child, Greer! What else did you expect from me?"

Greer went quiet and Celeste felt a wave of triumph crest in her chest. Greer shifted her bag higher onto her shoulder and muttered, "Just...I'll see you later, mom." She turned and walked from the hotel room, her shoulders slumped dejectedly.

As soon as the door shut, Celeste let out a cry of rage, throwing the crumpled paper into the bathroom. It soared over the threshold and landed on the white, marble floor, skittering to a stop under the countertop. Her chest heaved as she panted, her eyes wide and wild.

That stupid fucking vampyre. She had warned him what would happen.

Celeste dressed in record time and removed the silver blade from the top drawer of the bedside table, tucking it into the waistband of her jeans. She barely remembered hopping in her car, let alone the drive, and she was roaring into the gravel driveway of the vampyre's den nearly fifteen minutes later.

The morning sun was burning away the dew clinging to the grass, light fog rolling over the serene lawn. She marched through the grass, the hems of her socks soaking in the mist, and stomped up the porch steps. The stain coating the wood at the base of the front door had faded in the last week, but it was still visible enough.

She yanked open the screen door and gripped the door handle, the window panes rattled as she shook it. "I know you're in there," she seethed, hammering the door with her fist, "and I know you can hear me, *Cian.*"

The door flew open, the dark-skinned vampyre standing in the mudroom. "He's not—" he began, but Celeste had already moved.

Lunging forward, she swiped the blade from her waist- band and thrashed it at the vampyre. He lurched backward just in time to miss the tip of her blade. His eyes wide, he extended his hands in an attempt to yield her away, but she slashed the blade again and caught him in the forearm.

He hissed in pain, dark blood slowly dribbling from the cut. It had already begun to heal, the skin knitting together just as fast as it had been sliced apart. His fangs punched through his gum line and he bared them at her as a warning.

Celeste didn't listen. She lunged again, pushing him further into the house as she entered the mudroom. The two began a dance of teeth and blades, the vampyre desperately trying to fend off Celeste.

"Where is he?" she screeched, aiming the blade for the man's heart. "Where is Cian?" She was panting, sweating, and angry. So, so angry. "I'm going to rip out his heart."

The vampyre backed into the kitchen, his sneakers shuffling on the linoleum floor. "I told you. He's not— Jonas! No!"

The back of Celeste's neck was burning and a hot, sticky liquid was running down the shoulder of her tee-shirt. She spun on the balls of her feet and the second vampyre, who must have appeared from the cellar door behind her, smiled down at her. Blood dripped from his fangs and onto his chin.

Celeste made to sweep her blade at him, but Jonas caught her on the wrist and twisted until the blade popped from her hand and clattered to the floor. His breathing grew ragged as he eyed the pulsating veins beneath her skin. His eyes darkened to a distant, hungry.

"Jonas, *stop*," the third man begged, but it was too late.

Jonas had sunk his fangs into Celeste's forearm.

Celeste screamed in pain and terror before ripping her arm away from Jonas' unsuspecting grip. His fangs ripped a jagged line from her elbow to her wrist, blood spurting onto both Jonas and Celeste.

His eyes widened at the sight as Celeste tried to stumble away, holding her torn arm clamped in her opposite fist. He plunged forward like a viper as Celeste dove, slipping on the puddle of blood leaking from her arm. She hit the wooden floor, smacking her head against the edge of the foyer table on her way down.

Clammy nausea overtook her body like a wave as black spots exploded in her vision. She groaned, feeling the throbbing wound now open on her head. Her hair became matted and slicked with blood.

"You need to get out," a voice said, muffled and marbled, as if she were under water.

Celeste was slow to move, rolling onto her back. Her throat was dry, and swallowing felt like a dozen knives ripping at her from the inside. She pulled herself onto her knees, hands trembling and pale. As if she were a rubber band, she snapped back into her own body. Vision clearing, the gnashing of Jonas' teeth came into full volume.

She managed to crawl toward the front door, looking behind her long enough to see the dark-skinned man holding a thrashing, snarling Jonas in a vice grip. "*Go!*" he roared, his arms banded around Jonas' chest, pinning his arms to his sides.

Celeste's palms scraped against the unsealed wooden porch, splinters puncturing her skin, as she crawled out of the house. She knew she had lost too much blood, her head was floating, vision prickling once again. She attempted to right herself, using the handrail of the stairs to pull herself to a standing position. Her knees buckled beneath her and she tumbled headfirst down the five stairs that led to the porch.

She landed hard against the gravel pathway, dirt and blood coating her like a second skin. At least, she realized, she was in the sun.

Jonas broke free from the man's grip and busted through the front door. He paced the porch, watching her with a sharp stare. He made a single attempt to reach her, but his skin cracked and burnt under the rays of the morning sun. He let out a shout of pain, withdrawing back into the shadows of the porch.

Celeste inched her hand toward her pocket, pulling her cell phone from her jeans. Still lying bloodied and broken on the gravel path, she used a tremoring finger to punch a phone number into the dial pad of the screen.

"9-1-1. What is your emergency?" a woman on the other end of the line answered.

Celeste said nothing as darkness formed, finally succumbing to the pain and blood loss that had been threatening to take her.

"Law enforcement officials discovered a grisly scene today after a 9-1-1 call placed by a woman doing a welfare check on her elderly aunt and uncle was found in the front yard following a knife attack.

"The elderly couple, a local Mister and Missus Camper, were found with stab wounds to the chest and had been deceased for some time. Their bodies were discovered in an adjacent field.

"The victim, fifty-six year old Celeste Myers, was taken to the hospital with life-threatening injuries. She is expected to make a full recovery.

"No information has been released at this time about any suspects or persons of interest.

"If you have any information, please call the local police at—"

Celeste switched off the television, letting her head drop against the pillow. She winced, having forgotten the stitches at the back of her skull.

The emergency operator had managed to track her through the location on her cellphone. She didn't know how long she had laid in the gravel path, nor did she remember being loaded into the ambulance. She woke up in the emergency room, cringing against the harsh lights and the beep of monitors in the hallway. It wasn't long after that when she was moved to the intensive care unit for closer monitoring of her injuries.

The doctors had washed out her arm and stitched it back together, along with her skull, as the nurses hung bags of blood and fluid from the metal pole next to her bed. Celeste was itching to leave the hospital. Once the sun went down, she would be a sitting duck.

The vampyre had tasted her blood; he would be tracking her now.

She didn't know how the two hid from law enforcement, though she assumed it was both carefully and in the cellar. They wouldn't have been able to flee the house, due to the sun, and would have had to bunker down somewhere while the police conducted their investigation.

A small knock on the door pulled Celeste from her thoughts and her expression tightened at the sight of Greer in the doorway. Greer was fumbling nervously with her fingers, a habit Celeste had tried hard to break when Greer was a child, as she shifted her weight back and forth on each leg.

"I— I brought you some flowers," Greer started, gesturing over her shoulder. "But the nurses said I couldn't bring in any live plants."

Shame, flowers could have made the bare, white walls and fluorescent lighting livelier. The only thing remotely close was a copy of a painted picture of flowers set into a golden picture frame. It hung from the wall directly across from Celeste's bed, and she had found herself wanting to toss it from the third story window.

"It's fine," Celeste said instead, gesturing with her eyes toward the empty chair next to the bed. "The thought was nice."

Greer got the hint and she lurched forward, slowly walking toward the chair before sinking into it. "How are you feeling?" She looked down at Celeste's shredded forearm, taking in the swollen, puckered skin between each stitch.

"I've been better, but I'll be okay."

Greer nodded her head as she sucked in a breath. "Mom, what were you doing at that house? We don't have an aunt or uncle here."

Celeste sighed. She knew the question would come and she had already prepared. "Honey, it was Cian."

At the sound of the vampyre's name, Greer reeled back. "Wh—what?"

Celeste had decided to go with a half-truth. She could use this attack to her advantage, to divert her daughter away from the vampyres. If Greer knew how evil, how dangerous they were, surely, she would stay away.

Celeste sat forward and extended an arm to grasp Greer's knee. "We both know what he is," she dropped her voice to a whisper, forcing Greer to lean forward in order to hear. "We both know what he is capable of. He took me to that house. He wanted me out of the way, to have you all to himself."

Greer rested her forearms on her thighs. "You knew all along what he was and you didn't—"

"I'm sorry I lied to you," Celeste let her voice grow soft, her eyes turned down as if she were ashamed. She wasn't. "There are things in this world that want to hurt us, Greer. Things we need to protect ourselves from."

"They said I'm a...I don't know. Some sort of witch," Greer replied, sagging in relief as if the weight of the world had been removed from her shoulders. "I can do things, mom. Things I can't—"

"You have to stop," Celeste interjected. This was worse than she had thought. "You are my daughter, Greer Myers, and nothing more. If you are doing magic, it's because you are tapping into something you don't understand. It has *nothing* to do with what Cian said. Do you understand me?"

Greer's lip trembled as she nodded her head. "I'm sorry about earlier." A single tear dripped onto her cheek, leaving a small smear of make-up.

Celeste leaned back again, this time careful of her matted hair. "Thank you. Now, would you help your mother get cleaned up? I want to get some of this dried blood and dirt off me."

Greer silently stood, depositing her bag onto the floor next to the chair. Celeste watched her warily, knowing that sooner or later, Greer was going to learn the truth. She only hoped she could control the situation until then.

TEN

Celeste was still in the hospital receiving blood transfusions and antibiotics. She was expected to stay a few days and, in the meantime, Greer decided it would be best to steer clear of the hospital. She would be spending more than enough time with her mother when the discharge occurred.

The guilt tugged at her when she really thought about it. Her mother had almost died— Greer should be jumping for joy at the thought of taking care of her. Because her relationship with Celeste was equal parts complex and tenuous, she was having a hard time deciphering how she felt.

Then, there was the added mix that Celeste had known about Cian being a vampyre. How, she didn't know. She didn't know her mother had ever even seen Cian. Something wasn't adding up, and Greer was determined to unearth it.

She volunteered to pick up takeout from a local Chinese restaurant, one of Paige's favorites, and dusk was approaching by the time she, Paige, and Delia decided on what to order. She made her way to her Jeep, parked closer to the edge of the forest than she liked, and unlocked the doors with the key fob in her hand.

Before she had the opportunity to pull the door open, Cian was leaning against the side of the Jeep, his arms crossed over his chest and one ankle over the other.

"How is mommy?" he asked, a smirk that radiated superiority on his lips.

A shot of anger boiled over. "You have some nerve showing up here after what you did." Greer yanked the door open, tossing her wallet onto the front seat. "Attacking her, taking her to that house. She could have died."

Cian sent her an incredulous stare, his smirk slowly transforming into a tentative smile. "That little minx," he said, his voice taking on a giddy tone. "Is that what she told you? Maybe she still has it after all."

"What are you talking about?" Greer asked, pinching the bridge of her nose in frustration.

"Your mummy showed up at our house with her guns blazing, as you Americans say. She attacked my two mates, had the jump on one of them too."

Greer stilled, her hand wrapped around the edge of the car door. "You had nothing to do with her attack?"

"Me? No. I was too busy hiding from the sun in the forest. Picked off an unsuspecting jogger for a meal while I was at it. Compelled him to forget and sent him on his way."

Greer opened and closed her mouth, almost chastising him, when she turned her gaze up to meet his. "She said your name, she told me it was you."

Cian blew out a breath, stuffing his hands in his pockets. "About that. Your mother and I did have a meet cute one other time when we came across one another." He paused to lean forward. "She's very protective when it comes to you. Most members are when it comes to their young, anyways. Probably why the Paladin Society needs to track down their members so often."

"You met her before?"

"Just once."

Greer scoffed, the anger ebbing and flowing between Cian and her mother. What else hadn't Celeste told her? "Regardless, your *mate* almost killed her."

"That he did and he would have too if Isaac hadn't intervened."

Greer stared at him, the summer evening breeze ruffling her hair. She tucked the locks behind her ears. "There are three of you?"

"Did you think we traveled alone?" He frowned. "What a terribly, boring existence."

At that, Greer swung her leg into the Jeep and pulled herself onto the seat. Behind her, she could hear the opening of the back driver's side door and the subsequent ruffling of canvas as Cian settled himself into the backseat.

She whirled around, eyes narrowed as she glared at him. "What do you think you're doing?"

His eyes lifted as he clicked the buckle into place. "I assumed you were in a time crunch and needed to get moving, my mistake."

"Why are you in my car?" she asked through gritted teeth, her eyes closing in frustration.

"We aren't done chatting."

"I think we are. Get out."

"How are things progressing with your magic?"

Greer's heart lurched as she looked away. The street lamp above them flared on, illuminating the parking lot in a dull, yellow glow. "I've decided to stop. I'm messing with things I don't understand—"

Cian's eyes flashed. "Your mother talked with you. Very interesting. Very Paladin Society response of her."

Greer tucked her foot underneath her to turn complete- ly. "The Paladin Society. What is that? You've mentioned them twice now."

His irritating smirk returned. "I told you the parameters of our deal. If you want to know, show me your magic."

Greer's knuckles whitened as her nails bit into her palms. "And I told you that I won't perform any more magic."

"Consider yourself dead then," he snapped as his eyes tightened at the corners. There was silence between the two for a long moment before Cian spoke again. "If your mother is mentioning your magic, then she knows what you are. It is imperative that you learn."

Greer let out a huffed laugh. "You've already told me that you want to walk in the sun. It's not imperative that I learn anything."

"It is imperative. If you are no longer alive, the Mage line ends, and I am stuck living in darkness until the Earth gets sucked into a black hole."

She clicked her tongue. "So sweet, you thinking of my well-being. Now, get out of my car."

He crossed his arms over his chest. "No."

She leaned forward to unbuckle his seatbelt. "Out. Now."

"Just show me one little spell."

Greer felt her blood heat, the rage rising in her body. It filled her, every crack and crevice under a solid wall, overflowing with power. "I. Said. Get. Out." she hissed between gritted teeth, forcefully punctuating each syllable. She allowed the power to flow from her, to the space between them.

A loud crack sounded, followed by an ear-splitting shatter. Greer ducked her head between her hands for protection as splinters of glass rained down on them. The shards dug into her exposed skin, sticking to her clothing. When the glass had settled, she glanced toward Cian, wide-eyed and heart thumping. A breeze flowed through the car, followed by the sweet scent of pine cone-covered forest floors. Every window in the Jeep had exploded, the glass covering the interior of the car and the pavement surrounding them.

"I didn't hear you mutter a spell," Cian said. It wasn't a question.

"I didn't," Greer responded quietly. Her hands shook as she lowered them into her lap, brushing off the glass shards with careful sweeps.

Cian was studying her with a sudden focus that made her uncomfortable. Greer squirmed in her seat.

"Agnes needed to say an incantation before performing it."

Greer tilted her head in question. "Who is Agnes?"

"Your ancestor."

Greer choked.

"This requires a bit more assessing, I'm afraid," he said, as he opened the car door and stepped out. He paused to brush the glass from his shoulders and thighs. "Keep practicing, I'll be back soon."

"Wait!" Greer cried out as Cian entered the brush at the edge of the forest. "What about my car?"

He shrugged a shoulder. "Refrain from doing magic that you can't control? I'm not sure what to tell you."

He was gone before Greer's screech of incredulity echoed between the trunks of the trees.

Greer drove Paige's truck to pick up the Chinese food. She floated a lie that someone had broken in, but the lie sat heavy in her gut. Her and Delia had told each other everything, the good and the ugly.

Which was why, amongst the steaming heaps of orange chicken and beef with broccoli, Greer pulled the grimoire from its hiding place in the closet. She plopped it on the table between the plates of food, looking at Delia expectantly.

"What's this?" Delia asked, her mouth full of fried rice. She reached forward and grabbed the book, unwrapping the leather strap with ease. She thumbed through it, each page quickly passing. She didn't stop to look at a single one. "What do you think about that?" Greer said, leaning forward to set her elbows on the table.

Delia passed the book to Paige, who set down her fork to do the same.

"Hmmm," Delia started, before taking a sip of the red wine she had poured for herself. "I think it'll make a great journal? The leather is nice? The aesthetic is right up your alley?"

Greer dulled her gaze, sending Delia a blank look. "I'm serious. Open it to a random page and tell me what you think about the writing."

Paige cracked the grimoire back open, shuffling to a page mid-way through. "Okay, what am I supposed to be reading?"

Greer stood and leaned over the table, reading the page upside down. In the looped, inky black handwriting was a potion recipe for wolf shifters to shift outside of the equinox or solstice. She glanced back up, her gaze darting between Delia and Paige.

"The potion ingredients," Greer said, shoving a finger onto the parchment. "Wing of a songbird, skull dust of a field mouse, lemongrass, the list goes on. Can't you read any of that?"

Paige and Delia exchanged looks of alarm before Delia spoke up. "Greer, have you been getting enough sleep? Are you stressed with what happened to your mom?"

"Nothing is written on that page, G," Paige reiterated quietly, her brows knitted together.

Greer sat back in her seat as her heart dropped to her feet. Cian had told her that no one else could read the grimoire, that no one else possessed the magical ability to break through the grimoire's protection. She hadn't believed him. She had truly thought he was making it up.

Delia and Paige, on the other hand, had no reason to lie to her.

"You know, nevermind," Greer said, as she reached over and picked up the book.

"Greer—"

"G, what's going on?"

Greer shook her head. "I think you're right; I just need a bit more sleep." She lifted her plate from the table and stood from her seat. "I think I'll just eat in my room. I just need to relax."

Delia reached forward as if she were going to grab Greer's arm, but stopped herself. "You know we're here to talk if you need anything, right?"

"Yes, of course," Greer replied, but her smile was tight and unconvincing. "I'll be in my room if you need anything." She didn't see the second exchange of glances between Delia and Paige, but could feel them nonetheless. She tempered down the frustration that began to boil her blood, afraid that she would shatter the windows or burn down the apartment— this time with her two best friends inside.

ELEVEN

Her mother had told her to let it go, but Greer couldn't. Something tugged at her gut when she thought of Holly Hawkins. She found herself looking at the crime scene photographs late into the night, reading the autopsy report over and over again. She had tried to talk to her mother about it, but Celeste brushed her off. Then became bitter. Then became very angry.

Greer had stopped asking.

But she needed answers, ones that her mother was not willing to give no matter how hard she pressed. Alternatively, ones that Cian was also not willing to give unless she proved she was working on her magic.

And she still didn't know if she wanted to work on her magic. It had been a catastrophic disaster every time she tried.

She did the only thing she thought of to do. She booked a short flight over to the international airport nearest Polson, Montana and decided to check things out for herself.

The town, small and on the edge of a lake, was nestled into the valley of the white-capped mountains. She passed two mom-and-pop restaurants and a single gas station on the main throughway through town. She completed a few circles around the town in her rental sedan, where she discovered the rest of it consisted of residential homes that seemed to have been built fifty years previously. Based on the appearance of the roofs and the collapsing porches, she suspected some of the homes hadn't been updated in those fifty years either.

She trundled into the lot of a motel that, in a town any bigger than this one, would have been best described as seedy. Her eyes narrowed against the bright sun as she drew her gaze over the peeling paint of the motel exterior. After checking in with the front desk attendant, a blue-haired college student who took this job for seasonal work, she grabbed her weekend bag from the back seat of the car and made her way to the room. Her sandals crunched against the broken pavement as she crossed the parking lot.

She kept her head down as she passed a family of four with fishing poles arched over their shoulders. The youngest was chattering excitedly as he hopped from one foot to the next in a test to avoid the cracks in the cement. She climbed the outside stairwell and exited on the second-floor landing.

The door opened with ease when she unlocked it, and she dropped her bag onto the worn dresser as soon as she entered. The room was old and outdated with water stains marking the tiled ceiling. It smelled faintly of mildew and strongly of bleach, but it was the only room she could find in town on such short notice. It was, after all, located an hour and a half from one of the larger national parks in the country and guests were streaming in from all over to experience the summer activities Montana had to offer.

It was a quick turnaround. She wanted to rest, but she was already on her way out the door again. She had an appointment to make.

The police department was located inside of a one-story building that faced the lake. When Greer pulled into the parking lot, unpaved and set with loose gravel, she could see the metal boat docks empty and bobbing in the water. It was a beautiful day with the sun shining over the mountains and the gentle breeze wafting in cool air over the water. Many of the boats had been chartered for fishing and would return in the evening.

She shifted her canvas bag onto her shoulder and headed into the building, where she was immediately met with a countertop. A desk was set behind the thick glass that filled in the space between the counter and the ceiling. A woman sat there, dressed in a police officer uniform, her badge gleaming under the bright lights.

"How can I help you?" she asked through the speaker, eyeing Greer's mid-length skirt and blouse.

"I'm here to see the police chief. My name is Greer Myers; I have an appointment." Greer began to fumble in her bag for the fake journalist badge she had printed off the internet in the days before, but the officer waved her through the side door without a second look. It seemed they didn't get many journalists in Polson, Montana.

The officer stood from her seat as Greer pulled the heavy, metal door open and led her to the back of the station. It was small; four desks set together in the middle of the linoleum tiled room with one office set nearest the rear. Even with the windows ajar, she could smell old coffee in the air. A narrow hallway split off the main room on the right-hand side, and Greer assumed that it held an employee break room as well as a jail cell or two for rowdy travelers.

"Chief?" the woman said as they approached the office, rapping her knuckles on the doorframe. "Your three o'clock is here to see you."

The chief stood from his desk with a smile and gestured toward the chair opposite his own. He was a beefy man, shorter than average with a thick neck and broad shoulders. He bore a dark mustache and a military style haircut, the edges uneven as if he had done it himself.

He stuck out his hand as she approached and she shook it before taking a seat in the chair.

"When you called you had said you had some questions regarding a cold case file," he started, sinking into his own chair and adjusting his belt. "What can I do for you?"

"First, thank you for meeting with me," she said, reaching into her canvas bag and taking out the recording device she used for work. "Do you mind if I record? It's easier to listen back to something rather than review notes taken in the moment."

He hesitated for a brief moment, shoulder stiffening, before he relaxed. "Not at all. I hope you understand if there are questions I can't answer."

"Of course."

She set the recorder on the faded laminate desk between them and pressed the record button. The red light blinked on. She felt in her element; now she was just a researcher for the anthropology department, digging through files and interviewing experts. It was journalism, of sorts. She was a voice for the ancient dead.

"This is Greer Myers on July the fifteenth at three in the afternoon, here with the Chief of Police from Polson, Montana." She paused to reach into her bag and pulled out a notebook and pen. "Chief, I'm here to talk about the Holly Hawkins murder from 1996."

The chief nodded his head, eyes growing solemn. "I had a feeling that was the cold case you were referring to. There aren't many." He leaned down to open a drawer in his desk, retrieving a file from inside. He placed the folder in front of him, licked his forefinger, and began to rifle through it. "I was still an officer when this happened. Newly out of the academy. First murder investigation of my career."

"I was able to get a hold of some files including her autopsy report and subsequent photographs. Do you have any additional information regarding her injuries?"

The chief took a deep breath. "We do know that it wasn't a quick death." He thumbed through the file. "We believe that she was tortured. For what? Still a mystery." He turned the crime scene photograph around and pointed to the thin marks on Holly's limbs. "These were made by a blade similar to a paring knife. They were located on her arms, back of her knees and ankles, everywhere."

Greer swallowed. "And those were in addition to the multiple stab wounds?"

The chief nodded. "One to the abdomen. It would have been very painful. I remember asking the coroner about it. Holly would have had a large amount of blood lost from that wound alone."

"Why cut her throat then? Surely she would have died from the liver injury."

He sighed, sitting back in his chair. "Another mystery, but the detective at the time believed it was a message." He grabbed the photograph and lifted it up to look at it again. "It wasn't in the coroner's report, but in the murder investigation. Whoever killed her was looking for something in her neck."

Greer jolted, tearing her gaze away from her notepad. "Did you say looking for something?"

His nose wrinkled as he pulled out another photograph.

This was one Greer hadn't seen before. Holly's body was laid out on the black bag. Investigators had taken photographs prior to her being zipped into the body bag. "The throat was cut to the spine and there was evidence that the murderers were—" he paused to clear his throat "—digging in her flesh. With their fingers."

Greer felt sick. "Digging for what exactly?"

"The coroner found something interesting in her bones. Black speckles, as if they were partially made of stone."

"Stone?"

"We had it sent to the lab for testing. Turns out, her bones were laced with obsidian."

Greer sat back in her seat. "Obsidian? The volcanic stone?"

"The very same. We sent it for testing three times at two different labs to confirm."

She clicked her pen against the notepad. "How did that get there?"

The chief shrugged. "Your guess is as good as mine." He interlocked his fingers and placed them behind his head. "I remember this case well. There were lots of odd things surrounding it."

"Odd like what?"

He blew out a breath. "This woman— Holly. We know from birth and school records that she lived most of her life in North Carolina. Disappeared off the grid for nine months at the age of twenty-eight and reappeared in Montana with a five week old baby. No record of the child's birth, at least that she carried with her. Holly had no family, and I mean none. Mother died in a car accident under suspicious circumstances when she was nineteen, no record of a father. No siblings either. She was utterly alone."

"And all of that is unusual?"

"Well..." He trailed off and stared at the desk for a long minute before continuing on. "After her death, things started happening around here."

Greer felt her stomach drop to her feet. "Things like journalists and true crime fans?"

He shook his head. "I'm not a conspiracy theorist, okay? I don't believe in aliens or ghosts, but-" His face contorted into a grimace. "I'll tell you if you turn off the recorder. Off the record."

Greer leaned forward and pressed the record button. The red light immediately ceased blinking. She looked at him expectantly.

"A month following her death, a fellow comes along. Good looking man, thirty years old or so, blonde hair. He started asking around, wondering where she was. When he was informed of her death and of the child's disappearance—"The chief shuddered. "A bad disease swept through the local farms and killed off all the livestock. And then there were the locusts."

"The locusts?"

"Swarms of 'em. Looked back at the records. This area hasn't seen anything like that since the late 1800's. Lots of people started praying, and the local churches filled up every Sunday. A few people became really paranoid. Blamed Holly's death. The community came together to bury her in the cemetery just outside of town. Got her a real nice headstone too. The town wanted to appease God, I guess. Groups of people showed up from out of town and began asking more questions. The man disappeared after that, and we never saw him again. Shame, too. We thought he knew something. Matter of fact, we thought he was involved. Found blonde hairs at the crime scene, but the lab tests indicated the hairs were female, so that never added up. The plagues stopped when he left. Maybe it worked after all." He gestured toward the recorder. "You can turn that back on."

She leaned forward and pressed the button. The red light began to blink once again. "And the child? Any hits on her?"

The chief shook his head. "We looked high and low. Swept the lake with a net, had mountaineers look in the passes, submitted it on the national level. Never heard anything about it." He studied her as he rubbed his hairline. "The description of her from the neighbors was fairly vague and she was too young to age up. I think even you could pass as the baby."

Greer tapped her fingers against her thigh. "Thank you for meeting with me," she said. She pressed the recording

button once more. "You've given me quite a bit to think about."

"You're welcome," he replied, standing from his own seat when Greer did. "Anything else I can do for you?"

"Where can I find the cemetery? I was hoping to visit Holly's grave."

Greer was back in the rental car within five minutes of the police chief giving her directions. She punched her finger on the automatic window button, the cool breeze caressing her face as it rolled down. It should have felt good, but the breeze hit the cold sweat that began to coat her face, making her stomach turn from nausea. She took a deep, shaky breath before pulling out of the parking lot. The cemetery was just a ten-minute drive outside of town and, had she been in the area for anything else, the view of the lake and mountains would have been spectacular. When the terrain opened from neighborhoods to endless fields filled with long grass, her stomach continued to roll.

She swallowed back the bile that crawled up her throat.

She began to slow as the rusting, wrought iron gate appeared before her.

The cemetery was small with only a few dozen grave- stones adorning the neatly clipped land. She parked the car near the entrance and began to explore by foot, examining each gravestone carefully. Greer recognized repeating family names indicating the multiple generations of families that were buried there. Flowers adorned some of the newer gravestones, while the older ones sat covered in dirt and moss, forgotten to time.

Holly Hawkins

Greer stuttered forward when she spotted the name. The grave was located near the back in its own secluded corner. The chief of police appeared to be right, none of the townspeople wanted Holly's body near their family members.

She barely realized what she was doing before she knelt at the grave, brushing the dirt away from Holly's etched name.

"You deserved better," Greer whispered to the cracked stone, gripping the top of it as if it were the woman herself. She pulled a chunk of moss from the stone as she withdrew her hand, tossing it away from the grave.

She should have bought flowers. It didn't occur to her at the police station. Seeing the state of Holly's gravestone compared to the others, it was clear that the townsfolk still held some paranoid belief of the mysterious woman who had appeared in their ranks.

Greer stayed for some time. She knelt at the foot of the grave as she picked at the grass. There was no reason for it. There was no confirmation that Holly was her birth mother, but Greer found herself spilling everything to the headstone. Her childhood, her first kiss, the first time she drove a car, the first time she was caught drinking a beer, when she met Delia. She recounted her life as if the woman sat next to her, as if she were a daughter telling her mother what they both missed.

It was only when she felt an unnatural crackle in the air that she stopped. Greer pushed herself up to standing, darting her eyes around the cemetery. The silence that swelled in the graveyard was deafening, the loss of birds twittering and crickets chirping falling still. Her skin prickled with the thought of being watched and she made a beeline for the rental car.

Greer made one final sweep with her eyes before dipping into the sedan, seeing nothing for a moment. But she could have sworn, as she drove away, that a glimmer of a squat, dark-haired man appeared in the rearview mirror. The image was gone in a blink, and Greer didn't see it again.

TWELVE

"**M**om, I was on a work trip," Greer said through gritted teeth, as she helped Celeste into the hotel bed, "I'm sorry I couldn't be here when you got discharged. I didn't think it was going to be over the weekend."

Celeste sighed, as she settled onto the bed, the mattress sinking under her weight. "I thought you would be there, that's all. I got attacked for you."

"Mom, I was—you know what? Okay, you're right. I'm sorry."

Celeste sent her a sweet smile. "See, honey? Not so bad to take accountability."

Greer clenched her jaw, but said nothing. "Do you need me to pick up some food for you? Go to the pharmacy?" Celeste tucked her legs under the sheets. "I'm not sure how else you expect me to live here, Greer. You won't let me stay in your apartment."

"Delia still lives there, mom. We don't have a third bedroom."

"Well, that does seem convenient, doesn't it?"

Greer clicked her tongue, but decided against engaging. "Text me a list of the things you need, okay?" She handed Celeste the remote to the television and filled the bottle of water from the sink. "Do you need anything from this room before I go?"

"I wish you would stay. We haven't spent much time together."

"You and I both know that would be a terrible idea. I have to finish up a report for work."

"It's a Sunday, Greer," Celeste said in agitation. "You and I both know that you're using that as an excuse."

"Then you and I are at an impasse," Greer replied, as she tugged the hotel door open. "Don't forget to text me your list. I'll stop by the store this evening." She stepped into the carpeted hallway, and let the door swing shut behind her.

The overnight trip to Montana had been useful for two reasons.

One, if Greer had not shown the ability to perform magic, she would have thought the chief of police was reading too much into a run-of-the-mill murder. Knowing that she could perform magic, however bad it was, reaffirmed the gut feeling that she was connected to the murder of Holly Hawkins one way or another.

Two, she needed more information from Cian. It was not information he would give readily, and she was no longer willing to bargain with him. She needed to take it by force if she wanted it.

Which was why she had swiped the keys to her mother's car on the way out of the hotel room. Clicking the key fob to unlock the door, Greer ducked into the passenger side and opened the glove compartment. A car manual, a pile of napkins, the insurance and registration for the vehicle were the only things in there. She sighed, tipping the compartment door back up with a push of her hand. Nothing.

Next, Greer carefully tucked her hands into the cracks between the seats and the center console before looking in the pockets sewn into the backs of the chairs.

Nothing there either.

She let a sigh of frustration escape her parted lips before circling the sedan, and throwing open the driver's side door. Ducking her head under the steering wheel, she craned her neck to peek under the seat.

Bingo.

Greer nestled her hand in between the wires, and felt around for the hilt of the blade. Cian mentioned her mother showed up to the house with one, and if she wanted to get information, she needed to dig deep to pull out her inner Celeste. Her fingers wrapped around the metal, and it slipped from its hiding place with ease. She lifted the dagger into the air, studying it with narrowed eyes.

The dagger was silver and small, the blade extending only seven inches above the hilt. There were carvings etched in the blade— Latin perhaps? Greer removed her cell phone from the back pocket of her jean shorts and snapped a quick photo. She would run it through a translation application for confirmation at a later time.

She locked the car, careful not to set off the alarm as she was sure Celeste would recognize the chirp from her hotel bed, and hopped into the Jeep. She carefully laid the blade on her passenger seat and typed the address into the map function of her cell phone.

Celeste had been found at the house outside of town. Cian said Celeste had come looking for him. Greer deduced that Celeste somehow knew Cian was staying at that house. Whether he was still squatting there, she didn't know, but it was a start.

When Greer parked her car in the gravel driveway and assessed the farmhouse. Yellow caution tape cloaked the front door in a giant X and a lock-box hung from the knob. The house had still been under investigation over the past week, as police collected evidence for the murders of the couple and the attack on her mother. Greer doubted any of the vampyres would have been able to stay hidden for long with the foot traffic.

She turned toward her left, seeing a pole barn set a few hundred feet back from the house. Both of the large, hydraulic doors were closed. A weathervane in the shape of a rooster standing on an arrow sat atop the peak of the roof, the dull copper glinting in the bright sun. It creaked with each push of the breeze, the eerie squeaks rustling on the otherwise phantom wind. With no indication the police had been investigating the pole barn, Greer decided that would be the best place to begin.

She exited the Jeep with the blade clutched tightly in her fist. She followed the gravel driveway beyond the house, the tall grass flanking the path like a maze. It hadn't been cut in some weeks, more than likely since the deaths of the owners, and it was tall enough that the seed head on each blade appeared. Wild flowers had begun to sprout amidst the weeds, and Greer was surprised to realize how quickly nature took over when the humans were no longer there to landscape.

Greer trundled deeper into the long grass, passing a black stake with a red flag on the end. The thin, cheap plastic bent under the weight of the flag, and Greer assumed it was a placeholder for where one of the bodies was found. She gave the site a wide berth, not wanting to disturb the area. Heart hammering in her chest, she reached for the metal knob of the side door. It was unlocked. The door stuck in the frame, enough that Greer needed to shove her shoulder into it, and it finally broke free from the rubber door gaskets. The weather stripping tore at the top, and she brushed it aside as she entered the dark pole barn.

She reached her hand on the inside wall, flicking on the light when her fingers grazed the switch. The interior of the barn was bigger than she thought it would be, and it was clear the couple cared deeply for it. The cement was sealed and smooth, maybe even newly poured, and the metal walls were adorned with tools. The walls were lined with wooden workbenches, each containing a different project, and a compact tractor with a mower attachment was parked nearest the far hydraulic door.

The sawdust and pollen coating the equipment became dislodged when the breeze swept in with her, and she sneezed as it tickled her nose. Old motor oil and the tang of burnt wood filled her nose, her sneeze transforming into a cough against the sudden shift on the air. Her skin pebbled with the sense of being watched, and she swung around to find the doorway behind her still empty.

"Hello?" Greer called out, adjusting her grip on the blade. Her palms were slick with nervous sweat. "Cian?" She stepped deeper into the pole barn, her ears ringing against the silence permeating the space. "I know you're there."

"You're either the bravest woman I've ever met," a low voice spoke from behind her. "Or the stupidest."

Greer whipped around as she raised the blade to chest level.

A man stepped from behind the tractor. The door in the background was cracked open, revealing a television settled on a cardboard box and a tattered, leather couch. The man was handsome with rich, brown skin and coiled, dark hair. His eyes were a deep shade of brown, and the layering of the color was evident in the sharp lighting of the barn. The sleeves of his cotton shirt shifted as he lowered his hands to his sides and he flashed a set of white teeth at her. "You're her," he went on when Greer said nothing.

"You're the Mage."

Greer adjusted the hilt in her palm again. "How do you know who I am?"

The man stayed still, his sneakers rooted to the spot. "To us, you have a...light about you. A glow. We can sense your power." He sniffed the air. "And you have the smell of your kidnapper on you."

Greer bristled at his words. "She's not my kidnapper." The smile shifted from uncertain to amusingly confident. "We both know that's not true." He watched her closely for a moment. "Why are you here?"

"I want to know more about the death of Holly Hawkins," Greer said, keeping the blade raised despite the numbing bark in her shoulder. "I want to know what Cian knows."

"Cian isn't here. He stays in the woods during the day. He prefers the shade of nature, gives him more freedom." The man cocked his head in interest. "I do believe he gave you an ultimatum, though."

"I'm done with ultimatums. This is my life and I want information."

The man gestured toward his pocket and slowly withdrew a cell phone. With a swipe, he opened the screen and lifted it to his ear. "Cian. You have a guest at our residence." He made to take a step forward, arm extended, but Greer took a large step backward. The man stilled again. "I need to come closer for you to take the phone. I can't harm you."

Greer hesitated, the sawdust mixed with anxious anticipation drying her mouth and throat. After a long, silent minute, she nodded her head. The man took a tentative step forward, then a second, until he crossed the cement flooring of the pole barn.

"Here, Cian." The man tapped a finger on the screen, turning on the speaker function.

"Greer," a throaty rumble sounded, his Irish brogue recognizable even through the device. "To what do I owe the pleasure?"

"How did you know about Holly Hawkins?" Greer asked, loudly enough that the microphone could pick up her voice. "I went to Montana and talked to the chief of police. He said there were…plagues when she was killed."

"That was concerning when I heard it had happened," Cian replied, the rustling sound of feet on dead leaves echoing through the phone. "I had never seen that before and I've witnessed many a death of a supernatural creature."

"Holly had…magic?"

"Did Holly have magic? No. She possessed the capability to be the Mage, only through her matriarchal line. She was never chosen. Holly had no more powers than the mommy who raised you."

"Stop calling her that," Greer spat in irritation.

Cian chuckled. "You can thank Isaac for saving her life. He was the one who pulled Jonas off that decrepit shrew still trying to hunt me down. At the very least, Jonas got her off my back for the time being." He paused to heave a dramatic sigh. "It's too bad, really. Jonas has her scent now and with her injuries, well—" He clicked his tongue. "It's only a matter of time. Jonas is a truly magnificent hunter."

"Cian—" Isaac started, running a hand over his hair, but Greer interjected.

"You'll keep your cabal of oversized mosquitos away from her."

"Oh?" Cian must have stopped walking, because the underfoot crunching had ceased. "And why should I do that?"

"Because I'm the Mage and I said so."

Isaac tipped his head back, and let out a loud crack of laughter.

Cian chuckled again, a tone of amusement infiltrating his next words. "That's not going to work on me, love. Agnes, yes. You? The floral skirts don't demand respect."

"How about this?" Greer adjusted her strategy, her lips pressed in a tight line. "If you want my help walking in the daylight, you're going to need to be more upfront with me about the information you have. Otherwise, I'll leave and you'll never step foot on a sunny beach again."

The other end of the line went quiet, as Isaac's brows rose. A warm feeling of triumph shot through her body, and Greer felt safe enough to lower the blade back to her side. The feeling of pinpricks tingled her fingers with the reintroduction of blood flow.

"Okay, witchling," Cian said in a tone that struggled to convey light-heartedness. "What do you want?"

"Proof. I want definitive proof that my mother was involved in the death of Holly Hawkins."

Isaac shifted on his feet, still holding the phone in the open palm of his hand.

Greer heard Cian swallow. "And how do you suppose I do that?"

She bit the inside of her cheek, as her forehead wrinkled.

Cian caught onto her silence. "You want to have the power, Greer, but you need to provide the leverage." He sighed through his nose. "When I was a hundred or so years old, there was a sudden increase in wolf shifters getting slaughtered in the Kingdom of Bohemia. Agnes used their bodies to perform an incantation from her grimoire that led her straight to the group doing the killing."

"So, let's do that?" Greer said, bouncing the blade off the skin of her thigh.

"Did you hear me?" he asked, a bite of impatience reflected in his question. "I said she used their bodies. Or the pieces that were left, anyways. We will have to do something very unpleasant to get you what you need."

Greer's heart jolted, as her eyes connected with Isaac's.

He was nodding, his lips pursed in solemn agreement. "You mean to say dig her up?"

"Yes."

Greer continued biting the inside of her cheek, deep in thought. The idea of someone digging up Holly made her stomach churn, but the thought of the unknown for the rest of her life seemed unbearable.

"What do you want for it?"

"You know what I want. I want to walk in the sun. I help you do this and the first thing you do when you figure out your magic is to make that potion." He paused, the crunch of leaves echoing through the phone once again. "You are a means to an end for us. After I get that potion, we are gone."

"Fine, you have a deal," Greer replied in a sickly, sweet voice, but her teeth were clenched so hard she thought her molars would soon shatter.

Cian hung up without saying another word.

Greer looked up at Isaac and shook her head. "He's insufferable." She huffed a breath of irritation. "Thank you for saving my mother. That was kind of you."

Isaac peered down at the dagger still hanging loosely from her hand. "What was your plan with that?"

"This old thing?" She lifted it into the air, examining it under the bright lights of the pole barn. "I have no idea how to use it."

Isaac smiled, a broad and genuine one that crinkled the corners of his eyes. "Jury is still out then," he said, as he tucked his phone into the pocket of his jeans. "On whether you're brave or extremely stupid."

THIRTEEN

Cian

"I don't know why we're bothering with all of this," Jonas said, as he leaned against the handle of the shovel and looked into the newly-dug grave. "We could just kill her and wait for the next Mage to be more receptive."

Cian tossed his own shovel onto the grass above him and hoisted himself from the hole. "Assuming she hasn't had a daughter, there would not be a new Mage. The line ends with her if she's killed."

Jonas heaved a heavy sigh. "And we couldn't find someone else to make the potion?"

"She's the only one who can read the damn book," Cian hissed in irritation, wiping the sweat from his hairline. "There is no one else."

Jonas let out a humorless chuckle. "Sounds like she does have the leverage, Cian."

Cian turned to look at his friend, the first one he had made when he was turned into a vampyre all those centuries ago. Jonas' bright red hair was dulled only from the clouds that covered the moonlight.

The freckles that adorned his nose and cheeks were offset by his sharp, hazel eyes. Combined with his lazy smile and the barbed personality he possessed, it was no wonder that he preferred to hunt on the university campus. It had been easy for him to persuade college kids to let him take a bite from their necks, wrists, groins— whatever he was allowed to have access to.

Cian preferred to feed on the homeless, where the police wouldn't look too closely into their deaths, but Jonas— it was personal for him. He wanted their bodies, for them to remember the pain, and the fear, and the pleasure he could induce. Cian followed up when Jonas was done playing and removed their heads or staked them in the heart soon after.

The only way someone was turned into a vampyre was to die, body intact, with the venom from a bite in one's system. If they turned, Jonas would leave them to rot in the new forms they owned. Cian, on the other hand, had only turned one person in the centuries he had been plagued.

Isaac.

All this time later, it made Cian sick to think about what he had done to Isaac. What he should have done instead.

"I got through!" Isaac called from the hole. A loud crack sounded, echoing through the cemetery and rolling through the empty fields of grass surrounding them. "She's just a skeleton now."

Cian grabbed the flashlight from Jonas and peered over the edge. Isaac stood on the wooden casket, his feet bracketing the body below him. A single shovel mark had punched through the worn and deteriorating wood, revealing a heap of dust, ragged clothing, and bones beneath.

"Grab her skull and let's get out of here," Cian said, angling the flashlight for Isaac to have a better look inside.

"Well, I certainly didn't expect you three to be here grave-robbing."

Cian swung around; his fangs bared. Jonas followed suit, gripping the shovel handle in his fist.

A man appeared from behind a sun-bleached stone angel, his body dark against the moonlight that was bathing the cemetery in long shadows. While this man appeared to be human, Cian had known for the entirety of his existence as a vampyre that he wasn't. He was merely possessing the body of a newly dead human. Otherwise, he was a spirit made of anger, and wickedness, and death.

"Eligos," Cian said, as Jonas lowered the shovel and returned to casually leaning against the handle. "What brings you here?"

Eligos scrubbed a hand down his shaven face as his overhanging belly lifted with his breath. "Curious that you're here soon after another visit not even days ago. Young, brown hair, gray eyes." His gaze upturned as he took a step away from the shadows. "I should have been able to sense her presence, even if she was just human. Even more curious that I could sense nothing from her. It was as if she wasn't even there."

"Perhaps your power as a djinn is waning," Cian said cautiously, lowering a hand to help pull Isaac from the grave. "Does that happen as you age or did you just do something else to piss off the princes?"

"Careful," Eligos warned, eyes flashing. He tucked his hands into the pockets of his black coat. "I know you've been tracking the Mage line through the centuries. I know that this woman—" He paused to pointedly stare at the skull Isaac had set in the manicured grass. "—was the last to give birth to someone in said line. I want to know where she is."

Cian cleared his throat as he picked up his own shovel and began to move piles of dirt back into the hole they had dug. The dirt brushed against the casket, plinking on the wood like droplets of rain on a glass window. "I don't know what you're talking about."

"Oh, don't you?" Eligos went on, taking a menacing step forward. Cian felt the hair on the back of his neck crackle. Djinn were powerful. Easily the most powerful of the daemons when comparing sheer force. That was part of the reason only a handful of them remained. There had been a war amongst them nearly two thousand years ago, a war that sunk cities and ended civilizations. They had been punished by their creator, who had only allowed for a few to remain. Eligos was the only one Cian knew by name.

The others were whispers on the wind, but Cian knew they possessed the power to open portals and enter realms. If the remaining djinn were smart, they were in hiding.

"I just want to talk with her," Eligos went on as though he were commenting on the weather. "Find out where she grew up, who raised her. The normal things one would ask a twenty-six-year-old woman."

Cian shook his head as Jonas looked on with an interested gaze. "Sorry, Eligos. I don't know what you mean. I have no knowledge of any woman acting as the Mage."

Eligos was at his front in a flash and, despite the fact that the top of his head grazed the underside of Cian's chin, Cian felt a twinge of fear in his stomach. Eligos sniffed, smiling at the sudden shift in Cian's scent.

"I just want to know what you know; see what you've seen." Eligos reached up to brush the dirt from Cian's shirt. "It's been so long since I've seen the glow of the Mage. I just want to look upon it again." His smile turned dangerous, dark.

Cian pried Eligos's hands away from his chest. "Your role in Agnes' death is something I cannot forgive."

Eligos reached into the inner pocket of his knee-length coat, pulling out a vial from inside. He held it between his thumb and pointer finger, the contents swirling and twirling within. It seemed to emit its own glow, one that was brighter than even the moon that had come out from behind the streaks of clouds.

"I think you'll find that you can."

Cian glowered. "I'll take the bait. What is that?"

Eligos' smile returned, the wicked humor not quite reaching his eyes. "This is yours. Well, it was yours. Agnes discovered the cure to vampyrism before she died. Made this little potion for you." He threw it into the air and caught it in his hand. "I found it in one of the hideaway hovels she used."

Cian and Isaac stilled as Jonas shifted on his feet. Silence fell between the four men; even the air had turned stale and the crickets ceased their chirping. A car drove by, the headlights a quick flash against the otherwise dark night.

"Even if that was a cure," Cian said, as he began to shove the dirt back into the hole again, "Agnes is dead. It wouldn't work."

"Agnes had help," Eligos went on, "*Primordial* help." He tossed the vial over to Cian, where it arced across the space between them. Cian caught it with one hand. "The only power to withstand the death of the Mage is one that doesn't come from this world."

"You expect us to believe a cure is in that vial?" Isaac piped up, his arms crossed over his chest.

"I don't expect you to believe anything, dear man."

Eligos waved his hand and the vial disappeared from Cian's grip and reappeared in his own. A second wave and Eligos held a dead crow, the body filled with squirming maggots. He unscrewed the dropper from the vial and plunked three drips of the swirling liquid onto the bird. They waited for a long minute before the crow took a sweeping breath in, filling the once extinguished lungs with new air. It shook the maggots from its body, flinging them in all directions, and ruffled its feathers as it perched on Eligos' wrist.

It lifted its wings and flew off into the night, caws echoing across the decorative flower beds and well-tended headstones.

Silence fell once more.

"What do you want?" Cian asked breathlessly, his eyes fixed on the vial in Eligos' hand.

Eligos swept his gaze over the worn, faceless statues of winged angels and praying hands. The chilled wind that came off the mountain pass ruffled the hem of his coat. "I want her dead, Cian."

Cian recoiled as if he had been struck. "Kill her yourself, then," he shot back in disgust, peeling his eyes from the vial. "Nothing is worth my conscience."

"Is it not?" Eligos retorted, his head tilted curiously. "I remember you breaking that little rule for your friend Isaac, here."

Isaac's own eyes flashed as his gaze darted between

the two of them. "I've forgiven Cian for that," Isaac said, his head shaking slowly. "I will not allow you to use me for your schemes."

Eligos panned over to Isaac. "I'm quite sure you're not telling the truth. Anger and resentment pebble your soul, vampyre." He returned his attention to Cian. "You and I both know that I cannot kill her without her magic coming out. I may be powerful, but—" He trailed off for a moment before taking in a deep breath, "—there are other forces at play here."

"If you cannot kill her, how do you expect me to?" Cian asked.

Isaac shifted in discomfort as Jonas' lips turned upward in a smirk.

"I don't. I said I wanted her dead, not that you need to kill her. Keep up." Eligos raked his stare over Cian's filthy clothes, the shovel still in his hand, the dirt smeared on the front of his neck and left cheek. His eyes fell to the skull still on the grass. "I need you to convince her to give up her power. Then, I can kill her."

Cian's eyes widened as his knuckles whitened under the grip of the shovel handle. The wood began to splinter, the crackling ebbing beneath his fingers. "If we convince her of that, she will never be able to recover from it. Taking her power alone would kill her."

"I know," Eligos said gleefully, rocking on his small feet. "Energy like that does not end, but shifts. I will be able to come in and take it for myself."

It was Isaac's turn to scrub his hand down his face. "What do you want with all that power, Eligos?" he asked warily, as his posture perked under the scrutiny.

"I have plans for it," Eligos replied. "Plans you are now made aware of." He turned to Cian. "If you simply want to walk in the sun, then stay with her." His wicked smile returned. "However, if you want to return to humanity, continue aging, have a family...stick with me."

Cian hesitated for a fraction of a moment, but his mind was made up just as quickly. "Deal. Done."

Isaac opened his mouth to protest, but Jonas shoved an elbow deep into his gut. He doubled over in pain, groaning filling the still and silence.

"One more thing," Eligos said, as he began to fade into the night. "There is a faerie by the name of Odette. She lives somewhere in the area in which you are now residing. I was hired to track her down by someone who very badly wants her dead too. Bring her to me alive."

"What will you do with her?" Cian asked, his mind flashing back to her leathered wings and red top knot.

"None of your business," he snapped. "Odette alive and the Mage's power gone. Those are my terms. Work quickly, I'm not a patient daemon."

FOURTEEN

"You got it?" Greer asked, looking up from the grimoire opened on the kitchen table. She took a sip from the glass of wine as she pinched the phone in-between her shoulder and ear. "How long did it take you?"

"A fair few hours," Cian said from the other side of the line. "We're about an hour out of town now. We're headed straight to you. What is your apartment number?"

Greer stilled as her lips parted in hesitation.

Cian must have sensed it, because he went on with, "If we're going to do this, we're going to need to trust each other. Have I given you a reason to not trust me?"

"Well, no, but—"

"The apartment number then, if you please."

Greer sighed. "Number five. It's on the second floor." "We'll buzz when we get there."

With that, he hung up the phone.

She had scoured the grimoire to find the spell Cian told her about and gathered the ingredients required for it. Most of it was easy-cinnamon, daisy root, dried thyme, a map, four candles. The most difficult ingredient, by far, was a piece of the person killed. Cian was bringing that back. Greer hadn't bothered to ask what piece he had chosen.

Nerves wracked through her body. She had only tried using her magic once, the other two times by accident, and hadn't attempted anything since. It was even more trying that each section began with the simplest potions, incantations, or blessings and spanned to the very hardest at the end. The potion she needed to make was near the difficult side, easily over midway.

Greer flipped through the grimoire, curiously skimming the pages. She grimaced when she realized it was within her best interest to try one more incantation, a simple one. Something to get her warmed up.

She closed the grimoire and reopened it near the front, where the section of incantations resided. Greer skipped right over the incantation to create flames and landed on another simple one. Levitation.

She pulled the bundle of candles toward her as she looked over the incantation. She cleared her throat and readied her hands in front of her when she paused. A thought occurred to her.

The times she had performed magic and wielded it the way it was meant to be, both with the attacker and with Cian in the car, she had not said an incantation. In fact, the one time she had said an incantation she had nearly burnt the apartment down.

Greer turned her attention toward the bundle of candles, forgoing the grimoire entirely. Her eyes narrowed as her focus turned inward. *Float, float, float.* She chanted the words in her head as she dug deep into herself, remembering the feeling of the magic coming out of her.

This time, she allowed only a sliver of that power to break from behind the wall where it resided.

Suddenly, the candles shot into the air, hovering a few inches above the dining room table. Greer smiled; a true and genuine smile. *Light, light, light.* The candle wicks flickered before bursting into appropriately sized flames. The lit candles bobbed in the air as if strung from the ceiling. Greer stood from her seat and walked around the table, studying the candles from each angle. It had been much easier for her to use the magic without the incantation, and she wondered for a moment whether she needed the grimoire at all.

"Greer, are you— oh my God."

Delia burst through the unlocked door, Paige following behind her. Delia's steps jolted as she looked at the scene in front of them, and Paige almost fell forward as she ran into Delia's back.

Greer dropped her concentration, whipping around to see Delia and Paige's shocked faces. The candles winked out and clattered to the floor. "I— I can explain—" But she couldn't. Her mouth opened and closed a few times as she struggled to form said explanation.

Paige, the ever pragmatic person that she was, walked over to the table and ran her hand over the surface, as if she could find the trick wires that hung from the ceiling. She turned back to Greer. "How—how did you do that?" Delia's lips parted as her eyes dropped down to the grimoire. "You were trying to tell us something, weren't you? A few days ago with that book?"

Tears pricked the corners of Greer's eyes as the truth came flooding out of her. How the attack brought up some hidden magic, how she had been tracked down by a vampyre and given the name Holly Hawkins, how she looked into the death of the woman and found out about the missing child.

With every word spoken, Greer felt the weight lift from her shoulders and, when she finished, she polished off her wine in one swig. Delia and Paige had listened with unbroken attention, Delia in one of the dining room chairs and Paige on the counter, her feet dangling toward the ground.

Delia took in a deep breath and blew it out slowly. She grasped the grimoire and pulled it over to her. She rifled through the book once more, closely studying the pages. "There is writing on this page? Really?"

Greer nodded her head, sniffling as she dabbed at the corners of her eyes with a tissue. "It's filled. You just can't see it."

"And what were you trying to do when we walked in?" Paige asked. She tried to keep her hands from trembling, but Greer saw the effort.

"Something simple," Greer sighed, sitting back in her seat. The empty wine glass was still held in her hand. "I made a deal. Information exchanged for a potion to allow the vampyres to walk in the sun." Greer gestured toward the book still in Delia's hands. "I haven't been able to do much. The first time I tried was a category four hurricane."

Delia pressed her hand to her cheek in realization. "When you said you knocked the candle over?" She reached forward and grasped Greer's forearm. "Why didn't you tell me the truth?"

"I thought you would think I was insane," Greer replied miserably. She set the glass down with a clink on the wooden table. "And I'm still trying to figure all of this out. I'm trying to use some sort of locator spell that one of my ancestors designed. Cian, one of the vampyres, said that it could help give me proof that my mother had a hand in the death of Holly Hawkins."

Paige, who had been filling a glass of wine, lowered her hand slowly. "A locator spell?" Her eyes widened before making a sideways glance toward Delia. "Can you do one?"

Greer lifted her head. "I'm going to try for the first time tonight. For this particular one, I need a piece of the person killed. Then, it'll lead me to whoever killed her. But..." Greer trailed off, recognition sparking in her eyes. "Are you wondering about Delia's brothers? Would I be able to find them?"

Delia jaw dropped before she snapped it back together again. "I— would you? Is that possible?"

Greer squinted in thought as she shrugged a shoulder. "I don't see why I couldn't. I just— I'm not very good at magic." She pointed at the new coffee table. "I almost burnt the apartment down, and it still smells like mildew in here. But if this goes well, I'm willing to try."

Delia tightened her grasp around Greer's forearm, her gaze unabashedly fixed on Greer's face. "What would you need?" she asked in a hushed whisper.

"Something of theirs, I would expect. For me to track them. A map. More ingredients. I would need time to make sure I did it right." Greer paused, rocking her head back and forth. "I think I would have to destroy whatever belonged to them. I have to destroy a piece of Holly anyways."

"A piece of—"

At that moment, the buzzer on the intercom chirped. Greer twitched in surprise, leaping out of her chair. With Delia and Paige watching her, both women pink and flushed with the new information, Greer made her way to the door and pressed the microphone. "Yes?"

"Open the door, Greer. It's hot. Isaac is melting."

Greer pressed the unlock button on the intercom and heard the lock click through the speaker.

"Who is that?" Delia asked, as Greer opened the apartment door, awaiting the two vampyres.

As if on cue, Cian and Isaac appeared in the doorway. Cian in his usual leather jacket and dark pants, Isaac comfortable in a loose, cotton shirt and jeans. Greer could smell the stale, apartment hallway mixed with the humid forest air. Cian held a folded paper bag in his hand.

"Are you going to let us in?" he asked, holding up the bag with a casual flare to his wrist.

Greer made to reach for the bag, but he jerked it back- wards and hid it behind his back.

"I thought we talked about trusting one another," Cian chided, as Isaac chuckled. "If you want this, you're going to have to let us in."

Greer scowled. "The door is open, just walk in." "Can't do that, love," Cian responded after clicking his tongue. "Most creatures need to be invited into a dwelling. Vampyres, wolf shifters, the fae." Isaac sent a glance over to Cian, who ignored it. "None of us can get in without explicit permission from the humans that live there. It's an annoying little thing."

Delia stood from her chair as she crossed her arms over her chest. "Did you kill that couple in the farmhouse?" she asked bluntly as she narrowed her eyes onto Cian.

"Technically Jonas did," he said, bracing a forearm against the doorframe. "He's not with us." He turned back toward Greer. "Your choice, witchling. Do you want to know the truth or not?" He re- moved the bag from behind his back and dangled it between his point- er finger and thumb.

Greer hesitated as Delia said, "Think about this, G. They'll have access to the apartment."

Greer turned back toward Delia and sent her an apologetic look. "I have to know, Dels. I have to know if my mom was involved in all of this." She glanced at Cian, who continued to stare expectantly at her. "You can both come in."

"Excellent choice," Cian said, shoving the paper bag into Greer's chest as he crossed the threshold. "You wouldn't have gotten that skull without it."

"Skull?" Greer asked faintly, as Isaac dipped past her.

Delia's body stiffened as Cian entered the dining room and collapsed at the table.

"Is this your set up?" Cian asked with a smirk, as he glanced at the candles, the map, and the ingredients still in their packaging. "Conjuring times have changed."

"Is this your shtick?" Delia sank into the accent chair she had pulled from the living room, her uncomfortable glare set on Cian. "This overconfident smugness?"

Cian turned his gaze toward Delia with his head cocked. "I don't believe we are here to discuss this with you." He paused, looking at her from her sneakers to the top of her curly-haired head. "Who are you?"

Greer crossed the living room to open a window. The apartment had begun to grow stuffy with the extra bodies in it. The moonlight poured in as she separated the curtains, and the fresh mountain air came in with the window cracked. She felt the sweat on her neck cool instantly, leaving behind sticky residue.

"Greer is my best friend. I have her best interest at heart." Delia returned the motion, sliding her gaze along his leather jacket, ringed-fingers, and black boots. "Something I doubt you do."

Cian tapped his fingers on the dining room table as he narrowed his eyes on her. "You don't know of my intentions. I could be here to save her life."

"I doubt it," Delia snorted in derision. She crossed one knee over the other and let her foot bob in the air between them. "What is going to keep you from killing us in our sleep the moment you get what you want?"

Cian sucked his teeth in irritation. "Greer can't be killed by anything supernatural, that's how her magic works. As for you…" He pressed his lips together. "You aren't my type. I don't think I would bother."

Delia sneered, opening her mouth to get in her next jab, when Greer cut her off.

"Let's move on for now, shall we?" Greer unfolded the paper bag before making a noise of surprise from the back of her throat. She reached in and grasped the top of the skull, feeling the stray hairs still attached, and pulled it out.

"Is that thing real?" Paige asked as she slipped from the countertop and edged into the dining room. Cian's head lifted, as he turned his focus to Paige, not realizing she had been there. Paige bent down to further inspect the skull. "It looks like a Halloween decoration."

"I can assure you it is real," Cian replied. "The calluses on our palms from digging her up are in agreement."

Delia stood from her chair and joined Paige at the table, placing a hand on her shoulder as she bent over to glance at the skull.

"We are so fucked if they trace this back to us," Delia commented, as she peered up at Greer. "My law career would be over."

"Think of your brothers," Paige said soothingly, as she tucked a lock of hair behind Delia's ear. "If Greer can get this right, we can find your brothers."

"Yes, Delia. Relax," Cian prodded, and Delia sent him a scathing look. "I got the skull. You've got what you need. Are you going to do this or not?"

Greer sent him an equally scathing look as she wove through the four surrounding the table. She reached forward to grasp the large, folded map of Oregon. She unfurled it, a corner sticking from the wine she had accidentally spilled earlier, and slapped it back onto the surface before them. Greer paused as she looked at the map for a long moment, the internal debate roiling within her. She needed to get this over with. She smoothed the fold lines down as best as she could.

Next, Greer positioned the four candles in each corner of the map. She took the grimoire from Cian's hands and began to portion the ingredients into a stainless-steel stock pot she had bought for the occasion. She put the stock pot onto the oven and turned the knob for the burner. The stove went through a series of clicks before the ring of flames erupted.

Taking a deep breath, she palmed Holly's skull and studied it one more time. Dirt and grime crusted the top and into the eye sockets. The majority of the teeth were still intact, though a few had fallen from their sockets. More than likely, those teeth were located back in the casket in Montana. The strands of hair still attached threaded over her hands. Greer realized they were a beautiful shade of brown, much like her own.

With care and ease, Greer lowered Holly's skull into the stock pot. The skull floated on the water for a moment before sinking through the clump of cinnamon and falling to the bottom of the pot. She cleared her throat and turned inward as she had with the levitation and focused her attention on the stock pot. The contents hissed and bubbled before Greer heard a sharp crack followed by one more hiss. She grabbed a wooden spoon and stirred the contents clockwise seven times.

Greer was able to smoothly drag the spoon through the liquid. The skull had disintegrated under her power, and the bone dust fizzled to the surface. In a flash, the liquid turned a brilliant shade of orange, and steam plumed from the surface. The steam rolled over the edge of the pot like a misty smoke, covering the counter in a thick fog.

"Keep going," Cian said quietly. Greer turned to see him leaned forward with his forearms braced on his knees. "This is what happened when Agnes made the potion."

Greer cleared her throat, her head suddenly buzzing from the restrained control. "Delia, could you light the candles?"

"Why don't you—" Cian started, but was hushed by Delia when she passed behind him. Delia dug in the kitchen's junk drawer as the potion bubbled once again, and a second plume of steam unfurled from the stock pot.

When the candles had been lit, Greer grasped the handles of the pot and slowly walked it over to the dining room table. "Here goes nothing," she said under her breath, as she shook her head. In one quick motion, she poured the liquid in a counter-clockwise direction over the map, allowing it to drench completely from corner to corner.

Greer knelt at the edge of the table and decided to forgo the grimoire for the incantation. She channeled all of her power and energy into the map, focusing completely on the set-up in front of her.

"You're supposed to say an incantation," Cian started, "Agnes would—"

He stopped when a spark lit the corner of the map. It began in the northeast corner of Oregon and swept to the southeast corner. It marched over the middle of the map with ease before curling from the northwest and southwest corners, until they met halfway up the middle. The flames danced around the city Greer lived in, encircling it completely. Slowly, the flames licked inwards until they halted in an area of the map nearly ten minutes from her apartment.

The flames snuffed out as if someone had sucked the oxygen from the room.

"How did you do that?" Cian asked, as his lips parted in awe. "Agnes always needed to speak the incantation to get something to work. I don't understand."

Paige swept her hand over the wooden table, touching it gingerly at first as if she were expecting it to be hot. The table was just as it was before the spell— undamaged and dry.

"I'm on my phone looking at what is on that block," Isaac started quietly, as he scrolled his finger over the screen. "It's pretty bare. A McDonald's, a dollar store, and a hotel." Greer straightened and turned to look over Isaac's forearm to peer at his screen. She recognized the name of the hotel, and her body stilled. Her gaze became unfocused, the screen blurring in front of her. She took a stunned step backwards as her hand flew to her throat.

"Greer?" Delia asked, as concern rippled through her eyes.

"That's the hotel my mother is staying at," Greer finally said through stuttered breaths. "It's true, she killed my birth mom."

FIFTEEN

"Greer! Greer," Delia said as she tugged on Greer's sleeve. "It's nearly nine o'clock at night. Don't you think you need time to—"

"She's been lying to me, Dels," Greer seethed through gritted teeth. She was pacing the kitchen, the remaining piece of the map clutched tightly in her hand. "I've been asking, and she made me feel like I was wrong, like I was crazy for even thinking it."

Greer headed toward the front door and grabbed her keys off the hook bolted to the wall. She shoved her feet into her Birkenstocks and yanked open the door.

"Greer, if your mom killed someone, it's a bad idea to—"

"I'll go with you," Cian piped up, as he stood from the chair he sat in, clapping his hands together. "I have a bone to pick with her anyways."

Delia glanced alarmingly at Greer, but Greer was already over the threshold of the door and marching halfway down the hallway. The lightbulbs popped as she passed each one, bathing the hallway behind her in darkness.

"Greer, wait—" Delia started again, but was cut off by the door slamming shut behind Cian.

Greer heard his hurried footsteps as she jogged down the back staircase. She threw the metal door open, not bothering to see if Cian was still behind her, and unlocked her Jeep with the key fob in her hand.

"Maybe I should drive—" Cian started, but Greer sent him a sharp, rage-filled look. He held up his hands in surrender. "Passenger side it is then."

Greer threw open the driver's side door and climbed in before shoving the key into the ignition with enough force that the plastic wrapping on the end of the key cracked beneath her hand. Cian climbed in after her and, as soon as his door was shut, Greer rolled down the windows. She had them replaced while she was in Montana and didn't need to spend another few hundred dollars to have them replaced a second time.

Students crossed the entrance of the parking lot, dressed in casual summer outfits and headed toward the group of restaurants a few blocks away. Greer heard their chattering as they passed and watched as a woman jumped on the back of a man, her hair draping over his shoulder as she leaned in to kiss his cheek.

Their lives weren't falling apart. But Greer's was. Only Greer's.

Greer punched the gas and sped onto the main road. Cian grasped the handle on the ceiling, but said nothing as she increased her speed to keep up with the traffic.

"Do you want to talk about it?" Cian asked over the roar of the wind through the open windows. He kept his eyes trained on the road in front of them.

"Nope," Greer said, popping the 'P' dramatically. "Everything I have to say, I'll say it to my mother."

Cian clamped his lips shut, bracing his left elbow on the center console between them. Greer felt his forearm brush against hers. Her chest heaved with panting breaths as she took a right-hand turn at the next intersection. The tires screeched against the pavement and a group of men turned their heads at the noise.

Greer pulled into the parking lot at full speed, slamming on her brakes as soon as she turned into a lined spot. Cian jolted against his seat belt at the sudden stop. Greer threw the car into park and reached under her seat, feeling around for the blade.

Cian arched one eyebrow in disbelief as he looked at the dagger in her hand, the metal glinting under the parking lot light. "Where did you get that?"

Greer said nothing as she approached the glass front doors. They split as she walked forward, and she entered the lobby to the hotel. The red carpet under her feet was old and worn from years of traffic. Two green couches and two green armchairs sat near a large window bordered with thick golden curtains. No one manned the beige-colored desk near the front door, but Greer could hear fingers clacking on a computer in the back.

She turned off the main lobby and headed toward the elevator in the hallway. She passed the in-ground pool, the lights turned off and the water calm. Her senses were awash with the smell of chlorine that only grew stronger as she passed.

Greer pressed the button to the elevator and she heard the familiar jerk of the cables as the car descended to the ground floor. The doors opened with a ding, and she walked on, her teeth still clenched tightly together. Cian followed her, though eyed the blade in her hand warily.

The car jerked once again as the cables brought them to the third floor of the hotel and Greer pushed through the slow-opening doors as soon as the elevator quaked to a stop. She marched down the hallway, the plush carpet sinking with each forceful step, and stopped at the door marked 3022.

Greer lifted a fist and pounded on the door, not letting up until she heard, "I'm coming, I'm coming," from the interior of the room.

Behind Greer, another guest opened their own door and peeked into the hallway before shutting it upon seeing Cian's glowering face.

Greer's body trembled with rage and anticipation as she heard slow movements approach the door. The bolt clicked, the door cracked open, and Greer was already over the threshold as she pushed past her mother.

Celeste was left in stunned silence as she looked at the back of her daughter's head. She turned to close the door and spotted Cian. Her lip curled into a sneer as she said, "You are not invited in." She made to close the door, but Cian held it open with a single splayed hand.

His grin was overly sweet, and his tone dripped with sarcasm as he said, "I can't possibly tell if you're out of practice or not." He swung the door open and stepped over the threshold. "We're in a hotel, lovely. No residents; vampyres welcome." He entered the hotel room with a swaggering confidence. "You should thank your daughter you don't need a protection spell. She haggled for Jonas to stay away from you."

Greer watched as her mother slowly stepped into the room. "Greer? It's late, what could possibly—"

"You lied to me," Greer interjected, her face flushed and her hands clenched into fists at her side. "You told me you knew nothing about Holly Hawkins and you lied to me."

Celeste crossed her arms over her chest and shifted her weight to one foot. "I told you that I don't—"

Greer thrust a hand into her pocket and came out with the remaining piece of the map. She held it into the space between her and Celeste, her hand trembling. "I did a spell. A locator spell. Cian and his friends dug up Holly's skull for me, and I used it to track her killer. Imagine my surprise when it led me here." She tossed the map piece into the air, keeping her eyes trained on Celeste as it fluttered to the floor.

Celeste's face turned red hot before the blood cleared her cheeks, leaving the skin mottled and gray. "What did you do—" she started, but Greer tossed the blade onto the ground between them. It thudded to the carpet and bounced once before stilling. Celeste's gaze flicked down to the blade, her expression blank as she was stunned into silence.

"I thought that might look familiar to you," Greer went on as her nostrils flared, "I looked up the etching in the blade. *Paladinus Societas*. It translates to Paladin Society from Latin." She paused, her chest tightening to the point of pain. "You were involved with them, weren't you?"

Celeste's eyes were wide as she bit the inside of her cheek. She gave off the appearance that her life was falling apart around her and she didn't know what to do. "Generations of us," she finally said after a long minute, her dark eyes not leaving Greer's gray ones.

Greer's heart thumped wildly. "What did you say?"

"Generations of my family were part of the Paladin Society and we were proud to be so."

Greer felt her body go rigid. She had never heard Celeste talk about their family. She claimed they all had died before Greer was born.

"I was part of it when I was younger. I trained with my father and sister. We learned everything from the Paladin Society. We were tasked to kill monsters to keep humans safe." She stopped to take a shaky breath. "My father spent his entire life chasing the Mage lineage. I don't know how much the vampyre told you, but the Mage line was given power by Lucifer himself to protect his daemons. The last one's name was Agnes."

Greer saw Cian shift behind Celeste, his arms folding over his chest. His gaze turned feral, deadly as he watched the back of Celeste's blonde head. Celeste pressed on, none the wiser.

"What we understood about the Mage was that the energy the women could access was passed from mother to daughter through the same line stemming back thousands of years. Only one Mage could manifest at a time, and we never knew when the next could crop up. Problem was, Agnes had her daughter before she accepted the energy and became immortal. That was nearly seven hundred years ago. My father spent most of his adult life trying to track down the line of women from Agnes and he found it. Twenty-six years ago."

Celeste's voice hardened with every word spoken and she began to pick at the invisible lint on her shirt. Greer's anger roared at her mother's indifference and she couldn't control the burst of power that shattered through her. The television screen cracked, bifurcating the picture playing on the device. Glass skittered along the counter, dropping down onto the marble floor with loud *plinks*. The mirror in the bathroom had shattered, along with the lightbulbs lining the top of it.

Greer's body shook with adrenaline as she turned away from her mother to look out of the window. The dim lighting from the parking lot cast an orange hue onto the cars below. In the silence, she heard a neighboring door open and close. The noise was followed by footsteps walking down the hallway.

"You killed her," Greer said, as she lifted her head and looked back at Celeste. "You killed my mother."

Celeste was shaking her head vigorously, her blonde hair pulling from the ponytail she had secured it in. "You don't understand. I started, I made the first series of cuts, but my father wanted to take over. I was charged with searching the house for you. But when I saw you swaddled into that crib, not even five weeks old, I knew that I couldn't do what my father wanted me to do. I took you from your crib, wrapped you in my jacket, and escaped through the window in your bedroom."

"To leave those monsters to kill Holly," Greer spat, her voice trembling.

Tears pricked at Celeste's eyes for the first time Greer could remember. "To save your life." She choked back a sob as she placed a delicate hand over her mouth. "No one knew to look for you. Holly, she was alone. Likely didn't even know she was part of the Mage line. She had no family, she had just moved to Montana. I researched until I found the perfect identity we could hide under. The woman died in the late nineties in a car accident, no husband and no children."

Greer's face contorted from rage, to hurt, to betrayal. "I could have known who I was all along." She paused to take a deep, shaky breath. "You don't know that Holly didn't know where she came from. You and your family took that away from me. I don't even know who I am—"

"You are Greer Myers," Celeste interrupted. "You are my daughter—"

Greer splayed her hands out to her side. "But I'm not, am I?" She lifted one hand and ran it through her dark locks. "We've made each other miserable for years."

"Greer, that's not—"

"Yes, it's true! We've made each other miserable. Absolutely fucking miserable." Greer's voice was strangled as her head shook, slow and disbelieving. "And I thought it was my fault." She tapped her chest above her heart. "I thought something was wrong with me. I thought it was my fault that we couldn't connect. I spent years in therapy wondering why I couldn't bond with my own mother." She felt a flush creep up her neck. "I *hate* you."

Greer saw her mother briefly crumble beneath the posh, cool demeanor she proudly displayed. Celeste recovered quickly, lifting her chin in defiance. "I'm sorry you feel that way. One day, you'll understand. Right now, there is another matter at hand." Within the blink of an eye, Celeste bent over and grabbed the knife from the floor. She whirled around and plunged it into the stomach of an unsuspecting Cian.

Greer screamed as Cian doubled over in pain. Celeste quickly withdrew the blade, the metal dripping with dark, red blood.

"I told you to leave it alone," Celeste hissed as she readjusted her grip and made to plunge the dagger into him once again. "I told you to leave her alone. And look at what you did. You fucked it all up."

"*Stop*," Greer cried out, thrusting out a hand to grasp onto Celeste's forearm.

Celeste froze as if she were a stone statue. Her arm was extended, the knife mere centimeters from Cian's heart. Greer circled around to face her mother, whose eyes were wide with terror and ricocheting around the hotel room. Greer bent down and pried the blade from her mother's tightened hand. Cian collapsed face-first to the carpet in pain, groaning as he held pressure on the stab wound.

"You are nothing to me," Greer hissed to Celeste, as she bent down and helped Cian to his feet. Greer snapped her fingers and Celeste fell forward, able to move once again. "Stay away from me. Stay away from Cian and his friends. Stay out of my life."

Greer hadn't realized how tall Cian was until he was using her as a crutch. His body weight leaned heavily against her shoulder, and she wrapped an arm around his waist to help keep him upright.

"Greer, Greer wait," Celeste said from behind, as she crawled on the carpet in an attempt to reach them. "Please, Greer, wait—"

Greer allowed the door to shut with a snap behind them, focusing entirely on keeping Cian upright. They made their way to Greer's car, and Cian stumbled into the seat, gritting his teeth against the pain.

"Let me see," Greer said, picking at the hem of his shirt. He let her lift it, revealing the deep puncture mark just below his heart. It leaked blood and fluid down his abdomen, running over his waist and into the band of his pants. "We should get you to a hospital."

Cian chuckled before hissing in pain once again. "And tell them what? The reason I don't have a blood pressure is because I died three hundred years ago? No worries." He tugged his shirt down and used the handle on the ceiling to right himself in the seat. "I'll heal in a few hours."

Greer hovered awkwardly at his side, picking at her cuticles while she watched him. "I'm sorry about Celeste," she said earnestly, looking up at him with wide eyes.

"This is nothing compared to the wounds I got fighting for the Union Army."

Greer tilted her head. "The Union Army? Really?"

He nodded his head. "Bayonets are far worse than a few inch blade."

Greer cleared her throat. "Why don't— why don't you and Isaac stay at our apartment tonight. It's the least I can do to say thank you for helping me tonight."

A smirk quirked the side of his mouth upward as he said, "Am I growing on you, love?" He laughed at her disgusted expression. "We'll call it mutual respect then."

Greer rolled her eyes as she shut the door of the Jeep, not letting him see the smile that perked on her lips.

SIXTEEN

T he first thing she did the night before was block her mother's phone number. Greer had no interest in hearing what Celeste had to say after what she did to Cian.

Cian and Isaac stayed long enough for Greer to head to bed. Delia had already locked herself in her bedroom, followed in solidarity by Paige. Greer knew she needed to talk with Delia, and she was especially curious about Delia's reaction to Cian. Normally, Delia was the first to invite someone into their apartment.

The second thing she did happened the next morning. "Polson Police Department."

"Hi, this is Greer Myers. I had a meeting with the chief of police last week."

"What can we do for you?"

Greer pinched her phone between her ear and her shoulder as she unlocked her car. Swinging her canvas bag into the front seat, she next placed her lavender cream cold brew into the cup holder.

"I was hoping I could get DNA tested to confirm my relation to your cold case murder, Holly Hawkins."

The line went silent for a long moment before the woman said, "I'm going to transfer your call to the Chief. Please hold."

The line clicked as Greer started her car. A swirl of jaunty music filled her ear as she pulled into morning traffic. Cloud coverage cast the daylight in a gray hue and the subsequent rain came down like bullets, thick and loud against her windshield.

"Greer Myers," a familiar voice came over the speaker a moment later, and Greer imagined his mustache twitching with every word, "I heard you wanted a DNA test for the Holly Hawkins murder case?"

"I came across some information that led me to believe I might be related," Greer answered, as she turned onto the highway, heading into work. Sheets of water covered the road as she sped up, sending small waves cresting over the painted lines. "And I was hoping I could find some information on how to get tested."

The Chief was quiet for a moment before he said, "We can run a sample of your DNA through CODIS. It's a storage system in the state and federal government for crime scene evidence. If we run your DNA against CODIS and it is a match to Holly Hawkins, we can put that piece of the puzzle to bed."

"Do you mind emailing me the information for how to do that? I would like to take care of it this week, if able."

"Sure thing, kid. Should take a couple of days once we get the test going."

Greer rattled off her email as she pulled into the parking lot of the library and hung up shortly after. She placed the Jeep into park before reaching over to grab the umbrella from the floor of the passenger seat, opening it just outside of the driver's side door.

The rain dropped onto the tight fabric in heavy patters as she stepped from the car. In a hurried walk, she crossed the parking lot and entered the building with only the tips of her shoes soaking through. She tipped the to-go coffee mug in Roger's direction, the lid covered in water droplets, as she made her way into the library.

"Greer, I found some information for you to index," Daniel said as soon as she entered the office, lifting a stack of files into the air for her to grab. He didn't bother to look up from his computer monitor, and Greer was pleasantly surprised to see a steaming mug of lemon and honey tea seated on his desk.

Normalcy. That's what she needed. Normalcy.

"Thank you, Daniel," Greer said, as she tucked the documents under her arm and continued deeper into the office. "What are you working on today?"

"Henry wants me to talk with the leaders in the Pacific Northwest tribe community to see if they are comfortable with us creating a digital catalog of different aspects of their culture. I'm creating a presentation for what that would look like, and how they would have continued access to the research we're doing here."

"Sounds important," Greer said, as she placed the documents on her desk.

"It is. Very."

"Where is Erin today? She usually beats me here."

"Called in for an early appointment this morning. Said she'll be here later this afternoon."

"Ah. Well, don't let me keep you. I am going to head upstairs and grab a couple of books Henry wanted me to look through. I'll let you know if I can find anything you can catalog."

He made a noise at the back of his throat that told Greer he heard her, so she grabbed her coffee off the desk and headed to the second floor.

Part of her job, pulling newly delivered books for Henry to study, wasn't something she was entirely excited about. She did enjoy looking at the new selection, though, and it gave her time away from a small space where two of her office mates bickered for large chunks of the day.

The clock above her ticked as she walked between two tall, metal shelves, her heels sinking into the musty carpet. At the study tables around the corner, she heard the frustrated sighs of students and the quiet turning of pages. Greer reached above her to pull a book from a shelf above her head when another caught her eye. The spine, a forest green with golden lettering, stood out amongst the grayscale covers that surrounded it. She rested her wrist on the cool metal as she tilted her head to read the spine.

Mythical Creatures: An Encyclopedia of Faerie Folklore

Greer pulled the book from the shelf and flicked through the pages. Wings, feathers, horns. Tall creatures with pointed ears. Small creatures resting on mushrooms. Warnings to never make a deal with a faerie, to leave offerings of honeywater and candy, to the stealing of human children.

She stopped on a page nearest the middle of the book and began to read a passage.

In Celtic lore, faeries are powerful beings known to provide both assistance to humans and lead them astray. While they appear humanoid, faeries have supernatural magic that they use in mischievous ways.

Faeries claim to have the best of intentions, though tales warn to never make a deal or accept a favor from one. A per- son must be careful when dealing with a faerie, as they turn irritable, sullen, and dangerous when not treated in a way they find acceptable.

Many cultures and religions speculate that the power of a faerie is a gift from celestial beings, such as gods or angels. Their capriciousness may be a holdout from a time long past.

Greer read the last passage twice more. The third time with Odette in mind.

She had known Odette was a faerie, had also known that she knew very little about the creatures who were supposed to be under her charge. She needed to connect more pieces and that meant tracking down Odette.

Greer spent her next three days waiting to find Odette at various places around town. The coffeehouse, outside of the hospital, at different breweries the nurses went to after their shifts. She was afraid the faerie had moved onto a new location since her vehement reaction to being discovered by Greer.

Greer had a feeling, though, that the faerie was just laying low.

On day four, Greer was in line at the coffeehouse to get her usual lavender flavored coffee when she heard the bell of the door jingle behind her.

"Thanks so much," she said to the barista, a college aged woman with pink hair and a bandana, as Greer grabbed the coffee from the wooden countertop.

Greer turned to leave, her canvas work bag hitched onto her shoulder, when she spotted Odette. The faerie was preternaturally still near the door, her hand still splayed on the glass insert as if she were ready to run at any second.

"Odette," Greer said in a soft voice as if she were talking to a spooked animal. "I want to talk to you."

The faerie's eyes widened before she turned and fled through the door, her wing tips twitching with irritation and fear as she marched down the sidewalk.

"Stop," Greer commanded as she, too, stepped from the coffeeshop. "I asked you to stop." She felt that push of power burst from her and Odette froze in place, still as a stone statue. Guilt flooded through Greer as she approached Odette, her red hair ruffling in the early morning breeze. "I'm sorry," Greer said, releasing the faerie from her frozen state. "I didn't mean to. I'm trying to get control of my magic."

Odette's eyes were narrowed as she straightened and adjusted her scrub top. "I told you to stay away from me."

"I half expected you to leave town."

Odette bristled. "Tomorrow. I needed to put in my required two week notification in order to get a good recommendation for my new employer."

Greer blinked. "You're a faerie. Can't you just compel them to get what you want?"

"Not that I can." Odette sighed and shook her head. "I wouldn't want that done to me, so I wouldn't do it to others. Look, I don't want to get involved. I really don't. I just want to go."

That familiar spike of irritation shot through Greer again and, this time, she projected it toward Odette. The faerie stilled again as she was walking away.

Greer followed slowly, coming to a stop next to Odette. Passersby heading to the coffeeshop briefly pointed their gazes over the scene, but the waft of freshly brewed grounds and vanilla flavoring was over-taking enough for them to move on.

Greer reached Odette and casually stood next to her, as if they were both watching the light at the crosswalk. "This is what's going to happen," Greer said, putting her hands into the pockets of her rain jacket, "you are going to tell me about faeries. Everything you know about faeries and then I will let you go. Until then, we can continue this game." Greer shrugged. "Maybe the next time you freeze is in the middle of the street."

"That's filthy," Odette managed to say through gritted teeth, her eyes flashing with rage.

"First was the vampyres, then my mother. You're just the happy individual who gets the beginning of my anger. Now, are you going to cooperate or not?"

Odette was quiet for a moment until she muttered a quick, "Fine."

Greer released her power. It was something that has been coming with ease in the few days she had been practicing.

"What do you want to know?" Odette asked, straightening herself out for the second time in so many minutes.

"I've been reading books on faeries and—"

"You can throw it out." Odette's tone was sharp and decisive. Greer blanched as the crosswalk turned green and Odette began her walk. "Follow. We don't want to be caught mingling."

The early morning traffic began to line up at the red light. Talk radio blared from one of the cars as the driver sipped coffee from a stainless steel to-go mug. They headed in the direction of the hospital.

"There are four faerie courts," Odette rattled off quietly. "Court of Mist and Tide, Court of Flame and Ember, Court of Storm and Wind, and Court of Cedar and Sand. Each faerie court has their own magic based on the elements. Water, air, land, and fire."

"And you were?"

Odette sent her a dull look. "Court of Storm and Wind, air. Did the wings not give it away?"

Greer made a sound of annoyance as they crossed a side street lined with knee-high bushes.

"The Fae King is named Adair. He oversees all of the courts." Odette adjusted her large wings as they walked, the radiant white gleaming against the rising sun.

"Your magic. Where does it come from?"

"The Primordials. The gods and goddesses. The archangels. Whatever you want to call them. They're all the same."

Greer's head began to spin. Primordials, plague-like instances when Holly had died, and the talk of her having powers given to her line by Lucifer himself.

They began passing students in short, white coats with backpacks slung over their shoulders. A gaggle of young nurses giggling as they crossed the circle drive in front of the hospital, each with a lunchbox in hand. A screaming ambulance screeched past, lights flaring, as it spun into the parking bay by the emergency department.

"And what do you know about the Paladin Society?" Greer asked, as they stopped to the side of the hospital's main entrance.

Odette grasped her arm and pulled her to the side. "If you know what's best for you, you'll walk away from all of this. The Paladin Society has done nothing, but ruin the lives of everyone in its path."

"I don't even understand what they are."

"And you won't get it from me." Odette sighed, gesturing toward the hospital doors behind her. "Can I go? And will you stop tracking me down? I'm leaving tonight and I'm hoping we won't see one another again."

"But, I'm the Mage," Greer said slowly.

"Not everyone will be happy to see you. In many cases, the daemons will want nothing to do with you."

"I thought I was here to help," Greer replied quietly.

Odette snorted unkindly. "Agnes was a busybody who refused to get involved when she was truly needed. I expect you to be the same." She turned to leave.

"If you change your mind," Greer said to the back of Odette's head, "I have a feeling you're someone I want on my side."

Odette said nothing to Greer as she joined the throngs of people entering the hospital for the morning shift.

SEVENTEEN

ODETTE

Odette watched from behind a potted plant in the lobby as Greer turned away from the front doors of the hospital and walked away. She blew out a breath, her heart pounding in her chest, as she worked to settle herself back down. She had been living as a human for the past two hundred years, flitting from city to city in search of nothing, but in an escape from everything.

She was wanted and hunted to this day. Having the Mage in her town was going to cause her nothing, but trouble.

"Hi Odette!" a voice called to her from the front doors, and Odette whipped around to see one of the medical residents waving to her as he entered.

"H-hi, Dr. Taylor!" Odette replied with a short flick of her wrist, but she felt nothing except apprehension as she looked around.

She didn't feel safe. She wasn't safe. If the Mage was here, that meant Adair would show up at any moment. And if Adair found her—

Odette thought back to running through the woods, her bare feet slapping against the jagged rocks, blood dribbling down her back as the bandages covering the stumps of her wings fluttered in the winter wind behind her.

She imagined Adair's scream of rage as she ran, the pounding of hooves behind her. How she felt like nothing when she leapt into the air and entered the portal to the human realm, the phantom wind between worlds whooshing around her as she fell, fell, fell...

Odette couldn't wait until the end of her shift. It was imperative that she left immediately. She should have left in the weeks before; should have followed her gut when it was screaming for her to go. Instead of following the crowd deeper into the hospital, she turned on her heels and marched through the front doors.

The loft Odette rented was directly above a hair salon and, through the large window at the street level, she could spot the trendy waiting area with faux leather couches, a white coffee table piled with fashion magazines, and a serving table tucked in the corner filled with carafes of coffee. Despite the early hour, stylists dressed in black aprons were already bustling around the salon, one pumping the padded swivel chair to height.

The slim, steep stairs that led from the street to the loft over the salon creaked as she jogged up them, and her wings brushed against the narrow walls with every step. She could already smell the herbal shampoo and conditioner mixed with the overheated blow dryer motors seeping into the stairwell.

When Odette reached the landing, shared by three doors, she stuck her key into the door on the far right and unlocked it before using her shoulder to shove it open. The loft was minimally furnished with only one low-backed chair and a bed large enough to sport her wings. Not a single decoration adorned the walls or countertops and, if she had opened the cabinets, she would have found nothing save for one set of dishware and one set of silverware.

It was easier to stay disconnected that way.

Odette crossed the loft, her heart still dancing in her chest, and threw open the hallway closet door to reveal a single trunk tucked into the back. She pulled it forward with a tug and opened the lid once it crossed the threshold into the hallway. Her hands ran over the navy cloak, the fighting leathers, and the sword she had escaped with.

"You sure have been on the run for a long time for someone who has keepsakes to reminisce."

Odette whirled around as she pulled the sword from its scabbard, seeing the sharp metal glint in the early morning rays of the sun. It hadn't seen the light of day in nearly twenty years and was still just as clean as the last day she took it out.

A man slunk from the shadows of the kitchen, the one room she had by-passed without a second look, and his swaggering gait into the room alerted her to who he was immediately.

"I know you," Odette said, sheathing the sword with a smooth movement. "What are you doing here?"

"Name's Cian," he said with a smirk, ignoring her question.

"I didn't ask."

He tucked his hands into the front pockets of his jeans as he took another step forward, glancing around the bare apartment. He side-stepped the sun's rays now streaming in through the front window. "Nice place. Simple. Were you going for minimalism?"

Odette crossed her arms over her chest as she narrowed her eyes. "I asked you a question, vampyre. What are you doing here?"

Cian picked up the only thing in the room easily held, a single potted plant that Odette had gotten as a gift from a patient's family member, and studied it for a long minute before replacing it on the side table. "I need the assistance of someone who has been far more involved in the politics of the daemons than I have."

"The answer is no," Odette said pointedly, as she gestured toward the front door.

"See, I thought you would say that." He paused to click his tongue against his teeth and lean his shoulder casually against the far wall. "I've been teaching Greer about leverage and it's helped me brush up on my own negotiating skills, which I know will come in handy working with a member of the fae."

"Get to it or get out," Odette said dismissively, as she picked at her nail beds.

Cian tilted his head as he dragged his stare from her red bun to the soles of her gray work sneakers and back up again. "Greer needs some assistance being—" He seemed to struggle finding the right word for a beat, rocking his head back and forth as if he were in deep thought. "—persuaded with her magic. As the Mage, she can do plenty to help us out—"

"You, perhaps," Odette countered, "could do plenty to help you out. I have no interest." She crossed the room and yanked open the door, pointing into the stairwell. With the door open, she could hear the water spraying against the porcelain sinks and clients laughing with their stylist. "I happen to think she could help you, though by proxy.

Because by helping her, you help yourself." Cian pushed off the wall. "By that, I mean, I won't go running to Adair or Darragh to tell them of your whereabouts."

Odette snorted as she rolled her eyes. "Why do you think they have any interest in where I am?"

Cian took a few steps forward, and Odette could feel that he was building to something.

"Perhaps not you, Odette the faerie nurse who takes care of humans, but definitely Odette Milne for the former general to the Fae King's army and lost princess to the Fae throne."

Odette felt her face drain of blood and her features slacken. Cian raised his brows as if he were pleased by her reaction. She struggled to compose herself, but she still said, "You have the wrong person. My name is a coincidence." She knew she was convincing no one.

"Is that so? I'm sure the Fae King would—"

"He is not the king," Odette shot back.

Cian bowed his head. "My apologies. The death of your father all those centuries ago must still be weighing on your mind. Especially as Adair slit his throat as he slept. The right hand to the king, killing him in his bed." He clicked his tongue again. "Shame. I do wonder how badly he tortured those loyalists who snuck you from the forest and to the portal opening on the equinox."

Odette's chest tightened at his words, and her mind wandered to the man she had loved all those years ago. How he had been cut down by the king's guards as they ran, his head rolling down the grassy knoll as she bit back sobs, but left him behind.

"I could just slip into the night, you know. Leave all of this behind without a second look."

Cian nodded his head as he tapped his chin in thought.

"You certainly could." He took a deep breath. "Do you think Greer knows that the woman who goes by Deborah helped to shelter you for all of those years? Until her own tribe was driven out of their lands. Her Fae blood has been failing, I see. She's aged. It must be nice being so close now, I bet her movements aren't as quick as they once were."

"You're a bastard," Odette said quietly, as she narrowed her eyes and lifted her gaze to meet Cian's. "You're a fucking bastard."

"The Court of Mist and Tide doesn't tolerate *half-breeds*, I bet they would love to know—"

"Stop it," Odette said, as she clenched her jaw together. Odette unsheathed the blade and pointed it at him, her chest heaving with breathy pants. "What do you want?"

"Your help preparing Greer for what's to come," Cian said bluntly, as his eyes flashed with a haunted torment. "We both know a war has been brewing for centuries. Since the death of Agnes. We need to—"

"Agnes deserved the death she got," Odette bit back. The sword shook in her trembling hand. "She might have been killed by the Paladin Society, but she deserved to have her head spiked at the Vatican like it was." Odette lowered her sword, letting the tip dig into the wooden flooring.

"You don't mean that," Cian said in a dangerously low voice.

"When my father was killed by Adair, and I was run out of my kingdom, I went to Agnes to ask for her aid. I wanted an army, and I needed her magic to get one. She refused. Said she had no interest in getting involved. And my people have suffered for centuries since then. So, no, I will not take back what I said."

Cian said nothing as the two watched each other, but Odette was the first to break the silence. "Why are you doing this?"

It was Cian's turn to shift uncomfortably on his feet. "If I don't do it, someone much worse will step in and do it for me."

"Eligos," Odette said with a sigh, as she rubbed the back of her neck. "He's already here, isn't he?"

"No," Cian replied, and Odette knew from his tone it was the truth. "But he's close to finding her. I'm trying to keep her safe, and I don't know how to play the game. You have centuries of experience doing just that."

The only thing between them for a long minute was the soft indie music playing from below.

"What are you expecting to happen?" Odette finally asked, as she twirled the nose of the sword deeper into the hole she had created in the wooden flooring.

"All of our deaths if I'm being honest," Cian replied. "But I can't let Eligos win. Not again."

Odette didn't have a chance to ask what he meant before he said, "I'll be in touch." Then, he slunk through the door.

EIGHTEEN

Greer needed to hike. She needed to get into nature and clear her head and it was the perfect day to do it. The sun had fully risen by the time she had left Odette at the hospital and returned home to change. She stood on the meandering dirt trail, rock piles and crisscrossing tree roots lining each side of the path. Greer adjusted the straps of her backpack as she stood near the trailhead.

The birds that flew overhead chirped before landing on the bushes of fresh berries growing on the overlook at the top of the valley. Fresh, clean air. Summer sun on her skin. Not a cloud in the sky for the first time in days.

She began her ascent up the first hill, feeling her hiking boots gain traction on the loose gravel beneath her. The first mile was a series of smaller hills followed by plateaus, and by the second mile, a sheen of sweat had coated her forehead. By the third mile, her calves had begun to burn and her breathing turned to deep pants.

She kept going, enjoying her awakened body and the heat and the sweat.

It was when Greer had crossed the shallow creek running down the hillside that she stopped in her tracks. A sudden feeling of unease filled her with dread and she turned on the spot in an attempt to find the source. She could see nothing, could hear nothing, but hearing nothing was the biggest problem.

Where the rodents had been skittering in the bushes and the honeybees had been buzzing by, not a single sound remained. It was as if the world had stopped, had gone completely still and silent with her.

Greer took a large, quiet inhale as the hair lifted on the back of her neck. There was no one around, at least for miles, but she couldn't shake the quiver in her chest. She took one step and then another as she sent sidelong glances around her.

There is nothing wrong. Everything is fine. Stop overreacting.

She repeated the words over and over in her head, but was unable to shake the sense that something was watching her. She needed to leave, needed to get off the mountain. She turned on her heel to go back the way she came, but a ripple of the trees caught her peripheral vision.

The dead leaves off the trail swirled into the air as if picked up by a phantom wind. A tangle of brown and green filled the space in front of her. The crunch of pinecones under feet, a split second of forceful pounding.

Something burst through the tree line and onto the trail. Greer barely got a glance of it before she was flying through the air. Breath entered her chest with a sharp gasp and was expelled painfully as she hit the ground, the whoosh escaping her lips in a cough-like bark. Her head whipped to the side as she caught movement from the corner of her eye, and Greer screamed in shock.

At first glance, the creature could have been human.

It stood on two thin legs, each covered in leathery, gray skin. The tissue had been shredded and healed, but left long ropes of sinew dangling sickeningly from the backs of the knees and ankles. The abdomen was concave and devoid of any fat; the ribs showed through the thin skin of the chest, and Greer could easily count each one.

Greer's eyes widened as her eyes lifted to the top half of the creature.

Two arms jutted from the shoulder joint on each side and long, powerful nails erupted from the tips of each finger. The nails were filthy, bits of flesh melded with the dirt that were stuck in the undersides. The shoulders were capped with hundreds of white quills, fine appearing, as if it were fur, and Greer knew they were sharp enough to shred skin if they made contact.

The head, shaped like that of a coyote, was devoid of any tissue. The white bone of the skull was fractured and split in some places, the jagged bone rubbing together as it moved.

Sharp teeth lined the jaw and, without the flesh in place to hide them, Greer was able to see each finger-length canine and molar gnashing as it smelled for her. She didn't know if it could see or not, as the eye sockets were empty, leaving only the carved bone remaining. Large antlers protruded from the top of the skull, each fastened into a sharp point.

The creature roared and Greer scrambled to her feet. Ignoring the throbbing pain in her ribs, she began to run down the path. Dirt gravel and dirt formed a cloud behind her as she urged her legs to run faster, faster. The creature let out a second roar as it lurched forward, chasing after her with a clunky, unnatural gait.

The earthy smell of stagnant water mixed with the sun-heated dirt passed her as she flew into the meadow nearest the first set of climbs. Her chest burned as her heart raced and she felt her legs grow weak as her stomach turned rock hard. The fear coursed through her and, in an attempt to throw the creature off her track, she fled the trail to enter the long grass covering the mountainside.

The swish of grasses blowing in the breeze did nothing to mute the squelch of her hiking boots sticking in the heaps of mud made from the recent bouts of rain. Shadows drifted over the distant mountains as the clouds passed overhead and that's where she focused her attention as she moved. Greer didn't dare send any magic toward the creature chasing her for fear of setting the entire mountainside on fire. Instead, she dug deep and forced her legs to pump faster as she raced toward the valley below.

The creature sped up too, leaping over the tall grass when it came into range and tackling her to the ground once again. Greer felt her body sink into the thick, stinking mud. Her hair stuck to the back of her neck in matted clumps as mosquitos and large, black flies shot from the standing water snaking through the grassy meadow. She felt the creature pin her to the ground by her shoulders, one of the clawed hands wrapped around her arm and forcing her deeper into the mud.

It bent down to sniff her, and she imagined the snout working, the nostrils flaring as she heard air whistle through the empty sockets of the bony nose. The rancid smell of the creature was that of rotting meat and sewage on a hot summer's day, making her stomach un-clench and the bile threaten to crawl up the back of her throat.

Greer struggled to free herself as she attempted to pull her magic from deep within herself, but it was stuck as if behind a brick wall. The creature tossed its head back and swiped a clawed hand at her from its second arm, slicing her chest open. Blood spurted down the front of her shirt. It licked the thick, gushing liquid from her wound, the taste sending the creature into a wild frenzy.

Smoke bellowed from between its teeth as if her blood had burned it, but the creature seemed to relish the pain.

Oh, god. Somebody, anybody.

Throwing its head back, it made to tear at her again, but a flap of leathered wings and the zing of a sword being unsheathed surrounded her as two feet landed into the mud near her. Greer only saw the flash of metal against the sun as it lashed through the air and the sword came down with a mighty blow.

Blood sprayed from the neck of the creature, covering Greer in the viscous black liquid, as the creature crumpled into the grass at their sides, dead.

Greer wiped her eyes, smearing mud on her face from the backs of her hands as she looked up. The female was sliding her sword into the sheath strapped between two iridescent, leather wings.

Greer shot to her feet, the black blood dripping into the pooling water covering her ankles. "Odette?" she managed to say, surveying the faerie with wide eyes. She glanced down to the creature, split in half and entrails leaking onto the roots of the bent grass. Her eyes darted away, catching the faerie in front of her. "Wh—what are you—? What was—? You saved me."

"Yes," Odette replied simply in an unaffected tone.

"How did you know where I was?" Greer asked, her eyes narrowing as she took a step away from the creature. Water poured from the side of her hiking boot as she took a step into the untouched mud a few inches away. "And what was that?"

"I was high-ranking to the Fae King," Odette replied elusively. Her wings fluttered under the afternoon sun, sheen against the bright rays. "You weren't supposed to know I was around. Funny you're supposedly the more powerful person between the two of us and you can't even fight off a simple devil."

The two surveyed each other cautiously, each unsure of the next step to take. Greer's bravery gathered under Odette's scrutinizing stare. "If I wasn't supposed to know you were around, then why did you come find me? I left you at the hospital hours ago."

Odette crossed her arms over her chest. Greer looked at her. What Greer thought were lithe limbs were strong muscles, thinly strapped against her fae body. Her core was clad in a simple tank top and spandex shorts. Though her sneakers had already been dunked in water, Greer noticed that Odette was standing atop the thick mud as if she weren't heavy enough to breach the top layer.

Odette let out a sigh of exasperation through her nose. "I was alerted a devil was in the region, and I had a feeling it was here for you. I left work to find you, which led me to the devil. I couldn't let the Mage die, now could I?" Odette glanced down. "You're bleeding."

Greer followed her gaze and lightly touched the laceration on her chest. Blood still trickled from it, creating tiny rivers of red between the clumps of dirt stuck to her skin.

"Just heal it," Odette went on, watching Greer with a wrinkled nose. "Quit playing in it."

Greer scowled as she clenched her jaw, though she dropped her hand to her side. "If I could, I would. This is painful." She paused as she raked a hand through her dirty, wet hair. "It feels like I have a brick wall inside of me, keeping my magic locked away. I can only access it in bursts and then—"

"Then what?"

"It comes out in a wave of fury I can't control."

Odette was quiet for a moment as Greer, heavy-footed in the mud and long grass, made her way to the trail. Odette followed after her as she easily navigated the terrain.

Greer managed to step onto the gravel path, the loose dirt adhering to the mud. She collapsed to the pathway and the rocks scratched shallow cuts into her palms. She wiped the pebbles away with swipes against her thighs.

"Agnes was able to access her magic from a young age."

"That's great for Agnes," Greer mumbled, as she pushed herself to stand once more and began to limp down the trail.

"Where are you going?"

"Back to my car so I can go home." Greer made a sweeping gesture down the front of her ruined clothing. "Take a long shower and forget this ever happened."

"You need to work on your magic. Defeating a devil like that should have been a snap of your fingers."

Greer kept walking, but she said, "What's a devil?"

"A creature from Samsara. Hell. Hades. That's what happens when human souls crawl from the river after their death." Odette's wings twitched as she adjusted the sheath strapped to her back. "Are you going to walk the entire way back to your car?"

"That thing is what human souls become?"

"The ones sent to Samsara to atone for the lives they led, yes. Greer, we are two miles from your car."

"Are you offering to fly me there?"

Odette bristled. "I'm no carrier pigeon."

"Then why did you say something?" Greer snapped as a retort. Her agitation grew with every throb from the cut on her chest.

They began a descent down the hill. The landscape shifted from a mountainside meadow to the beginnings of the valley forest. The path ahead was demarcated by the tree line and Greer could see large boulders dotting the terrain. A man and a woman emerged from around the curved path. Both smiled and waved as they passed Odette and Greer. The man had a sheen of sweat on his reddened face.

"What about the—?" Greer started, but she was hushed by Odette until the couple was far beyond them.

"You don't know who might be working for the Paladin Society," Odette explained as they entered the forest. Birds chirped high in the trees, calling their return after the appearance of the devil. "It's best to not speak until we're alone. Besides, I've glamoured both you and the body. Your injuries and the devil will be invisible under my magic until I lift it."

"You talk about the Paladin Society as if they're something to fear."

Odette was quiet for a moment as the two tramped through the undergrowth, pinecones crunching beneath them. Greer noticed a dagger was still clutched tightly in her hand.

"Shortly after the Primordials invaded this world, there was a war between the two leaders. Michael wanted the humans to stay under the rule of the Primordials whereas Azazel wanted the humans to have free will. The two sides fought, but it was a draw."

"A side didn't win?" Greer asked, as she stepped over a large root jutting from the forest floor.

Odette shook her head. "Azazel, in response, took a handful of humans and gave them to his generals who imbued them with powers similar to creatures in their home realm. He wanted the humans under his rule to know true free-will. That was the beginning of the daemon factions you know today."

"And Michael?"

"Michael was furious that Azazel broke their pact and, knowing his brother, gave the humans in his army the knowledge of how to kill the daemons. Those humans named themselves the Paladin Society."

"And where are the Primordials now?"

Odette shrugged her shoulders. "There's been rumors of sightings. Rumors of demi-primordials. Nephilim, if you will. A true sighting hasn't happened in centuries though. There has been no contact between daemons and primordials that I know of."

Greer stepped over a root jutting from the trail, her attention still focused on Odette. "And how old are you?"

A smirk pulled at Odette's lips. "Nearly eight hundred."

"So you've seen quite a bit of human history."

"No. I spent most of my life in the Fae realms. I didn't come to the human world until a couple of centuries ago."

"And why are you on the run?" Greer asked, as she spotted her Jeep parked in the lot from the top of the hill.

"You're as much of a busybody as Agnes too."

Greer managed to temper her eye roll. "Don't tell me then. I was just trying to get to know you."

Odette narrowed her eyes. It was clear she was wary of Greer. "Why? What do you have to gain for it?"

"Nothing," Greer replied, as she reached her car and pressed the passcode into the keypad under the door handle. She pulled the door open before saying, "Something tells me we'll need each other before the end of this, that's all."

Odette was quiet as Greer climbed into the front seat.

"I suppose I should thank you again," Greer said, resting her arm on the top of the steering wheel.

"I'll follow you to your place," Odette said, as she took a step back and spread her wings. "I'll make sure nothing else is going to come along too." She shot into the sky, and her wings flapped once, twice, three times before she was able to steady herself in the air.

Greer shut the door to her Jeep, turned the key in the ignition, and she was off.

The drive was fairly stop and go. Students getting out of their last class before the end of the summer semester littered the roadways. A few of them paused to gawk at Greer's appearance as they passed by, pointing and whispering to their group of friends. Greer was equal parts irritated that Odette had lifted the glamour so soon and glad when she finally pulled into the parking lot of her apartment building.

Odette touched down on the pavement next to her car and tucked her wings tightly into her body.

"How did they not see you?" Greer asked, as she pressed the lock button and jangled her keys in her hand. She finally came up with the building key.

"Glamour. I can make them see what I want to make them see."

"But not me?" Greer pushed the key into the lock and opened the metal door.

"No, not you." Odette followed her up the old, carpeted stairs. "I expect there are many things you can do. Heal from a vampyre bite, see through fae magic, trap your mind against succubus."

Greer tripped on the last step at Odette's words. "A succubus?"

Odette's amber eyes shifted toward her. "You have much to learn before any daemon will take you seriously."

Greer silently agreed as she unlocked the door to her apartment and stepped inside. She was surprised when she found Cian and Isaac sitting at the dining room table. Cian, dressed in his usual black cotton shirt and leather jacket, tapped his fingers against the wood grained surface.

"What are you doing here?" Greer heard from behind her. She glanced over her shoulder to see Odette's sharp eyes gazing at someone in the shadows of the hallway.

Jonas appeared in the doorway and leaned against the wall. "We've been here waiting for quite some time." He took a sidelong glance toward Greer and the large cut on her chest. "Aren't you going to invite us in, sweetheart?"

Greer tilted her head and narrowed her eyes at the red-headed vampyre. "Odette, you can come in. Jonas, you may not."

Odette sent a simpering smile toward Jonas as she sauntered over the threshold.

"And why can't I come in?" Jonas asked. His lips pressed into a tight, white line as his hands clenched into fists.

Greer walked up to the door and stopped just before the threshold. "You attacked my mother. You've been hunting these university grounds for weeks now. There is no way I am going to allow you access to my apartment when Delia lives here."

Jonas' stare turned glassy as he glowered down at her, but Greer was already turning back to the group behind her. Isaac and Cian were discussing Greer's magic, Odette keeping a fair distance from both vampyres seated at the table. Much to Greer's chagrin, Odette had removed a dagger from her waistline and was absent-mindedly spinning the pointed end into the kitchen countertop. She was busy flipping through the spread of documents Greer and Delia had been going through the night before and had failed to notice Greer's pointed stare.

"Did you not read these?" Odette interrupted Cian as she squared herself to face them. She held the autopsy report in her hand.

Cian blinked. "Unless the murderer hid a secret message in the stab wounds, I don't necessarily care."

Odette clicked her tongue. "There is an elementary reason in here as to why Greer can't access her magic all the time." She paused to slap the document onto the table in front of Cian. "Let's see if you can figure out why."

Isaac had reached forward and slid the paper toward him, scanning it with a fierce focus.

"What's in there?" Greer asked, as she glanced over Isaac's shoulder. She half-expected something new to have appeared on the page.

"Something these three half-witted leeches should have figured out on day one." Odette dropped her gaze to look at Cian.

Cian shot up from his seat, the legs scraping noisily against the tiled floor. Rage clouded the lines of his face as he pulled himself to a threatening height.

Odette appeared unfazed. Her hip leaned casually against the edge of the counter as she continued to spin her dagger into the surface. A small hole had formed under the point and Greer was itching to grab the dagger from Odette.

"Obsidian?" Isaac said, breaking the tension that formed in the room. He looked over his shoulder to Odette. "The obsidian in her bones?"

"Ding, ding, ding." Odette pushed herself off the counter. "Someone, rather, something, put in an extraordinary effort to hide Holly. If we were to open you up and look at her bones, Greer, I would expect similar findings."

Confusion clouded Greer's features. "Obsidian?"

"Dims magic. Makes it nearly impossible to perform if you're wearing it." Odette pushed herself forward. "The Fae use obsidian to make shackles—"

"You would know all about that wouldn't you, princess," Cian simmered. It was clear to Greer that he didn't appreciate being upstaged by a newcomer.

Odette ignored him and continued on. "If one practices long enough, one can break through the bonds of the stone for short periods of time. It's not consistent, though, and it usually takes more effort. Magic will come out in blasts."

"We should have caught that," Isaac said quietly to Cian. "That's why Eligos can't—"

"Enough, Isaac."

Cian's tone was stern and conversation ending.

Isaac clamped his lips closed, but sent Greer a look. She didn't know what it meant, but was desperate to find out what Isaac had begun to say.

"You should have caught it," Odette replied with a nod. "And you would have if you three shared more than one brain cell." She leaned forward to pluck the report from Isaac's hands. "The next question that needs to be answered is how to get it out."

"If we get it out," Cian said, ignoring the jab from Odette, "more daemons will show up. More than there already are, I mean." He sent Odette a knowing stare.

"I don't think it matters much that I have the obsidian," Greer interjected quickly. "I can still perform magic. Like you said, it takes a bit more effort, but I can do it. Besides, when I called the sheriff to claim Holly's body, I didn't—"

The three stiffened in unison, slowly turning to view Greer with wide and frightened eyes.

"Repeat that last part, sweetheart," Jonas said from behind her. He was still leaned against the threshold of the door, unable to enter. "Did you say you claimed her body?"

"Yes, I submitted a DNA test through the police station. I don't know why—"

"Do you realize what you've done?" Odette asked in a horrified, hushed voice. She looked ready to bolt from the room. "You've killed us all."

"What are you talking about?" Greer said, her brows knitting with confusion.

"Did you ever think of the possibility that the people who killed your mother, tried to kill you, would be watching the legal parameters surrounding the case? Would see if anything has moved? Had been solved? If, perhaps, her long, lost daughter reappeared?" Cian went on. He leaned onto the dining room table, splaying his hands on the surface. His head hung in exasperation; his chin dipped to his chest. "And you just gave them a trail to follow you here."

Greer opened and closed her mouth. "I didn't, I didn't know, didn't think—"

"No, you didn't think." Cian's hands had curled and his knuckles whitened under the stress. "You didn't think at all." Greer turned to look at each daemon, trying to see if one would come to her aid. Isaac was staring out of the window, the serene view of the sunlit forest cut a far more beautiful picture compared to what was happening inside of the apartment.

Greer turned to look at Jonas, her last holdout, only to realize that he had disappeared from the doorway, fleeing into the shadows once more.

NINETEEN

"**Y**ou've been working on that all weekend, GG. Why don't you take a break?"

Greer felt the couch cushion shift as someone sank onto it. She sat back and blew out at breath. Turning her head, she spotted Delia looking at her with concern.

Delia's normal curly hair was piled to the back of her head and pinched with a large claw clip. Tanned skin, a thanks to her Latina heritage, seemed to glow against the setting sun streaming into the room.

"I'm nearly done with the potions section. There doesn't seem to be a rhyme or reason to the order, so I need to put it into something I can easily navigate." Greer paused to thumb at the old parchment, crinkling under her touch. "Plus, I'm getting increasingly worried something will happen to this thing while it's in my possession."

Greer had been meticulously working to catalog the various potions, spells, and curses into a database on her computer. A database that could be searched by ingredient, by use, in alphabetical order, by category. It was one she used for the anthropology department, and one that she knew well.

At the very least, it was easier than flicking through the book every time she needed to find something.

"If there is anyone who is best suited for taking care of an old book, it's you."

"Yeah, perhaps." Greer went quiet for a moment. She scrubbed a hand down her face. "Did you have something in mind for tonight?"

"Well," Delia started with a ghost of a smile on her lips, "I did think we could go out and celebrate my last weekend being a single lady."

Greer whipped her head toward Delia once again to see her best friend holding a thin, silver ring between her pointer finger and thumb. The band was intricately carved and an oval-shaped diamond sat in the four-pronged casing. More diamonds lined the band, and they seemed to glitter under the living room lighting.

Carefully, Greer grasped the ring from Delia and held it up to eye-level for closer examination. She noticed that Delia still held the purple, velvet box that usually contained the ring.

"Delia, this is absolutely stunning."

"I contacted Paige's mother and got the stone from her great-grandmother's ring. I worked with a jeweler in town to create the piece." Delia shifted in her seat. "I wanted it to be a complete surprise for everyone, but I couldn't keep it to myself anymore."

Greer leaned over and wrapped her arms around Delia's shoulders. Her heart was floating in her chest, her cheeks pinching from the large smile on her face. "I'm so happy for you, Dels." Greer pulled back, but kept her hands planted firmly on her best friend's shoulders. "When are you going to propose?"

Delia took the ring from Greer and nestled it safely back in the box. It snapped shut in her hand, and she tucked it back into the pocket of her jacket. "Next weekend. We're going to that fancy Italian place in the town over. She's always wanted to go, but you need a reservation months in advance."

Greer excitedly clapped her hands together as she squealed. "I can't wait to hear all about it."

Delia's smile faded slightly. "G, I wanted to talk to you about something else."

Greer felt her stomach flip-flop. Delia went on.

"Celeste has been calling me. I know you have her number blocked, but she's still in town. I've been telling her to stay away, but she's absolutely distraught. I think she's leaving town in a few days. Don't you think it's time to have a second talk with her? Now that things have blown over a bit?"

Greer's lips pursed before a hard smile and a humorless laugh passed over them.

"I know she did some bad shit, G," Delia pressed forward quickly. "Some really bad shit. I don't think there is an explanation in the world that can make this better. But...she did raise you. Get some more information from her, at the very least."

"She killed—"

"I know, G. Just— just think about it, okay?"

Greer blew out another breath as she collapsed back into the couch cushion behind her. In truth, she had been contemplating talking to Celeste more. Without Cian overseeing the interaction. Without her mother feeling that immediate threat and reacting the way she had been raised to.

"Yeah, I'll think about it." Was all Greer said in response.

Delia sent her a small smile before pushing herself off the couch and walking toward her bedroom. Greer saw Delia open the velvet box and peer at the ring inside as she rounded the corner.

Greer waited until the sun had set behind the trees and the breeze had turned cool, blowing away any remnants of sunny warmth. She waited until the crickets chirped loudly, echoing against the trees lining the forest. Lastly, she waited until her stomach roiled with nerves and the smell of the dinner she was helping Delia cook nearly sent her running to the bathroom. Greer didn't say a word as she turned from the kitchen and grabbed her keys off the ring by the door.

Delia didn't bother to ask where she was going.

The scent of earthy pine was strong against the wind that creaked the thick branches on the trees. It melded with the smell of impending rain and Greer wasn't surprised when she felt a few droplets of water grace her forehead. A screech from an owl rang out; the sound eerie against the inky sky. Not a single star could be seen above her and the misty air created a glowing ringlet around each streetlamp. The drive to the hotel was just as eerily quiet with the lack of students flooding the campus nearby. Most had gone home following the end of the summer semester, though it was only six weeks of a break before they returned.

The rain began, coming down in pelting sheets, bouncing off the black pavement, and creating tiny rivers that ran toward the drain nearest the intersection. Greer ignored the prickling of her skin and the twisting of her stomach. She could attribute the feelings to her nerves, but this felt different. Her body screamed at her to *go back, go back, go back*.

She kept on.

The first thing she noticed when she turned the wheel into the parking lot were the flashing blue and red lights illuminated against the wet ground. *Whoops* of oncoming police cars joined the scene as they peeled into the parking lot after her, and they screeched to a stop near the glass doors at the front of the hotel.

Greer shivered with anxiety as she threw her car into park and hauled herself from the front seat, standing on the wheel guard to get a better look at the scene.

Crime scene investigators carted plastic boxes into the hotel, stopping briefly in the lobby to don blue show covers and gloves. A woman was seated on the metal bench near the glass doors, a maid by the looks of her uniform, and she had wrapped a blanket around her shoulders. Greer could tell even from a distance that the woman was crying. Her shoulders were slumped and her head bobbed as she wiped her tears with a corner of the blanket. A police officer had knelt next to her, the rain-slicked sidewalk soaking the knee of his pants.

The scene was a chaotic masterpiece of flowing bodies, loud sirens, and flashing lights.

Greer hopped down from the wheel guard, the pool of water that had gathered near her tire splashing into her sandals. She crossed the parking lot and fixed her eye on a lone officer standing guard near the stone column, holding the flapping awning in place.

"Sorry, ma'am. No one in the hotel at this time," he said on her approach.

"What happened?"

"I'm not at liberty to say," the officer responded.

At the same time, a woman in a large, blue coat labeled 'coroner' swept past them pushing a gurney, toting a black, plastic body bag.

The officer began to gesture toward the crowd of hotel guests gathered in the rain on the other side of the yellow caution tape, but Greer had already conjured a piece of her magic.

This power felt different. It coated her tongue with a metallic taste and electricity crackled against her skin. The hair on her arms stood on end as she waved a hand toward the officer.

A dreamy, confused look flashed over his gaze and, when he looked down at her, Greer knew that her attempt at a glamour had worked. "Grab a box, Mullins, and follow the coroner inside. I heard this one is grisly."

Greer's glamour mimicked that of the crime scene tech she had seen earlier and she struggled to hold it in place as she yanked a box from the back of the crime scene van, tucking it against her side. One of the detectives did a double take as Greer passed by. Greer knew it was the glamour shimmering, her true appearance flickering in and out, but she ducked her head down and quickly pushed past. She reached the elevator just as the car dinged it's arrival, and Greer settled into step next to the coroner pushing the metal gurney. The cart clanked as it entered the elevator, and the coroner had to angle it just right for it to fit.

"Mullins, I thought you were ahead of me," the coroner, a curvy, middle-aged woman with wisps of brown hair peeking out from under her fitted cap, said. "Prepare yourself. The detective down in the lobby said this was the worst one he's ever seen."

"What happened?" Greer asked, not recognizing the voice that left her lips. Whoever Mullins was had a throaty tone to her.

"Hotel guest was murdered. Shredded, by the sounds of it." The elevator jolted into place as it reached its destination— Celeste's floor. "The detective said he had a hard time determining where she started and ended."

The doors opened and Greer stepped out, followed by the coroner who had to re-angle the cart to retrieve it from the elevator car. Greer followed the woman down the hallway and her heart dipped further into her chest with every step. It plummeted to her toes when they rounded the hallway in the direction of Celeste's room.

It took every piece of Greer's energy to temper the primal cry of horror and grief when she realized a second officer stood next to her ajar hotel door.

Greer stepped over the threshold, the plastic box still tucked under her arm, and placed a foot into a clearing free of debris. She followed the wreckage around the corner of the small foyer peppered with glass from the shattered full-body mirror that had once doubled as a door to the closet.

"I told you it was bad," the coroner said, as she stepped past Greer.

Every surface of the room was clad with some spatter or smear of blood. It was as if her mother had tried to escape, but was forced high onto the wall by some unknown power. Smudged hand prints, too high for Celeste to reach on her own, were plastered across the corners of the ceiling, onto the upper doorframe leading into the bathroom.

Greer's shoes sunk into the thick carpet and they crunched against the tiny shards of glass littering the ground, possibly from the shattered glass top of the wooden desk. The skeletons of the desk and dresser lay haphazardly on the carpet, each forced into a charred ball, as if it had been melted and twisted.

The hotel art that had been placed on the walls were slashed and thrown across the room.

Torn pieces of canvas mixed with the shards of glass. Greer looked around in horror as she followed the smears of blood that evolved into puddles on the white tile of the bathroom. She turned toward doorway, where the pools of blood had morphed into rivers flowing in thick lines through the grout of the tile.

It was there, shoved in a heap under the countertop, where the lifeless body of Celeste lay.

Greer let out the scream she had been holding in, dropping the glamour she had carefully pinned into place with a whoosh of power, as she fell to her knees.

"How did she—"

"Get her out of here!"

"She just appeared, Sarge, I swear—"

A hand wrapped around Greer's arm and hoisted her to her feet. The last thing Greer saw before being marched from the room was Celeste's unseeing brown eyes staring at her, the neck at an unnatural angle.

Greer was perched on the edge of the plastic chair in the interrogation room with shivers running up and down her spine. She clutched a small cup of water between her hands as an officer, balding with kind, brown eyes, peered at her from across the cold metal table.

His gaze was filled with pity as he waited for her to say something.

The lump in her throat restricted any sound that threatened to escape, even the guttural sob or scream that was on the tip of her tongue. A rap on the door had the detective standing from his seat, and he opened it with a squeak that sent another shudder through Greer.

A second detective, the name Flecker etched into the gold bar pinned to his uniform, entered the room, and both men took seats in the plastic chairs across from her.

"Celeste was found this evening by a maid who was performing a turndown service," the second man, Flecker, started. "Her throat was cut to the spine, nearly decapitated, before her neck was broken. The perpetrator, it seems, only broke in for the murder. Nothing of note was taken."

Greer said nothing. She continued her inspection of the grooves carved in the metal table, imagining her mother's blood running through them like it had the grout.

"The coroner finished her first inspection," Detective Flecker went on. "She believes, based on body temperature, that your mother died three to five hours before the maid entered the room." He took a deep breath through his nose. "We've already checked your alibi against that of your roommate's. She and your other friend, Paige, are in the waiting room."

Greer blinked.

"Greer," the first officer started gently. He began to reach forward as if he were going to pat her hand, but then decided against it. He awkwardly retracted his hand back into place, resting his forearms on the table. "We have a few more questions to ask you." Silence filled the space between them for a moment. "There was writing on the wall in the bathroom of the hotel room—"

She drowned out his voice as the vision flared into her mind. Her mother's body, broken and bloody, shoved under that countertop. Blood still moved from her neck in a slow, macabre march across her skin. A story of Celeste's final moments in the struggle before the attacker pulled her head back by her hair and slit her throat from ear to ear.

Whoever killed her had dipped their fingers in her blood, swiping large letters across the white walls.

Holly. Anna. Greer.

Greer made a non-committal noise from her throat, glancing up at them with blank eyes.

"We know your name is there," he started again, clicking his pen against the metal interrogation table. "But a picture is beginning to form with the other two names. Are you familiar with either of those?"

Greer tried to swallow back the knot forming in her windpipe before nodding her head, not wanting to delve into the intricacies of the relationship between Holly and Celeste. Or that Celeste was not Celeste.

The detective clicked the pen again as he cleared his throat. The florescent lighting hummed in the background. It was a noise Greer focused on in an effort to calm her body. "The detectives believe Anna might be your mother's real name. They attempted to run her fingerprints in the system to confirm her identity, but the tips of her fingers had been burnt off. Did she ever tell you of how she got the injuries on her hands?"

Greer's mouth was dry and chalky as she parted her lips to answer. "A— a house fire when she was younger."

"The coroner suspects it was at least twenty years ago from the healing patterns on her hands. Do you remember a house fire from when you were younger? Any injuries that you might have?"

Greer shook her head.

"The social security number your mother used matched that of Celeste Myers. She was a widower who died back in 1994 at the age of eighty-six. They suspect Anna, your mother, stole her identity shortly after in 1997." Flecker paused as he watched Greer's reaction closely.

Something inside Greer cleaved in two, leaving fractured pieces of her soul littered deep within her.

That metallic taste rose in her mouth once again and the electricity skittered across her skin. Greer shot from her seat and let out a guttered scream. The bright lights above her popped and sent sparks raining down on them. The officers jerked in surprise as they looked at Greer with bulging eyes.

A sickening thud emitted through the room as her kneecaps hit the floor and she was emptying her stomach onto the cold concrete. Over and over and over.

When she was finished, the room was dark and silent once again.

TWENTY

"**I**s this the daughter of Celeste Myers?"

Greer stopped in the living room as she answered the phone. Delia lifted her head from the thick pile of documents she had set in her lap.

"This is her." Greer felt her heartbeat quicken from the unknown male voice on the other end. "How can I help you?"

"Hi. This is Blake O'Neill from the Lamplighter Inn that your mother was staying at. The police have finished their investigation of the room and have released her belongings. Would, erm, would you prefer to come pick them up or have us mail them somewhere?"

Greer rubbed her temple with her thumb as she let out a sigh from her nose. "I can come get them in a few minutes. Thanks, Blake." She hung up the phone with a press of the home screen and looked at Delia with a defeated stare.

It had been a week since Celeste's murder and Greer had taken a leave of absence from work to take care of everything from the will, to the cremation, to the selling of the condo her mother owned in San Francisco.

"I know what you're thinking," Delia said, as she lifted the stack from her lap and pushed herself off the couch. "This is not your fault. You did nothing wrong by filing for that DNA test."

Greer shifted on her feet. The guilt that had been gnawing at her in the last week twisted her stomach into knots. "It doesn't feel like that, Dels. I should have withdrawn that fucking request. Cian said—"

"That something would happen to you," Delia emphasized. "Celeste lived under a fake name. You needed to know where you came from and you found that out with that letter from the sheriff in Montana. You couldn't have known this would happen."

Greer sniffed then sighed again. "The hotel is ready for me to come pick up my mother's stuff. I'm going to head up there now."

"Wait for me, I'll come with you."

"Dels, I appreciate you. But I have to do this alone."

Delia stopped in her tracks. "You don't have to do this alone, GG," she said quietly, folding her arms over her chest. "Paige and I are here for you. Always."

Greer sent her a small smile. "I know." She reached up to grab her keys from the hook. "I'll pick up Chinese food on the way home, yeah? Sweet and sour chicken for you and chow mein with beef for Paige?"

Delia hummed in disapproval as she sank back down on the couch. "Chinese food won't make me worry less for you." Her arms were still wrapped tightly across her chest. "I'll call Paige and have her come over for dinner anyways. She's been texting all day to check in on you."

Greer felt her chest swell. She turned to leave before Delia spotted the tears pricking the corners of her eyes.

The evening was warmer than she anticipated, and the dry heat washed over her as soon as she stepped from the apartment building.

The grass must have been feeling the same way, as the lawns surrounding the area had turned crunchy and brown with the lack of rain.

The drive back to the hotel felt like a dream. Greer half-expected for the line of police cars and caution tape to still be there when she pulled up, but the parking lot was merely dotted with a handful of cars.

Two men, both dressed in athleisure wear, were at the trunk of a car, and they each tossed a duffle bag over their shoulders before slamming the hatch shut. Their fingers intertwined as they approached the hotel and the glass doors split open upon their arrival.

Greer slowly followed the couple and waited behind them in the familiar hotel lobby. They received their room keys and Greer stepped up to the desk. The receptionist was a young man, college-aged, with thick, blonde hair. His face was speckled with acne, red and angry, and his nose was crooked, as if it had been broken a few times. "Welcome to the Lamplighter Inn. Checking in?"

There was a gap in his stained front teeth when he smiled. "My name is Greer Myers. I received a call earlier from the owner about my mother's belongings?"

The smile slid from his face just as quickly as he hitched it on. He cleared his throat in discomfort before saying, "That was my father. We have her belongings in the back room. Did you want to take a look?"

"Yes, I do."

Greer wound the corner of the desk and followed the man into the back room. The pile was nestled under the desk containing two television screens playing live footage of the front door and of the pool deck. The man's laptop was set amongst the security screens, a window maximized to the latest German tennis open.

"Sorry it's a mess," he went on as he pointed out the pile Greer had already noticed. "We didn't really know what to do with it all."

Celeste's black suitcase was half-zipped. Clothes hung from the side and it was obvious they had been shoved inside. A smaller bag, also black, contained her toiletries and a white garbage bag was stuffed to the brim with dirty clothes. Greer could tell through the opaque plastic that the clothes were covered in sprays of blood.

Lots of blood.

"Sorry about that too." The receptionist reached up to scratch the back of his head. "We were going to launder them, but we didn't know if you wanted the account charged with the extra fees."

Greer almost made a snide comment about the hotel just doing the laundry free of charge, but decided to bite it back instead. She sent him a tight smile before grasping the plastic bag in her hand and slinging it over her shoulder. "I got it, don't worry about it." She bent down to shove the loose clothing deeper into the suitcase and zipped it shut. The suitcase wheels caught on the fibers of the carpet when she attempted to pull it, and it took her just as much energy to not yell out in frustration.

"Have a good night," the receptionist said, as he led her from the back room. He turned to check-in a new guest at the desk.

This time, Greer did bite out, "I appreciate you holding my murdered mother's things. Though, it would have been nice if you, at least, washed the blood from her clothing." She thought she would feel a sense of triumph at the wide-eyed look of terror on the new guest's face, but she only felt a roil of shame in her gut.

The receptionist's lips parted in shock as his eyes slung between Greer and the new guest.

Greer mumbled a quick apology before dipping her chin to her chest and walking through the sliding doors once again. She left the receptionist to deal with the new guest, who looked like he had half a mind to find a new hotel for his stay.

That same guilt followed her when she loaded the trunk of her Jeep and all the way to the Chinese restaurant on her way back home.

Paige was already seated on the couch by the time Greer hauled the three bags to the apartment, her legs curled under her as she leaned against the armrest. Delia sat next to Paige with her hand rested on Paige's thigh just below the hem of the cotton shorts she wore.

"GG, why didn't you call me?" Delia asked as she shot off the couch and stumbled forward to grasp the garbage bag and the Chinese food from Greer's hands. "I could have helped you bring all this up the stairs."

Greer groaned in pain as the tight plastic unwound from her palm, leaving behind a deep indentation from where the straps had cut into the skin. The relief of the third bag gave her a free hand to pull the suitcase over the metal threshold. She gave a quick and firm tug against the handle, realizing too late that the zipper had been wedged in the crack between the door and the frame.

It tore free with her yank, spilling the contents of the suitcase at the doorstep and into the foyer of the apartment. Greer swore under her breath, dropping the handle and allowing the suitcase to crash to the floor.

Paige was off the couch at the sound and stepped into the hallway, the toes of her bare feet curled against the old carpet. She bent down and picked up an armful of clothing, shoveling it back into the open suitcase.

A second crash drew Greer's attention from the apartment, and she lifted her head to find Paige with one foot in the air. Her hand was clasped around her ankle and blood leaked from under the nail of her biggest toe. Near her other foot lay a black and silver lockbox. The metal of the seam clanged loudly against the thin, old carpet when it bounced off Paige's foot.

"Paige, Jesus, are you okay?" Greer asked, forgoing the open suitcase still on the floor.

Paige waved her off. "Fucking thing was folded into the clothes. It slipped from my hand," she hissed, as she wiped the blood from her toe. A second droplet had already formed.

Greer stepped over the suitcase and bent down to pick up the lockbox. It was heavy in comparison to how small it was, and there was no key in the lock. Greer toed through the pile of clothing in the suitcase in search of the key, but found nothing. She held it up to her ear and shook the box, expecting to hear a rattle.

Nothing sounded.

"What is it?" Delia asked, as she padded from the kitchen into the hallway. She twirled the plastic fork from her dinner between her teeth as she held an icepack for Paige in her other hand.

"I'm not so sure." Greer bit the inside of her cheek as she examined the lockbox. "I'm not so sure how I can open it."

"Magic, perhaps?" Paige asked as she gingerly set her foot back onto the carpet. She tested putting weight against the already bruised toe and winced in response.

"I've been through every spell of the grimoire and haven't found one to open anything that looks like this." Greer paused to kick a path through the clothes, making it easier for Paige to navigate toward the couch.

Delia made a noise at the back of her throat as Paige said, "What about calling that vampyre? Aren't they strong?"

"I don't think we should involve them in anything we don't need to," Delia responded as she leaned against the doorframe. She picked up a wayward shirt by scooping it with the top of her foot and flicked it into the suitcase. "I'm sure we could find another way to open the box. Come on.

Why don't we take a break and eat this food while it's still hot. Paige, I'm going to grab a band-aid for you."

Greer helped Paige limp forward, settling her onto the couch, as Delia returned with the first aid kit from the hallway closet. Greer grabbed the Chinese food from the kitchen table, before kicking the suitcase over the threshold and shutting the door behind her.

Following dinner, Greer spent the majority of the evening attempting to open the lockbox. Various bouts of magic, both controlled and not, as well as picking at the lock with a hairpin. The magic bounced off the top and embedded into the drywall behind her. After a handful of attempts, and new gouges in her bedroom wall, Greer tossed the box back onto her night stand in frustration.

She eyed her phone on the nightstand and, remembering the warning Delia had in her voice, picked it up anyways. She swiped her thumb against the screen and typed in the passcode, waiting for a brief moment for the home page to load.

The mattress sank under her weight as Greer perched on the edge of the bed. She bit her lip in thought, wondering if she was making the right decision, before searching Cian's name in the address book.

She laid back against the burnt orange fleece blanket that sat atop her white down comforter and lifted her phone toward the ceiling for a better view. Clicking on the message icon, she quickly typed, *I need some help opening a box I found in my mother's belongings. Do you mind stopping by?* and sent it off before she could second guess herself.

Greer dropped her hand to the mattress.

Her phone buzzed less than a minute later, and Greer picked it back up to read, *Now? What could be so important that it needs to be done now?*

Greer rolled her eyes. *If I knew what was inside and didn't think it was important, I wouldn't be bothering you.*

She pushed herself so sitting on the edge of the mat- tress again and surveyed her bedroom as she waited for the next reply. Greer had worked to make her bedroom a safe haven over the past year or so, collecting the macramé hanging art and wooden bookshelves that suited her style. The wicker chair with the white cushion that sat in the corner was the newest item, and it was the one that she spent the most time reading in.

Her phone buzzed again. *Be there in five. You owe me dinner.*

She chuckled as she rolled her eyes and typed quickly. *I have nothing to offer except my utmost gratitude. Don't ring the bell when you get here.*

I'll find someone on my way then.

Can't you find a nice rabbit or something? Maybe a raccoon? No.

Greer shut off her phone and flicked it into the corner of her bed, where it promptly got lost in the pile of patterned throw pillows. She sighed as she pushed herself to standing and leaned over the desk, peeking through the blinds that covered the windows. It was raining again, the first time since the night of the murder, and water ran over the dry dirt that couldn't soak it in fast enough. Lightning flashed in the distance, and a roll of thunder followed a few seconds later.

Grabbing the lockbox from the nightstand, Greer cracked the bed- room door open and intently listened into the hallway. She heard nothing except the squeaks of a bedframe and the soft moaning that only meant Delia and Paige were enjoying each other's company. Greer tip-toed past the second bedroom and into the dark living room, illuminated in flashes of light from the storm.

She held the unlock button to the front door until she heard the lock click through the speaker. Only then did she turn the bolt on the apartment door. Cian's silhouette took up the space in the doorframe, shadowed against the hallway light that hummed with every roll of thunder.

"Where is it?" Cian said, as he moved past her and into the dining room. He picked at his elongated fangs dramatically. The sleeve of his leather jacket was dripping with rainwater.

Greer glowered. She held the lockbox out in front of her.

He grasped it for a moment, his fingers wrapping

around the cool metal. He withdrew his hand just as quickly, and the box clattered to the table with a loud *thunk*.

Greer hushed him as she picked up the box once again and tried to hand it to him, but he shook his head.

"That box has an obsidian coating. I could feel it pulling at my strength."

She turned the box over and looked at it. "That explains why every spell I threw at it just bounced right off."

Cian leered at her. "That would have been handy to know before I came all the way over here."

"Can you get it apart or not?" Greer placed the box on the table, quietly this time, and lifted her gaze toward him.

"With brute force maybe," Cian replied, though he gestured for her. "Hold onto the sides. I'm going to try and use you as a brace."

Greer did as he requested and wrapped her hands around the edges of the lockbox, holding it into place. He leaned over the other side of the table. His hands brushed over her wrists as he rested one palm atop hers. His leather coated scent wafted over her and she felt a shiver go up her spine at the contact.

Cian stiffened slightly at the increased patter of her heartbeat, but he cleared his throat and murmured, "I'm going to do this quickly. The longer I touch it, the longer it will take for me to recover."

Greer nodded.

He let out a breath and flexed his fingers before grasping the handle of the lockbox. He yanked it upward in one smooth pull, and the metal pulled apart with a grinding snap of the lock. He dropped the lid onto the table, but his hand held onto Greer's.

She cleared her throat as she hesitantly withdrew her hand from underneath his, reaching into the box. The in-side was the same, cool metal, but Greer felt thick paper between the tips of her fingers. She grabbed onto the item and removed it, turning it over in her hand.

The item was an envelope, sealed at the top and folded once in the middle. Greer unfolded it and pulled at the seal by slipping her pinky in the gap. The envelope gave easily and tore at the tug of her wrist. The smell of old paper and dust replaced Cian's scent as she opened the envelope and glanced inside.

"What is it?" Cian asked in a hushed voice.

Lightning flashed once more, lighting up the brown of his hair and the green of his eyes.

Greer reached into the envelope and pulled out a business card. The paper was thick in comparison to the envelope. One side was written *to Greer in case of Celeste's death* and the other contained a label for Indiana Bank and Trust, along with a telephone number in smaller font underneath the label. A key was nestled inside the corner of the envelope.

"What is that, do you reckon?"

Greer looked at him, realizing that he had been studying her face. "I—I didn't realize my mother had any ties to Indiana at all." She turned the card over again and ran her thumb along the indents the pen made into the business card. She could imagine the way Celeste held the pen be- tween her thumb and fingers, the way the ink would swirl onto the cardstock under Celeste's direction.

Greer jumped as Cian placed a gentle hand onto her forearm. "You should focus on your magic." His eyes dropped to the business card still in her hand. "This is just another dead end."

Greer sighed as she tossed the card onto the table. It slid across the smooth surface and came to a rest near the lockbox. "You're probably right."

He was quiet as he reached into his back pocket and pulled out a silver flask. He twisted the top off and took a long swig before extending his hand toward her.

"That's not blood is it?"

The corners of his lips tugged upward as he softly laughed. He shook the flask at her and it glinted under another flash of lightning. "No blood, just good Irish whiskey."

Greer took the flask and held it to her lips, taking a deep drink. The whiskey had a nutty aroma with a smoky finish, balanced and rich against her tongue. She shivered again as the alcohol sharply coated the back of her throat, but she reveled in the feeling. "It is good."

"If there is one thing I know, it's whiskey."

It was Greer who smiled this time. "I'll remember that when I need a recommendation for a drink."

"You seem to need one now."

She took another swig from the flask, tipping her head back to finish off what was inside.

TWENTY-ONE

"**G**reer, a few of us from the anthropology department are headed to that new bar down the street. Carter's, I think?" Erin said, as she shut her laptop and safely stored it in her leather work bag. "Did you want to join us?"

"I don't think I can, Erin. I've got so much work to catch up on from my bereavement leave."

"And it'll be here when you get back," Daniel weighed in. He hitched the strap of his work bag onto his shoulder and held his empty coffee mug in his hand. "It's been weeks since you've come out with us. Come for dinner at least?"

The end of the day bustle in the hallway broke over the hum of the fluorescent lights as fellow researchers took toward the elevators in a rush to head off the evening traffic. Greer opened her mouth to respond when her cell phone vibrated across the table. She turned to ignore it when it vibrated for a second time.

She reached for it to flip the phone over when she glanced at the screen. It was an incoming call.

With a furrowed brow, she swiped her thumb on the screen to answer and put the phone up to her ear. "Hello?"

"Greer Myers?" The other end crackled from the library basement's bad connection.

"This is she."

"Greer, this is Robert Mills. I am the estate lawyer for your mother, Celeste Myers. Her will and testament have been released and are ready to be filed in probate court. I am currently working in the state of California, but I am able to send the will to a lawyer of your choosing to look over. I understand that you're in the state of Oregon?"

"Yes, that is correct." Greer cleared her throat. "Could you send the documents to Delia Savas at Quincy and Astor Law Firm?"

"Yes, I certainly can. Do you happen to have the fax number for encrypted documents?"

Greer fished Delia's business card from her work bag and rattled off the number before hanging up the phone. She sent a quick text to Delia warning her to watch out for the will coming her way.

"I'm really sorry," Greer said again, looking up, "I just—"

Erin and Daniel had left the office in the time it took for her to take the phone call. Her heart sunk in her chest. A month ago, they would have waited.

Now Greer just felt removed. Removed from her job, removed from her friends, removed from her old life. She felt as though she were an outsider looking in, a mere observer into a changing environment that she wasn't able to run from.

Quietly and tearfully, Greer packed her laptop into her bag and slowly joined the crowd lined up at the elevators. Erin and Daniel were already long gone.

Delia had the will spread neatly on the coffee table by the time Greer walked through the door of the apartment. Leaned forward to inspect the document closer, she was tapping her nails against the side of the soda can in her other hand. Greer wrapped the strap of her work bag on the back of a dining room chair before collapsing on the couch next to Delia.

"Long day?" Delia asked absent-mindedly as she bit her inner cheek.

"You could say that." Greer sighed as she sank deeper into the microfiber cushion. "What did you find?"

"Do you know who James Whittley is?"

"No, I don't." Greer took the soda can from Delia's hand and took a swig, tasting the sweet strawberry and vanilla syrups. "Why?"

Delia lifted the last page of the document from the table. "The first page is everything we expected. She left all of her belongings to you. Since the condo was sold, the estate money will be released to you when we get this filed in probate court." She pointed to the last sentence at the bottom of the page. "The successor executor of the will is a Mister James Whittley. It gives his address out of Iowa."

Greer leaned forward to place the empty can on the coffee table. "My mother never mentioned anyone of that name." A humorless chuckle escaped from the back of her throat. "She never mentioned anyone, truth be told."

"I can file this in the court tomorrow. That won't take too long." Delia paused as she reached to the top of the table and slid a small business card from under the first page of the will. "This, on the other hand."

Greer felt her mouth go dry and she dropped her gaze from Delia's.

"I found the box on the table this morning. It appeared to have been wrenched open," Delia pressed on despite Greer's silence. "The way it was warped, I figured you took Paige's advice and called the vampyre." She sighed. "I just want to make sure you're safe, Greer. These— these creatures are playing a game centuries old. We don't know what they want."

"Dels, he just wants that potion—"

"To make him walk in the sun, I know." Delia rubbed at her temple. "Your biological mother was killed. Your adopted mother was killed. This is serious and dangerous, GG. Please make sure you're being safe."

Greer plucked the business card from Delia's fingers. "I'm being safe, Delia, I promise. I just— I need to know who I am. What does all of this mean?" She ran her thumb over the indents from the pen, the same way she had done the night before.

"Have you called the number yet?" Delia asked.

Greer shook her head and lifted her gaze to see Delia holding her cell phone forward. Greer scraped it from Delia's outstretched palm and quickly toggled the phone number into the keypad. She lifted the phone to her ear as it began to ring.

"Indiana Bank and Trust. What can I do to assist you this afternoon?"

Greer sucked in a breath. "Yeah, hi, I'm looking to find some information on an account you might have?"

She heard the woman on the other end clack her fingernails against the keys on the keyboard. "Can I have the account number?"

Greer froze and her stomach dropped to her feet. "I—I don't have the number. It's for my deceased mother, Celeste Myers? She would be the account manager."

There was a pause with more typing on the other end. "I'm sorry, ma'am, but we don't have an account under that name. Are you sure you have the correct bank?"

"No," Greer said with a scoff, "My mother was killed a few weeks ago. I found a business card of yours with an inscription on the back in her personal effects."

"I'm sorry for your loss. But, even if we did have some- one with that name here, we would need a death certificate in order to divulge any information to you."

Unexpected anger swirled beneath Greer's skin, but she tempered it. "Oh, okay. Thank you for your help."

"I'm sorry I couldn't be of more assistance. If you find the necessary documentation, please feel free to reach back out." The woman hung up before Greer could get another word in.

The timer on the oven dinged to signify the completion of the frozen pizza, the scent which had been from the kitchen. Greer felt herself internally drop as she closed her eyes, using the rage, heartbreak, and grief as a guide. It was the first time she really let herself feel in weeks.

Greer felt her energy push against a barrier, as if she had descended down a shaft and reached the bottom. Exhausted and frustrated, she took a deep breath and let out a cathartic scream. Delia's hand reached over and clenched around Greer's in solidarity. Greer felt a pinprick of power breach that barrier, then...

The six empty beer bottles on the counter from the night before burst in unison, sending shards of glass across the kitchen. Greer and Delia let out screams of shock as they threw their forearms up to protect their faces. Greer felt the flying glass scrape at the skin of her elbows and knees, sticking in the fabric of her shirt.

She lowered her arms to study the scene. The brown- stained glass covered the kitchen countertop and tile floors. It certainly wasn't the first time Greer had unintentionally created magic, but it was the first time she had affected several items at once. She turned to look at Delia, who was busy brushing shards of glass from the front of her spandex leggings. Delia lifted her gaze to connect with Greer, both women wide-eyed.

"Was that—"

"Me." Greer's voice was cracked and hoarse after the scream.

A pounding on the door a moment later had both Greer and Delia jolting in their spots on the couch, letting out additional screeches of surprise.

"Greer? Delia? Is everything okay? I heard shouts."

Delia lunged toward the apartment door and yanked it open to reveal their neighbor, Mister Kulikowski. The front of his vest was buttoned incorrectly, as if he had been in the middle of dressing when he heard their yells. His thinning hair stuck upwards at an odd angle.

"Hi, Mister Kulikowski," Delia managed to say. Her chest was still heaving while struggling to breathe. "I dropped a six pack of beer and shattered the bottles. I'm so sorry that you heard us. We were just startled, that's all."

Their neighbor peeked around the corner of the doorframe and Greer gave him a tiny smile and wave.

"I've been hearing loud noises coming from here the last few weeks. Strange men traipsing in and out of the apartment at all hours, including last night." His dark eyes were sharp as he surveyed the two women. "Are either of you in some sort of trouble?"

Greer and Delia quickly shook their heads. "Everything is fine, Mister Kulikowski," Greer said over the back of the couch. "We'll be sure to quiet down."

"That's not— I'm not— I'm not worried about the noise level, girls." His thick eyebrows lifted toward the top of his balding head, the long hairs far overdue for a trim.

"I worry about both of you."

Greer felt her heart tug as Delia sent him a dazzling smile.

"And you know we worry about you, too." Delia leaned her head against the edge of the door. "We haven't had dinner with you in quite some time. Why don't you come over next week? I can make some lasagna, and Greer can pick up wine on her way home from work. She passes by that grocery store that carries the Merlot you like so much."

His eyes softened. "I would like that very much. It's been lonely since Marlene died."

"We miss her too," Greer said, her chin resting on the back of the couch. "She made the best biscuits and gravy for breakfast. Sent me with my fair share in the mornings before work most days."

His smile was warm. "She loved you both. And Paige. She loved her, too." He heaved a sigh and a curt nod. "Well, if everything is okay, I'll leave you girls to it. Be sure to be careful when cleaning up that glass. Wear shoes until you know it's all up from the floor."

"We will," Greer stated.

"Thanks, Mister Kulikowski," Delia said with another smile.

He swept his gaze over the two of them one last time before turning toward his apartment.

His indoor slippers shuffled against the carpet as he went.

Delia shut the door behind her and rested the top of her back against the wood. "We need to work on your magic. It has to stop coming out with every emotional outburst. Oh shit." Delia pushed off the door and jogged toward the kitchen, smoke unfurling from the oven. She hissed in pain as she tripped forward, and Greer realized Delia had stepped on a shard of glass.

Greer lurched off the couch and ushered Delia into a seat at the table. She grabbed a pillow from the couch and began to preemptively wave it underneath the smoke detector. It would be their luck telling Mister Kulikowski that everything was fine, only to have the alarm trill less than a minute later.

"I swear, between you and Paige," Greer said, as she tossed the pillow back onto the couch, and handed Delia the first aid kit still on the countertop from the night before. "We've got foot injuries covered, that's for sure," Delia responded, placing her foot on the opposite thigh to pull the small shard of glass from the skin.

The bottom of the pizza was charred when Greer took it from the oven and dropped it on the stovetop. The stinking smell of burnt cheese filled the small space, and Delia wrinkled her nose as Greer waved her oven mitts to reduce the smoke.

"I think we should order take out for dinner," Greer finally said, slapping the oven mitts down as she assessed the burnt pizza. The crust had bubbled and the pepperoni was black. "I owe you for the glass from the beer bottles."

Delia clicked her tongue, as she tossed the unopened first aid kit back onto the counter. She stood from her seat. "Pad Thai?" She grabbed the broom from the empty slot next to the refrigerator, running the fibers against the floor to sweep the glass into a pile.

"Anything, but pizza." Greer swiped the back of her hand across her sweating brow. "It's going to take forever to get this smell out of here. And we just got the smell out from the mildew."

Delia said nothing as she continued to sweep.

Greer's mind wandered. Delia was right, she was going to continue to hurt people if she didn't get her magic under control. Her best friend inadvertently stepping on glass was the prime example.

But, she thought back to that feeling, that puncture through the blockade and the rush of power that blasted through. She reached out to that barrier once again with tendrils of her magic, trying to sense the tiny hole she had created.

As if made of an elastic band, the hole had already snapped shut.

Greer closed her eyes and shook her head as she picked up a washrag to assist in cleaning the kitchen. She would have been lying to herself if she said she didn't love that burst of power and the feeling of it rushing through her veins.

TWENTY-TWO

The name James Whittley plagued Greer.

She stared at the dark ceiling at night and contemplated who the man was or what connection he had to her mother. During the day, she spent more time than she should have searching his name on the internet.

Greer learned that the man was well into his seventies and had lived at that address for the last twenty-five years. She even paid a website fifty dollars to reveal the phone number associated with the address. The line was disconnected.

Delia had her hesitations about Greer making the trip alone. She had even offered to go with her over the baked ziti dish they made for dinner that Friday night.

Greer promised her that it wasn't necessary. It was a quick two-day trip to Iowa. The flight was a handful of hours. The drive was only an hour after that. There was no indication, other than her internet searches, that James Whittley still resided there. It was entirely possible that she would find an empty house when she got there.

Bugs leapt from the long, swaying grass as Greer trundled down the dirt road. The sweetly scented, late summer breeze removed any wisp of cloud that may have gathered in the afternoon sky. She bounced in the front seat as she drove to avoid the potholes that littered the dirt road and the dust cloud created behind her was briskly carried away.

Greer squinted her eyes against the bright sun as she assessed the lone house at the end of the road.

Old and in desperate need of repairs, the sagging porch was cast within a deep shadow created by the leaky roof held aloft by three wooden pillars. The paint on each pillar was considerably chipped and seemed to have retained damage from both extreme weather and termites. The light fixed to the siding adjacent to the front door was still lit and it flashed dully as it swung with the wind.

There was a red barn fifty yards from the back of the house. Though by the condition of the structure and the vines growing up the wall, it seemed that the roof had caved in years before.

Greer cut off the engine of the car and exited the vehicle. The dirt driveway crunched beneath her sneakers as she walked over the dying weeds stifled by the cracked, dry mud.

The rotting wood of the porch bowed under her weight as she carefully climbed the stairs.

Reaching the landing, Greer lifted her hand. She hesitated as she stared at the faded blue door. There was movement on the other side that sounded like someone shifting on a couch. The creak broke her free of her thoughts, and she rapped on the door with a knuckle.

She took a step back as the breeze streamed through the porch, ruffling her hair. She noticed, for the first time, strange etchings carved into the doorframe. Swirls and dips and lines made in a pattern unfamiliar to her.

Greer stared at it in interest as she reached a hand forward to trace the nearest carving with a fingertip when a shuffle sounded beyond the door. Her hand dropped back to her side.

Hunched in the upper back and using a cane, Greer was surprised to see a white-haired man clad in a long night shirt and slippers. The lenses in his glasses were thick, aiding his milky eyes. He had the air of a man who was once powerful in his prime. Now, with his twisted skeleton, he looked like someone to be pitied.

He looked up at her as his eyes cleared slightly with his adjusted focus.

"James Whittley?" Greer asked.

He rubbed the top of his head to smooth his thinning hair, but said nothing. Waiting.

"My name is Greer Myers. You were the second executor on my mother's will. Her name was Celeste Myers." James placed both hands on the cane for balance.

"Doesn't ring a bell." His voice was gruff, as if he hadn't spoken aloud in some time.

"The name Celeste is a stolen identity. I'm not sure what her real name was."

The man went to turn away. He placed a hand on the door knob as he readied himself to slam the door in her face. "Holly Hawkins," Greer said quickly as a way to stop him. "She had a hand in the death of a woman named Holly Hawkins."

James stilled.

Greer took the opportunity to glance over his shoulder. She spotted an old, stained couch with a pitted middle cushion. It clashed heavily against the orange, shagged carpet and paisley wallpaper. A yellowing lamp was in the corner on an antique end table, where he had placed a book filled with Sudoku puzzles. A pencil was tucked neatly into the crevice of the spine, and a magnifying glass rested across the open page.

"You know who I'm talking about," Greer stated as she returned her gaze to watch the old man.

"Yes."

She felt her breath hitch in her chest. "Then you know who I am."

"She was supposed to kill you, my Anna."

"That name was painted in blood on the wall of the hotel room she was found in. Along with mine and Holly's." James slowly sank into the armchair closest to the door.

The wood creaked under his weight, and he groaned as he leaned the cane against a matching antique side table. "Can I come inside?" Greer asked. Frustration had begun to grow inside of her. "I want to have this conversation with you."

"I don't allow creatures inside of my home."

"Creatures?" she replied and her thoughts pinged back and forth with questions. "I'm not a creature, I'm your granddaughter—"

"If my Anna raised you as her own then she is dead to me." James reached into the breast pocket of his night-shirt and pulled out a folded handkerchief. "If the Paladin Society caught up with her, it was what she deserved." He wiped his nose before replacing it. "And you are certainly no granddaughter of mine."

Greer made to move through the open doorway, but smacked against an invisible barrier. She bounced painfully off the wall and rubbed her throbbing nose with the palm of her hand. Flabbergasted, she lifted a hand and pressed against the barrier. "What is this?" she asked in a hushed voice. She swept her hand toward the markings, but found herself unable to touch them.

His Adam's apple bobbed as he swallowed. "The sigils on the doorway are of a different world. Given to the Paladin Society by our creators to keep out unwanted Primordials." He turned his milky gaze toward Greer. "If you can't get through, that confirms my long-suspected thoughts of your ancestry."

Greer took a step backward and felt the wood bend dangerously beneath her footing. "My ancestry?"

"Tell me. How did my daughter die?"

A fly buzzed near her ear and she batted it away with a flick of her wrist. "Terribly."

"Bloody?"

"Very." Greer paused for a moment as she tilted her head in confusion. "Why?"

"Could you identify her body?"

Greer didn't understand. "Why are you asking me these questions?"

James went silent for a moment, and when he finally spoke, it still wasn't to answer her question. "When she died, did you see her soul? Who came to retrieve it?"

Greer shifted to lean against one of the wooden columns behind her. The wood was soft and wet against her forearms. "She had been dead for hours by the time I saw her." Her clothes felt suddenly uncomfortable against her skin. "Who would have come to retrieve it?"

"It's a shame that I'm mostly blind. I would like to gaze upon the face of the woman who will bring the end of the world."

Greer pushed off the column to approach the open doorway, coming as close as the barrier would let her. She felt her breath rebound against an invisible glass. "If you step outside, I could heal you," she said in a hushed lie, "I could allow you to see. If you know who I am, you know what I am capable of."

"I am living on borrowed time whether you heal me or not." James removed his glasses to clean them on the sleeve of his night shirt, before replacing them on the bridge of his nose. "One day, he will come for me and he will not allow me to die quickly. I was merely curious if he caught up with Anna."

"Who are you talking about?" Greer asked quickly. "Who is he?"

"Your father." James scratched the stubble on his sagging cheek. "Peeling the skin from one's bones is his calling card."

Greer felt a sudden cold expand in her gut as her face grew sweaty and chilled. "My father?"

"He comes here every so often." James's gaze drifted away as he stared, unseeingly, into the television screen. "He's long since given up trying to get through my wards. He'll sit on the porch chair and whisper through the door-way. Telling me exactly what he'll do to my soul when I die. How he'll strip me down to bare nerves and flay me open; inflict pain until I no longer know my own name."

Greer shivered as she glanced at the empty rocking chair to her left. The faded paint, the torn, purple cushion. She imagined a faceless man seated there, his fingers tapping against the armrest as he gazed over the open fields before him.

James went on. "It's to be expected. Killing the mate of a Primordial."

"Mate?" Greer lifted her head to look at the old man again. "What does that mean?"

"A string connecting them through time and space. The bond transcends all, so deep that a Primordial could shed their created purpose if the mate asked." His gnarled hand rested on a knee. "What of my youngest daughter, Joy?"

Greer opened and closed her mouth for a beat. "My mother never said she even had a sister. Back to my father-"

"No," James said with a shake of his head. "I'm no longer interested in entertaining you." His rise to standing was slow, and a wince clouded his face as his lower back cracked in response. "Leave now, child, and don't return here."

"Wait— my father, who is my father?"

James wrapped his contorted fingers around the edge of the door. "If you are lucky, girl, you'll never need to find out."

With that, he swung the door shut, leaving Greer on the porch with the sun beaming against her back.

TWENTY-THREE

CIAN

G reer was stewing. Cian could tell.

She hadn't mentioned to him her plan of seeking out James Whittley, and he felt a pang of exasperation when she finally did. She should be working on that damn potion. They had a deal.

Cian didn't know why she had called him instead of the roommate or the roommate's girlfriend. He also didn't know why he agreed to meet her at this saloon on the outskirts of town. The Sunday night regulars behind them had already begun dancing a two-step, leading each other in an intricate pattern around the open floor.

It had taken far too long for Cian to pry out of Greer why she felt the need to call him. A margarita and two shots of tequila later, to be exact. She had slammed them back with ease, and Cian watched the column of her throat work as she swallowed.

When Greer lowered the second shot glass to the bar top, the *clink* barely audible over the background twang of upbeat violins and guitars, the first question she had asked him was about Primordials.

Cian had felt his stomach twist in response. The knot that had hardened in his gut soured the freshly consumed alcohol. He hated tequila to begin with, and he especially hated it now. "Did he fess up and say who your father is?" Cian asked, as he took a long swig of the beer in front of him.

Greer shook her head, and Cian took the opportunity to look at her.

The light freckles that adorned her nose and cheeks. Her gray eyes, a stormy dark against the dim lighting. The brown locks curled with a natural elegance that fell down her back. How her breasts pushed against the low-cut sundress.

He looked away and took another swig of beer. If Greer was half-Primordial, it certainly connected a few loose ends. Specifically, why her magic seemed to work better when she didn't use a spell. Cian briefly wondered if that would make a difference when it came to his potion.

Greer lifted her second margarita to her lips, readying for a sip of her own, when she was knocked to the side of the stool by a drunken man pushing toward the bar. The drink splashed over the edge of the rim and soaked the front of her sundress, the ice spilling to the floor.

She let out a yelp of surprise.

"Watch where you're going, mate!" Cian shouted over the music, as he shot to his feet and gripped the front of the man's shirt.

The man took a stumbling step backward in a failed attempt to break away from Cian. He swung a fist upward, a poor and clumsily aimed punch, as he slurred out a string of colorful swear words. Cian rebuffed it easily and his fangs pressed painfully against his gum line, begging for release. A hand shot out of the darkened bar, and Cian glanced down to see a familiar set of blue painted fingernails clasping his forearm. Lifting his gaze, he caught Greer's cautioned eye.

Cian pushed the man away, marking him for another time, and the man fell to the floor as he tripped over his own shoes. The crowd that was gathered around the bar chuckled and jeered as the man pushed himself to standing before disappearing into the mass of bodies.

Cian turned back to Greer, who had busied herself by blotting at her sundress with a handful of cocktail napkins provided by the bartender. The mango-flavored drink stained yellow against her cream-colored dress. He reached across the bar and grabbed a second handful, holding them out for Greer to take. She laughed as she grabbed a few more before shrugging and tossing the wet napkins onto the bar top.

"It's no use," Greer said, as she assessed the dark blot seeping into the fabric. She picked up her drink and tipped the rest of it into her mouth. "I'm only making it worse."

Cian linked his gaze with hers, and he felt the bass from the song playing over the speakers thrum through his chest.

He didn't know what came over him. Maybe it was the lights jetting out over the dance floor. Maybe it was the thinly veiled sweat scent covered by floral perfume. It could have even been the way her skin felt against his when she clamped her fingers around his arm.

Regardless of the reason, he held out his hand for her to take and tilted his head in gesture toward the dance floor. "Now?" Greer asked dubiously, as her gaze dropped to his hand.

"Come on," Cian said with a smile. He opened and closed his fingers playfully. "What are you afraid of?"

Greer's eyes steeled over as a smirk lifted the corner of her lips. She reached forward to grasp onto his hand, and Cian pulled her onto the dance floor. "I don't know how to do this," Greer said nervously, as Cian placed a hand on her waist, wrapping his fingers in the fabric of her dress. He lifted his other hand, still clasped firmly within hers, and rested her hand on his shoulder. She wrapped her second hand around the back of his neck, and Cian felt her fingers lightly tangle in the scruff of hair near the base of his skull.

"Follow my lead then," Cian responded with a wink.

Then, they were off.

Cian led her to the right, the music filling the gap of space between them. Cian watched Greer's gaze study his shoes, and she laughed when she stumbled over her own sandaled feet. He swept them backward with the crowd, his hand tightening against her back to hold her steady. She bumped into another couple as Cian spun her outwards, both of their arms extended before he pulled her until her back was against his chest.

His hand returned to her hip as the coconut scent of her hair wafted upward toward him. He felt the curve of her ass against his groin, and he twisted her around to face him.

Greer's arms wound around his neck once again, and he pulled her closely against him, keeping his hand flush against her lower back. Cian glanced down to look at her as he led them to the left this time, bumping against a second couple in the crowd. She was looking up at him through her thick lashes, and Cian felt his cock twitch as her thighs brushed against his own.

The floor was sticky against the soles of Cian's sneakers as he twirled her around, her sundress lifting at the hem with the movement. The air was hot and stuffy as more people joined the dance floor, some still clutching condensation-slicked glasses. The lights flashed across country-themed decor on the walls— the horseshoes, leather saddles, and whiskey barrels perched on the large shelves above the bar.

The strum of the guitar and the beat of the drums pulsed through them. Cian swooped her backward, and her back arched as the tips of her hair danced against the wooden floor. He gripped her under her lifted knee, and his hand roamed up her smooth thigh. She let out a peal of laughter as her fingernails dug into his upper arms for balance.

Cian reached down to grasp the back of her thighs, his nose brushing against her bare chest, and hoisted her into the air. Greer wrapped her legs around his waist, resting her forearms against the crook of his neck, and threw her head back in laughter as he spun them both around.

"How did you learn to dance like that?" She asked.

He shrugged, enjoying the feeling of her backside against his forearms. "Jack of all trades."

The music slowed, and Cian returned his hands to her waist as he let her down. Greer slid her body against his, and Cian couldn't help his roaming hands as she did so. His finger tangled in her dress, feeling the arcs of her hips and sweeping over her waist until her sandaled feet were settled back onto the sticky floor.

They swayed to the music, the plucking of the guitar strings rhythmic and unhurried. Cian reached up and brushed away a lock of hair clinging to Greer's sweaty forehead before resting his hand against her neck. He felt her thumbs hook in the waistband of his jeans as her fingers lightly caressed the skin of his lower abdomen. His hands trembled with stifled urgency as they tightened against her hip and neck.

Time slowed, and the dance floor narrowed as the lights from the stage containing the live band glided over them. Cian dipped his gaze down to her full lips and watched as she bit the bottom one between her teeth. He felt her back arch against his hand as she pushed her hips into his own. Her head tipped back to expose the column of her throat, and Cian could no longer help brushing his lips against the fair, tender skin of her neck.

He felt it pebble beneath him as the tip of his nose bowed upwards toward her ear and followed her along her jawline until he hovered before her. Cian smelled the mango flavoring and tequila on her breath as he waited, their eyes hungrily searching one another. It was Greer who closed the gap between them, clasping her hands around the leather of his jacket and pulling him toward her.

The kiss wasn't hesitant or soft, and Greer's lips immediately parted as Cian's tongue swept across them, demanding access. He tasted her— mint, salt, and alcohol melding together. Cian felt the rumble of her moan in his mouth, and he wished they were somewhere more private, just so he could hear it cut through the silence of an empty room. Breaking apart from her, seeing the redness of her lips and the fiery glow in her eyes, he pulled her through the crowd and into the shadows of the saloon's back hallway.

He hauled Greer's lips into his own again as he pushed her against the brick wall.

Greer sank her teeth into his lower lip, biting and sucking as Cian's hands tugged at her dress, cupping her breasts, gripping her thighs. He felt his callouses scrape across the smooth skin of her shoulders, and her hips pushed into his own, wanting and needing.

Cian felt a light tap. He ignored it for a moment before the pressure and persistence grew with each thud against his back. He broke away from Greer, agitation flitting over his face, and turned to glance over his shoulder.

And came face to face with a well-muscled bouncer.

Bald headed and clad in a white t-shirt, the bouncer had his arms crossed over his chest as he looked at them, unimpressed. "Get out and find a room," he said, thumbing over his shoulder toward the door.

Cian heard a light laugh covered by a cough escape from Greer as he grabbed her hand to lead her back through the crowd. Dancing bodies bounced against his own, jostling his shoulders. He tucked Greer's hand under his arm to keep her from being torn away.

They burst from the dance floor and through the front doors, bypassing the line of people waiting to gain entry. The misty evening air kissed their sweaty skin and created illuminated rings around the streetlamps posted within the parking lot.

Greer's giggle grew to a chuckle, then a full-on belly laugh, as Cian looked on at her. She threw her arms to the side and spun in the rain, her sandals slapping into the puddles and mudding her toes.

Cian tucked his hands into his pockets as he watched her approach the Jeep and plug the key code into the driver's door.

"So your place then?" He asked, as he followed her. He leaned forward to pin her hips to the side of the car with his own, and bracketed his hands around her head.

Greer lifted onto her tip-toes and kissed him lightly on the lips before reaching behind her back and pulling the door open. "Maybe next time," she retorted playfully, as she hopped into the Jeep and shut the door with a snap. Cian ran a hand through his dark hair, wet from the rain, as he watched her turn on the engine and drive away.

Water splashed up onto the tires as she rolled over cracks in the pavement.

The night had taken an unexpected turn, Cian certainly knew that. His lips still tingled and stung, swollen from the heaviness of their kisses. It was his stomach that flip-flopped when he thought of betraying Greer to Eligos and what it would mean for him if he couldn't stop it.

Cian smiled to himself as the Jeep turned onto the main road, the tail lights disappearing into the trees flanking the pavement. And he realized that, perhaps, for the first time in over four hundred years, he was going to get himself into more trouble than he was ready for.

TWENTY-FOUR

G reer needed to find release twice that night before she could relax enough to sleep. She had even tossed and turned after that; the covers felt entirely too itchy against her sensitive skin. When she finally did drift off, her sleep was marred by her usual dream of the winged man.

This bad dream was new, though.

He sunk his cock into her, fucking her into oblivion, before thrusting the dagger between her ribs and throwing her from the cliff.

She awoke from the dream with a start, sitting straight up in bed as her chest heaved. Greer felt her fingernails scrape against her skin as she clutched at her heart— as if she could grip it and hold it steady.

Having already made the mistake of checking her phone first thing, she was almost surprised to see two texts from Cian that read: *you looked beautiful tonight* followed by *the taste of your tongue on mine was intoxicating*.

Greer's anxiety had her skipping her morning almond honey flavored coffee, but she regretted that decision by early afternoon. Despite the tap of her heels echoing against the metal shelving units in the library archives, she struggled to keep her eyes open and mind attentive.

She needed a distraction. One that didn't involve exchanging lewd and dangerously dirty messages with Cian— something she had been doing since that morning.

The hour spent with James Whittley over the weekend had her thinking. She searched the library for information on Primordials and found nothing. She briefly remembered Odette rattling off other names, including archangels, and searched for that instead. The internet was equal parts too vague, too definitive, and Greer had a hard time sorting one from another.

This was part of the reason she paced the empty aisle, breathing in the scent of dust from the dry air pouring through the vent in the ceiling. The clock ticked in the background and she found herself focusing on that as she walked.

Greer paused in front of a shelf labeled *Religions of the West* and pulled the first three books on her handwritten note from the front of the row. The leather bindings were rough against her fingers as she marched back to the circle of computers in the middle of the archives.

A graduate intern was seated at one of the desks, her blonde hair pulled into a tight bun and her hazel eyes raking over the computer screen as she scribbled onto a notepad in front of her. Greer dropped the three books in her hand onto an empty desk, the sound jolting the intern from her concentration.

The intern glared at Greer, who ignored her in turn.

Greer pulled the first book, *The Fallen Angels: An Encyclopedia of History and Origins,* toward her and opened it, flipping to the table of contents. She scanned the page before flicking to the first chapter.

The hierarchy of Angelic-like creatures vary from religion to religion, spanning dozens of cultures. Some are considered spirits or guardians to humans while others are attendants to God. In this text, the focus will be on Judaic-Christian views.

Dozens of cultures. Greer rubbed her temples with her fingers and began to wonder if this was going to be a waste. Glancing up, her eyes ran along the shelves upon shelves, all lined with books, all filled with centuries of religious lore. There must have been hundreds.

Greer continued reading.

While the orders of angels depend on the choirs in which they fall, the types of angels that are considered the most well- known are archangels and guardian angels. Each archangel has a specific role or gift that works as an extension to God while guardian angels serve as messengers and offer support to humans. There are contradicting texts that categorize fallen angels within the hierarchy as well, though some scholars argue that these angels would be considered demons.

She snapped the book shut and blew out a loud breath as she leaned back in her chair, ignoring the intern's exasperated looks for the second time.

"Greer!"

She lifted her head at the voice and perplexity tugged over her face when she spotted Henry emerging from the shelves. His shoes echoed across the cavernous sub-floor as he approached her.

"Erin told me that I could find you here." His eyes dropped to the books that sat in front of her, and he reached down to pick one up. "Angelology?"

Greer cleared her throat as she looked up at him. "Just looking for some late nineteenth century connections is all." The lie was smooth, but the guilt twisted in her gut nonetheless. "What are you doing down here?"

Henry replaced the book onto the table and fixed his gaze on her. "I come with great news. The directors at the history and art museums connected to the university read your research on the artist from Washington State— Deborah. They were very impressed and expressed interest in doing a joint exhibit featuring Deborah's work and cultural notes from the leaders of the Modoc and Klamath tribes." He tucked his hands into the pockets of his gray pants. "I want you to head it."

Greer blinked. From the corner of her eye, she saw the intern raise her brows as if she couldn't believe it either.

"I— I— that's quite the honor, Henry," Greer started, her mind scattered and clumsy as she struggled to form a single string of thoughts. "Do you think I'm ready for that?"

The corners of Henry's lips pulled down in surprised bewilderment. "Absolutely, Greer. You've been giving us exceptional work for the better part of a year now. Your interview with Deborah was phenomenal, and the subsequent paper you authored was sublime. Why wouldn't you think that you were ready?"

In truth, Greer didn't feel she had been as focused as she could have been. She scraped a hand into her hair to tuck a lock behind her ear as she gave a quick shake of her head. "It's just a big step is all."

"It is," he agreed. "And I'm counting on you to bring it to life." He paused for a moment before continuing. "As you know, we have a partnership with the National and Kapodistrian University of Athens in Greece. There is a position coming up soon at the National Archaeological Museum that coincides with the current archaeological team digging in a village west of the city— over the bay. It comprises of cataloging new Mycenaean findings that the dig discovers and assisting the university to research the surrounding villages. If this goes well, I want to nominate you for the position."

Greer contemplated pinching her arm to make sure she wasn't dreaming. "Are— wait, what?"

"It's an eight-month transfer beginning in November. The current dig season ends at the end of August and they will ship the findings to the museum for restoration after that. Is it something you would be interested in?"

Greer shot out of her seat, her face heating. "Henry, that— it's something I've always wanted."

"Fantastic. Get started with a proposal and have it on my desk Wednesday morning. Contact Deborah. I'll give you the phone numbers for the tribal council; they will expect a proposal as well to make sure the exhibit is respectful at every step."

"I'll get on it right away."

Greer made no attempt to hide the ear-to-ear grin she sported as she followed Henry from the archives, abandoning the books and her personal research on the desk behind her.

She was the last from their ten-strong college friend group to make it to the restaurant that evening. Having been motivated to stay later than her contracted hours to work on the proposal, Greer felt as though she made good headway with an outline by the time she waved goodbye to the evening guard posted at the front door.

The Italian restaurant was downtown— a mom and pop establishment held over from when the developers began to build modern office buildings amongst the main strip. Iron sconces with built in gas lines bracketed the black front doors and benches with intricately patterned armrests were bolted nearest the brick exterior.

Her stomach grumbled as the smell of freshly baked pasta, bread sticks, and olive oil sat on the humid, summer air and Greer quickly hurried inside.

Cool air blasted at her, sweeping her hair over her shoulder, and she followed the gradual arc of the hallway around the hostess stand and by the bar lined with leather counter height seats.

Knives scraped against plates and the mumbled sounds of soft talking accompanied her as she passed through the trendy dining room.

Her heels clicked against the terracotta stone pavers set into the floor, uneven against her thin pumps. The black dress she had changed into after work was tight to her hips, and Greer noticed more than one man's gaze tracking her.

The room was already packed when Greer entered, and she was immediately met by her freshman year dormitory neighbor, Meredith, who smiled at her. Meredith was a curvy brunette with thin lips, a wide nose, and a cottage-core style that involved chunky sweaters and overalls. Meredith had already turned to continue her conversation with Kassie, a taller-than-average woman who had played on the university basketball team. Kassie waved a hello to Greer, who returned it with a grin.

The first to hug Greer was Imani, a black woman and third grade teacher Delia had met during sophomore year.

Imani had transferred from the local community college near her hometown of Arizona and was the first from their friend group to get married. That night, she was dressed in a stunning teal jumpsuit that complemented her dark skin beautifully.

A buffet was already set on the long tables pushed against the wall, each clad with silver trays of steaming pasta, chicken dishes, salads, and dinner rolls. Bottles of wine sat uncorked in ice baths on the small bar nestled in the opposite corner.

"Finally!" Paige called from across the room.

"Jesus, GG, it's about time." Delia pointed to her watch, dramatically thrust into the air.

"We've been waiting for you!" Imani said with a soft chuckle as she took a sip of the cocktail in her hand.

Paige took the opportunity to greet Greer by pushing a glass of red wine into her hand, showing off the glimmering diamond under the light of the chandelier.

"Look at that thing! It looks stellar, Paige, truly. Delia could not have done better!" Greer exclaimed with a laugh, as she took Paige's hand and examined the ring closely.

She paused to lean to the side and hug another black woman named Angela, who had shared a dormitory all four years with Meredith. Angela's signature box braids were intricately twisted into an elegant bun, and her floral perfume was light against Greer's nose.

Greer kissed Angela on each cheek.

Greer felt her phone buzz in her clutch, and she fished it out with her thumb and forefinger. The message opened with a swipe of her thumb to reveal a response to a picture she had sent Cian of her backside in the black dress she wore.

I want to take that off you. Now I can't stop thinking about how you might taste.

She swallowed thickly, heat pooling in her core, as she shot off a quick: *please find out immediately* in response to Cian before sliding her phone back into place.

Greer managed to inch through the rest of the group and up to her best friend, snaking an arm into the crook of Delia's. "I have an engagement gift for you." Greer bumped her hip playfully against Delia's.

Delia took a sip of her white wine as she looked up. Her dark eyes shone with happiness, evident even through the dim lighting. "You didn't have to do that."

"Of course, I did. Your new fiancée helped me anyways." Paige crossed the room and planted a long kiss on Delia's lips before intertwining their fingers together as Greer turned toward her clutch, pulling out an envelope.

Delia handed her wine glass to Paige as her brow furrowed. "What is this?" She took the envelope from Greer and snuck a finger in to pull up the flap. Slowly, she retrieved the small piece of paper from the interior of the thick envelope. "Wh—is this what I think this is?"

Her eyes widened as she snapped her gaze up to Greer.

Greer looked down at the fold of map clutched preciously in Delia's hand. She had been working on keeping the promise she made to Delia. It was only when Paige was able to find an item that belonged to Delia's brothers that Greer could use it to track them using the same type of locator spell she used for Holly and Celeste.

The spell, along with the map, indicated they were still in the state of Texas on the outskirts of Austin. It was the closest Delia had come in years to finding them.

Delia's eyes pricked with tears as she wrapped her arms around Greer's shoulders, squeezing tightly. "GG, this is— I can't—" She let out a watery laugh. "This is the best gift I could have ever gotten." Delia lifted her hand, gently cupping Paige's cheek, before tilting her chin upward to capture her lips against Paige's. "Thank you, both of you."

"You deserve to find them, to know them," Paige said, as she returned the kiss. "We promised we would help, and that is one promise we refuse to break."

Greer agreed as Delia burst into tears, clutching the piece of map tightly against her heart.

TWENTY-FIVE

Greer called a meeting between the three vampyres and Odette at the breakfast diner nearest her apartment complex. Finding the time and place was easy enough— getting the four of them to agree to meet in the first place was the difficult part.

Bribes, threats, and compensations were involved.

The corner booth was the best place for them to view the skyline; in the shadows enough that the rays wouldn't burn the three vampyres if they sat through the sunrise, but open enough that Greer felt safe in the presence of Jonas. He still made Greer feel uneasy, though she couldn't quite put her finger on why.

Cian leaned over to draw a smiley face into the condensation coating the window, smudging the newly cleaned glass. The movement broke Greer from her thoughts, pulling her back to the group seated in the cracked booth.

Odette scoffed at Cian, her eyes rolling. "I had to be here, why, again?" Odette drawled, tapping the empty coffee cup against the well-scratched tabletop.

"You're part of the team. Plus, I need your help figuring out this Primordial business and *all of you*," Greer seethed the former few words, "are knowledgeable with it."

She paused as a plate-laden waitress clad in a graying apron stopped at their table and deposited a Corned Beef Hash in front of Odette and a French Toast platter in front of Greer. A second waitress followed behind and refilled their mugs, the newly brewed coffee steaming and fragrant.

"You're lucky we're in public," Jonas said, as he leaned forward to place his forearms on the chipped edges of the table. His predator's eye turned to Odette, who sent him a sharp, warning look. "Daemons tend to not get along with one another."

Odette flashed her teeth in a snarl and reached toward her hip for a dagger Greer made her forgo at the door. "Careful, bloodsucker. I bite too."

The silence between them was charged and tense, garnering the attention of a group of elderly men at a table mere feet away. The sizzle of potatoes on the grill top and the scent of bacon grease filled the spaces as Greer picked up the glass dispenser filled with maple syrup, the handle sticky with residue.

"Greer, what would you like to know?" Isaac asked, his deep voice slicing through the strain.

Greer glanced up to zip her eyes between Jonas and Odette. "Oh, are we done? I thought we were still comparing our genitalia."

The quip earned a snort from Isaac and a second growl of warning from Jonas. This time, it was Cian who shot him a sharp look.

"You're meddling in things you don't understand," Jonas said, as he picked up his steaming mug and took a quick sip. Greer wrinkled her nose as he smacked his lips. "There isn't a soul who knows our world who would put us at the same table as her." He gestured toward

Odette, coffee mug still in hand. Some of the liquid dripped over the edge and onto the surface below.

"Agnes would," Cian responded quietly, his arms crossed over his chest.

"Agnes was a two-faced twit who couldn't tell her head from a hole in the wall," Odette snapped.

Cian clenched his jaw as a cool cloud of anger passed over his features. "Agnes did wonders for the daemons. We were on the brink of war for centuries—"

"Agnes did wonders for the daemons Agnes wanted to do wonders for." Odette angrily stabbed her fork into the hash, the tips of her dull fork scraping against the plate. "May I remind you; she was no friend to the Fae who opposed Adair."

"Adair?" Greer asked, as she took a sip of her coffee. "The current Fae King," Cian responded.

Odette hissed under her breath and shook her head. "He is no—"

"No king," Cian bit back, his tone aggravated. "Yeah, we know."

The table went silent once again. Greer took a bite of her French toast and chewed slowly before saying, "Odette, the last time we truly spoke you told me how the Primoridals invaded this world and a war broke out between the two leaders. How did—"

"That's incorrect," Jonas interjected, as he tore his gaze from Greer to Odette. He seemed to revel in the correction— evident by the arm he threw over the back of the booth and the condescending smirk quirking the side of his mouth.

Odette placed her fork on the edge of her plate and looked him over with eyes filled with unimpressed carelessness. "No, it isn't. Those are the tales told to us as Faelings. The Primoridal who created us was a member of the Fallen. They—"

"Are just stories," Jonas shot back. "You know nothing of the world outside of what was told to you as a child." He ran a hand through his red hair as he sat back in the booth. "The Fallen came to this world looking for an escape after losing the War of the Sixteen. The leader brought followers here and it was then he created the daemons, each in the image of the Primordials that followed him through the portal."

Greer's lips parted. "How do you know this?"

"I am old."

"How old?" she pushed, and Cian snapped his eyes over to Jonas.

Jonas cocked his head. "Old enough to know Stonehenge was built as a temple to the Primordials when they still came to Earth. That humans were sacrificed in their names and buried under the stones with high honors."

From the corner of her eye, Greer saw Odette bristle. Greer stayed quiet as the waitress made a second pass to check on the levels of their coffee before marching off, her shoes squeaking against the sticky floor.

"Have you met one before? A Primordial, I mean."

"No. They don't pop up for Sunday brunch." Jonas swallowed and shifted in his seat. "Much like other daemons, vampyres stuck to one corner of the world. The British Isles, Scotland, Ireland. Our villages would expect attacks every few months. We started with war prisoners and eventually began casting members out as punishment, tying them to posts outside of the village."

"From what I understand, villages weren't that big. What happened when you ran out of prisoners?" Greer asked.

Odette's ears twitched forward, the only indication Greer noticed to show she was listening.

"That's how I turned. I volunteered to protect my mother and sisters." Jonas' stare was cold, calculating as it studied her. Greer suppressed a shiver. "What they don't tell you about is the hunger. How quickly you lose your humanity. How nothing and no one comes between you and your next meal."

Isaac was nodding his head, his gaze fixed to a crack in the table. In the background, Greer heard the kitchen bell *ding* as newly plated food appeared in the warming window. One of the waitresses bustled over, grabbing each plate in a hand.

"And your mother and sisters?"

"Died in their beds nearly four thousand years ago."

"So, you did save them."

Jonas snorted unkindly. "I said they died in their beds. I didn't say how."

Greer glued her lips shut, forming a thin, white line to hide her grimace. Pink stained her cheeks, a flush that was not lost on Jonas. She watched his jaw clench, his eyes glaze over with hunger as they dropped to her exposed neck.

Cian must have noticed it too, as he quickly changed the subject. "Jonas, since you know all...why don't you tell Greer what other daemons she can expect to stumble upon. Where they originated, perhaps."

Jonas ripped his gaze away from her throat and re- connected his stare with Greer's. She shrank back as her stomach twisted and his lips curled into a sneering smirk. "Of course." Jonas clicked his tongue against the fangs that had erupted from his gum line. "Wolf shifters from the Germanic region. Sirens, a pod from each of the seven seas. The four realms of the Fae." He nodded toward Odette who remained silent, shoving her fork into the pile of hash. "Shtriga from Eastern Europe. Dragons from China, Japan, and southeastern Asia. Basilisks from the Amazon Rainforest and India." He paused to send a know-ing look to Cian. "Djinn from Sumeria. Ghouls from Arabia."

Greer almost missed the exchange of glances between Cian and Isaac.

"And you can still find most of them right where they were created," Odette said, as she pushed the remainder of her corned beef hash around with her fork. "Which is why we all hate each other."

"It's always been about territory." Isaac shook his head. "Territory and control."

"Agnes could, at the very least, control Adair," Cian said, as he turned a critical eye toward Odette. "Keep him from encroaching on the mortal world. Since her death, though, he's made strides to overtake it."

"The war you were talking about?" Greer piped up as the waitress made a third pass with the coffee carafe. "It's coming from the Fae?"

Odette picked up her napkin to dab at her lips, as she let her fork clatter to the plate. "Yes. Yes, it is. Been in the works for centuries now."

"And you as the Fae general to the old King—"

"That piece is not up for discussion," Odette snapped, her amber eyes flaring.

Greer felt a pulse of frustration shoot through her.

"Maybe not right now, but it will be."

Sparks flew between the two females as they stared at one another.

"Careful, Mage," Odette responded in a hushed voice. "Don't burn your bridges before they're built."

Greer opened her mouth to reply, but Cian pressed in, "I think we can all agree that Greer is more than just the Mage." His eyes bore into Odette's. "And, as the child of a Primordial, it is imperative we have her on our side."

"Why wouldn't she be on our side?" Isaac asked, a forefinger tracing the rim of his coffee cup.

"There are sixteen Primordials, fourteen of which are males. Half of those are Fallen. We know Greer's birth mother was a descendant from the Mage line, and we also know she was the mate of a Primordial. There is no guarantee that her father was a member of the Fallen."

Greer blew out a breath, her head spinning.

"We should ask Eligos," Jonas tacked on, a glint to his eye that made Greer squirm in her seat. "He's got most of the information on the Primordials. He would be easy to summon—"

"We are not summoning Eligos," Cian said through gritted teeth. "There is nothing for him to offer." There was a second exchange between Cian and Isaac that Greer was sure she wasn't supposed to witness.

Additionally, Greer was just as confused by the vitriol response by Cian. "Who is Eligos?"

"Suit yourself, then. Stay in the dark," Jonas skimmed right over Greer's question, drumming his fingers against the side of the table.

"Can I get you guys anything else?" The waitress asked, as she approached the table. Despite her wording, she was already ripping the paper off of the pad she carried in her apron.

Greer glanced out of the smudged window and spotted the orange-hued sky. Tall, purple clouds hung suspended amongst the early rays of the sun.

"I think we're all set," Isaac said, as he glanced over his shoulder.

"You three go ahead. I'll take care of it."

Greer pulled the paper toward her before reaching into her wallet and extracting her debit card. Jonas was already standing on the booth as he clambered over Isaac, his red hair bright against the fluorescent lighting.

"We should meet up soon to work on your magic," Cian said as he, too, hopped over the back of the booth. He sent her a knowing wink, and Greer felt her core heat.

"Ugh, ew." Odette popped out of the booth, batting her wings to let the kinked leather straighten out. "At least let me leave before shifting your scent around. I thought you were better than that."

Greer's cheeks flushed again as Cian and Isaac split from the restaurant, the sun beginning its ascent over the top of the tree line.

Clutching the bill in her hand, Greer wove through the maze of tables, each now filled with commuters grazing the front page of the daily newspaper. Others chatted with office mates as they sipped coffee or dug into scrambled eggs. The two waitresses were bustling through the restaurant, delivering steaming plates of food and refilling coffee mugs. A line had already formed near the front door; groups awaiting a table to open.

"What do you think of Jonas?" Greer asked, as she handed the bill and her debit card to the waitress manning the register.

"I think he's old, and that makes him dangerous," Odette replied, as she tucked her wings tighter to her back to allow a waitress to scoot past.

Greer was only mildly surprised by the response. "Why would being old make him dangerous?"

Odette shifted on her feet as the waitress ripped the receipt from the register and handed it to Greer. "He's been around long enough to learn how to pull the strings."

Greer glanced thoughtfully back at Odette. "Haven't you?"

Odette narrowed her eyes at Greer, though the action was in consideration rather than irritation. "Not well enough to keep Adair off the throne. Not well enough to stop him from flooding into the human world." The door chimed as they stepped from the restaurant and into the late summer morning. "And not well enough to know how to fix it."

Greer assumed the last sentence was said more to herself than to Greer. She watched as Odette spread her wings, thrusting herself into the air, wings shimmering against the sun.

TWENTY-SIX

JONAS

Fat raindrops *plunked* against the bowing veranda as Jonas sat in the armchair at the old, abandoned house he moved the vampyre coven into. It was another farmhouse, this one uninhabited, and it bore a cobblestone front covered in ivy and vines. The windows had long been broken and the previous owners left the window casing clumsily boarded. Thick gaps separated the soggy planks of wood and, it was there, Jonas noticed the jagged glass lying in large pieces in the overgrown garden.

The inside was just as broken as the out. Abandoned furniture littered each room and the patterned wallpaper hung in large strips, showcasing the spotted mold, water stains, and chunks of glue that had been hidden beneath. The electricity had long since been disconnected and someone had scavenged for the copper wiring, leaving the blue and green jacket covers to dangle like worms from each light socket.

The storm clouds that gathered on the horizon only grew taller and taller against the mountain peaks. Jonas kept an eye on them, enjoying the breeze wafting in through the boarded windows. The gusts blew away the mustiness from the water leaks, bringing it fresh scents of impending rain. The only thing he worried about was the hole in the roof, but even that wouldn't be enough to deter him from his find.

The house was quiet, neglected, and, most importantly, isolated.

"Again." Jonas steepled his fingers together as he rested his elbows on the armchair. The old, yellowed stitching pulled under the pressure.

Greer's brow was slicked with a thin layer of sweat, her concentration on the eagle feather in front of her stilling her features.

"You're not breathing."

Greer let out the air she had been holding, her chest puffed under the thin t-shirt she wore. "I'm trying to focus," she replied, not taking her eyes off the feather.

Thunder rolled in the distance, echoing across the wildflower field. The breeze picked up again, fluttering through the barbules and lifting the feather from the end table. Greer slammed it down with a palm, and Jonas scoffed at the childlike reaction.

He had been put on babysitting duty. At least, that's how it felt. Jonas could think of a host of things he would prefer to do than help the human learn how to control her magic.

Cian and Isaac were three towns over raiding the local blood bank. They would bring back coolers stuffed to the brim with blood bags and give him excuses as to why he shouldn't have to go out and hunt. Jonas would have to swallow his pride and down each stale, over-processed bag of blood.

He preferred to hunt. To feel the bodies squirm beneath him, to smell the fear under the skin, to see the wide-eyes of his victims when they realized what he was going to do. Most of them pissed themselves, a few of them ran, but he enjoyed the taste of their warm, surging blood nonetheless. If he were being honest with himself, he particularly enjoyed watching Cian and Isaac clean up his messes.

Removing the heads from the bodies was the closest thing to a religious experience he was sure to ever get.

Unfortunately, this was part of the reason Greer— *the Mage*— had forced them to move to a different part of town. Three missing girls was bad enough. The bodies of three missing girls washing up on the banks of the river that ran through town, each missing their head, was the work of a serial killer.

Not that Jonas could dispute it. He had been keeping a canine tooth from each victim since the day he had been turned.

Jonas needed to correct himself. Running his hands through the bag filled with thousands of teeth he had collected over the years— *that* was the closest thing to a religious experience he was sure to ever get.

Jonas would worship at that altar for hours. Would wrap his hand around his cock and remember the pain, the fear, the panic that filled his senses with every bite he took. He was quiet for a beat before speaking again. "If you focus anymore, you're going to pop a vessel in your brain."

Greer sat back on her heels and glowered at him. An enchanted eagle feather was the first ingredient to the sun potion Cian wanted and, luckily for Jonas, Greer was having a hard time with the first step. He never understood why his friend wanted to walk in the sun so badly.

Jonas reveled in the dark, in the silver moonlight, in the shadows. That's where they belonged and that's where he wanted to stay.

"Do you have anything constructive to say?" Greer asked, frustration lacing her tone.

The room grew darker as the storm rolled in and thunder echoed for a second time, shaking the floor beneath his feet. The breeze played in her hair, pushing the locks over her shoulder and uncovering the side of her neck. Jonas watched as the artery pulsed just beneath the skin, and he felt himself twitch at the ratcheting of her heartbeat.

"Do better?"

Greer closed her eyes and, for a moment, Jonas thought she was going to throw something at him. He wished that she would.

"This is really difficult," Greer finally said, her gray eyes opening to connect with his. "It's like there's a block in my mind stopping me from accessing anything." She lifted her hands over the feather. "I can feel it, I...just...can't..." She trailed off and groaned, letting her hands fall into her lap.

"Remove the block," Jonas responded, as if the answer were obvious.

Greer sucked in an agitated breath and stared at him with a blank expression. "My God, I wonder how I functioned before I met you."

It was his turn to glower. "Agnes could—"

Greer slammed her hands onto the end table and the eagle feather fluttered to the dirty carpet she knelt on. "But I'm *not* Agnes," she said sharply. "I'm not this five hundred years old amazing witch who could manage her magic or stop wars. I'm just a nobody who can't seem to do even the simplest of spells from that damn grimoire." She pressed her palms against her eyeballs, scrubbing down her face until the skin under her sockets pulled to reveal the pink tissue underneath.

Jonas watched her swallow, the lump in her throat bobbing. "Are you done?" he asked, boredom slicing through his voice.

Greer's head snapped to the side as she turned to look at him, jaw clenching. Thunder cracked through the house as those fat droplets of water fell harder, bouncing off the wood of the veranda, but Jonas still heard that hissed, "Fuck you," escape from her lips.

Jonas was on her in less time than it took for the lightning to follow, illuminating the room with a bright flash. His hand clamped tightly around her jaw as his fangs jutted downward, exposed and snarling.

"Get off of me," Greer said, slowly enunciating each word.

Jonas was pleased to see not a shred of fear flash in those eyes. "Or what?" he said, his tone critical and condescending. He tilted his head, but kept his gaze tight onto her. "You're alone out here, kitten. Why don't we see how you purr?"

Sizzling flesh filled the space between them, in both sound and smell. Smoke unfurled from under his fingers in white curls, rising into the air. The pads of Jonas's fingertips began to burn hotter and hotter the longer he held on. He felt his jaw clench reflexively against the pain, and a pang of anger twisted in his chest when he saw her eyes sink down to his clenching jaw.

A smirk grew on her lips, and it took every ounce of his restraint to not rip them from her face. His grip tightened on her as the smoke rose faster and thicker with each passing second. His fingers beginning to blacken, Jonas let out a roar of rage and pain as he yanked his hand back from her jaw. Hand shaking, he glanced down to study the taut skin. It was brittle like old leather.

Greer, however, remained unscathed.

She shot up from her kneeled position and approached him, thunder rolling louder and deeper now, her stare intense and unblinking. She reached out and, this time, it was her hand that clamped around the scruff of his jaw. He felt the skin beneath her fingers begin to burn, and he let out an instinctive aching grunt.

Greer leaned in close, her breath tickling the lobe of his ear as she said, "Touch me again, Jonas, and I'll make sure it's your dick that burns off. Do we understand one another?"

He attempted a smirk, and her fingers cemented even further against his jaw. So many calculating thoughts eddied through his mind. He liked seeing her this way, liked the power she held and the way she wielded it. Liked how she made him hurt, made him burn.

Cian couldn't pull this from her, couldn't shape her the way that he could.

"Understood," Jonas simmered out, disappointed that Greer immediately released his cheeks. He dropped to the floor, and his knees cracked against the wood.

It didn't take her long to gather her things and walk out the door, the engine of her Jeep barely audible over the storm raging just outside. Jonas laughed, low and throaty, as he assessed the tips of his fingers. The burnt patches were

already healing, thick scabs coating the skin.

"I would say that went well," a voice said from behind. Jonas' gaze slipped over his shoulder in time to see the short, stout man emerge from the shadows. "I wonder who would kill you first if you tried that again. Her, Cian, or her father."

Jonas pushed himself up to full height, adjusting his shirt and jacket as he did.

The rain came in droves now, a wet wall of water thundering onto the damaged roof above them. Jonas could hear the rain dripping into the second-floor bedrooms.

"Eligos," Jonas greeted the djinn. He took a moment to look over the receding hairline, the too-short pants, and the overhanging belly. He wasn't surprised that the male found Greer; it was only a matter of time. "To what do I owe the pleasure?"

"Came to see how Cian's plans are going," Eligos said with a casual air, though his voice was edged with something much darker.

Jonas snorted with derision. "Cian's plans are non-existent if that answers your first question." He paused for a moment to think and a roll of thunder sounded, so violent that the walls of the house rattled. "I would hope that Greer would try to kill me first. She made a promise."

"She sure has her father's temper. Could be a draw." Jonas stilled. "You know who he is?"

"Of course. There's a reason her power is overtaking the magic of the Mage." Eligos clicked his tongue. "It was really only a matter of time before it all came tumbling out of her, poor dear. All it took was a hole the size of a pin-prick, and her father's power infiltrated her soul like a tangled web. I daresay he gave her too much of it."

"Gave her too much of it?" Jonas asked.

"Oh yes," Eligos was beaming, clearly enjoying himself, "Primordials can decide how much of their power to give their offspring. Didn't you know?"

The pattering rain was the only thing that stood between them for a heartbeat.

"You said you knew who her father was. Are you going to share with the class or would you prefer me to guess?"

"The guesses are limited, but if that's the little game you'd prefer to play, then sure. Be my guest." Jonas stared blankly at him.

"You ruin all the fun," Eligos pouted, but Jonas felt that scalding wrath creeping just under the surface. "I will tell you, but only if you agree to a tiny deal. Just a favor. Quid pro quo, if you will."

Jonas sighed as he leaned his forearms on the back of the lumpy, orange armchair. "Depends on the favor, you know this."

"I want that girl dead."

Jonas slowly raised his brow. "I remember you telling Cian that you wanted her power. What changed?"

Eligos took a step forward. "Energy is energy, magic is magic, it can neither live nor die, but it can be transferred." He grabbed a horse figurine off the fireplace mantel, looked it over for a moment, then tossed it over his shoulder. Jonas heard the *tinkle* of porcelain against wood as it shattered. "And nearly thirty percent of a Primordial's power being transferred to me would be...well, it would surely help the plans I have with the Fae King."

"Thirty percent?" Jonas drew his head back. "That's—"

"Unheard of," Eligos finished for him. "The largest cache of power outside of Samsara itself."

Jonas turned away, his fingertips tingling with discomfort as the scabs loosened and fell to the floor. "What Primordial would give away that much power. Which Primordial has that much power to—" He paused and whirled back to face Eligos. "No, it's not—"

"*Him?* Yes."

Jonas stared at Eligos with a blank expression long enough for a smirk to appear on the djinn's face. But then, Jonas let out a laugh so loud that Eligos jolted, his smirk falling into a scowl of agitation. Jonas doubled over, banding an arm across his belly as he laughed, and laughed, and laughed.

"You...you expect me to kill the daughter of *Azazel?* Lucifer himself?" Jonas howled, clapping a freckled hand against his knee. He managed to sober, sighing deeply. "Even if I could kill her, Azazel will scent me on her immediately. There is nothing in this world I want worth having him on my tail for the rest of my very numbered days."

Eligos took another step forward, and Jonas felt awash in the dread and wickedness that came with being in the vicinity of a djinn.

"What if I told you, dear man, that I would be using her power to close the portals to Samsara? That we would be opening the Fae realms and enslaving every man, woman, and child on this godforsaken planet?" Eligos took in a breath. "And what if I offered you the one thing I know you've always craved— power."

Jonas tilted his head. "I'm listening."

Eligos gestured for Jonas to take a seat in the armchair that still boasted his forearms. "You are a rare creature, Jonas. Created by Darragh, the first vampyre himself— considered a first generation to the original. Only three of you left in the world. Kill Greer, close Samsara, and kill Darragh. Be the commander to the vampyres. Have every human at your absolute disposal."

Jonas let his imagination run wild. He could feel Eligos watching him. "Terms," Jonas said swiftly, as he sank into the armchair. "I told Greer I would contact you for information on the Princes. I need to hold that bargain to remain trustworthy."

"Done with a counter."

Jonas waited silently; his hands folded in his lap. "I need that grimoire. Find it, and bring it to me."

"The grimoire is protected; it always has been."

Eligos smiled, a toothy grin that spelled fear to most of the daemons in the human realm. "Her power dims with each day the Primordial side of her takes over. Soon, the grimoire will be unprotected. Just any other leather-bound book."

Jonas leaned back and steepled his newly-healed fingers, the smile finally spreading on his face too.

TWENTY-SEVEN

Greer leaned against Delia, her arm thrown tightly around her best friend's shoulders, as they stumbled across the parking lot. Delia hadn't stopped giggling the entire walk back from the Mexican restaurant, even after she tripped over the curb and skinned her knees on the asphalt.

"It's too bad Paige had to work late," Greer managed to slur out. "She's always the best after shots of tequila."

"I get to have Paige for the rest of my life," Delia declared, yelling the last few words at the top of her voice. She stopped walking to splay her arms to her side in a dramatic fashion, still ignoring the blood trickling down from the gravel-filled laceration. "But you...I only get the Sage for how much longer?"

"It's Mage, M-a-g-e," Greer spelled it out as they crossed the grassy lawn toward the front door of the apartment building. She grasped the handle and yanked, dismay filling her when it didn't budge. "Oh, shit. A key. The door— Delia, the door needs a key."

Delia wasn't listening. She was busy unbuckling the straps of her heels. She groaned as she set her foot down onto the cool, wet sidewalk. "That feels like heaven against this blister." Her head slowly lifted at Greer's voice, but she was thrown off balance by the height difference from her missing shoe. Delia staggered back in a poor attempt to catch herself and landed flat on her back in a mud puddle.

Thunder crackled in the distance, echoing against the mountains surrounding the city. The lightning that followed was dull behind the clouds. Greer felt the humidity against her skin as she let out a drunken cackle at the sight of Delia's parted lips and wide eyes.

"You even laugh like a witch," Delia lamented, pushing herself out of the mud and attempting to wipe the dirt off her backside. She succeeded in merely smearing it further. Delia lurched toward Greer, lifting a hand to point toward Greer's upper lip. "I think you have a wart right—"

Greer smacked Delia's hand away, and they broke into another peal of giggles when one of their neighbors unlatched the door with his key, holding it open for them to enter the stairway. Delia's single black pump remained on the sidewalk.

Both women watched their neighbor, a college-aged man with shagged blonde hair named Tyler, climb the staircase. Greer looked on with a dizzy head and spinning vision, as if the stairs were Mount Everest, grand and looming.

Greer was the first to move. She stumbled forward and wrapped both hands around the handrail mounted to the exposed brick wall. *One foot up, haul herself upward with her upper body strength. Second foot up, haul herself upward with her upper body strength.* Greer cleared four stairs and, swaying, she glanced over her shoulder to see how Delia was fairing.

Her brow pulled together in confusion when the stairway was empty, but then Greer glanced down. Delia had fallen to all fours and was attempting to crawl up the stairs, one foot bare and the other still strapped into her heel. Greer let out a second cackle as she pulled herself onto the fifth step, then the sixth.

Delia didn't seem to know, or particularly care, that she was giving herself carpet burn on her already serrated knees. Greer reached the landing of the second floor before Delia did. She was so screwed— they were both so screwed. It would be a miracle if they weren't still drunk for work in the morning. Greer watched as Delia lugged herself onto the edge of the landing before pressing her cheek against the dirty, old carpet.

"Leave me here to die," Delia moaned before a deep hiccup reverberated from her chest. Her usual pristine curls fell into a jumbled mess on either side of her face, sticking into the smeared mascara that bled down her cheeks.

Greer stooped down, pausing for a moment to throw out a hand and catch herself against the wall, before grasping Delia under the arms and giving her a good tug.

Delia didn't budge, but Greer slipped backward and fell clean onto her tailbone.

Eyes closed with her cheek still pressed against the edge of the landing, Delia let out a tittering snicker before moaning a second time. "God, GG, what is that smell?" She snuck her hand from where it was pinned beneath her to cover her wrinkled nose.

"You're covered in mud."

Delia scoffed. "No, it's not that. It smells...rotten."

Lightning flashed through the window, brighter and closer in proximity this time around. It illuminated the landing, casting long shadows onto their faces. Greer realized the ceiling light was blinking and she momentarily wondered when that had started. Or if anyone else had noticed.

"I showered today," Greer said, remembering the conversation she was in. Her chin dipped as she swung it around to look at Delia.

"It's not you, Hermione Granger."

Greer cracked a smile.

Delia managed to stagger to her feet, catching herself against the wall as Greer once did. She glanced down to take in her torn and swollen knees before stumbling into the hallway. "Keys, I need keys. Keeeeeeeys," Delia was mumbling under her breath. She walked as if the hallway were tilted, her shoulder rotating between brushing and bouncing against the scuffed drywall.

Greer used the windowsill to pull herself to standing and the lightning flashed again, forking across the sky. She squinted with the sudden brightness as she braced against the glass. A handprint smudged the clean window.

"GG, thank God," Delia said loudly, as she reached their apartment door. "We didn't latch the door." There was a pause before she went on, "I don't think I could work a key." She giggled, and Greer heard the door squeak as Delia swung it open.

Greer blinked furiously. Something nagged at the back of her skull. Something was wrong. What could be wrong? The night had been so fun. Why was the hallway so blurry? Her mind was swimming in tequila. She floundered after Delia, her surroundings spinning around her as she moved.

Greer let out a long exhale as she crossed the threshold of the apartment, using the doorframe to balance herself when she rounded the corner.

"Dels?" she croaked.

Something was definitely wrong. Greer couldn't quite put her finger on it. Maybe it was the twisted and broken furniture. Perhaps it was the smashed vases, the patterned pieces littering the floor. Flowers that had previously resided in the smashed vases were torn apart and peppered the couch cushions.

And the smell...*the smell*. A rancid, rotting mix of saltwater fish and the juice that sat at the bottom of a garbage bin.

"Dels?" Greer was covering her nose now as she ventured deeper into the apartment. "Where are you?"

Delia popped her head around the corner of the kitchen. She was clutching a garbage bag in her hand, tied together with the orange, plastic ribbons. Her shirt was pulled halfway up her face, a poor attempt to stave away the smell.

"It's not this—" Delia trailed off, following Greer's horrified gaze.

Only darkness was there...until it wasn't.

The ceiling in the back corner of the hallway moved as a scratching scuttle sounded across the drywall. Greer spotted the hairy legs as it stepped from the shadows, the gray armored shell covered in thick spikes, the sharp claws that ended in pincers. It stood on the ceiling, upside down, and Greer could see a metasoma similar to that of a scorpion dangling toward the ground. It ended in a sharp stinger and, in the back of her drunken mind, she knew that it would be fatal to be stuck with it.

The creature moved in a flash, scurrying across the ceiling in a race of pincers and claws. Delia let out a sharp scream as she swung the garbage bag at it, knocking it from the ceiling. It hit the floor with a sharp thud, righting itself just as quickly.

Greer's body froze as she watched the quick legs hurry toward her. Faster and faster it moved, and the sober part of her brain, hidden away by the four margaritas she had downed at dinner, yelled at her to *run, run, run!*

She threw herself backwards, staggering into the living room and tripping over a broken leg of the accent chair.

Her mind spun, the room with it, as she struggled to move away from the creature. The smell gagged her, punching down her throat and infiltrating every sense she had. She could taste it, the rotting scent coating her tongue. She felt something snap beneath her sandal and a sharp pain blasted through her heel and up the back of her leg. Her knee buckled and she fell to the floor.

A piece of vase stuck from the bottom of her foot, thick and jagged. Blood poured from the wound, dripping off the edge and staining the carpet.

"*Greer!*"

She snapped her head up in time to see one of those sharp pincers slice at her. She dodged the claw with a roll to the side, and the creature emitted a harsh, angry click. The sound was otherworldly, and her skin pebbled when she heard it. More glass punctured her arms and legs as she pushed herself to standing, managing to clear the back of the couch with a stumbling jump.

"Duck!"

Greer hit the floor, covering her head with her hands. An ear-splitting *pang* resounded through the apartment, followed by another set of angry clicks. Greer lifted her head to see Delia standing above her, the garbage bag replaced in her hand by a large saucepan.

Delia held it by the handle and the first hit had chipped the black paint from the side. She swung it at the creature once again, catching it in the head. A dent the shape of a pincer formed in the cookware and a crack split the side, cleaving the handle away. The pan clattered to the floor, bouncing away from her.

The creature seemed to sense that Delia was now defenseless, as it quickly turned its attention toward her. The sharp stinger at the back thrust over the back of its body, aiming for Delia's exposed upper thigh. She jumped back and hopped onto the counter with expert dexterity. It scuttled after her, and Greer realized that Delia wasn't quite out of range from the stinger.

Delia realized that as well. She kicked forward, scooting herself over the counter. Coffee mugs, loose silverware, and the black paper towel stand clattered to the floor in her wake, raining down on the creature. With every *thunk* of an item on the back of its armor, the creature grew increasingly agitated. The thrusts of the stinger became erratic and disjointed. It stuck into the cabinet doors, splintering the wood and sending shards flying across the small kitchen. Delia's back flushed to the side of the refrigerator.

Greer reached down and wrenched the glass from her foot, letting it clatter to the floor. She launched herself forward, sliding across the surface of the dining room table and leaving bloody footprints behind her. She threw her hands toward the creature and let out a shriek of panic as the stinger drove up, aiming for Delia's calf. Greer willed the creature to freeze, pushing all of her might into the release of energy.

The air around them thrummed and pulsed, waves of power flowed from every exposed surface of Greer's body. It shimmered and swirled, distorting the room into a kaleidoscope of shapes and colors. Time slowed to a crawling pace as a whoosh of wind surrounded them, rushing past her ears as though she were in a tight tunnel. The energy narrowed and, in an instant, focused entirely on the creature.

The room shuddered into a vacuum of silence and then...the creature exploded.

Piles of rotting meat and blackened blood enveloped the apartment, coating every surface in a gooey consistency. Shards of the armor bolted from its back like missiles, and Greer dove into the hallway to take cover. She could still feel the splinters poking her back, ripping into her legs.

The dust settled and for a moment, it was quiet. A heap of flesh, hanging precariously from the top of the fridge, fell in slow motion before slapping to the floor with a stomach-clenching squelch.

"What...was that?" Delia asked, her cheeks pale as she scanned the apartment with wide eyes.

"A devil. I think." Greer put light pressure on her heel. She was surprised when the expected throbbing never came, and she lifted her foot to inspect the sole. It had already healed, the skin painted red with her drying blood.

Delia slowly uncurled from her position on the counter

and toed her way down to the kitchen floor. She had lost her second shoe in the assault. "Was that...was that thing here for you?"

Greer nodded her head. "Yes, I think so." She was more surprised that none of her neighbors had heard. Heading toward the front door, she stuck her head over the threshold and looked to the right, then the left. Every door remained closed, unbothered.

Greer took a step back to study the doorframe, her eyes sweeping across the threshold.

It shimmered as Delia switched the living room light on. Subtle and iridescent.

"What is it?"

"I— I think someone sound-proofed the apartment," Greer responded, uncertainty lacing her tone. "There's an odd glimmer here." She glanced over her shoulder, eyes connecting with Delia. "And Mister Kulikowski isn't banging on the door."

Delia cleared her throat as she bent down to scoop a chair leg from the floor. She held it for a moment, deep in thought, before tossing it onto a ripped couch cushion. "GG, if Paige had been here waiting—"

"I know."

"...If we had been here for dinner—"

"I *know*."

Delia fell silent, clamping her lips together. They formed a thin, pale line against her tanned skin.

Greer took in a deep breath before blowing it back out. She spun on her heel and marched into her bedroom, throwing open the door. It hit the wall behind it with a bang. She sighed through her nose as she assessed the scene in front of her.

The bed was turned over and thrown into the corner of the room. Every article of clothing she owned ripped from the dressers and strewn onto the floor. The mirrors were shattered, the glass covered with piles of shirts, as if the person didn't want to see their own reflection. The curtains had been torn from the rods, hanging limply from the snapped metal.

A small gasp escaped Delia's lips as she halted behind Greer.

Greer picked over the carnage, kicking debris to the side as she waded through the ocean of trash and clothes. She rounded the corner toward the bathroom, spotting the closet doors. They had been yanked from the metal tracks and thrown into the bathroom, where they leaned haphazardly between the toilet and the shower.

That wasn't what caught Greer's eye, though.

A soft glow emanated from the back of the closet, a resonating blue. The light had no source that Greer could see, but it completely encircled the grimoire she had hiding in the back corner. This must have been what that person was looking for. It was the only thing that remained untouched. She glanced down, seeing that the floating shelves had

been removed from the walls and used as a battering ram against the fiery blue. The ends of the shelves, originally painted white, were charred black. The smell of burnt charcoal wafted from the closet, and Greer could see that the smoke curled from the carpet where the shelves had been thrown.

"GG, be careful," Delia said in a hushed tone, as Greer took a step into the closet.

Greer approached the blue hue, anticipating to be washed in a bath of warmth from the light. Her brows rose. She bent down and scooped up the grimoire, her hand entering the blue light as if it weren't there.

At her touch, the light winked out.

TWENTY-EIGHT

T he week was the busiest one Greer had experienced in quite some time. Between spending more and more time at work trying to balance the exhibit opening, one that Deborah had enthusiastically agreed to, buying new furniture, and debating about how to handle the devil in her apartment, Greer felt like she was burning the candle at both ends.

While the exhibit planning was coming along, and she had decided to connect with an event planner through the university to help her with layout and design, there was one piece that Greer didn't realize she needed to navigate.

Erin.

Her officemate had become increasingly distant since Greer had accepted the exhibit position from Henry. It started with little things: not showing Greer new research, snorting with derision when Greer got off the phone with the event planner or tribal council, making comments under her breath about Greer being a sellout by not focusing on her research any longer.

It escalated over the weekend when Erin waited until Greer went to the archives to grab a coffee from the café with Daniel— something she the two women had done as a team at two every afternoon.

"She's just jealous she wasn't picked," Paige had said over dinner one evening after Greer had voiced her frustrations. "I bet she was expecting to get the job after everything that happened with your mom."

Delia took a sip of wine. "Are you sure you didn't do anything to upset her? I thought your working relationship was good."

Greer sighed. "I thought so too. Daniel just sends me these sad little smiles. I think he's trying to stay neutral, but doesn't quite know how."

The situation came to head early Monday morning when Greer asked Erin if there was anything she did to upset her officemate. To which Erin looked down her nose, shuffled a stack of papers on her desk, and proceeded to tell Greer that the only reason she received the promotion was because she had two dead mothers. Daniel's eyes had widened, though he stayed quiet, and immediately turned to his computer to appear busy.

Greer's lips parted in surprise as she looked at Erin, who returned the stare with a smug, humorless smile. Greer cleared her throat before telling Erin that she had been planning to bring Erin on as a co-host for the exhibit in hopes they would both get chosen to transfer to Greece, but now Erin could kiss that opportunity goodbye.

While that wasn't necessarily the truth, Greer still felt a zing of satisfaction as she watched that smug grin slide to Erin's sandal-clad toes. Greer left the office soon after and had been working from the silent floor of the library that overlooked the distant mountains ever since.

"I'm going to beat her ass," Delia had said that night when Greer filled her in over a beer at an establishment called Brass Cannon Aleworks.

The brewery was a cute place— small with long tables akin to a German beer hall rather than a standard brewery. A large, circular chandelier dressed in faux greenery hung from the white ceiling. On the weekends, live bands played on the stage located in the beer garden. They had been giving a wide berth to the Mexican restaurant since the night of the devil, though Greer suspected that was due to how shitty they felt the next morning after four margaritas each.

"Tell me where she lives, I'm going to—" Delia finished her sentence by sliding into Spanish, something she only did when she was spitting angry.

"If anything, I can have a go at her first," Greer said as her magic prickled at her fingertips. "Though I might accidentally burn the library down or summon a giant squid. Truly, it's all up in the air."

It was in that same conversation that Greer tentatively brought up the devil and mentioned, while swirling her beer around the stein, that she had made the decision to move out of the apartment. She felt a heaviness lift from her shoulders as she voiced it aloud for the first time and knew that, had she been standing, her knees would have been wobbly and weak.

Delia was silent for a minute and watched her with a keen, steady gaze. Greer focused on the thumps of the beer glasses against the wooden table tops as the group behind them talked and laughed. A gurgle of foam sounded from the beer tap behind the bar as the keg emptied and a sizzling plate of freshly baked pretzels was delivered to the table to their left.

The group of men descended on it like a pack of ravenous hyenas.

"You don't need to do that," Delia finally responded, though she didn't quite look like she had convinced herself of that.

Greer scanned Delia's features, half in shadows from the dim lighting of the brewery. "Dels, we both know that I do." She leaned forward to take Delia's hands into her own. "You said it yourself. What if Paige was home, what if we hadn't gone out for drinks. Whoever sent the devil came to steal the grimoire. It, and I, have to go."

Delia adjusted in her seat, looking toward a group of women to her right who were absorbed in a quiz printed in a women's love and fashion magazine. From their giggles, Greer thought it was a sex quiz.

"Where will you go?" Delia asked, her bright, brown eyes shifting back to Greer.

"I already put in an application for a house on the other side of town. It's small and further from campus, but it'll work. It was accepted this afternoon, and it'll be ready tomorrow. The previous tenant moved out two weeks ago."

Delia picked up her beer glass and took a long gulp, her throat bobbing as the tears pricked the corner of her eyes. "We've lived together for the better part of ten years. It's going to be strange being without you." She chuckled as the empty glass clinked against the table.

Greer's chest constricted as her throat grew thick, a lump forming that she struggled to swallow past. "It had to come to an end sooner or later. Paige is moving in and you two deserve to start a life together."

Delia let out a wet laugh, her eyes leaking down her cheeks. "We talked about that last night, actually. We just assumed you would be coming with us."

"Let me rephrase then." Greer's eyes brightened as she imagined the conversation between her two best friends. "You and Paige deserve to start a life together. Alone. Without the looming threat of death from the Paladin Society breathing down your necks."

"Fine, fine," Delia lamented. "It's only twenty minutes away." Her features grew solemn. A grim twist formed from her smile. "Promise me one thing."

Greer took a sip of her drink as laughter blasted from a rowdy group toward the rear of the brewery. "Anything."

Delia hesitated as if she were weighing her words. Her gaze dropped as she picked her fingernail against a groove in the table. "Be careful with Cian, okay?" Greer opened her mouth to object, but Delia quickly went on. "I know, GG, I know you like him. It's been a long time since you've met someone you liked. But—" She paused to sigh. "You tend to jump first and ask questions later. I'm not so sure he would be there to catch you."

Greer leaned away, her posture stiffening as she licked her lips. She was going to argue and had even steeled herself to it. But Greer looked into Delia's eyes, pleading and full of care, and she felt herself soften. "I promise. I will be careful, Dels."

Two days later, the last box was packed and taped shut.

With the help of Cian, Greer had been working long into the night to make sure everything was ready to move. She remembered back to the conversation she had with Delia at the brewery and didn't quite meet her eyes when Cian walked through the door. Delia said nothing, merely greeted Cian with a tight smile before returning to help Greer pack.

Greer knew that her best friend was swallowing back any comment with difficulty.

Paige was in the process of loading a box onto the moving van as Greer stood from her slouched position, massaging her tight lower back. She surveyed the empty bedroom, her heart cleaving in two for the umpteenth time that day. It was quiet, save for the late summer, early autumn rain pattering against the window pane. She was going to miss this place; the sun shining through the slit of the curtains in the morning, the forest visible from the balcony off of the living room.

"I think everything is packed up," a voice from behind echoed into the empty space. Greer turned, spotting Delia leaning against the door frame. Delia's eyes were red- rimmed with frequent tears, and she shoved off the frame with her shoulder. "I didn't think this would be so hard." Greer held her arms out and Delia walked into them.

She wound her arms around Delia's shoulders and tightened them into a hug. "You have to let me fly the nest," Greer said with a chuckle.

Delia sniffled as she pulled back to wipe her cheeks with the sleeve of her shirt. "The only positive to all of this is Paige moving in this weekend."

"She should have moved in years ago."

Delia laughed and sniffled once more. "You're right, she should have." She closed her eyes tightly in a poor attempt to keep her tears at bay. They dripped from her lashes, sliding down her cheeks. "It should have been the three of us living here. I'm so angry we didn't have that. I feel like it got stolen from us."

Greer placed a comforting hand on Delia's back. "She lived here half of the week anyways. Now she's finally contributing to all of the water and groceries she uses."

"Oh, thanks, GG." Paige crossed the threshold into the bedroom, stepping over a small pile of trash that still needed to be bagged. She threw an arm over Greer's shoulders, nonetheless. "I'm going to miss you too."

"Come on," Greer said after a beat of silence. "You two being my people means you are obligated to help me move."

Delia and Paige groaned as Greer hooked her arm around each of their elbows.

"I hate moving," Delia moaned, as she dragged her feet across the empty bedroom.

"But we're so good at it," Greer retorted. "That's why we've done it every year since college."

Greer and Delia had begun to pull on their shoes when Cian jogged into the apartment, his silver rings reflecting against the overhead light as he rubbed his hands together.

"Ready?"

Delia finally broke and scoffed in response. Their relationship had barely thawed in the last few weeks, remaining nearly as icy as the day they met. Delia had never voiced it, but Greer had a sneaking suspicion that Delia blamed Cian for everything that happened with Greer. Delia marched past him, fixing her curly, dark hair back into the claw clip. Cian turned to look at Greer and Paige. "What now?"

Greer shrugged and grabbed her keys from the counter. "She thinks you're a walking red flag."

Paige snorted with laughter and followed Delia down the hallway of the building.

"You can't sense anything when you live in a cave and sleep upside down," Cian grumbled, closing the front door behind him.

"Takes one to know one," Greer said in a sing-song voice, as they made their way down the stairs and into the parking lot.

The sun was setting earlier and earlier now that autumn was knocking on the door. The breeze had turned cooler in the last few days, and it plucked the wet leaves from their branches where they fell to the pavement in thick clumps. Students had moved back to campus, and the new semester at the university was due to start in the following weeks. The town had come alive again and Greer reveled in it.

The house she decided to rent was truly only fifteen minutes away. She maneuvered through the side streets, their lamps gleaming like bright orbs off of the damp asphalt. The boxes in the trunk of her Jeep shifted with every turn of the wheel.

She rolled into the gravel driveway, spotting Isaac and Paige in the front window as they situated boxes from one room to the next. Greer half-expected Jonas to be lurking in the shadows and was only a little surprised that he wasn't. Delia had already parked her car and was carrying a box up the steps of the wooden porch.

The house, though outdated, was cute enough; a small, two-bedroom on the outskirts of town and partially paid for with the estate money from her mother's death. Greer certainly would not have been able to afford it on her university salary alone.

The flower planters at the base of the porch were over- grown, as was the backyard, but that was fenced at the very least. The light fixed to the side of the house flickered, the bulb probably old. The gutters were clogged with old leaves. The sodden wooden porch sagged under her weight and the sheeted, aluminum exterior was peeling in places. Aside from that, she had a beautiful view of the mountains and a stream ran just outside of the fence line, the soothing sound of trickling water weaving into the house. Her closest neighbor was half a mile away, giving her immense amounts of privacy that the apartment couldn't afford.

Greer made her way to the trunk, where Cian had already opened the hatch of the Jeep and was pulling a box toward him. He placed it in her arms before she crossed the yard, the grass squelching under her shoes.

She bumped the front door open with a hip.

"That one goes in the bathroom!" Paige was calling over to Isaac. He slid the box toward the hallway, kicking it with his foot across the wood floors.

Greer set her box down on the kitchen counter. The pale, yellow laminate was going to be a big change from the marble of the luxury-style apartment. She glanced at the white cabinets, the paint chipping from the corners, and sighed.

Cian entered the kitchen and set his box down next to hers. "Yellow, classic." He pointed up to the strip of wallpaper that lined the wall near the ceiling. "And chickens. I didn't know an eighty-year-old woman was your inspiration."

"If I owned the house, I would just have you fix it for me." She opened the box in front of her and reached in to pull out a stack of plates.

"I have excellent taste." His arm brushed against hers as he reached into the open box, and Greer felt her stomach clench. "I'm thinking of bright green everything. We can keep that chicken wallpaper though."

Greer laughed.

They worked in silence for a while, unpacking the boxes that Isaac slid into each room. The air felt heavy between them as they stood side-by-side. She would shoot him a sidelong glance through her curtain of hair, studying the curve of his nose and the way his lips quirked when their hands touched. She could feel his gaze on her when she turned away. A few times he opened his mouth to speak before clamping it shut once again.

"I almost forgot." Delia walked into the kitchen, dropping a small envelope onto the counter in front of Greer.

She ignored Cian completely, keeping her back to him. Cian pushed out his fangs, flashing them at the back of Delia's neck. "I found this going through the living room after the devil attack. It got knocked to the floor."

Greer put away a set of coffee mugs and wiped her hands on her leggings before picking up the envelope, moving to open it. Delia leaned a hip against the counter, picking at a loose thread on the sleeve of her sweatshirt.

"I'm pretty sure that's the business card from the box Leeches McGee over here broke open for you. I didn't want to throw it away in case it was important."

Cian snarled at the nickname, but Greer heard Isaac laugh from the room over.

Greer went completely still as she pulled out the small card with the key taped to the back with a trembling hand. Her mouth fell open, and she felt equal parts light-headed and nauseous. She gently scraped the pad of her thumb over her mother's writing, a ringing sounding in her ears. Greer had forgotten about the business card and the sudden reemergence of it was shocking.

Greer's head whipped up as a thought crossed her mind. The business card. James Whittley. Anna. It was a long shot, an impossibility. But she had to try.

She leaned forward to grab her cell phone off the counter, ignoring the curious stares from Cian and Delia, as she swiped against the screen to turn it on. Glancing back and forth between the screen and the business card, she punched in the phone number and placed the call on speaker.

Cian watched her with a hyper-alerted focus as a woman on the other end picked up the line. "Indiana Bank and Trust, how can I help you?"

"Yeah, hi," Greer said, bending over to rest her forearms on the edge of the countertop. "I was wondering if you had account information for an Anna Whittley? She has recently passed away. I'm her daughter."

"Hold on one moment," the woman responded, the clacking of her keyboard sounding over the line, "Hmm...I don't see anything." Greer dropped her chin to her chest in defeat. "Oh wait, yes." Her head shot up. "It seems she has a safety deposit box that requires a key." She paused to type again. "There is a second name on this account. You said you were her daughter?"

Greer's heart ratcheted up as her chest tightened. "Greer Myers. My name is Greer Myers."

"That is the joint holder here, yes. We are in the process of closing the bank for the night, but we can have the box pulled for you first thing in the morning. We do require a government photo ID and the key to the box. You will also need to fill out a signature card upon your arrival. A second banker will be in the room when you open it and you will be able to empty the box if you so choose at that point. Will that work for you?"

"Yes," Greer replied hurriedly. "Yes, I'll be there."

"Great, we'll see you then," the woman responded before hanging up the phone.

Greer would buy a plane ticket that night if she had to. She was getting to that deposit box one way or another.

TWENTY-NINE

Greer was on the next plane to Indianapolis, accompanied by Cian, his volunteering surprising both her and Delia. She paid a pretty penny for the flights, using a sum from the estate money she was trying to save, and they didn't land until nearly three in the morning.

None of that mattered.

She buzzed with adrenaline when they exited the terminal and found herself increasingly more nervous by the time she took the hotel room key card from the bleary-eyed receptionist when she checked them in. They passed through the lobby, the smells of freshly brewed coffee and cigarette smoke wafting past the desk, and Cian followed her toward the first floor room.

The walk down the hallway was relatively short and Greer spotted the fire escape placard glued to the wall as they approached the numbered door. The smooth plastic card slid into the key slot with ease before Greer pulled it out to disengage the lock.

She pushed the door open and, from the corner of her eye, she saw Cian's ring-clad hand shoot forward to brace it enough for her to slip through. The air conditioner hummed as the fan clicked on, blowing frigid air from the unit underneath the window. Greer dropped her overnight bag onto the red carpet before marching over to yank the curtains shut.

She heard Cian chuckle behind her.

The room was small and clean enough for a last minute place at the airport. Muted stains dotted the patterned carpet and ding marks scuffed the walls nearest the door. There was only one king sized bed situated against the wall. The bed was bracketed by nightstands, one containing a bedside lamp and the other an alarm clock. The wooden desk, surfaced by a pane of thick glass for easier cleaning, held a tray with complimentary tea bags, instant coffee, and paper-wrapped mugs.

Greer could hear the canned laughter from a television on the other side of the wall where soft snoring emanated through the patched silence of the show.

She collapsed onto the bed, feeling the give of the mattress beneath her, and kicked off her sneakers. They flopped unceremoniously to the floor as Cian set his own backpack down onto the floor next to the bathroom.

Greer swept her gaze over to him, taking in his sig- nature leather jacket and tousled dark hair. The air felt suddenly charged as he lifted his eyes to meet her own. Her heartbeat pounded against her chest as her body became flushed and sensitive. She shot up from the bed, clearing her throat.

"I—I'm gonna jump in the shower. I need to wash the plane smell off me." She grimaced to herself as he nodded and grabbed the remote for the television, but she had already rushed toward the bathroom and snapped the door shut behind her.

Greer let out a slow breath as she leaned against the door and closed her eyes, letting her head fall back to rest against the faux wood. What was wrong with her? She felt like an idiot. She could do this. It was just Cian.

She opened her eyes to assess the dirty grout in the corners of the tiled floor, the metal rack above the toilet holding folded, white towels, and the small bottles of shampoo and conditioner set near the chrome sink fixture. Pushing herself from the door, the tile was shockingly cool beneath her bare feet as she made her way toward the shower and turned the handle to the left.

The water jetted on with a sputter and echoed across the empty, plastic tub. It didn't take long for steam to rise behind the curtain and the mirror fogged by the time Greer stripped off her clothes. She stepped into the shower and sighed at the rush of warm water coating her skin, closing her eyes and taking another deep breath.

Greer felt sensitive down to her very bones and a tingling of pleasure had taken root in her lower belly. Her hands ached with the need to touch herself, and she repressed the desire to rub her thighs together just to feel the friction between her legs. She shuddered, thinking of his hands exploring her breasts, his fingers coaxing her.

Greer quickly shook her head and cleared her throat. *Get ahold of yourself,* she thought, as she reached down to grab the washcloth resting on the side of the tub. She held it up to the shower head and allowed the water to soak through before grabbing the soap from the corner of the rim. She picked at the corner of the cover, her wet fingers slipping against the paper, but managed to successfully unwrap it. Greer lathered the soap against the washcloth, the aromatic citrus bar blending with the rolling steam, and pressed the cloth against her chest. She bit back a moan, not of pleasure, but of relief.

She hadn't lied to Cian— she hated the grimy, sweaty layer her skin had after flying.

Greer swept the washcloth over each limb, scrubbing her skin until she was raw. She let the water beat at her back, run in rivulets down her legs, and pool at her red painted toes.

Cian was outside the door, Cian was outside the door, Cian was outside the door.

Greer tried to control her rapid heartbeat, the fluttering nerves in the pit of her stomach. She stayed in the shower until her fingers pruned and her skin had turned a blotchy red. Once realizing she could no longer hide in the bathroom, she shut off the water and grabbed a towel from the rack off the wall.

Pressing her face into the cloth, Greer took a calming inhale, taking in the faint smell of bleach from deep in the fibers. The towel felt rough as she swiped it over her chest and arms, quickly dampening by the time she reached her abdomen and legs. She bent over to wrap her hair into the towel, piling it atop her head, when she reached forward to grab her clothes off of the countertop.

Greer's heart seized in her chest.

In her rush to flee the hotel room, she had forgotten to grab the duffle bag from the end of the bed. She leaned against the edge of the counter as she craned her ear toward the door, intently listening over the bathroom fan. Greer heard nothing, save for the fan, and figured he had stepped from the room when she hopped in the shower.

Greer pulled the towel off her head, wet hair slapping her shoulders as water dripped down her back, and wrapped the towel tightly around her chest. She bunched the ends of the towel in one hand as she opened the door a crack and peered into the room. Empty.

Sighing a breath of relief, she yanked the door open the rest of the way and confidently marched toward her bag, only to run headlong into Cian. The desk, Greer realized, had been hidden from her view. The pamphlets Cian had been rifling through dropped to the floor with a light thud.

"What in God's name—" he began, extending his hands to catch Greer's open arms. His gaze became glossy and

fixed as he swiped down Greer's front, taking in the wet hair, the bundled towel, her bare legs. "Why—?"

"I—I forgot my clothes in my bag," Greer managed to say, her voice feeling tight and hoarse against the lump that had grown in her throat. "I thought you left the room—"

Cian loosened his grip on her arms, but kept his fingers wrapped around her. "You should have yelled out," he said, his own voice dropping to a low hush. "I could have brought it for you." His fingers curled, grazing the skin of

her triceps.

Greer felt her skin pebble.

"Would you like to get your duffle bag?" Cian went on, taking a step closer to her. She felt the leather of his jacket graze her skin, the spiced aftershave replacing the citrus smell in her nose. He reached up to tuck a tangled lock behind her ear before cupping her jaw.

Greer turned her head, taking the opportunity to nip at the palm of his hand. She felt her teeth scrape over the calluses of his hand as she looked up at him through her thick lashes. Cian's eyes hardened, a dark wildness taking over the glossy glaze that made a heat pool in Greer's core. He raised a hand to brush against her own, where she held the bundled towel closed around her, and his fingers grazed her collarbone.

Greer wasn't sure who broke the plane between them or whether they met in the middle, but her lips collided with Cian's in a ferocity they had yet to explore. She bit his lip, sucking on it, and he groaned in response, opening his mouth to let his tongue swipe with hers. The hand on her collarbone moved, threading into the tangled, wet hair at the back of her head as his other hand hooked into the band of the towel around her chest.

"I need to hear you say yes," Cian said, as he broke away from her, panting.

Greer locked eyes with him, stormy gray into deep green, and whispered, "Yes. God, please, yes."

The hooked thumb shoved the towel downward and it tore from her hands, the breeze from the air conditioner puckering her skin and hardening her nipples. She let out a breathy gasp as his fingers caressed between her legs, sliding into the wetness that had nothing to do with her shower. Cian groaned as he bent down to lift her into the air before spinning them both and depositing her onto the bed. His gaze fell to her open legs, to her knees slumped to either side of her, and crawled between them. He cupped her neck as his lips found hers once again, this time deepening the kiss, and she felt him push a finger inside of her.

Greer felt him hardening against her hip, his jeans tenting as another breathy gasp escaped her.

There would be time for pleasantries, but it was not then.

"Cian— Cian," Greer managed to break away from him as she tapped him on the shoulder. He lifted his gaze to meet hers, adding a second finger and thrusting into her once again. She moaned a response and his green eyes went feral with need, fueling her as she entwined her fingers into his hair. "Play later."

Cian responded by lifting her lower body and hooking her ankles around his waist. She rolled her hips, grinding against him without abandon. He moaned her name into her mouth, his tongue stroking her as he pulled lightly on her hair. Her head craned back as her chest pushed forward, exposing the column of her throat. He tore away from her to clamp his teeth around her nipple, swirling his tongue around the taut flesh. Greer cried out at the sensitivity as his lips grazed up her chest to the base of her throat, and bit at her neck on his way back up.

Greer's hands thrust under his shirt, exploring his bare chest. Her fingertips ran against the bands of muscle that made up his torso. She heard his breathing deepen as he clumsily took off his jacket and tossed it into the corner of the room.

Cian took the opportunity to unhook her ankles from around his waist and yank her forward, draping her thighs over his shoulders. Greer felt her heart stutter as the vampyre planted slow, artful kisses up her thigh, stopping at the apex. She held her breath as she felt Cian clamp his hands around her thighs, and she nearly leapt from the mattress at the first swipe of his tongue against her core.

Greer moaned as the vampyre lapped at her entrance, dipping his tongue into the slick folds. She closed her eyes, a sharp moan crawling up her throat as Cian slowly thrust two fingers back inside of her. He pressed hard and curled them against her front wall, catching Greer's sensitivity from the inside.

Greer looked up her body, Cian catching her eye in the valley between her breasts. Her eyes locked with his as he dragged his fingers through Greer's core once again. A shot of arousal zinged through as she watched Cian slowly extract those fingers, place them between his lips, and suck the wetness from them. She whimpered, her thighs trembling, as Cian descended on her once again, nipping at her before slowly flicking her sex with the tip of his tongue.

Cian placed his fingers back at Greer's entrance, slip- ping them inside as he continued the patterned assault on the nerves between Greer's thighs. The pressure built there, begging to crest like a tall wave, and she wasn't sure how long she could take it.

She glanced back toward him, thrill zapping through her when she realized the vampyre was still watching her. Cian reached up with a hand that had been clamped around her thigh and pinched an exposed nipple.

That did it.

Greer moaned as her core shattered. She plunged a hand up, grasp- ing Cian's hair as she rode the vampyre's face. Her sex pulsated, her inner muscles clenching around Cian's fingers as she unraveled in sharp tremors that rocked her body and tore her breath from her chest.

Still reeling, Greer dropped her thighs from his shoulders and sat forward to grasp at his belt buckle, desperately pulling at the leather strap. Cian reached to grasp the back of his shirt and tugged it over his head. She saw, for the first time, the trail of hair that led beneath the waistband of his jeans. Greer heard his breath hitch in his throat as she popped the button open on his pants and shoved them down. He sprang free, and her hand immediately went between his legs, caressing the velvet steel of his cock.

He shuddered at her touch, feather light, as she slowly circled her fingers around the enormous shaft and pumped it once...twice...

"Greer," Cian panted, grasping her chin to lift her gaze. "Play later."

She smirked at his turn of the phrase as she scooted back against the sheets. He crawled onto the bed after her, never taking his eye off the glistening flesh between her legs. "Don't hold back," she commanded, cupping his cheek as he nestled his hips between her own. He nipped at the palm of her hand as he pushed against her entrance. Greer felt the tip of him expand her, and her inhale eclipsed into a moan as he worked into her, inch by inch. Her legs fell wide to accommodate him and, she realized, it had been a long time since she had felt so deliciously full.

He trembled above her, his body and mind seemingly at war, as he continued to ease into her, pull out to her entrance, and ease back in once more. Her breath stuck at the back of her throat as Cian worked toward seating himself, but Greer's breathy gasps turned into a loud groan when he thrust in, sheathing himself fully inside of her.

Cian leaned down to kiss her as she lifted her hips to meet his. His thrusts were deep and punishing, the sweet mix of edging pain and ecstasy. Greer's legs wrapped around his waist as he sunk deeper into her with the new angle. With each drive into her, he sent them propelling toward the bedframe and Greer shot a hand up to catch herself from hitting the wall completely. She didn't care, she wanted him undone.

"Fuck, Greer," he groaned into her mouth, and she bit at his lips once again. Greer met him thrust for thrust, their bodies in sync, as the heat in her core began to build once again. His head dipped down, his teeth painfully catching her nipple.

Her core exploded, sending waves of pleasure coursing through her body once again. Shudders wracked her spine as Cian gripped her hips to pull her upward and pounded into her, pistoning her through the eruption as her inner muscles clenched against his cock. He removed a hand from her hip and pressed his thumb against her sex.

Greer was moaning his name, digging her fingernails into his upper back. She hadn't felt this good in a long time; no one had made her feel this good in a long time. She gave herself over to him, whimpers and moans eliciting from her throat with each stroke of his cock, each pressured brush of his thumb.

Cian's climax was building, his thrusts becoming erratic and wild, as he thickened inside of her. Greer threaded her fingers into his hair and pulled from the base of his neck. She planted her lips on his throat, her teeth on his shoulder, her tongue on his collarbone as he found release. He plunged into her with one final thrust before pulling out to spill on the sheets underneath them. Their lips caught once more as he jerked with each thrust into the sheets as he finished. Cian's kisses turned slow and erotic as they came down from the orgasms they shared.

Greer was panting, sweat dripping down the valley of her breasts as he sat back on his heels, his knees denting into the mattress. She felt suddenly cold and empty with- out him inside of her. Cian rolled to the side and perched himself on his forearm as he gently scraped a wet strand of hair from her forehead. Greer's chest still heaved as she turned to look at him. His own breath sawed in and out of him as he struggled to calm his trembling body. He cupped her cheek, leaning down to kiss her softly.

"You feel even better than you taste." Cian kissed her again. "I am very eager to do that with you again."

Greer's core turned liquid as she felt her thighs pool with moisture. "What are you waiting for then?" she asked in a husky tone, as she flipped onto her belly, wriggling her ass playfully in the air.

Cian let out a throaty growl as he pushed to his knees and grasped her hips, hauling them toward him. He sheathed himself with one mighty thrust as Greer let out a cry from too sensitive of pleasure. This time, he took no prisoners as he slammed into her, pulling deep moans from the center of Greer's chest as she buried her face into the mattress.

THIRTY

Greer was pleasured and spent by the time the bank opened a few hours later. It took every piece of her to untuck herself from Cian's grasp and roll out of bed, though Cian had successfully pulled her back down once to bury his face between her legs for the final time. She had gotten a later start than she wanted and, by the time she closed the hotel door behind her, the sun had already risen above the airport.

On the taxi ride over to Indiana Bank and Trust, her mind flashed back to waking up that morning, his mouth on hers and his hands roaming her body.

Greer pulled the heavy door of the bank open when she arrived and was immediately greeted by the security guard, his hands folded at his front and a gun tucked into the holster strapped around his hips. She sent him a small smile and nod as she joined the line stretching from the counter.

She glanced around as she waited, taking in the glass table holding deposit slips in wooden cubbies. A man dressed in a suit was hurriedly filling out a form, the chain anchoring the pen to the surface lightly clanking against the glass with every movement of his hand. To her right was the waiting area filled with purple cushioned couches and beyond that were small cubicles clad in investment account and credit card posters.

The woman in front of her shifted her weight from side to side as she peeked over the shoulder of the man in front of her, sighing deeply when the line hadn't moved. Greer put her hand into her pocket, running her thumb along the grooves of the key. The rustle of paper bills running through a counting machine sounded over the low chatter from the bank manager, who was on the phone with a client asking about their savings account.

Feet shuffled as the line moved forward and a couple exited the bank, the woman's perfume mingled on the air as she went by. Greer didn't reach the front of the line for another ten minutes and, by the time the impatient woman stood at the counter, Greer was anxiously tapping her foot on the tiled floor.

"Next in line!"

Greer's head shot up as the coffee maker gurgled and hissed in the waiting room, new coffee dribbling into the carafe.

"Welcome to Indiana Bank and Trust, what can I do for you this morning?" A friendly, older woman waved her forward.

Greer returned the smile as she leaned her forearms onto the beige counter. "Hi, my name is Greer Myers. I had called last night about my mother's safety deposit box." She reached into the pocket of her jacket. "I have the key with me."

"Ah, yes!" the woman exclaimed as she pushed her tortoise shell glasses higher on the bridge of her nose. "You talked to me. I just need to see your government issued photo I.D., and then myself and my bank manager can bring you to the box."

Reaching into her wallet, Greer retrieved her driver's license and plopped it onto the counter. The woman slid it toward her and glanced over the top of her glasses to peer at it, the rhinestones of her eyeglasses chain twinkling under the bright ceiling lights. She compared it against the computer screen for a moment before glancing up and handing the license back to Greer. "The bank manager is waiting in the back, come this way."

Greer pushed off the counter and followed the woman as they walked through the waiting room and into a darkened corridor. The woman's thick, black shoes were heavy against the tiled floor and Greer noticed a camera positioned in the corner of the hallway, the red light rhythmically blinking as they passed it. The two women entered a private room at the end of the hall and Greer took in the small windows, worn carpet, and veneer table.

It reminded her of the interrogation room where the police held her after she found her mother's body, down to the musty smell. On the other side of the table stood the bank manager, her black hair pinned into a knot at the base of her head and an accordion keychain wrapped around her upper arm. Greer took a deep breath and blew it out, trying to calm her frantic heart.

The bank manager leaned down to verify the number engraved to the front of the box, the bank teller reading off the code from a slip of paper. "Key?" the bank manager asked, as she straightened, her dark eyes turning up to look at Greer, the accordion keychain jingling when she moved.

Greer stepped forward and shoved the key into the lock, turning it with a twist of her hand. The lock popped, and the subsequent grind against the metal of the old box was sharp against her ears. The bank manager lifted the lid, the hinges squeaking, and both her and Greer looked into the box.

There was nothing, save for a small, dark rectangle nestled against the velvet lining. Greer contemplated it in confusion for a moment before reaching down and pulling the item from the box. A zip drive.

"I just want to remind you that the rental fee on the safety box is due in three weeks if you plan on continuing to store it here," the bank manager said, as Greer closed her hand around the drive.

"No, no thank you," Greer said, as she pocketed it. "You can close the account. I'm taking this with me." Desperately ready to see what was on the drive, she turned and marched from the room.

"Wait, we need—" one of the women started, but Greer was already halfway down the hall, leaving both women behind as she went.

Greer was itching with nerves during the taxi ride back to the hotel, and she nearly jogged to the room, fumbling with the key card as she struggled to slip it into the lock. Cian must have heard her, because he threw the door open and leaned against the frame with a wide smile on his face. She ducked under his arm and walked straight to her duffle bag, rifling through it until she dug out her laptop.

Greer heard the door slap shut as Cian came up be- hind her, resting his chin on her shoulder. She peeled the computer apart as she set it on the desk and pressed the power button. The computer booted on and ran through a series of updates. Greer tapped her red fingernails on the glass covering of the desk as she anxiously awaited the home screen.

As soon as it appeared, she inserted the zip drive into the port and the folder materialized on the screen. There was one file located there, labeled: for Greer.

Greer double clicked on the icon, and it opened in the video player, the thumbnail of her mother paused on the screen. Her chest tightened at the unexpected sighting. Cian reached over her shoulder and entwined his fingers with hers, squeezing her hand gently. She pressed play and her mother began talking.

"Hi baby," Celeste began, her blonde hair flowing over her shoulders. "If you see this video then you already know that I'm gone. You probably also know that I died violently, and that's why you're looking for answers. I'm not sure what I told you before I died, but it was probably a lie—"

Cian hissed under his breath behind Greer.

"—I lied to you, because I knew that this video would be the end of your search for answers, and I needed to protect you, even in death, until you were completely ready to hear them."

Greer recognized the background of the video. The condo in San Francisco, where she had spent the majority of her childhood, was just as she remembered. She spotted the white, marble tiles of the floor, covered every few feet by rugs of various shades of gray. The walls were white as well, though expensive artwork her mother had collected over the years adorned them. No personal effects could be found. Not a single yearbook photo tacked to the wall or family portrait tucked onto a shelf.

It had felt sterile and barren when Greer was growing up. And, through the video screen, it felt just as sterile and barren now.

"When I was growing up, I never wanted to be a mother," Celeste went on. "I knew how to kick ass and kill monsters, but raising a child? No interest. It wasn't until I saw your face, your cheeks, your cute little feet, that I knew I couldn't let my father kill you. I saw the plans he made in secret, but there is so much more that he doesn't know."

Greer swallowed back the tears that pricked the corner of her eyes. She felt Cian place a soothing hand on her shoulder, gripping his fingers against her jacket.

"Robert Mills was the lawyer that drew up my will. Of course, that wasn't his name then. I snuck him out and helped him gain a new identity. He was a member of the Society. I met him nearly twenty-eight years ago when I was instructed to kill him. He had seen too much, stolen documents that he didn't realize were vital to the plans the Paladin Society had. I know he read them, but it wouldn't have made any sense to him. He showed them to me when I came to his door and those documents made sense to me."

An overlay appeared on the screen where her mother had edited the video, and Greer leaned in to read each one as they scrolled by. Dated and time-stamped, each document detailed the course of Holly Hawkin's life, Greer's birth, and the plot to kill them both. Greer's breath grew heavy as the lump in her throat seemed to double in size. "When you were conceived, the power in Samsara shifted. Demi-Primordials have the power to change reality. Your birth father, he was thrilled. There was so much he wanted to do with Samsara and with the creatures that came from it. There were others that wanted it to stay traditional and didn't want to bring change to the current order."

Greer noticed a seal at the top of one of the documents— a seal that was labeled for Vatican City. As the papers scrolled by, she realized the label was affixed to the corner of each one. *Paladin Society— Vatican City. Paladin Society— Vatican City. Paladin Society— Vatican City.*

"In those documents stolen by Robert, there was a plan created between the Paladin Socity, a djinn named Eligos, and the Fae King. Eligos reached out to Paladin to tell them of a powerful child who had just been conceived by a Primordial, a Primordial who wanted to make those changes to Samsara. Eligos and the Fae King wanted to work with Paladin to close Samsara completely, locking the Primordials into their own realm for good. In order to do that, he needed to find the Mage ancestral line. That line is the only connection holding open the portals between realms. When the Mage is alive, those portals are strong and, with her line in-tact, those portals remain. Weakened, but they remain."

Greer glanced over her shoulder to see Cian's face, pale and drained of blood. His lips were parted in shock, and Greer scanned his features in an attempt to read what he might be thinking. His grip tensed against her shoulder, and she cringed away from him, his strength biting painfully. "When the Paladin Society got word from my father that the Mage line had been found, and a child had been born, they put the two together. A Mage child with Primordial blood who had the ability to keep the Samsara portal open needed to go. My father was dispatched to kill you and Holly Hawkins."

A photograph of the order, the letter crinkled as if it had been pulled from the trash, flashed onto the screen.

"When I realized what my father was there to do, I left with you and never looked back. Robert owed me, and he helped us hide in plain sight. I became a different person; a person I hated, though. I kept you at arm's length. I didn't want to get close to you. I was terrified that your powers would show— that Paladin would find us and kill us both."

Greer watched as Celeste placed a trembling hand over her mouth and dipped her forehead toward the desk as she doubled over. Celeste let out a quiet sob— the cry of a woman who spent over half of her life running and could finally tell her story. Tears dripped down Greer's cheeks as she looked at Celeste, who had lifted her head.

The pain in her eyes, the worry lines around her frowned mouth, the slump of her shoulders.

Celeste drew in a deep, shaky breath to calm her voice. "As you got older and nothing came from it, I thought my father was wrong. You were a happy child, you had friends, you were popular and successful. I didn't know how your powers worked— maybe it was something you needed to grow into. Maybe you didn't inherit any at all." She paused to take in another shaky breath. "You just left for college today, but I wanted you to know the whole story. And that I love you—"

Greer let out her own sob now, clamping a hand over her mouth to stifle the sound.

"—Even if I had a hard time showing it, you were the best thing that ever happened to me. I wish you had been able to get to know me, the real me. I think we would have loved each other. I had so much to teach you. I'm so proud of you and I'm so proud to be your adopted mother. I'm sorry that I'm not there to tell you this myself, but I hope you know how I feel. I'll see you on the other side, my love."

Anna Whittley, also known as Celeste, reached forward and the camera went black.

Silence filled the space between Cian and Greer as Greer stared at the computer screen. The video had automatically returned to the thumbnail, the smiling still of her mother underneath the play symbol overlaying the picture. Rage grew in Greer's gut. She kept her lips clamped shut, her eyes twinging with tears.

Then, she exploded.

Power slipped from every part of her, detonating from her as if she were ground zero of a bomb. Every screen in the room cracked as every lightbulb popped, the shattering glass falling to the floor. Sparks flew from the lamp, still plugged in, and fell against the nightstand. They scorched holes into the mattress, the acrid smell of burnt fibers suddenly filling the room.

"Greer, you have to take a breath," Cian said, as Greer continued her silent rage. "You have to calm down so we can figure out what to do next."

Greer was seeing red as she whirled to face Cian. "You know him. You've mentioned that name. Eligos. Who is he? How do I find him?"

Cian let her rage for a moment before answering. "We don't know anything for sure, this is all conjecture. If we—"

Greer whipped to point at her broken computer, pieces of hair pulling free from her bun with the sudden movement. "Cian, seriously? Holly, dead. Anna, dead. How else would the Paladin Society have known about my birth? About my mothers...both of my mothers." She stepped backward, her sneakers crunching against the glass from the television screen that had fallen to the floor. "They had someone on the inside. It makes so much fucking sense now."

"What are you going to do?" He asked. He crossed his arms and leaned against the dresser. "You can't just confront him."

Greer stopped pacing and racked her mind, remembering the dagger still lying at the bottom of her mother's suitcase. She hadn't unpacked it, but stuffed it in the back corner of the coat closet in the rental house. "I'm going to kill him."

A laugh burst forth from Cian before he was able to stifle it back down. She glared at him, crossing her arms defensively.

"Oh, you weren't kidding." He ran a hand through

his dark hair, and Greer noticed he had placed his rings back on his fingers. "Greer, Eligos is thousands of years old. Thousands. He—he might not look like it, but he is incredibly dangerous. He..." Cian sighed. "He would kill you in an instant."

Greer contemplated this for a moment, rocking back and forth on her feet. "Come with me then," she finally said. "You can be there to help me if things go sideways." Cian opened and closed his mouth a few times. "I—

I'm not going to do that."

"Why not?" she cut in, exasperatedly throwing her hands out to the sides. "You've killed other creatures before. You told me yourself."

"That's different," he replied, a bite to his voice now. "Killing another vampyre and killing a djinn are two very different things. I wouldn't get close enough before he made me a pile of meat and a mist of blood. I won't take that chance."

Greer let out an angry hiss. "You can't take that chance, or you don't want to take that chance?"

"Yes!" Cian yelled back. "Both!"

Her body quivered in anger. "You're a coward. You saw that video; you know what he did." She took in a breath. "I hope you're ready for him to turn me into a pile of meat and a mist of blood, then."

"You don't mean that," he said in a hushed, angry voice. His fists were clenched at his sides, his gaze burning with

rage. He may have towered over her physically, but Greer was ready to match his energy with ease.

She lifted an eyebrow, not backing down despite the menacing glower he was sending toward her. "Why? You were the one that said I would die if I tried to go up against Eligos."

"I will not stand by and watch you die." He punctuated each syllable with a heated inflection. "And you can't die. You owe me a potion."

Greer felt like she had been kicked in the stomach.

Cian sighed, rubbing at his forehead. "Greer, I didn't mean—"

"Yes, you did." Her jaw tightened as her eyes went from dark and angry to filled with agony. "You absolutely did." Greer didn't give herself time to feel the pain, anger, or sadness from their argument. Or his unwillingness to help.

Greer darted toward the bed and began shoving her dirty clothes into the bag.

"What are you doing?"

"Leaving." She shoved the shattered laptop and the zip drive on top of her dirty clothes before zipping the bag shut. "Now."

"Greer, the flight is tonight after the sun goes down. I can't leave this room until then."

Greer looked up at him, the pounding in her ears narrowing as her heart thumped against her chest, her throat dried, sawing painfully as she breathed. "Exactly.

I'm going back now to figure out how to find him." She made to swing her duffle bag over her shoulder, hitching the strap around her head.

"That's an absolutely terrible idea," Cian said, as he reached out to grab onto her arm, but let out a seething hiss of pain as he yanked his hand back. The tips of his fingers sizzled, as they had with Jonas, from the burns he received from touching Greer.

"It might be a terrible idea," Greer said, straightening with resolution as she opened the door. Sunlight streamed in from the window in the hallway, sending Cian scrambling deeper into the room. "But at least I'm not a fucking coward."

Cian was readying himself to yell back at her, but she slammed the door shut on her way out.

THIRTY-ONE

Greer walked through the front door hours later, mind still racing, and made an immediate beeline for the closet in the narrow hallway that led to the bedrooms. She deposited her duffle bag on the carpeted floor before rifling through the coats hung on the rack to reach the back wall where Isaac had stored the suitcase. Wrapping her fingers around the handle, she yanked the suitcase from its holding place and let it drop in front of her.

Taking a deep breath, Greer leaned forward to unzip the top and flipped it over, revealing the bloody clothes and toiletry bag still crammed inside. She pulled everything out and sorted through it until she found what she was looking for— her mother's dagger.

Someone had wrapped the blade in an old shirt and only the leather-covered hilt was visible. Greer grasped it, feeling the hard metal beneath the leather, and pulled it from its fake sheath. The blade was just as she remembered it— silver with those etchings along the blade. She sat back on her heels as she held it, admiring the swirling letters.

"What do you think you'll be able to do with that?" a voice behind her asked.

Startled, Greer pushed herself to standing as she whirled around, swiping the blade through the air. There was a *zing* as a sword left its sheath and it came down on the blade of the dagger with staggering force. The dagger left Greer's stinging hand, landing with the point embedded into the old carpet. Gripping her wrist, where the collision sent a shudder up her arm, she lifted her gaze toward the intruder.

Odette.

Her red hair had been pulled back into a loose braid and her sword, the metal shining under the hallway lights, rested casually on her shoulder. Greer spotted the sheath strapped between her iridescent wings.

Greer sent her a scathing look as she bent down to jerk the dagger from the carpet. "What are you doing here?" she asked.

Odette shrugged. "Cian called," she replied simply, and she let out a chuckle of impatience as Greer tightened her grip on the dagger once again. "What do you plan on doing with that?" Her head tilted in a gesture toward the dagger.

Greer's cheeks flushed. "I'm going to use it," she began, but her voice strengthened as she went on, "to kill Eligos."

Odette was quiet for a long moment, contemplating Greer with a cocked head. She let the sword swing down, its own point lodging into the carpet, and used it as a crutch as she doubled over with laughter. Greer glared at her, arms crossed over her chest and dagger bouncing against her waist, as she waited for the faerie.

Odette straightened back up and wiped the mirthful tears from her eyes. "Besides the fact that I'm confident you have no idea how to use that, Eligos is a djinn. You aren't going to get close enough to try."

Greer blinked. "I'm the Mage, I can—"

"You don't get it. A djinn is different." Odette shook her head. "Djinn have unfathomable power. That's why the majority of them were either killed or banished from this realm after the Three Hundred Years War." Odette looked at Greer, scanning her from head to toe. "You have Primordial power. You should focus on that."

Greer sighed through her nose, long and exasperated. "Both of us know why I can't do that, Odette." She turned her eyes toward the sword, the tip still buried in her carpet. "Teach me."

Odette choked. "I'm sorry? Teach you what?"

"Teach me how to use this." Greer held up the dagger, shockingly small compared to the blade Odette wielded. "My magic is not reliable enough, and I still need to learn how to defend myself. You were the general to the Fae King. You're the best person to do it."

Odette's eyes narrowed in contemplation. "Fine." She turned on the balls of her feet and stalked away, her wings tucked tightly against her back. She paused to glance over her shoulder. "Are you coming or are you going to just stand there?"

Greer lurched forward, keeping the blade to her side, as she followed Odette through the sliding glass door that led to the fenced in backyard. The late summer heat had crept in as evening approached, and the air was stifling hot with no breeze to circulate the humidity. Dandelions and clover threaded through the grass, the earthy moist soil scent fresh and pungent.

Greer hadn't had the time, or the extra income, to furnish the patio yet— only the prickly garden weeds growing between each brick enhanced the space. White daisies poked through the slats of the wooden fence, and the trees on the other side cast long shadows into the yard.

Odette kicked off her sneakers as they entered the grass, and she paused when her bare feet hit the soil, toes curling against the earth.

Greer followed suit, gingerly stepping off the brick patio. The dead grass was sharp against the soles of her feet.

"If you were anyone else," Odette started as she circled Greer, looking at her from every angle, "I would begin with hand-to-hand combat. However, a fast fist is nothing compared to a fast blade." She held out her hand, hilt first, and gestured for Greer to take it.

Greer dropped her dagger, where it clattered against the brick, and reached forward to wrap her hand around the hilt. The sword was heavier than she expected, and it slid from her grasp, thudding against the grass unexpectedly. Odette sent her a scathing look at the noise, and Greer quickly lifted the sword to rest on her shoulder.

Odette approached her and tapped Greer's foot with her own, gesturing for her to widen her stance. "Stability and balance are the first lesson." She bent down, picking up her front foot and pointed it forward. Moving toward her back foot, she picked it up and pointed it diagonally at a soft angle. "Here is the foot placement."

Odette stood, positioning herself in front of Greer. "Feel the bounce in your knees, the rotation of your hips as you move. Stay on the balls of your feet."

She squared herself in the same stance in front of Greer, who watched as Odette used her hips to drive a full power blow, swinging her shoulder around as if she were still holding a sword.

"This gives you the ability to move." Odette leaped forward and slashed her arm once again, this time from bottom left to upper right.

Odette came behind Greer, grasping her sword hand with one fist. She splayed her other hand on Greer's abdomen, a motion that made Greer squirm in discomfort. "Your core stays tight, otherwise the transfer of power from your hips to your sword hand will be diminished." Odette physically moved Greer to showcase the feeling, and Greer was suddenly grateful she had, even if the closeness was more intimate than she expected.

Odette removed her hands and quickly grasped Greer's hips, only to thrust one of her hips forward, forcing her core to twist. "Stay taut," Odette commanded, pinching Greer's abdomen. Greer braced her core as Odette thrust her hip forward again, and she felt the immediate shift in force as she swung her sword.

"That's cool," Greer breathed, as Odette released her hips. Greer practiced once more on her own.

"Not cool, just swordsmanship," Odette said, crouching on her haunches to watch her from a new angle. The bottom third of her wings lay against the grass, though she didn't seem to notice.

The two of them worked on foot placement for the next hour. Odette had Greer leap into the position from the front, side, and back. She critiqued each time Greer landed until the movement felt natural rather than forced. It wasn't until Greer was dripping sweat into the grass and barely able to hold up the sword that Odette called it quits.

For the day, that is.

Greer staggered into the kitchen and filled two glasses with water, handing one to Odette when she reached the backyard again. She sank into the grass next to the faerie, who had draped her wings behind her like a wedding train. Greer picked up the sword and settled it across her lap, studying the curved blade etched with a vine of leaves that seemingly grew from the hilt. The leather wrapping was just as intricately designed with flora and swirls stamped into it.

"I've studied weapons before," Greer started with a deep breath, as Odette took a long drink of the water. "Many of them actually. This is a beautiful example." She looked over to Odette, who wiped the water from her lips with the back of her hand. "I'm guessing it is centuries old?"

"Yes, it is."

Greer drew in a breath, still working to calm her heart. "Did you use this when you were in the Fae King's service?"

Odette stilled; the water glass clenched tightly in her hand. Greer glanced over to her, taking in the white knuckles and pale cheeks of someone who was surprised by a line of questioning.

"Odette?" Greer said after a long minute.

Odette cleared her throat and shook her head. "Yes, it was my sword when I was in the Fae King's service."

Greer nodded her head. "Why did you leave?"

Odette dropped her gaze toward the blades of grass between her bare feet, and Greer watched her throat bob as she swallowed. "I, erm, I didn't leave." Her hands reflexively went to her wrists, rubbing them as if she still had chains clamped there.

Greer felt her mouth go dry. "Can you tell me what happened?"

Odette sniffed and took another sip of water. This time, her hand trembled as she lifted the glass to her mouth. "The Fae King, the original Fae King, was my father," she started slowly. "I was the general to his army, as well as heir to the throne."

Greer withdrew her gaze from the faerie, fixing it on the golden details at the end of the hilt.

It was carved into a sun— fitting for the floral designs that bedecked the rest of the blade.

"One night, his right-hand snuck crushed Belladonna into his wine. For humans, it's deadly, but with our high metabolism and propensity for healing, it is used as a sedative. Still a strong one, but a sedative nonetheless." Odette's gaze was glossed over, lost in her memory. "When my father was asleep, Adair slit his throat. I was ripped from my own bed by his followers and thrown into the dungeon, kept there for two hundred and sixty-four years. My wings were cut off regularly, as they continued to grow back."

Greer felt hot, acidic bile crawl up her throat at the thought. She imagined Odette in chains, slumped against a cold wall, the floor laden with old straw. Nothing, save for a bucket in the corner and a drafty, barred window too high for her to peek through.

"I became close with a guard by the name of Eoghann. His father was executed by Adair for being a member of my father's guard, but Eoghann lived in the village and was recruited to take his spot. Eoghann was brought on to guard the dungeons and we became fast friends, eventually falling in love." Odette paused to take a deep breath. "He tried to lead a coup against Adair on my six hundredth birthday and managed to free me. We meant to run together, but he— he didn't make it."

Greer looked up to notice the sun setting behind the tall trees. It bathed the sky in deep orange, illuminating each cloud with a silver outline.

"I came to the human realm and went to Agnes first thing. Tried to get her to form an army and march against Adair. She refused."

"Is that why you hate Agnes?" Greer asked, her voice just above a whisper.

Odette nodded. "Yes, it is."

"Is that why you hate me, then?"

Odette snorted this time. "I don't hate you. I just don't respect you. There is a difference."

Greer sprawled her hands behind her, the grass tickling between each finger, and leaned back. Someone nearby had fired up the grill, the smell of burning charcoal and grilling meats light on the breeze that had begun to pick up.

"Why are you here then? If you don't respect me?" Greer felt Odette's eyes on her as she answered. "Cian."

Greer whipped her head to connect her stare with Odette's. "Cian? I thought you didn't know each other?"

Odette nodded her head. "We didn't know each other until a few weeks ago. He blackmailed me in order to make me stay— promised to tell Adair where I was if I didn't agree to help you."

"I'm going to kill him too," Greer bristled, a shot of anger filling her.

Odette let out a genuine laugh, the locks of red hair that had escaped her braid fanning over her wings. "Cian is no Eligos, but you wouldn't get much closer in hand-to-hand combat against him. He's a soldier after all."

Greer look down at her lap. "How did you know?"

"I've been in battle, Greer. Many of them, unfortunately. I know the sullen, haunted look of a soldier when I see one."

Greer looked towards the sky, the orange fading into a dark blue. Stars had begun to wink through, bright dots against the inky blanket. The barbecue smell had shifted into that of burnt leaves in a bonfire. Off in the distance, Greer spotted a plume of smoke rising above the trees.

"Could I earn your respect if I helped you take back your throne?"

Odette's eyes snapped to Greer. "What?"

"You said Agnes refused to help you and that's why you hate her." Greer took a deep breath. "If I agreed to help you, would that earn your respect?"

"Why would you do that?"

Greer chuckled. "If I don't have the respect of an eight- hundred-year-old faerie, how am I going to expect it from anyone else?"

Odette glanced away, but said nothing.

"It wouldn't come for free, of course," Greer went on. "If I agreed to help you, if I agreed to use my magic for that, you would need to use your influence to help earn the trust and respect of the other daemons."

Odette shifted, the grass crackling beneath her. "Your negotiating skills need work."

It was Greer's turn to laugh. "You're probably right." She paused to take a sip of her water, now warm in her hand. "You can teach me that too. Where would you start? If you were to hunt for an army?"

Odette leaned forward again, resting her forearms on her knees. She swirled the water in the glass, watching it slosh up the sides. "The Court of Mist and Tide, I expect. The Lord of Mist and Tide was a tight ally to my father. I think I could convince him to fight under my banner."

Greer nodded slowly. "And where would you need me?"

"Trying to find any vampyre Cian, Isaac, and Jonas can help you muster."

At the mention of Cian's name in that capacity, Greer's stomach clenched uncomfortably. She hadn't heard from the vampyre since she left him in Indiana, though she hadn't reached out herself either.

Greer grasped the hilt of the sword and swung it towards Odette, who took it in her hand. Odette picked up the dagger lying by her side, twirled it in the air once, before sticking it into the grass between them.

"You have a deal, Mage," Odette said, looking off into the distance herself. "You're going to want to hang onto that dagger. You'll need it before the end."

THIRTY-TWO

It was Greer's birthday, and Delia had come over while Greer was at work to decorate her little house. Streamers decked the walls and helium-filled balloons were pinned by the ribbon in every corner of the house. Two birthday cards, one from Delia and the other from Paige, were propped next to one another on the kitchen countertop. Delia had written that she had stuck a cake in the refrigerator of the apartment, and Greer was expected to come over for dinner that night.

Or else.

Greer laughed under her breath as she set the card back down. This wasn't exactly how she planned on ringing in her twenty-seventh birthday. If she had been told six months ago that this is where her life would be, she wouldn't have believed it. Yet, here she was...making deals with faeries and having sex with vampyres.

Great sex, she reminded herself, not that that mattered now. Her and Cian had barely spoken since their trip days ago, though Greer knew she was partially avoiding the male. If not completely avoiding him.

Heading into the back bedroom, still filled with unpacked boxes and dirty laundry, Greer opened the closet door to pull a pair of leggings from the built-in wire racks. She tugged on the pair she wanted, accidentally pulling a long coat and a dress off the hangers nearby. Her gaze dropped to the floor and, as she picked up the coat to hang back up, she caught sight of the grimoire lying in the back corner of the closet.

Greer bent down to pick it up, fingertips grazing the ancient cover. She had forgotten about it between the move and her exhibit planning at work, barely spending any time cataloging the book into her laptop for easier access. She tossed the leggings onto one of the boxes and, completely ignoring the coat still lying haphazardly on the floor, sank onto the edge of the mattress.

Opening the cover and working from the back of the grimoire, she thumbed through each section, feeling the wrinkled parchment beneath her fingertips. Vervain, Poppy, Henbane, Monkshood. Each with a small blurb written in a different loopy handwriting. Greer could tell each handwriting apart, generations of Mages that had come before her to scribble their knowledge into this very book. The pages clumped together and Greer accidentally turned toward a spell section—one that she hadn't quite cataloged yet. She almost skipped past it to return to plants when something caught her eye.

A djinn summoning.

Greer felt her breath catch in her chest. The ink was faded, much older than the surrounding pages, and the blocked handwriting matched that from the front of the grimoire. Greer deduced that this incantation was created during the time that djinn wandered the Earth, and if they had been gone for two thousand years...

The incantation looked simple enough. All she needed was her own blood, olive oil, fire, and salt. She eyed the dagger sitting on the nightstand next to her bed. If she could summon him and immediately stab him before he could get his bearings.

That— that might work.

The plan was already forming in her mind when she thought of Cian and Odette's warnings. A djinn's strength, his power. How Greer and her own magic could not compete right now, might not be able to compete *ever*. She could hear their voices in her head warning her against what she was about to do.

But she didn't need to compete, she just needed to win. Abandoning the leggings, Greer grabbed the dagger from the stand and hurried into the kitchen. Keeping the grimoire flipped open to the summoning incantation, she laid the book on the counter next to the birthday cards.

She glanced around.

The kitchen was small, but the space would work. She needed to make a circle made of salt on the floor, connected completely. Five drops of olive oil mixed with five drops of blood directly in the middle of the circle followed by the incantation. It was long and in Latin, but Greer thought her training in old languages would get her through enough to make it work. After that, she would drop a match into the blood and oil mixture, where Eligos would appear.

Theoretically, anyways. The incantation page itself stated that one should never summon a djinn without a plan. Greer had a plan.

Greer pulled the box of salt from the upper cabinet and diligently created a small circle on one side of the kitchen. She stepped into it, affirming that a man's feet could fit comfortably inside. Next, she pulled a bowl from the cabinet and placed five drops of olive oil inside.

She picked up the dagger and, with a deep breath, pricked the end of her finger with the tip of the blade. Blood immediately bubbled to the surface of her skin and she dripped five beads into the oil. They swirled around and pulled at one another, never mixing completely. Greer took the bowl and dumped it unceremoniously into the middle of the salt circle.

Swallowing back the nerves building in her throat, she braced her hip against the edge of the counter and picked up the book. She began to speak the incantation out loud. The Latin felt clunky and unnatural on her tongue, and she briefly wondered if the incantation was mixed with something darker, more ancient.

It took her nearly three minutes to finish the incantation, even with her stumbling over her words, and she immediately lit a match following her completion. Her body turned jittery with nerves as she held the match over the circle. Greer sucked in a deep breath before dropping it to the floor.

The match dropped in slow motion, or at least that's how it felt. She watched as the blood and olive oil were set ablaze, a much larger flame than Greer expected rocketed upward. The flame licked the ceiling, scorching it black under its touch. Wind whipped around, pulling her hair from her top knot. The sound was otherworldly, rolling past her ears in a horrifying blend of thunder, two trains colliding on the tracks, and a blaring emergency alarm.

The room grew cold. Dropping down, and down, and down until Greer was shivering, her arms wrapped around her body in a poor attempt to conserve warmth. She squeezed her eyes shut, doubling over at the waist to protect her body from the projectiles being launched by the wind. The kitchen felt just as it had during her nightmares with the winged man, and she realized, in that moment, that she had made a terrible mistake.

Suddenly, it all stopped.

Greer's ears buzzed as silence fell and the wind settled. The temperature rose and her skin began to warm, turning back to pink from the blue tinge her chapped lips had become. She unraveled her body, straightening up as she looked at the salt circle.

It was still intact, except…a pair of shoes stood there.

Greer wasted no time as she lunged forward, aiming the dagger directly at the man's heart. He faked a yawn and brushed a hand, sending the dagger flying to the other side of the kitchen. It stuck into the wall adjacent to the window that overlooked the backyard, the hilt wobbling back and forth.

Lips parted in surprise, Greer turned back to the man. He was dressed in a black suit and long overcoat, his black shoes shining and new. The shirt he bore was a size too small, the buttons pulling against his belly, and the collar was tight to his neck. Neither seemed to bother him. His hairline had receded, elongating his forehead, and his eyes were just as dark as his remaining hair.

The worst part, though, was the aura of power around him. It crackled through the air and sent the skin on the back of Greer's neck pebbling. Her stomach churned with nausea as she swallowed the bile threatening the back of her throat.

The man looked around, a slight frown on his face, as he surveyed the room. "You must be Greer," he said, plucking rogue pieces of salt from the arm of his jacket. "And you must know who I am if you called for me."

"Yes," she whispered, her eyes darting toward something, anything, she could use as a weapon.

His gaze turned toward her, predatorily and fierce. "You must know that was a very foolish thing to do." He sniffed the air, his nostrils working like a dog on a scent. "You are Holly's daughter, aren't you? I can smell the bond." He sniffed again. "There's a second bond there. Interesting." He paused to study her. "I can't sense your power though."

"Sorry to disappoint," Greer replied through gritted teeth. She was afraid to open her mouth for fear her lunch would splash onto the djinn's shoes. "I heard you were the one that ordered the death of my mother."

"*Mothers*, dear, both of them," he corrected her without any hesitation. "Let's make sure we have our story straight here."

Greer blanched. "I—I thought that was the Paladin Society. I—I thought—"

Eligos clicked his tongue against his teeth. "Oh my, we are behind, aren't we." He sniffed the air for a third time, and a cruel smile invaded his features. "I'm surprised Cian didn't fill you in while he had his cock buried inside of you. He's always been one to stick that thing in places it doesn't need to go. Though, I guess it would have ruined the mood, I daresay."

"Cian? What does Cian have to do with this?"

The djinn glanced down at his fingernails. "Who do you think brought me information on you?" He glanced up to her. "You should have worked much harder on making that potion, you know."

Greer felt her cheeks flush, her throat dry. "He wouldn't do that—"

"Wouldn't he though? Cian has been on this planet for nearly five hundred years. You are a naive child if you believe he didn't have an ulterior motive."

Her heart cracked open, then shattered completely.

Eligos must have sensed it in her silence, because his smile widened even further as he clapped his hands together. "Now, let's get down to the reason you summoned me here." From thin air, he conjured a roll of parchment and a quill pen. Pausing for a moment to make a note at the bottom of the parchment, he turned his wrist once again and both vanished just as quickly as they appeared.

"I want you dead," Greer managed to say through strangled breaths.

Eligos let out a low chuckle. "We both know you can't do that," he said, his dark eyes narrowing on her. "You can't even perform a correct summoning spell." He lifted his hands, and the salt circle broke, each grain of salt suspending in the air.

Greer's eyes widened as her heart dropped to her feet. "You forgot to bind the salt, dear." He dropped his voice to a whisper as he said. "It's the only thing that works to keep a djinn contained."

In an instant, Eligos flung his hands forward, and the salt shot through the air like tiny bullets, peppering Greer painfully on her exposed skin. She could already feel the welts forming, the blood trickling down her arms and legs.

Eligos took a menacing step forward as Greer cried out, "What do you want from me?"

He stopped in his tracks and cocked his head, sending her a contemplative look. "I want your magic. I want your power. Neither of those things can happen while you are still alive." He raised a hand and clenched his fingers into a tight fist.

Greer felt an invisible hand wrap around her throat, pulling her into the air. She gasped for breath as she clawed at her neck, her toes barely skimming the linoleum tile of the kitchen. She felt her own power build beneath her skin before blasting out of her. It collided into Eligos with a nasty crack, and Greer felt that tendril of power withdraw from her neck. She crashed to the floor, her kneecaps smacking painfully as she fell.

"We both know I can't do any damage to you," Eligos seethed, rubbing the spot on his chest where Greer's magic had hit him. "But you invited me into your home, into your life. I can find anyone who has been in here. I can kill them instead." He paused to sniff the air dramatically before sharply turning to the set of birthday cards that had blown off of the counter during the summoning. "Starting with her."

"Eligos, please—"

"Give me your power or I will start killing off your friends. One by one." Another wicked smile split his lips. "That actually sounds like great fun. I think I'll start now."

Eligos disappeared, leaving nothing behind.

Greer felt her chest constrict as she lunged through the kitchen and into the living room, searching for her cell phone. She had never felt true fear until that moment, had never felt her chest tighten to the point of dizziness, had never felt her stomach turn rock hard inside of her.

Her fingers were clammy and cold as she tried to swipe the screen upward. She had to pause to wipe her hand on the leg of her pants before continuing on. Arms trembling all the way to her shoulders, she managed to plug in Delia's number before putting the phone to her ear. Her hearing still buzzed as if a swarm of angry flies had taken up residence inside of her head.

"Happy birthday!"

Greer's head snapped up as Delia answered on the other end. "Dels, Dels! Where are you?"

Delia scoffed. "Cooking your damn birthday dinner, of course. Where are you? Are you on your way?"

Greer closed her eyes and rested her head against the back of the accent chair in the living room. "Delia, listen to me. You need to—"

"Hold on, GG. Someone is at the door."

"Delia, no! Stop!"

Greer heard the door click open on the other end. She heard Delia let out an ear-piercing scream. Then, she heard nothing at all.

THIRTY-THREE

"I — I did something really bad, Odette," Greer sobbed into the phone as she sped through town, spinning the wheel to screech around a corner. The wheels popped up onto the curb, and a man who had been mowing his lawn shook his finger angrily at her. She didn't slow down.

"What happened?" Odette's tone was sharp.

Greer recounted the story in under a minute, her voice garbled and raw. When she finished, Odette swore.

"Why— why would you— Greer!" Odette said, full of disbelief.

Greer only sobbed harder. "Please— *please*, I need your help. *Please.*"

"Where are you?"

"Headed to Delia and Paige's apartment, my old apartment. I'm five minutes away."

"I'll meet you there," was all Odette said before she hung up the phone.

Greer sped on.

The sky was dark now, rain falling in fat drops against the windshield. The wet season of Oregon had just begun, the clouds gathering over the coast tall and broad. The long grass swayed in the breeze and Greer saw a few forest critters dart across the road in a rush to find a hiding spot from the nocturnal animals who had just awoken from the day's slumber.

Greer sobbed again, clapping a hand over her mouth as her chest heaved, her throat thickened even further, and her cheeks had began to swell from the constant tears. She peeled into the parking lot, jolting as she threw her Jeep into park before it was done rolling forward. The gears ground in protest, but she was already flinging herself out of the car.

The handle of the front door melted under her grip, contorting to a molding of metal that she broke through with ease, and she was taking the stairs two at a time, sprinting up, up, up until she reached the landing of her former floor.

Isaac was already there, pacing with long strides in front of the door. "Greer, Odette called. What—"

Greer said nothing as she passed him, shouldering the door open. What she saw stopped her in her tracks.

Blood. Big, red letters made from blood. Enough blood to scrawl an address across the white wall of the living room. An invitation and a warning. Greer sank onto the center cushion of the couch, staring at the wall with a gaping, unfocused gaze.

"GG, what—" Paige gasped loudly from behind her, dropping her work bag to the floor with a thud. "Is that blood?" Her eyes darted to Greer, who had curved over herself, holding her stomach as deep cries wracked her core. "GG, *where is Delia*?" She crossed the apartment in record time, turning off the oven and pulling the smoking lasagna from inside.

Greer hadn't even noticed something was burning. "I think we know where she is," Odette said, as she entered the apartment, gesturing toward the address on the wall. She crossed the living room and ran her finger through the wet, sticky liquid before licking it off the tip. "She was still alive when this blood was taken."

"A-alive?" Paige asked, shock lacing her tone, as she thrust a hand into her hair and pulled at it. "You're lying. Where is my fiancée? What have you done with her?"

"It was all my fault," Greer whispered from the couch, keeping her eyes fixed on the address. "I— I summoned Eligos. I thought I could take him. He— he— I heard him take her." Tears leaked from the corners of her eyes. "I heard her scream."

Paige openly stared, her gaze darting around the room. "What are we waiting for?" She flung a hand toward the wall. "We have to go. We have to go right now before he hurts her any further."

"Eligos is extremely powerful," Odette said calmly, adjusting the sheath of her sword higher between her wings. She scanned Greer's face as she said it. "We don't know what he has up his sleeve—"

"He wants me." Odette clamped her mouth shut as Paige turned to look at Greer. Greer lifted her head as she stood up. "He wants my power and in return—" She stopped to take a deep breath. "He'll keep my friends alive."

Isaac let out a deep sigh as Paige rapidly blinked, scrambling to understand the gravity of Greer's words.

"I'm going," Greer continued on. She sniffled as she wiped the tears from under her red-rimmed eyes. "I have to go."

"Greer, if you die—" Isaac began, but Greer quickly interjected.

"The Mage line will die, I know." Greer shifted her weight back and forth, hands trembling as she picked at her cuticles. "I have to try. This is— this is my best friend."

"I'm going with you," Paige stated, her head dipping in a curt nod.

"You're insane. Eligos will tear you apart," Odette said.

"Delia is going to be my wife," Paige responded, her tone even and firm. "We have plane tickets to fly to Austin next week to find Delia's brothers." She turned to look at Greer. "I will not be left behind. I deserve to go with you."

Despite the sinking feeling in her gut and the roiling in her head, Greer slowly nodded.

"Just great," Odette spat. "Two humans and a vampyre to look out for." She threw her gaze around the room. "Where are the other two?"

Isaac shifted in discomfort, reaching up to scratch the back of his head. "It's—it's just me. Cian and Jonas— well, Cian, he—"

"He was working with Eligos all along," Greer finished for him.

Isaac swallowed, but nodded. "Eligos approached us when we were...digging up Holly Hawkins." He said the words hesitantly, as if he were afraid of upsetting Greer further. "He promised Cian a potion if he revealed your location. He didn't— then." His gaze turned toward Odette. "He was also told to bring you to Eligos alive."

Odette swore again. "I hope you proved what you wanted to prove," she said, turning her fiery gaze toward Greer, "because we'll get your friend back, but every single one of us might die in the process." She leaned forward to put her face within inches of Greer's. "And everything that happens tonight is on you."

Darkness had blanketed over the city as night settled in. It was the first chilled night of the year, the cold humidity layering dew on the grass peeking through the crumbling concrete of the parking lot.

The streets were just as empty— an unsettling sight for a college touch nearing autumn. At any other time, staggering students would be making their way from their campus apartments to the bars lining the main street. Her chest clenched as she thought about those nights she had with Delia. She certainly thought she would have more of them.

Greer briefly wondered if everyone could sense Eligos as she could and had taken to hiding instead.

She stepped on the gas, winding the car through the downtown area. The lights, blinking yellow, were a bright, stark contrast against the dark sky and dimly lit buildings. Greer arrived at the warehouse a few minutes later, pulling through the fenced parking lot and placing her car into park. The spotlights, posted above each door that led to the interior, were blinking as they swayed in the wind.

No humans, no daemons, nothing. The parking lot was completely bare. The silence, cut only by Paige's haggard breathing and Isaac shifting against the leather seat, set every nerve in her body firing. She expected devils to be guarding the parking lot, waiting for her. The anticipation filled her with dread.

With them being notably absent, this scenario was much worse.

Greer grabbed her mother's dagger, holding it tightly in her clenched fist as she slid out of the car. Paige and Isaac followed suit, the three of them jumping in surprise when Odette landed with a thud against the pavement. She held a spare sword out to Isaac, who shook his head.

He pointed his thumb toward Paige, who took it with a small, grateful smile.

Greer led the way toward the nearest door and climbed the metal-grate steps. Grasping the handle, the door pulled open with a tug, a horrible wrenching scrape resounding through the air. Paige winced as Odette clicked her tongue against her teeth. If Eligos didn't know they were here, he certainly knew now.

There was no turning back, and Greer felt a shiver go up her spine as she crossed the threshold.

The hallways were winding and the building was cold. By the thick layers of dust and debris, it had clearly been some time since anyone besides herself had stepped foot inside. She heard the pattering of tiny claws on the yield floor, seeing a rodent tail whipping around the corner as she passed.

Greer adjusted the dagger, playing with the hilt as she walked.

The hallway dead ended into a two-way turn. She glanced to the right, seeing a door with a metal push bar. From the skinny, wired window set into one side of the door, she could see that it led back to the parking lot. Glancing to the left, Greer saw long, plastic blinds hanging from the ceiling. They were eerily still in the silence. She took a deep breath and ventured deeper into the warehouse, the blinds clacking against each other as she went through.

It opened to a metal staircase that terminated on the concrete floor of a large, open garage. Planted directly in the middle of the garage, under a bright fluorescent light, was Delia.

Paige made to bolt down the staircase, but she was caught on the upper arm by Isaac, who pulled her back. She stumbled, tripping on her own feet.

"This is a trap," Isaac muttered to Paige as she regained her balance. "We have to figure out where Eligos is hiding. Or who else he is hiding."

"Oh, God, Dels," Greer whispered, as her free hand gripped the metal handrail lining the staircase. Her heart cracked as she saw her best friend, broken and unconscious, in that chair.

"I'll go first," Odette said in a hushed voice. "If nothing happens, Greer follows next. Then Paige, then Isaac." She turned to Isaac. "I trust that you'll have our backs?"

Isaac nodded his confirmation.

Odette vaulted over the rail before spreading her wings, allowing them to flutter her to the concrete floor. She landed lightly, almost soundlessly, as she tucked her wings close to her back. She held her sword forward, turning her head to take in each corner of the garage.

Nothing moved in the shadows. Odette lifted a hand and gestured for Greer to follow.

Greer bolted down the staircase and swept past Odette, falling to her knees as she reached the chair. She placed her hands on Delia's cheeks and tried to lift her head, but it lulled heavily in her hands. Rage and anguish filled those fissures in her chest as she reached down to untie the rope from Delia's ankles. With the cordage removed, Greer could see the bloody sores and irritated chafing created by Delia trying to free her feet.

Both eyes, bruised and swollen, were closed as her chin sagged to her chest. Blood seeped from the corners of her lips, cuts slicing down her cheeks and neck. Her lower lip was inflamed and split, as if she had been punched in the mouth. Delia didn't move as Greer grasped her shoulders and shook her gently. It took Odette walking over to lay a finger on her neck to confirm that she was still alive.

Paige let out a sob as she fumbled with the binds that held Delia's wrists to the armrests of the chair. "We're going to get you out of here, my love," she whispered, placing an arm around Delia's waist and hauling her to her feet. Isaac shot out an arm as Paige stumbled, taking all of Delia's weight against her body.

Delia managed a light moan, blood bubbling from her mouth.

"I can't imagine you'll get far."

The familiar voice made Greer snap her head up. She spun around to face Paige and Delia, her eyes locking on her best friend. Delia was no longer unconscious, but smiling viciously up at Paige. Greer felt her heart leap her into her throat.

"I've learned a few things in my time alone," Eligos purred.

Greer looked around, her mouth going dry as she saw devils of all shapes and sizes enter from the shadows, watching them with hungry, excited eyes.

"Where is Delia?" Greer called out, as Paige pushed Eligos away from her, glancing frantically around as if Delia would appear just as suddenly as the devils had. "What did you do with her?"

Eligos let out a gleeful giggle as he transformed back into the pock-marked man in the long coat. The laugh put a shiver up her spine. "I think you'll find that she's in this very room." He swept an arm behind him, a grand gesture toward the devils stalking toward them. "Let's hope you find her before you kill her." He chuckled again before disappearing and reappearing behind Greer and Paige.

Isaac and Odette had begun to move toward the devils, their swords glinting under the light.

"What do you want with my power?" Greer asked, trying to buy them time. She held her dagger tightly in her hand. "Why are you doing this?"

Eligos's smile returned, a Cheshire cat playing with a mouse. "As horrid and inconsistent as you are with your control, you have the ability to open and close the portals to any and all of the realms. You can control the size of them and what comes through. Primordials can only temporarily open portals they are associated with, but the Mage can use her magic to brace open realms for the daemons. As a demi, you can do all of that and more."

From the corner of her eye, Greer saw Paige begin to circle around the back of Eligos. "And the Fae King? How does Paladin fit into all of this?"

His smile grew wider. "Adair and I have an understanding. He gives me his legions to overthrow the Princes of Samsara, and I open the Fae realm using your powers. Adair takes over the human realm as his own." He chuckled. "Of course, I needed the Paladin Society to track down the Mage line, but they were none the wiser when I posed as one of their own. So naive those humans can be."

"And what happens to me?" Greer went on. Paige was creeping closer, the knife held high above her head.

"I assume you'll die a horrible and painful death having your magic torn from your body. But, it's that or watch all your friends get ripped to pieces by my friends." He raised his arms, gesturing to the creatures surrounding them. "Starting with your cute best friend, here." He spun around, sending out a tendril of his power like a whip. It wrapped around Paige's ankle, and he yanked back, as if holding onto a lasso. She went careening to the floor, smacking the back of her head against the concrete.

Paige groaned as she held her head, her gaze unfocused and bleary.

Greer let out a cry of anger as a flash of her power emerged, but it was easily blocked by Eligos.

"We aren't even at the best part, dear," Eligos called from his spot in the room, his voice echoing across the concrete. Greer spun around to face his new position, now seeing Cian and Jonas next to Eligos, the djinn's hand on each of their shoulders.

Isaac became distracted by the appearance of his two closest friends and a devil, who was four legged like a wolf with finger-length teeth, snapping its jaws at him. Cian made to move forward, but Eligos laughed.

Greer went still as Cian's face broke with devastation. "I'm so sorry," he said, as Eligos pulled a vial of liquid from inside of his coat.

"Cian here made the deal of an immortal lifetime with me, if you remember," Eligos said happily. "You should have focused more attention on that little potion to help him walk in the sun. He might not have been so eager to join my ranks."

"I—I tried to stop it," Cian finally said. "I tried to stop everything. I—I didn't communicate with him after your mother, Anna, was killed. I didn't know what he was going to do."

Greer's breath hitched in her throat as her focus narrowed onto Cian. "You? You...he killed her, because of you?" She spat at him, no longer able to keep her body still. She lurched forward, dagger in hand, and he jerked back.

Paige, having recovered just in time, nabbed Greer by the arm, pulling her away.

"It truly is hard to believe you, Cian, when you stand next to me holding the vial you've been bargaining centuries for." The vial appeared in his hand, the swirling contents glimmering.

Greer's gaze flattened, her vision splitting, blackening in the peripherals. Paige was still tightly clutching her arm. "When I'm done with Eligos," she said to Cian, who hung his head in shame, "I should have never— I shouldn't have—" She looked away from him in disgust, feeling dirty in her own body.

Eligos clicked his tongue against his teeth. "I certainly wouldn't have let Cian stick his cock in me, but who am I to judge?" He turned to the devils surrounding them. "Kill the rest, bring me the Mage alive."

In an instant, the throng of devils descended on them.

THIRTY-FOUR

The circumference of the circle shrunk with Eligos's words. Odette's eyes darted around the room, intently assessing each devil that came ever closer. Greer's heart stuttered as Paige removed her hand from Greer's arm, stepping forward protectively.

It was all Greer's fault. She stepped right into the trap she was warned about and dragged her friends with her. They were all going to die, and it was all her fault.

"We need to find Delia," Paige called out to the group.

At the same time, Odette yelled, "Backs to each other!"

Greer and Isaac obeyed, setting up in a square formation with their backs to Paige and Odette. Turning to look over her shoulder, Greer spotted the back of Paige's head, the hair matted and bloody from where she had knocked it against the floor. Greer held up her dagger as Isaac turned toward the chair, ripping two wooden legs from the bottom before tossing it aside. Odette was whipping her sword around artfully. It looked natural in her hand, her fingers flexing around the hilt.

"What now, general?" Isaac yelled over his shoulder to Odette, the thrashing and gnashing of teeth growing louder as the devils stalked closer.

"Don't die," Odette yelled back. "And Greer?" She paused to scan the Mage's features. "Now is a great time to bring out your magic."

"I—I'll burn this warehouse down," Greer shot back. "With all of us inside!"

"Then find Delia," Paige said, reaching back with an arm to clamp her fingers around Greer's wrist. "Find Delia for us. You're the only one who can."

Greer felt her body shake uncontrollably and thought back to various pages of the grimoire, her mind rifling through the limited knowledge that she had. She thought all the way back to the beginning of this, how she had seen Odette's wings when her magic broke through for the first time. A thought occurred to her. If Odette's faerie glamour couldn't hold under her magic, then certainly...

Greer fell back, grasping Isaac's shoulders and adjusting the formation to a triangle. "I'm going to try something to find Delia, but I can't do that and fight at the same time."

"You got—"

The first devil struck. The leathery, four-legged beast pounded, teeth flashing, toward Odette. It leapt into the air, the two front legs extending out in an attempt to tackle the faerie. At the last second, she lunged downward, flipping onto her back. She threw herself underneath the devil and stuck the blade into the soft flesh, thrusting it up as she slid. The devil yowled, his underbelly bursting open and flooding the ground with intestines and black blood. Greer's stomach turned at the sight.

Four more lunged forward.

Odette took on two, whipping and dancing around expertly as she slashed her blade through the air, carving up the devils and leaving their carcasses in ribbons on the floor. Isaac's approach was much more militant, as he used his training from previous wears to stab with the broken end of the chair leg, clubbing them over the head with the other, then retreating out of the way of thrashing claws.

Paige, on the other hand, had no style. What she did have was a faerie sword and a whole lot of nerve. She two-handed the hilt, bringing the blade down on the neck of the devil who had come near her. As the devil she was fighting fell to the floor, Paige turned toward Greer and panted, "GG, we have to make sure none of these are Delia."

Greer stilled, settling into the discomfort and fear of the battle raging around her. She closed her eyes as she allowed the gnashing of teeth and screeching of claws against concrete to grow silent. She imagined her power reaching forward, tendrils of magic wrapping around each devil. Her magic examined each one, surrounding them before moving on. Greer didn't know what she was looking for, but each devil felt empty.

A cold, nothing.

Odette yelled out as she was pulled into a third fight. This time, she clashed into a three-headed scaled devil with a forked tongue and four long talons that lined the tail. She opted to use her wings, flying around to distract the heads as she cut them off one by one.

Isaac was defending Greer as hard as he could, forgoing his military strategy and slicing the chair leg through the air. His left forearm was ripped to shreds, the sinew hanging onto his limb by threads of torn tendons, as he used it as a shield against the claws and fangs of the devils. Greer's focus was broken as Paige jostled her. Paige's hair and forehead were slick with sweat, her face covered in splatters of black blood and tissue. Greer tried to push back through Isaac, seeing one descending on Paige. Greer let out a sudden shout of pain as she made the mistake of standing in one place for too long. A claw had raked over her upper arm and it split open, blood soaking her sleeve and leaking down her skin.

Fear gripped at her, pulsing through her veins as she flailed. Completely forgetting the basics of fighting that Odette had taught her, completely forgetting Odette's instructions to stay in control. Panic rose as a group of devils overwhelmed her and, with a scream of horror, her magic ripped from the middle of her chest and flattened the three devils who had surrounded her.

Greer was knocked to the ground by her own power.

A long-limbed creature with a wolf-like head and fingers ending in long, blackened nails stalked over her, pinning her shoulder to the concrete. It became distracted by the river of blood flowing down her arm, and she took the opportunity to thrust the dagger in her hand upwards, catching it in the leg. It shrieked as the tip embedded in the fleshy thigh, and Greer let another flash of power leave her, using the dagger as a conduit. Magic pumped to its heart, the spiderweb veins turning from black to red as it contorted back. It let out another shriek of pain as its back snapped, sending it backwards at an unnatural angle.

The creature fell over, dead.

Greer shot up, seeing an opening in the horde, and raced toward the metal staircase.

A mountainous devil with a jagged back and clubs for hands had its eyes locked on her. Isaac must have seen it as well, as he tucked an ankle behind his thigh, sliding underneath the creature as if he were stealing home plate, and cut the back Achilles tendon of the devil. It roared once as Isaac jolted upward and thrust his chair leg through the roof of its mouth. It collapsed to the floor with a smash that shook the surrounding structure, writhing for a long moment. The rocky back scraped against the concrete before It stopped, lying unmoving next to Greer.

"Find Delia," Isaac yelled over to Greer, as he braced his foot against the creature's head, yanking at the chair leg.

"Isaac, here!" Greer held out her mother's dagger, gesturing for him to take it. "You need it more than I do."

He grasped the blade by the hilt just in time to force it through the eye of another devil who had crept up on them, wrenching it back out with a sickening squelch. The tang of rotten flesh and blood filled the air between them, then Isaac was off again.

Greer, protected only by the flimsy banister of the metal staircase, fell into her power once again. She shot out those tendrils, exploring each devil still alive, praying to whoever in the universe that could hear her for Delia to still be alive.

There.

Greer's eyes flew open as they fell on a creature in the corner of the room. Delia had been hidden by Eligos's power, transformed into a skeletal bird with fogged eyes. Feathers were missing in large clumps where brittle bone stuck out, only covered by light cords of dried flesh. She was trying to keep as close to the back wall as she could, out of the fray, and Greer could sense her terror as she clawed at the concrete with broken talons.

"Odette!" Greer screamed as she shot upwards, peering over the throng of the battle, "Keep it open! I found her!"

The faerie turned, hearing Greer's voice with her sensitive, pointed ears, and sent her a curt nod. She moved her fighting stance to guard the hole in the swarm Greer had pointed on. Greer scurried through the barrier, jumping over the first fallen devil. Blood still leaked onto the floor, and Greer's sneakers slid from underneath her when she ran through it. She dropped to the floor, landing painfully on her hip. It sent shock waves down her leg, but Greer didn't care.

She had to get to Delia.

Covered in the thick, black blood, she sent another shot of power to a spider-like creature who had sensed her, and it immediately burst into flame. Now that she knew where Delia was and how Eligos was hiding her, Greer didn't hold back her magic; it was fueled by hate, and fear, and rage. Four creatures around her combusted into nothing, but smoky shadow as she passed them. They were sucked into the fans at the top of the ceiling and dispersed through the room, the thickness plummeting low to the floor like a dense, dark fog.

Greer approached Delia slowly, unsure how reactive her best friend would be. Or if she was even still in there at all. Delia snapped her beak at Greer's outstretched hand, her fogged eyes widening. Greer's cheeks paled with the effort it took to send more probing magic outward, testing Eligos's magic. It was built like a cage around Delia and her soul, the very essence of herself, was trapped inside.

Greer tried to wind her power around it, infiltrate it, unlock it. She tried everything, failing again and again. The creatures behind her drew closer, headed off by Odette, but she was growing tired. Greer could see it in her movements, could see the pain reflecting in her eyes as she swung her sword, could see the blood pouring down her back on her sword hand side from where she was caught unaware and a devil had slashed its talons.

Greer's power was faltering, fading like a lightbulb that was about to go out. She dug deep within herself, but was met by that brick wall, that obsidian, that kept her at bay. She thought back to when she found out about Holly, about Celeste, about both of their deaths. Cian's betrayal... She pulled at those emotions, feelings, and experiences and managed to drum up the last piece of magic she could access.

She lashed it forward like an anvil on a chain, and it cracked into the side of that cage. It shattered, those last remnants of Eligos' power crumbling to the floor.

Greer rushed forward and dropped to her knees next to Delia. Hair askew and clothes dirty, Delia had curled herself into a tight ball against the concrete floor. Greer wrapped her arms around Delia in a tight embrace, rocking her back and forth. She managed to help Delia unfurl, noticing her split lip, the bruised eye, and the blood trickling from a laceration near her hairline.

"We have to go now," she said to her best friend, helping her sit up. "Can you walk?"

"Greer?" Delia asked, her hoarse voice no more than a whisper. "I was— I was stuck. I was this thing, trapped. I—I couldn't see." Her eyes darted around at the battle raging before her. "Oh God, where is Paige. Is she okay?"

"Paige is here, she's fine." Greer wound an arm around her waist and helped pull her to standing. "We have to get you out of here, she's going to follow us out—" Her lips clamped shut when she looked Delia over and noticed she had wet herself from fear, the stain snaking between her legs and down her left pant side.

"Greer?" Delia asked, a moan of pain escaping as she limped along. "Are we going to die?"

Greer didn't answer that as they reached the second break, held open by Isaac. Odette blocked the devils as Greer dragged Delia through, but dropped her unceremoniously to the floor as Greer took a blow to the right flank of her ribcage. The wallop sent her flying sideways, and her head cracked against the concrete floor as she fell. Her vision busted into stars before blurring, and her stomach turned over as her head exploded into a fit of pain. She struggled to get her bearings, blinking and shaking her head vigorously as the devil circled her, watching with a predatory gaze.

Greer rolled over onto her hands and knees, widening her eyes and taking deep, heaving breaths. She needed to move, needed to get to Delia. She desperately needed her head to clear in order to do both of those things.

Suddenly, with a burst of energy and speed that seemed to infiltrate the space around them, Cian appeared. He stood between Greer and the devil, still decked in his leather jacket and black boots. If Greer had thought she had imagined him fighting before, it was nothing compared to seeing it now. His movements were smooth and natural as he spun, whipped, and slashed the sword he held through the air.

Devil after devil fell to his blade and, what devils he didn't get to, Odette was close on his tail. Together, they danced in a battle so tightly regulated that it seemed they had been sparring partners their whole lives.

Odette's red hair had escaped from her braid, twirling around her like a wave of fire as they fought back-to-back. Cian's muscles rippled when he swung the sharp sword, the tendons of his forearms trembling under his grasp of the hilt.

Greer's head cleared as she sat up, kneeling back onto her feet. The goose egg forming on her temple was tender and sore, but that was the least of her problems now. Cian appeared before her, hauling her to her feet by her armpit. The swift motion upwards made her stomach weaken, but she forced it back.

"Get her out," he growled, pulling Greer behind him as another devil tried to sneak around her back. Greer let out a cry of pain as the devil's pincers managed to hook into her stomach, tearing out a chunk of flesh. Cian thrust his sword forward, lodging it into the creature's throat. The devil let out a wet, guttural gurgle before collapsing to the ground. He jerked the sword back, the neck opening when the blade released.

"Why did you come back?" Greer panted, assessing the tear in her abdomen. Fat and flesh poked through as it openly bled. This one would require medical attention if she couldn't access more of her magic to heal it.

"I needed you to know that I planned on betraying Eligos all along." He swung around to decapitate one of the last devils still standing. "Paige is outside. I got her out." He lifted the sword, covered in goo and the stinking, black liquid. "That's where I got this." Greer jolted in surprise at a loud smash and crash that echoed through the garage as Cian whipped around to assess the new batch of devils that had begun to pour into the warehouse. "Can't let the faerie have all the fun."

Greer's lips parted as she struggled to form words, but he had already disappeared into the throng. She saw the devils in his wake being torn apart, and he left a trail behind him as if he were a battering ram. Greer looked to find Delia, who had crawled to the metal staircase and was using the guard rail to pull herself up.

She hurried over, putting her arm around Delia's waist once again. "Greer?" Delia asked, mascara smeared down her cheeks. "We have to get Paige. We have to save my wife."

Those words split Greer wide open, cracking her heart in two. "Paige is outside, she's waiting for us. We have to focus on getting you out of here," she replied, helping Delia clamber up the stairs.

They pushed through the plastic blinds, the battle be- hind them quieting to a dull roar. Greer's ears rang in the silence of the hallway, the only sound being their blood-soaked sneakers against the tiled floor. They reached the parking lot, and Greer immediately spotted Paige. Delia tripped over a crack in the pavement as she attempted to move her feet faster, needing to get to her fiancée as quickly as she could.

"Paige, baby, you're okay!" Delia managed to get out through teeth clenched in pain. Her lip split further as she spoke, fresh blood trickled down her chin. She wiped it away with the sleeve of her shirt. She threw her arms around Paige's neck, who immediately pulled her into a tight hug.

Paige pulled away from her, smoothing Delia's curled and tangled hair. Delia looked her over with an assessing stare, but Paige sent her a small, grateful smile. A tear trickled down the tip of her nose as she cupped Delia's cheek. "Nothing major, a few scratches here and there." Paige swept a hand over the front of her shirt. "None of this blood is mine."

"What—what happened?" Delia asked, turning toward Greer with a fearful gaze. "Who was that?"

"I—I fucked up, Dels," Greer admitted quietly, "I—" She was interrupted by the appearance of a short, squat man. Delia screamed and pointed as Greer whipped around, taking a step backward. She had no weapon; she had no magic.

Eligos hit Greer with a wave of energy so powerful that it took her breath away. It sent her soaring across the parking lot, and she landed in a cold puddle of water, leftover from the recent rainfall that had filled each crack and crevice of the pavement. Greer clambered across the loose stones and concrete, but she was too far away to reach Eligos in time.

From behind her, Greer heard Cian shout a warning from the side door of the warehouse, but he was also too far away to reach Eligos in time.

Too far away to do anything as Eligos removed his own blade from the inside of his jacket. Too far away to stop him from aiming that blade at Delia. Too far away to stop him as he moved to thrust it toward her abdomen.

The only one of them who wasn't too far away was Paige. And Paige threw herself in front of that dagger, where it plunged deep into her chest.

THIRTY-FIVE

Delia let out an unearthly, primal scream so full of pain that Greer could feel it shredding her heart into ribbons. Cian's eyes were wild as he assessed the scene before him, seeing Delia on the pavement sobbing and Paige with the dagger protruding from her chest.

Greer could see the whites of Paige's eyes as she dropped to her knees. She knew Paige only had less than a minute before she died. Her breathing had already turned to short pants, the gurgling in the back of her throat becoming more and more pronounced with every gasp. Greer watched in horror as a venom spread through Paige, creating black webs out of her veins as it crept up her neck and down her abdomen.

The substance Eligos had implanted into the blade was poison, and it was spreading quickly.

"I told you what would happen," Eligos said, as he reached down and pulled the dagger from Paige's chest with a horrifying wrench. Paige lurched forward, landing on the palms of her hands. His attention turned toward the warehouse for a moment, where Isaac and Odette appeared on the top steps. Odette's hand, covered in blood, flew to her mouth as Isaac's jaw tightened. Eligos looked back at Greer. "I told you it would start with someone."

Then, it happened. The one thing that Agnes had written about for how to access magic.

Greer had read it hundreds of times, had tried to quiet her mind and meditate, tried to think back on memories tied with strong emotions. She used Holly's death, Anna's death. Every time, she felt as though she hit a wall in her mind, leaving her with inconsistencies in the strength of the magic she could use. This was the only thing she could think of doing as Paige's life came crashing to a close. One last chance to save one of her best friends.

Greer felt her soul drop in her body as she turned into herself. Every tremor, every thread of rage fueled her soul as she sped down, down, down toward that barrier.

The voices around her were muffled, and she may as well have been underwater. Paige's pants had turned into shudders. Odette sprang into the air, the front of her shirt covered in chunks of muscle and intestine, and snapped her wings open as she tried to reach the djinn attempting to disappear.

Time slowed as Greer neared that barrier, the one she could never break through to control her magic. She used the view before her, of Eligos standing in front of Paige with the dagger in his hand, to punch through. It shattered irreparably as her soul sped past it, accessing that pool of magic shimmering just below the surface.

Greer felt her bones crack, and she threw back her head, letting out a scream of unending, terrible pain, but then…there was nothing, but power. It filled her. Every cell of her body, every fiber of her essence was overflowing with unrelenting, untouched energy.

She opened her eyes to stare down Eligos with that same predatory stare she had seen on Odette, Isaac, and Cian— and unleashed herself. Greer extended her hand and sent a wave of power so absolute that it lifted Eligos into the air. He hung, suspended and unable to move, as she neared him. He opened his mouth to beg with her, but with a swift clench of her fist, she cleaved the djinn's spirit from the body he possessed.

The corpse crumpled to the pavement, unmoving. Greer held her stare on Eligos, not letting herself get distracted by the body rapidly deteriorating on the ground. The djinn, now a fog of darkness and smoke, roiled in the air. She felt his fear, his need to find a new body. She forced him to remain there.

Greer looked at him for a moment, watching the black shadow. She drew up a tendril of her power and found it begging to be released. She felt it pulsate as it left her hand, humming as though it had finally been reunited with its master. Her magic purred at her, bending to her will as she extended her hand and sent that tendril toward that roiling, dark fog that was Eligos.

The magic knew what she asked. It slid from her hand, hovering in the air, as it glided toward Eligos, still hanging in the balance by Greer. It circled, as if trying to find the best point of entry. Finally, it struck. Entangling itself with Eligos, her power took control of the djinn's spirit. Her power and Eligos became one, coiling around one another as Eligos attempted to tug himself away. He was unsuccessful as his black, fog-like spirit dissipated, leaving nothing but her power behind.

She reeled it back in, allowing it to permeate her skin and settling back into place within her soul. Home, it seemed to say. It was home when it was released within her. Greer dropped to her knees at Delia's side, seeing Paige take her final gasps of breath. She laid her hands on Paige's chest, willing her power to slow the poison before it reached her heart. It did as she asked, her power now creeping along Paige's veins. She pulled at the poison, asking it to withdraw its hold. The poison refused, already too interwoven within Paige's body and soul.

A surge of power crackled through the air and Greer, still holding the poison at bay, looked up in surprise. Two feet landed on the cracked pavement with a thud that sent shock waves through the earth beneath her. Greer felt her own heart stutter.

The man's body was clad in fighting leathers, the armor buckled over his broad chest. A sword, only visible by the sliver of metal glinting as he strode toward them beneath the parking lot lights, was strapped between two wings.

Wings.

Her eyes roamed across them. They were so different from Odette's that it took Greer a moment to process what she was seeing. The wings, covered in gray feathers, were massive. Tucked in as tightly as they could against his back, yet they still stretched nearly the length of Paige's outstretched body.

Greer's gaze raked up toward his face. A dagger was sheathed at his hip, three emerald gemstones lined the hilt. His arms were tattooed with shadowed markings that circled each bicep, and his long, dark hair was pulled into a bun near the back of his head with a leather wrapping that matched his armor.

Her gray eyes connected with his cerulean ones and the man stopped in his tracks. He watched her, curiosity glossing over his handsome features. "Can you see me?" he asked, as he took a step closer.

"Yes," Greer whispered in response. "Of course, I can see you. Who else—" She glanced around. Odette and Isaac were in the background talking amongst themselves, sending glances toward Paige.

Greer could hear they were talking about Isaac potentially biting her, but he didn't want to do anything against Paige's will. And Paige was too far gone for consent. Aside from that, Odette wasn't even sure if his bite would work against the poison, especially if Greer's power couldn't.

Delia, on the other hand, was staring at Greer through swollen eyes, her cheeks splotched red. She hiccupped. "GG, who are you talking to?"

Greer looked back up toward the man. "Help me save her."

"No," was all he said. His sword zinged from his sheath. Greer could see the etchings carved into the blade, a set of words she couldn't recognize.

"*Please.*"

The man stared at her, his blue eyes firm and holding.

He said nothing.

"Why are you here?" Greer asked, her conversation now catching Odette and Isaac's attention. They stopped whispering to one another, their eyes moving between Greer and the empty space Greer was seemingly talking to.

"I think you know why I'm here."

"Greer!"

She turned her head to see Cian approaching quickly, pulling the vial Eligos had given him from his pocket. Isaac was preternaturally fast on the best day, but this time, Greer had never seen him move so quickly. He reached Cian, the tip of his sword slicing into Cian's throat. Cian held up his hands, one of them still holding the vial of liquid he had traded for Greer's life. It was still full, the cork in place.

"Greer, I'm so sorry," Cian said, as he tried to move forward, but Isaac pushed the blade deeper into the skin. Greer watched as blood pebbled beneath it. "I...give her this. Please." He held up the vial to Isaac, urging him to take it. "Agnes made this before she died. It contains the Essence of the Primordials—"

"No, it doesn't," the man interrupted, but Greer sent him a scathing look.

"—It's the only antidote to anything made in Samsara, including the poison from a djinn. She never told me how she got it. I—I had been looking for it for centuries. That's how I got caught up in all of this."

Isaac withdrew the blade and snatched it from his hand, immediately dropping to the ground beside Paige. "Hold the poison where it's at."

Greer threw all of her focus into keeping the poison from spreading as Isaac carefully placed a hand behind Paige's head, tilting it forward. He pulled the corked top from the vial with his teeth, pouring the contents into Paige's mouth.

Greer's brow began to sweat from the strain. Nothing happened.

It wasn't working. Why wasn't it working?

"Greer. Is that your name?" The man slowly approached. His tone was not comforting nor was it unkind. He was merely stating what he knew. "Greer, that is no ordinary poison. That is Venom from a Primordial." He paused as her bottom lip trembled. "Greer, once the venom is settled, there is no way to extract it without the Essence. That vial did not contain it. It's her time to come with me."

"No, it's not. It's not her time," Greer shot back. "Get away from her!"

Odette and Isaac froze as they looked at Greer, but she was looking at the winged man, who had taken another step toward Paige.

Greer shook her head, her eyes filled with tears as she let out a sob. The knot in her throat bobbed, and she let the tears drip down onto her cheeks, smearing the dirt and muck coating her skin. She leaned forward, placing her on Paige's chest, listening to those gasps become further and further apart. From the corner of her eye, she saw Paige squeeze Delia's hand, as if giving her permission.

Greer lifted her head in time to see Paige's eyes open just enough to look at Delia. She struggled to pull her lips into a smile, the muscles wavering weakly as blood and saliva dribbled from her jaw to her neck. She opened her mouth, as if trying to say something, but Delia cut her off.

"Don't say anything, my love, please." Delia's voice wobbled as she spoke. She reached up to stroke Paige's hair. "You were the best thing to ever happen to me." Bending at the waist, she planted a kiss on Paige's pale, clammy forehead.

"Paige, I—I—" Greer started before breaking down into tears. She grasped Paige's hand, intertwining their fingers together. "I'm so sorry—" Greer thought her chest would cave in. Nothing had ever hurt this much, nothing else could possibly hurt this much. She hated herself. She hated what she could do. She hated who she was. "I would do anything, I—I—"

Paige squeezed Greer's fingers, her breath now sawing in and out of her chest. The stab wound, once gushing, now slowly leaked onto her already sodden shirt. The blood pooled beneath them, red and bright. She nodded her head, trying one more time to pull a smile onto her lips.

Delia leaned over, lifting her hand to grasp on to Greer's shoulder. "Please, please let the venom go," she whispered into Greer's neck. "She's in so much pain, please take it away."

Greer glanced up to the man, still standing over them, his sword tip resting lightly against his boot.

"Where will she go?" Greer asked him, the tightness in her chest unbearable.

"On."

Greer took in a deep, choking breath. And let Paige go. The man lifted his sword above his head and swung it down. Greer expected a devastating blow, perhaps an amputation of some sort, but the blade went straight through

Paige, as if nothing were there.

Delia gaped at the space above Paige, her mouth slackening. Paige took in one more rattling breath and then moved no more, eyes glazing over in death. Her hand weakened within Greer's as her chest deflated for the last time.

Greer watched as the man lifted Paige's soul from her body, a small ball of gleaming light, and sent it toward the sky. It danced in the air as it rose before finally disappearing beyond the tree line. Greer thought a piece of her died with Paige as Delia let out a mournful sob.

Delia braced herself against Paige's body, her shoulders curling over Paige's still chest. Her wracking sobs sounded painful as she screamed, and screamed, and screamed for Paige to come back to her.

"We weren't done yet," Delia said over and over. "We weren't done."

Greer was empty, devoid of any emotion. She wished it were her lying on the ground.

"Greer...Greer, I'm so sorry," Cian was saying, still standing behind Isaac. "Eligos, he...he told me how I could get the potion back. I thought he just wanted your power. I didn't know he would go this far. Greer, please—"

At the pleading sound of his voice, Greer's head snapped up. Wrath and revenge filled her, filled every space that Paige's friendship, kindness, and love had previously held. It all died when Paige did. Greer sent out a tendril of power like a whip, wrapping it around Cian's throat.

He let out a choking sound as he grasped for something intangible. His eyes, wide and full of fear, began to turn red with the blood vessels popping under the pressure.

"This is all your fault," Greer hissed. She knew it wasn't. It was hers. She tightened it around his neck anyways.

"Paige's death is all your fault." Cian let out another choking sound as his feet lifted from the ground. "You could have just come to me; we would have found a way to get it from him." His tongue lolled from his mouth as his eyes bugged from the sockets.

"Greer," Odette said slowly from behind her. "Greer!"

"Wh—" Greer glanced over her shoulder, immediately withdrawing her tendril of power, sending Cian crashing to the ground, coughing and clutching his throat.

"I heard you visited James Whittley. Pity you had to meet that sniveling little worm. One day soon those wards against me will fail and I will have so much fun peeling his skin from his bones."

Isaac stumbled back.

Standing there, mere feet away, was a second man...a second man with wings. Bright, white, feathered wings. His body, much like the first man, was broad and muscled with high cheekbones and full lips on his face. His golden hair was long, pulled back into the same style bun that the first man wore. The leather armor he wore was black, buckled straps criss-crossing his chest and shoulders. A dagger was sheathed at his hip and the hilt also bore three stones, though these appeared to be rubies rather than the emerald of the first man.

"Who are you?" Greer asked. She hoped her tone sounded confidently strong, but knew it came out waveringly meek.

"Most humans call me Lucifer, though I prefer to go by my name. Azazel. Not that you're human, are you Greer?" Odette stilled, her breathing fast and heaving. Isaac gripped his sword, bringing it forward in protection of him and Delia. Azazel merely smirked at the movement. "There's no need for that," he said.

With a pointed stare, the metal grew hot and red under Isaac's grasp, and he tossed the sword to the ground, swearing under his breath. Greer swallowed, flicking her eyes back toward the first man. He had stiffened in the time Azazel appeared, and had sheathed his sword to the strap between his wings.

"Azazel," he said through gritted teeth. "Why are you here?"

"I wish I could say I was surprised to see you here, Samael, but..." He trailed off, glancing down at Paige's body. He clicked his tongue against his teeth. "Pity." He took a step toward Greer. "You are precisely what I expected the daughter of Holly Hawkins to look like. You certainly look remarkably like her, if I do say so myself."

"How do you know about my birth mother?"

Azazel's wings twitched as agitation flashed across his face. "Your mother was my mate."

Greer laughed, low and humorless. "That's funny. No, she wasn't."

He sent her a look of impatience, one that she knew was mirrored on her own face. "And why not?" he asked, moving closer to her.

Greer stood her ground, keeping Paige's body behind her. "Because that would make *you*, my father." She licked her chapped lips. "That's ridiculous. I was told my father was a Primordial, not an angel."

Azazel's mouth upturned into a smirk as the impatient expression left his features. "I am both of those things, Greer. We go by many names, many titles, from many religions. I am the one who laced your bones with obsidian. I am the one that brought your mother down to Samsara while we awaited your birth."

"You're also the one who sent her away," Greer shot back.

Azazel's eyes darkened. "She could not be in Samsara without you inside of her, and I knew that I had someone in my midst who couldn't be trusted. We decided together that she was better off raising you with the knowledge of your magic and your power until you were strong enough to break through it yourself. So, we opted to hide you both away by embedding you with obsidian stone; not only hiding you from other Primordials, but also myself. I went searching for her when she missed our first check-in and, by the time I learned of her death, you were gone, and I had no way of looking for you. I could only hope that you would break through the obsidian before your mortal death."

"My mortal death?"

Azazel looked as though he were struggling to keep his composure. Greer found it unnerving. "Having access to the powers of a Primordial means having the lifespan of a Primordial."

Greer looked him over. She could certainly see the similarities between them. Their eyes were the same round shape and gray color. Her nose, slim and regal, was the same as his as well. The waves to her hair were the same curl pattern as his. Her heart sank.

"With your obsidian stone gone, other Primoridals will come looking for you," he began again. "And you are not ready to face them." He took a breath. "You are to come to Samsara with me and train. Learn how to use your powers and learn how to fight in combat."

Greer's lips parted in surprise. "No, no. I'm not going with you. My life is here, my friends—"

Azazel sighed through his nose. "Samael." He gestured toward the first man. "If you please."

Samael stepped toward Greer and clamped a hand around her upper arm. "Hey, wait—" she said, jerking to pull away from him. "Stop it. What are you doing? I don't want to go with you. Stop!"

Greer whipped her gaze around, desperate and hopeless. She saw Isaac and Cian attempt to push forward. Odette had unsheathed her blade, ready to spring into the air after them. Delia, still covered in the blood of Paige, didn't look like she was capable of taking another loss. She crumpled over Paige's body once more, not watching as Greer was stolen away.

"Delia?"

There was no response.

Greer screamed in pain and rage as a golden slit erupted from thin air twenty feet above them, dancing and shimmering against the darkened sky. Samael scooped her up, an arm behind her knees and an arm behind her shoulders, and shot up into the sky.

She was still trying to pull away from him when they entered the portal, still trying to get back to Delia, to find her way back to Paige. She felt a tug at her chest and a rush of wind pass by her ears.

Then, it was dark and silent, and Greer felt nothing at all.

EPILOGUE

DELIA

The funeral was beautiful, of course. Paige's parents picked a funeral home that overlooked the mountains from the back windows. The lawn was manicured, the decorative flower garden was properly watered, and the casket was a redwood one with brass handles. The director was nice enough, and the staff kept a discreet distance from the mourners. A video montage played on the television screen mounted behind the podium and, God, Delia hated nothing more by the end of the afternoon than the playlist Paige's mother had found to accompany it.

Paige would have laughed along with her at the hymns, the pageantry, and the scent of fresh snapdragons lining the wreaths that hung near the casket. Delia was quite sure the breath mints she was eating like candy were going to be a staple she remembered from the day. That and the feel of Paige's mother's hair against her cheek as she pulled Delia in close every other minute.

Delia cringed at every slightly moist palm that shook her own, and her back was stiff from sitting on that hard pew, but she would have endured it every single minute of every single day if that meant having Paige out of that redwood box.

And Greer...

Delia swallowed hard as she thought about her best friend. She still didn't know the whole story. Paige had been ripped away from her, and Delia thought, for the brief amount of time they had together, that she could lean on Greer for support. Now, she was alone.

She had their college friends who came into town every so often, and she had her co-workers, who had delivered an unnatural number of casseroles to her apartment when they heard the news. But they weren't Greer. And they certainly weren't Paige.

Odette had glamoured Paige to make her death seem like a robbery gone wrong. Had cleaned up the garage by setting fire to the inside, not knowing how else to discard dozens of rotting creatures. Had given Delia an alibi in case the police came sniffing around during their investigation.

They had, briefly, and then they left her alone too.

Delia walked through the cemetery following the end of the funeral. She looked at the gravestones, moss covered and cracked, and vowed to Paige that she would never let that happen to her.

The wind whistled through the trees, and the birds sang as they sat upon the branches. The air was crisp for the first time in months. Paige would have loved the weather. Her favorite season was autumn, and it wouldn't be long before the leaves changed.

"I'm sorry to hear about your wife," a voice said, as it fell into step next to her.

Delia turned to see an older woman, maybe seventy, with salt and pepper black hair. Her kind face was lined and wrinkled, bronzed from the sun. "Who are you?" Delia asked.

There was no reason for niceties any longer. Paige was the only one who cared for them anyways.

"Well, Greer knew me as Deborah." Delia halted in her tracks, the heels of her shoes sinking into the soft grass. "My name is Nerea." She paused to place a soft hand on Delia's arm, and Delia noticed her fingertips were stained with blue paint. "Odette told me that your wife's funeral was today. I am here on her behalf."

"And where is she?" The question came out ruder than she meant it. Or maybe she did mean it that way; she didn't care.

"Gone," Nerea said. "She had a duty she needed to accept. I'm sure we'll see her again."

Delia squinted against the rays of the sun, setting earlier and earlier now. "If you know who Odette is, then you know what Odette is. Right?"

Nerea looked over at Delia in contemplation. "Yes. I do know what Odette is. I also know *who* she is, if that makes a difference."

It didn't.

"Listen, it's been really nice chatting with you," Deila said slowly, brushing aside a low hanging branch as she reached the iron gates at the front of the cemetery. "But I—" She turned to look at Nerea. The woman was gone.

Delia's brow pulled together, as she glanced around. She spun in a full circle, spotting the mausoleum to her left and the mountains to her front. Nerea was nowhere to be found. There wasn't even anywhere for her to walk off too— the gravel drive was straight and narrow, as was the road that led to the cemetery itself.

She didn't think anything else about it as she drove back to the apartment. She didn't want to go back there. In actuality, Delia wanted to drown herself in a tub full of vodka while smoking a carton of cigarettes. She didn't want to feel pressured to go through Paige's belongings, to cry into a t-shirt that still smelled like her wife, to stare at the wall filled with their photographs and wonder *what if, what if, what if.*

Delia turned her steering wheel and made a quick U-turn, her tires squealing against the pavement. A horn honked at her as she peeled off in front of it, but she silently wished it would have just hit her instead.

The exterior light at Greer's house was still on and swinging in the cool wind. Delia jangled her keys in her hand as she walked up the overgrown lawn. She could hear the creek trickling in the background and crickets chirped in the adjacent field. She realized the front door was already unlocked when she pushed the key in and she turned the handle to enter.

"Ugh. What are you doing here?"

Cian's eyes snapped over to hers, narrowing as she crossed the threshold into the kitchen. He had pulled a barstool over to the breakfast counter and was watching a video on Greer's computer. The screen was shattered, distorting the images, but it worked just the same. Delia dumped her purse and coat onto the end of the couch, dropping into the accent chair nearest to Cian.

She glanced around the kitchen, spotting the birthday cards Paige had purchased on behalf of them both, scattered on the floor. Delia felt a pang of anger rise in her throat when she saw them. Paige had spent nearly an hour at their local stationary store finding the perfect ones. Pushing herself from the chair, Delia crossed the room and picked them up, setting them back onto the counter. She felt the crunch of grains beneath the soles of her shoes, and Delia briefly wondered if it were salt or sand.

"If you're going to squat here, you could have at least cleaned up."

Cian sent her a biting look before turning back to the computer screen. It was paused, Greer's mother Celeste was situated in the bottom corner of the video while a larger document was showcased on the player.

"What are you looking at?"

Cian let out a sigh of annoyance. "If you really need to know, it's a zip drive."

"I deduced that much for myself, thank you," she replied derisively. "What I wanted to know is what is the video that you are playing and pausing, and playing and pausing?"

Cian paused it again, an eyebrow cocked as he dramatically turned to look over his shoulder. "It's a video made by Greer's mother, Anna. Or Celeste. Anyways, she was a member of the Paladin Society, and I'm going through these documents she scanned into the video to see if I can find any information on the location of their headquarters."

Delia felt her heart stutter at hearing the name Paladin Society. "That thing, that djinn," she began slowly, "he mentioned having worked with them." Cian stared blankly at her before she went on. "When he had me hidden as that creature, I could still hear and comprehend. I just couldn't communicate."

Cian made a grunt of understanding as he turned back to the laptop and hit the spacebar. The video resumed and he leaned forward, placing his forearms on the edge of the countertop. Delia clicked her tongue in response, but sank back into the accent chair.

They were silent for a few minutes, and then Cian restarted the video as soon as it ended.

"What are you planning on doing with that?"

"Selling it to the highest bidder."

Delia narrowed her eyes. "Didn't you already do that? Didn't work out very well for any of us."

Cian glanced over his shoulder again, his eyes flashing dangerously as he ejected his fangs from his gum line. "I could still eat you; you know."

"You won't, because you need my help."

Cian snorted. "I do?"

"To find the Paladin Society? Yes, you do."

Cian pressed the spacebar to pause the video, and he spun to face her, crossing his arms over his chest. "I'll bite. Pun intended. Why do I need your help?"

"Jonas fucked right off as soon as Eligos died. I haven't seen Isaac since the day Paige died. You are completely and utterly alone." She paused to swallow. "And so am I."

"Maybe I prefer to be alone."

Delia let a humorless chuckle escape from her lips. "You wouldn't have traveled with Isaac and Jonas for the last few centuries if that were true."

Cian squirmed in his seat. "Jonas didn't just fuck off; he took the real potion with him."

"The one you traded Greer for?"

"Yes, that—" Cian scoffed, as he began to turn around. "You know, maybe I don't need your help after all."

"I saw Paige's ghost." The words slipped from her, though she didn't quite know why, and she felt suddenly freed by the admission. She cleared her throat. "When Greer, you know, when she let the poison take over and Paige died. I saw her spirit leave her body. She— she looked at me and smiled. She was whole and wasn't in pain and she mouthed 'I love you' before she moved on. I'm not sure anyone else saw her, but I did."

Cian was quiet, for once, as he listened. "I didn't see her," he finally said. He let out a sigh through his nose. "I wanted to find the Paladin Society to see if they knew of a way to get to Samsara. There is a repeating seal here that says Vatican City. I thought it was a good place to start."

Delia stared at him. "You want to...go to hell?"

"To find Greer."

Delia blew out a breath as she sat back against the cushion. "I'm coming too, then. When are we leaving?"

"The faster we can sort through this mess, the sooner we can leave."

Delia shoved herself from the chair, glad for the time being that she could distract herself from the pain, and the grief, and the sadness, and the anger. "We better get started then."

The Paladin Society had ruined her life, their festering cruelty had killed her wife. Now, Delia was going to make them pay.

Acknowledgements

I want to first start my thanking my husband, Joe, for the never-ending support and love he he given me. Thank you for letting me cry on your shoulder, for listening to me read passages out loud, and for helping to manage my anxiety when I questioned why I was doing this every other day. You are my life partner, my dream, and my heart. I love you forever!

Thank you to my close-knit family! My parents, who cultivated a creativity in me that still burns brightly to this day. You let me spread my wings and chase my dreams to the tallest mountains. There isn't enough gratitude in the world for me to express! To my sisters, who inspire me and challenge me. Thank you for being my first readers, for your *honest* edits and feedback, and for loving me through every stage of life. I'm so immensely proud to be your big sister!

Thank you to my amazing editor, Mozelle Jordan, for making me a better author. Your mentorship and feedback has been out of this world. Thank you to my just as amazing cover artist, Rebecca Frank, for reading my mind and exploring the depths of this story with me in ways that I didn't know were possible.

Finally, you can't read, because you're a doggo. But soulmates come in all forms and one of mine is in you. You, my Sadie-girl are an old lady now, but you have been my road trip partner, my running buddy, my college roommate, my rock during cancer treatments, and much more. You've sat at my feet every single day while I write these stories. One day you'll be gone and I'll endure a lifetime of missing you for the privilege of loving you. I stole your name, so everyone can know a piece of you forever.

About the Author

Sadie Hewitt is the author of stunning, fantastical mysteries that keep readers on their toes. She is an avid fantasy and thriller reader. Sadie is especially passionate about diverse representation and mental health recovery in fiction, allowing her to create wonderfully vivid and relatable characters who jump off the page.

When she's not writing or working as a full-time respiratory therapist, she travels the world, spends time with her two dogs and husband, and scarfs pizza like it's going out of style.

To be the first to know about Sadie's latest releases and upcoming projects, visit www.SadieHewitt.com

The adventure doesn't end with As the Fallen Rise!
Within the Solstice Cages, *the second book in the series, is hitting the shelves in January 2024.*

Three worlds on a collision course. A battle looming on the horizon. When the dust settles, who will control the realms?

Odette Milne—true heir to the Fae throne—has hidden away for two hundred years... until now. A sinister disappearance brings her out to face the truth of what her kingdom has become.

Delia Savas must team up with her enemy to get answers from Vatican City—answers that could save the life of an old friend. But she's about to find herself in the middle of a supernatural war that could cost her everything.

Greer Myers is watching her perfect life fall apart and it's all her fault. After contributing to a tragic loss, she's determined to make things right...even if it means crossing the underworld to do it.

War is inevitable, and in war, no one wins. But in the end, only one will rule.

Be sure to turn the page for a sneak peek!

PROLOGUE

Agnes

Year 1656

Agnes had forgotten how goddamn cold the Kingdom of Bohemia was during the winter. How frigid the air was when it passed through her lungs. How the icy rain stuck to her hair and froze, leaving her in a constant state of damp. How, no matter how many layers she put on, the wind still bit through the wool.

So. Goddammed. Cold.

Agnes had treated more than her fair share of human villagers the last month, many of whom would have lost fingers and toes without her intervention. Many who were willing to look past the tinctures, the rubs, and the potions she handed out just to get a taste of the healing warmth only she could provide.

Not one of them was screaming witch yet. Not in this weather. That possibility would rise when the storm cleared and the temperature rose.

Agnes approached the familiar house she had built before the freezing rains set in. It was so different from the timber-framed farmhouses in the village, mostly because the style of the one-room cottage was one she still preferred after all of these years. The hearth with an open flame, her dried herbs hanging from the rafters, her bed shoved into the corner. It reminded her of her youth; when her and her mother would sit by the fire in the dead of winter looking over the grimoire that only Agnes could read.

Growing up, her cottage was in the middle of a glen, muddy and typically awash with rainwater. Agnes would practice spellwork and her mother would sew thick spools of wool into skirts, shawls, and full-length shirts for the upcoming seasons. They would look up at one another and smile over the crackling flames and Agnes would wonder how life could get much better than it was in that moment.

Over five hundred years later, the cottage she now lived in backed to the river, fed by the mountains in the distance, and left her with plenty of room to plant her garden when the summer months allowed.

Not now though. Now it was too goddamn cold.

Agnes's fingers clasped the iron knob as she shoved her shoulder into the wooden door, a flurry of snow and wind following her over the threshold.

"I thought I was going to find your frozen body on the bank of the river."

Her eyes darted up to the man standing near the small table Agnes had set up for herself. She took in his handsome face, high cheekbones, raven black hair. And rolled her eyes.

"Next time I'm sending you out there," she retorted, lowering the hood of her green cloak before tugging the strings at her collarbones.

The man put down the knife he held. He had taken over chopping the dried herbs Agnes had started before she decided to venture out into the storm for a fresh bucket of river water. He sauntered over to her and grasped the wet cloak to pull it from her shoulders before hanging it on a peg near the hearth. The icy droplets were already beginning to thaw, steadily dripping from the hem.

"I distinctly remember telling you that I would go."

Agnes threw him a withering look, setting down the water-filled bucket near the front door. She paused near the hearth to hold her hands to the fire. The flames licked at the frozen tips of her fingers, sending waves of relief thrumming through her body. She sucked in a deep breath through her nose, taking in the scent of burnt, smoky wood and dried rosemary. The logs under her cauldron crackled merrily, sending sparks tumbling onto the stone floor.

The man returned to the table, picking up the knife once again. "The father of that werewolf pup returned this afternoon while you were gone."

"Oh?" Agnes asked, glancing over her shoulder. She spotted his black curtain of hair cascade over his chest as he focused on the herbs. A quarter inch cut- just as she liked it. "And did he pick up the potion as I told him to?"

He chuckled. "Not without grumbling how in his day he didn't have fancy potions to lessen the pain of the first transition."

Agnes scoffed. "One would think you wouldn't want your children in pain, especially needlessly terrible pain you've experienced yourself." Her heart stuttered as she thought back to her own daughter, now long gone centuries ago.

Agnes barely had enough time with Beatrice, certainly not long enough for her daughter to have remembered her. It seemed silly to ponder on, really, considering Agnes had purposefully gotten pregnant by the local farmer's son as a means to an end.

"The line needs continuing," her mother told her proudly when Agnes had barely been eighteen years of age. "I did it for you, my mother did it for me. We have a duty, my love, to provide for this world."

By the end of the month, it only took her and the farmer's son four half-hearted romps in a hay field. Well, half-hearted on Agnes's part. He certainly held up his end of the bargain by providing her with Beatrice.

And Beatrice was perfect. Large, hazel eyes. Wavy locks of brown hair. Freckles adorning her nose and upper cheeks. Agnes became the Mage nearing Beatrice's eighth birthday and never saw her again, steering clear in case the Paladin Society came sniffing.

The man set down the knife and looked over to her, assessing the sudden shift. Agnes swallowed as she shook her head, adding, "at least he picked it up." She promptly turned back to the fire, suddenly missing the humid rains and warm sun of Thailand and Cambodia.

She hadn't been back to this side of the world in nearly twenty-five years, opting to move around for the daemons to have equal opportunity access to her magic. Agnes reminded herself that she missed these wild winters while she was stuck traveling through India during monsoon season. Turns out, the grass was, indeed, not greener on the other side.

He seemed to be thinking the same thing as he bent at the waist and leaned his elbows against the table before absent-mindedly saying, "I seem to remember a summer. Mmm...ten years ago, perhaps? Where you complained every single day about the sweltering heat of Dai Viet."

Agnes looked over her shoulder at him once again and clicked her tongue. She rose to standing, taking a moment to adjust her skirts and woolen hair covering. "I don't seem to remember asking," she said pointedly and watched as his eyes darkened, glinting just like the heated flames behind her.

Their eyes connected and Agnes felt her core clench.

"You know," he began, not removing his eyes from hers as he straightened, weaving around the side of the table. "We've been together centuries now and I think I love you more today than I did then." He approached her slowly as he placed his hands on her chilled cheeks and leaned down to kiss her softly.

"I hope so," Agnes replied with a smile. "It would be a shame if you felt the need to trade me in for a younger Mage."

He nipped at her nose playfully as she ran her hands up the front of his linen shirt. "Maybe not the next Mage, but certainly a goat or two."

Agnes laughed as she stood on her tip-toes to plant her lips on his once more. His hands slid to the back of her head and waist, drawing her in closer as he deepened the kiss.

"You're still freezing," he murmured against her lips. "I may have a secret to warm you up."

"Is that so?" She asked, sliding her thumbs into the waistband of his trousers. "I may be open to you showing me."

The man smiled again as his hand cupped her breast. Agnes was just getting into the rhythm of her tongue sliding across his when a knock sounded on the front door. Not a knock, a pound. Someone pounding on the front door. The man twisted toward her bed, pulling the dagger he had provided her from under the mattress where she kept it hidden.

The three gemstones embedded in the hilt shone against the firelight.

"Agnes! Agnes. Let me in, will ya? It's cold enough to freeze the teats off a frog!"

The man groaned, walking back toward Agnes and resting his forehead on hers. "How did he find you so quickly?" He asked. He let go of her hand to lean against the wooden table.

"Cian makes quick work of anything he sets his mind to."

Agnes walked toward the front door and tugged it open, seeing the familiar vampyre on the other side of the threshold. He pushed past her, rubbing his arms.

"Fuckin' hell," Cian said in his thick Irish brogue, peeling his coat off and steering toward the fire. "Three months of walkin' to get here. Thank our Lord the fire is hot. Do you know how many villages I had to pass through? Jonas is in the forest still. Probably left a trail of bodies from--" He turned to warm his backside, spotting the man at the table for the first time. "Who are you?"

The man arched a brow at the vampyre, whose eyes had dropped to the dagger still in his hand. He snorted, tossing the blade onto the quilt. "I'm leaving," the man announced, taking his own cloak off the second peg by the hearth and wrapping it around his shoulders.

"So soon?" Agnes asked, her heart dipping in disappointment.

"I'll be back in a while," he replied with a wink, fastening the cloak's button and pulling open the door, sending in a third flurry of white. The flames in the hearth flickered with the cold breeze, the snow and sparks dancing together in a swirl of ice and fire.

He stepped over the threshold and spun to face Agnes just as Cian turned his back to plant his hands near the fire once again. The man released his feathered wings, large and brilliantly black against the white, winter landscape behind him. He pushed off the ground and shot into the air, flapping his wings when he cleared the top of the door frame. Snow billowed from the slanted roof, joining the flakes blown around by the storm.

Then, he was gone.

Agnes shut the door once he was out of eyesight, latching the lock with a stiff pull.

"Who was that?" Cian asked, reaching up toward the ceiling to pull down a bundle of tomatoes. He popped one off the vine and tossed it into his mouth.

Agnes sighed. "A...friend," she said, hesitating. She had been sworn to secrecy about his identity and, to be honest, their connection wasn't something she was willing to share. "A very, very old friend."